Judith Cook was born and brought up in Manchester. She began her career as a journalist for the *Guardian* and went on to become a freelance writer, winning awards for investigative journalism and having several highly acclaimed works of fiction and non-fiction published. She is a part-time lecturer in Elizabethan and Jacobean theatre at Exeter University. Judith Cook lives in the fishing port of Newlyn, Cornwall, with her partner and two cats.

The first and second entries in the Casebook of Dr Simon Forman, *Death of a Lady's Maid* and *Murder at the Rose*, are also available from Headline.

Praise for Judith Cook's work:

'Cook has written three other books set in the same period and she brings it effortlessly to life. She spins a fast and entertaining tale'   *Guardian*

'Cook roots her exciting and readable novel firmly in the world of the playhouses'   *Financial Times*

'A good, pacy read . . . Cook is keen on fine historical detail and has obviously mastered her subject'
                                         Evening Standard

'A well-balanced thriller . . . intelligent and entertaining'
                                         TLS

Also by Judith Cook

The Slicing Edge of Death
To Brave Every Danger
Death of a Lady's Maid
Murder at the Rose

Blood on
the Borders

Judith Cook

HEADLINE

First published in 1999
by HEADLINE BOOK PUBLISHING

First published in paperback in 1999
by HEADLINE BOOK PUBLISHING

10 9 8 7 6 5 4 3 2 1

ISBN 0 7472 5610 1

Printed and bound in Great Britain by
Clays Ltd, St Ives plc

HEADLINE BOOK PUBLISHING
A division of Hodder Headline PLC
338 Euston Road
London NW1 3BH

For Brian and Shelia
after all these years
and who live on the Borders.

ACKNOWLEDGEMENTS

First, people. My thanks to Ian Power, Curator of Carlisle Castle; to the staff at the Armstrong Museum in Langholm who helped sort out papers for me which have proved invaluable; staff at Edinburgh Castle and Holyrood Palace; also at the Tourist Offices in Moffat, Langholm and Hawick; and the people in the small towns and villages on the Borders who were so courteous and helpful.

The two books I found most useful were George Macdonald Fraser's seminal work on the Reivers – *Steel Bonnets*, and John Prebble's history of those turbulent times – *The Lion in the North*. Medical sources used include *Simon Forman's Casebook* (edited by A. L. Rowse), *Dr Hall's Casebook* (edited by Joan Lane) and *Culpeper's Herbal*.

Chapter 1

May Day

The night on which Dr Simon Forman opened the door of his house on London's Bankside to find a dying man on his doorstep followed one of the longest-seeming days of his life.

To be strictly accurate it was more than a day, for it had begun late the previous evening, on 30 April 1592, when he joined a party of friends riding out to Oxleas Woods to bring in the May, the hawthorn blossom. While clergymen regularly fulminated from their pulpits over the evils of continuing with such pagan practices which led, in their view, to debauchery and a general laxity of morals, they did so to little effect. In towns and villages all over England, parties of young and not-so-young people were riding or walking out to fetch in great swathes of blossom with which to deck the outside of their houses and the morning streets, while children continued to dance around maypoles.

This year the revellers were in luck for it was a mild and dry night. Simon's party had encamped in a woodland glade and, surrounding themselves with torches stuck in the ground, they ate good food and drank fine wine until the first streaks of dawn appeared in the east. It had been particularly enjoyable for Simon as Mistress Avisa Allen, wife to a worthy silk-merchant, had been one of the party, but without her older husband. The good doctor had been laying siege to Avisa for over a year, in spite of having had at least one brief sexual adventure elsewhere, and it was looking as if he might finally achieve his heart's desire for, under cover of the darkness and festivities, Avisa had whispered to him that her husband was to go to the Low Countries shortly on business and that this

1

might be an opportunity for them to get to know each other rather better. She had even allowed him to kiss her several times and laughed when he said that he was grateful for the opportunity May Day afforded, even though so far as he was concerned, may blossom smelled of cat's piss! Matters were definitely progressing.

By the time they rode back towards London, each bearing a branch of blossom, it was broad daylight. They fell in with other parties of riders and larger groups of walkers, all making their way home in the same direction. Some of the young men were obviously much the worse for drink and were finding the walk home difficult, while young couples, the girls with wilting flowers in their hair and their gowns stained with earth and grass, walked together still entwined, giggling and flushed. Simon mused on the likely numbers of February babies that would be born the following year and the hasty marriages that would be taking place in some three months' time when the results of the night's work became apparent. But in spite of what the parsons thundered, he believed such rare licence to be harmless; it was a celebration that winter had finally passed, and most of the young men would marry their sweethearts.

On reaching the Bankside he and some of the other single men went to an ordinary for breakfast, having waved off the rest of the party. The ordinary was busy and it was some while before they were served, by which time they were extremely hungry and fell on large pieces of pie served with pease-pudding as if they had not eaten for a week.

Simon was in no hurry to return home afterwards; he wandered through the streets full of people in holiday mood, stopping off for half an hour to watch a Mummers' play on a street corner, in which St George successfully fought off an ingenious dragon. The players were then moved on by the Mayor's Men – a group of young men in fancy dress, who were pulling behind them a cart in which sat a May Queen. To Simon's amusement, he saw it was Joan Alleyn, wife of the famous actor, her fair hair crowned with flowers. She waved and called to him that she had been abducted by the Mayor's Men and would have to write and tell her husband Edward of it (for he was away on tour), for fear he should hear she had become a loose woman in his absence.

Time passed almost without his knowing it, and he was surprised when he heard a church clock strike noon and so made his way home. He had given his servant John Bradedge and his housekeeper wife, Anna, the day off to visit friends downriver in Deptford with their two-year-old son (to whom he was godfather), telling them they need not return until the following morning, so his house was unusually quiet when he let himself in. But not for long. Scarcely had he got through the door when the first of the morning's casualties presented himself – a young man with a cut head and a bad headache.

'How did you do this?' asked Simon, as he cleaned him up.

The young man looked embarrassed. 'I'm not too sure. I did drink rather a lot – a good deal, in fact – and I remember arguing with my cousin when we went to pick the may, over who should sit beside our neighbour's daughter Viola, then aiming a blow at him, then nothing more till I woke up in a ditch to find everyone else had gone home.'

Simon wiped the cut with an infusion of rue leaves in water, then poured a liquid into a small phial. 'Go home and take this. It's water of lilies of the valley. I could have given you a draught made from ivy leaves but this is more pleasant to take. It's supposed to recruit a weak memory too,' he added mischievously. 'Perhaps it will assist you to recall just what did happen between you and your cousin!'. The young man looked sheepish, paid him his fee, then went on his way. He was followed by a mother whose child had severe colic – which Simon diagnosed as the result of having eaten too many sweetmeats – and a number of other revellers suffering from assorted injuries. He was already thinking longingly of sleep when two giggling girls knocked on the door, demanding he cast their horoscopes to see if the young men with whom they had become so familiar during the night were likely to fulfil their promises. At first he thought of sending them away and telling them to return the next day, but they were both clutching purses and he felt he was in no position to do so.

It was now nearly a year since the Royal College of Physicians had withdrawn his licence to practise medicine in the City of London, and almost as long since they had been informed, on good authority, that their decision for so doing was no longer valid as it had been based on their having been given false information about him. Indeed, the Physicians had agreed in principle months back that his licence would finally be restored to him, but so far they had still taken no action, their prejudice against him ensuring they would leave doing so until the last possible moment. For the past year, therefore, Simon had been cut off from most of his wealthiest patients – although of late he had been discreetly visiting some of them again when expressly called in. But the situation was far from satisfactory and he still lived very much from hand to mouth.

That being the case, he gritted his teeth, stifled his yawns, smiled and cast the girls' horoscopes, informing them afterwards as he rolled away his charts, that one of them at least would be a happy wife and mother within the twelve month, although he could not see early marriage for her friend.

After they had gone he went into the strangely empty kitchen, found the bread and cheese Anna had left out for him, washed it down with a quart of ale, then went to the room at the back of the house where he had a daybed and threw himself down on it for a nap. Hardly had he drifted off, however, when there was an urgent knocking on his door. At first he lay there hoping the caller would give in and go away, but when it became obvious that this was not going to happen, he groaned, got reluctantly to his feet and went to open his front door.

Outside stood a young woman whose tatty finery proclaimed her trade. He presumed she must be one of the numerous local whores, the Winchester Geese, who worked the streets and alleys of the Bankside. Simon's neighbourhood lay within the see of the Bishop of Winchester; hence the prostitutes' nickname.

The girl looked at Simon in some surprise for she had expected to find a venerable old fellow with a long grey beard, instead of which she was presented with a chestnut-haired man of pleasing appearance in his mid-thirties. 'I'm sorry to trouble you, sir,' she said, 'but I've come about Emma – Emma Ball. She's really bad with the childbed fever.'

Simon had known Emma Ball for some years, during most of which she was mistress to the poet and dramatist Robert Greene. A few weeks earlier, Greene had finally moved out of her little house, leaving her eight months forward with child and sickly with it. Simon had previously had an exasperated affection for the drunken poet who combined excess in all things with genuine charm, but he had seen nothing charming in Greene's treatment of his devoted mistress; he had not scrupled to live off her every time he was short of funds. The two had quarrelled continuously once Emma was unable to whore and the money began to run out, and finally, in an excess of drunken dignity coupled with his own growing sickness, Greene had left her for lodgings near St Paul's Church.

Simon was aware that Emma's child was expected any time, but he had been busy and it had slipped his mind. Telling the girl to wait, he pulled on his doublet then went into his study and poured various mixtures into small bottles, put some dried leaves in a packet, and placed the lot in a bag, along with a good candle in case he should need more light. Having organised everything to his satisfaction, he prepared to follow the girl to Emma's house.

'So the child is born then?' he asked, as they hurried past the Clink Gaol.

'Aye, sir. A boy – two days since.' Emma's labour had been prolonged and exhausting, she told him, and it had been all the wise woman who acted as midwife could do to bring mother and child through it alive. 'Though the babe's sickly, sir, and the woman doubts it'll live long. But all seemed well with Emma until this morning when I went to see her and found her lying there, the child crying beside her on the bed, and her hot with fever and wandering in her mind. I asked a neighbour what I should do and she said to come for you since you were a friend of Emma's.'

Within ten minutes they had reached Emma's small house (a gift from a former lover) and Simon was climbing up the ladder to the bedchamber on the upper floor. The room was shuttered and dark and smelled of sickness, and he threw back the shutters to let in the air and afternoon sun. Emma lay on a trestle bed, tossing and turning and muttering to herself while the baby had obviously cried itself to sleep. He put his hand on her forehead and she opened unfocused, unseeing eyes.

'Go downstairs and heat me some water,' he told her friend, 'so that I can make her an infusion of feverfew. In the meantime I'll try to give her some cinnamon in white wine – it's sometimes effective in these cases.'

He lifted Emma's head and carefully spooned some of the cinnamon liquid down her throat. It was a while before the girl returned with some hot water in a jug; apparently she'd had to ask the neighbour to heat it since there was no fuel in the house for a fire, and she'd also had to pull two pails of water from the pump that served the houses in the street. Then she shifted from foot to foot.

'If it's all the same with you, sir, I really ought to go.' She reddened slightly. 'It is a holiday and there are many people about. The folk will soon be coming out of the Bear Pit and I can earn good money – but I'll come back and stay with her tonight. I promise I won't bring any customers back here with me.'

Simon thanked her. She looked no more than fifteen at most and he wondered what had driven her to her present trade. 'I'll stay as long as I can,' he told her, 'but before you go, will you bring me up a pail of cold water and a cloth, and I'll see if I can cool her down.' She did as he had asked, and after she had gone he applied cold cloths to Emma's forehead and chest.

Time passed and the child stirred and began to cry feebly. The noise roused his patient and this time when she opened her eyes she recognised him and tried to speak but he stopped her. 'Drink this,' he said, offering the draught of feverfew, 'and lie still. I'll pass you the child.'

He picked the baby up. It was small, pale and looked like a wizened little old man. Emma took it and put it as well as she was able to the breast then sank back with exhaustion. Simon continued to wipe her forehead and after a little while gave her some more of the cinnamon mixture. Outside he could hear continued sounds of merriment and mayhem. One particularly raucous burst of shouting drew him to the window; outside, two rival bands of apprentice boys were fighting each other with staves until the constable appeared and sent them packing, threatening them with a night in the cells. A further influx of people into the street denoted that the entertainment at the Bear Pit must have ended.

Then suddenly there was great excitement as two young men

raced through the crowd, pushing people aside, even knocking them over in their haste without bothering to stop and see if they had caused any injury or damage. The reason for their hurry was obvious, for they were being hotly pursued by two or three stout fellows who looked as if they meant business. Cutpurses taking the opportunity presented by the holiday crowds, thought Simon at first, but when one of the pursued men glanced up towards the window he did not look like the usual shabby thief, for he was wearing a dark blue velvet doublet and had a sword at his side. Nor, for that matter, did his red-headed companion – who was equally well dressed and armed. More likely some personal feud then, Simon decided; perhaps the young men were thought to have taken advantage of the sisters or sweethearts of those in pursuit during a night in the woods. There was another, unarmed, man close behind them. At first Simon was not sure whether or not he was one of the pursuers, but it appeared that was not the case, for he stopped and stood still almost opposite Emma's window. As if aware of Simon watching from above he looked up at him, caught his eye for a moment, then turned and went back the way he had come.

Simon went over and looked down at Emma. She was dozing again but was breathing easier and had stopped her restless tossing and turning; the baby was asleep again beside her. He thought about going home but did not like to leave her until she had someone to stay with her. She was a brave soul and had in the past done him good service; indeed, she had directly helped him bring a villain to justice of a kind – a fact which set Simon recalling the past eventful year. He went back to the window, put the shutter to and found himself a seat on a rickety stool, which was the only piece of furniture in the room apart from Emma's bed, and waited for her friend to return.

For a little while his mind wandered on to his immediate problems, not least matters of finance. Some time before, he had quarrelled with the College of Physicians after a complaint had been laid against him by an influential City merchant, as a result of which the governing board of the College, who had always been suspicious of both his qualifications and his methods, had been only too happy to withdraw his licence to practise within the City. Since when, following requests from friends and grateful patients, they had finally promised to restore it but so far had not actually done so. He must stir himself to apply to them yet again, he told himself, after which his thoughts strayed to more pleasurable matters, not least his coming assignation with Avisa. It was still warm and he was exhausted. His head nodded and he dozed off.

Suddenly he became aware that Emma had woken and was calling to him. It was now quite dark. He took the candle from his bag, felt for flint and tinder, lit it and, after finding a holder for it, went over to the bed and lifted the flame so that he could see her. She looked up at the candle.

'Beeswax? I can't afford beeswax candles.'

'Don't fret – it's a gift. You must have some light in here. Are you feeling any better?'

'How long have you been here?' she countered. 'Who sent for you?'

'A fair while,' he admitted, explaining how her friend had come for him out of concern for her. 'You were burning with fever. I've brought it down somewhat. Do you recall me giving you various draughts?'

She shook her head weakly then felt for the baby, struggling to sit up. Simon helped her and put the bolster behind her head. She looked down at the child. 'Do you think he'll live, Dr Forman?'

She was not a woman to fool so he told her the truth. 'Who knows? The matter's in God's hands. You must know he's not a robust infant. He needs good nourishment.'

'Which I doubt I can give.' She sighed. 'I sent word to Robin that he had a son and would he come to me and give the child his name, but he sent word back that I might not claim my bastard was any child of his. Oh, I know what you think of him,' she added, looking at Simon's face, 'but in spite of all I still love him dearly. I've called the child Fortunatus.'

Simon, unable to comment on so inappropriate a name, hid his feelings by pouring her some more of the feverfew infusion and helping her drink it.

'Are you going to bleed me?' she asked. 'That's what the wise woman said I needed.'

8

'No, I'm not. I don't believe in it. As I told the Royal College, to their great rage, it seems to me a fool thing to do in at least two circumstances: where there is already a wound that has bled much, or after childbed when a woman has suffered similarly.'

'But will it not cure my fever?' she asked.

'No. It will only make you weaker. Trust me. I know no more than others as to what causes this fever after childbed, but I do not accept that it is due to a humour in the blood. I think it more likely that there is some poison in the body – but how it arrives there and why, I can't say. I've brought you some syrup of violets which you must take in the morning and twice a day thereafter for three days. It is an excellent but gentle purge. It will do you far more good than bleeding.'

'You look tired,' she told him.

Simon agreed that he was. 'It's my own fault, for I had no sleep last night. I spent it in Oxleas Woods with a party of friends bringing in the May.'

Emma smiled. 'Of course. I had forgot it's May Day. Did you have success with a lady of your choice?'

It was his turn to smile. 'More than previously. Let's say I now live in hope!'

There was a noise from below and the young whore appeared up the ladder, accompanied by an older woman. They both looked relieved at seeing Emma's improvement. 'I've brought Mary here,' the girl explained, 'as her own child was stillborn a week ago and she has much milk.'

'Since I've no little one of my own now, it seems a Christian thing to do to nourish yours,' Mary told Emma, 'so give him to me,' she continued, waving away Emma's weak thanks, 'and we'll see how he takes it.' At which she sat firmly down on the bed, picked up the child and put it to her breast where it sucked hungrily.

Simon marvelled at the sisterhood of such women who had so little but yet would turn to and help each other; relieved to see that Emma was now in good hands, he prepared to leave. She thanked him profusely, promising that she would pay him as soon as she was able, but he waved the offer away. 'You've helped me twice for little or no reward,' he said. 'Now I've left you the infusion of feverfew and the violet syrup. Take the first throughout the night and the second first thing in the morning. And let one of your friends stay with you now. I'll come back and see you tomorrow.'

He went down the ladder and out into the darkness, gulping in the outside air in spite of the staleness of the streets. A slight fresh sea smell told him it must be high tide. The streets and alleys were fast emptying of revellers though a few stragglers still roamed the alleyways, mostly the worse for drink. He was tired to death. All he wanted to do was go to bed and sleep for a week, but as he turned out of the narrow road towards the river bank and his house he heard the sounds of tramping feet coming in the opposite direction. His heart sank. It could only mean one thing: the Watch were out on their rounds. Soon they loomed up in front of him, the men armed with stout staves, the constable, holding a large lantern, marching at their head.

The Watch, made up of half a dozen honest and responsible local citizens under the command of the parish constable, was often made mock of, especially by young men. 'Nosy', 'self-important' and 'spoil-sports' were among the kindest epithets aimed at them by their critics (who, from time to time, also went so far as to aim other things such as the contents of chamber pots from bedroom windows), but most honest citizens were only too grateful that at least someone was willing to attempt to keep law and order on the streets. No doubt, this being a holiday, the Watch had spent a busy evening, and Simon resigned himself to being stopped and asked what he was doing out so late.

'Who's there?' shouted the constable, catching sight of him in the gloom. 'Stop and tell us your business and if it be honest or no!'

Resignedly Simon did so, rocking on his feet with tiredness. The constable came closer and held up his lantern, breathing the smell of onions into his face. 'Sorry, Dr Forman, didn't see it was you. But you can't be too careful on a day like today. It's been true bedlam here, hasn't it, lads?' The men nodded sagely and agreed. 'Broken heads, cutpurses, apprentice fights – we've had 'em all.'

Simon expressed his sympathy for the trials of the good men of the Watch and explained that he had just come from a very sick patient and was now in search of his bed. The constable was about to wave him off when a thought struck him.

'Just one thing, Dr Forman. You don't happen to have seen two young men running through the streets, do you?'

'I've seen many such,' replied Simon with a yawn. 'What is particular about these two that I should notice them?'

'One has carrot-red hair,' replied the constable, 'and the other dark.'

He must mean the two men he had seen that afternoon racing past Emma's house. Simon informed the constable that he had indeed seen two such fellows as described, but it was a long while back. 'They were making towards Rose Alley with others in hot pursuit. Have they broken the law then?'

The constable shook his head. 'I don't know the rights and wrongs of it. All I know is that a messenger came from up there,' he nodded upriver towards Whitehall, 'saying that if we see any such we must apprehend them. But if it's as you say, then they'll be miles away from here by now, I reckon.'

They parted company and Simon turned towards his home as the noise of the Watch receded into the distance. For the second time that day he let himself into his empty house then, without pausing to eat or drink, he climbed the stairs and, shedding his clothes on the floor, fell into his bed and straight into sleep.

The banging on his front door had gone on for some time before he realised what it was and that his servants were not there to answer it. Again he thought of ignoring it but then it struck him that possibly Emma had taken a turn for the worse and sent her friend again to fetch him. Cursing his fool generosity which had not only allowed John and Anna their day's holiday but had led him to agree that they need not return until the following morning, he groaned and put on his bedgown, found a candle, lit it, stumbled downstairs and opened the door. At first he could see no one and, assuming it must be some clown's idea of a merry prank, swore loudly and with imagination. Then he heard a groan from near by, coupled with the sound of someone making stealthily away.

He went outside and lifted up the candle. Sprawled across the path, his head towards the door, was a man lying face down. Simon knelt, set the candle beside him, and turned him over. It was the

11

young man in the blue velvet doublet he had seen running for his life that afternoon, one of the two the Watch had been asked to bring in. Simon felt a stickiness on his hand and holding it to the candlelight saw it was covered in blood. He opened the man's doublet and, seeing a dark and rapidly spreading stain on his shirt, ripped it open.

He was bleeding in two places from what looked like sword thrusts, one in the gut and the other near to the heart. The man was dying fast and it was patently obvious there was nothing Simon or anyone else could do. He looked around to see if there was anyone else about, but the street appeared deserted. He was just considering whether or not he should attempt to get the dying man indoors when he groaned and opened his eyes.

'Who are you?' asked Simon gently. 'Who did this?'

Blood trickled from the corner of the man's mouth. He made several attempts to speak but at first no sound came. Then he made a sound that could have been a name but Simon was unable to understand what he was saying, for not only was the voice faint and fading but the man spoke with a strange accent. Was he a foreigner then? The man made another attempt to communicate.

'Musna tell,' he managed. 'Musna tell . . . Carey.'

'Mustn't tell what?' urged Simon in desperation. 'I can't understand you. Do you mean Sir Henry Carey? The Lord Chamberlain?'

The injured man nodded feebly. 'Carmichael knows . . .' he whispered.

Simon put his arm round the man's shoulders and raised him up. 'Who's Carmichael?'

The victim summoned up all his strength and made one final effort.

'Hermitage!' he said. And died.

Chapter 2

Treason

Simon was shaken into wakefulness by the sounds of voices and movements downstairs. God be praised, the Bradedges must have returned! The previous night had seemed endless. Left with a corpse lying at his feet in a pool of blood and no sign of the Watch which had proved so tedious when he hadn't wanted them, Simon had sat beside the dead man for several minutes wondering what he should do. Try to drag the body into his yard and leave it until the morning? Set off, exhausted as he was, to see if he could find the Watch who might be anywhere in the maze of streets and alleyways that made up the Bankside?

Fortunately it was then that he heard footsteps and saw through the first streaks of his second wakeful dawn a stout fellow whom he recognised as one of the wherrymen who regularly plied his trade from the bottom of the nearby watersteps. He was obviously in search of early custom.

'Have you seen any sign of the Watch?' Simon called out to him.

The man stopped, turned, then came over to Simon. 'Matter o'fact, I have,' he said. 'They're sitting in a shelter about three streets away, drinking hot possets. I reckon they've earned it tonight. Why?' Simon motioned towards the man lying beside him on the path. The wherryman bent over to look.

'Is he . . . ?'

'Dead? Yes, he is.'

'What happened?'

'I've no idea,' Simon responded. 'All I know is that there was a knock on my door and I opened it to find him lying here. He died almost at once, apparently from a sword wound.'

The wherryman grunted. 'Some foolish young blood involved in a quarrel. Well off too, from the looks of him.' He rubbed his hands, for the dawn wind was chill. 'Did you want me for something then, sir?'

'Do you think you could go back to where you saw the Watch, tell them what's happened, and ask them to come here?' The man looked doubtful, but seeing there appeared to be no immediate custom in view, he gave a resigned nod and set off back the way he had come. About ten minutes later, to his profound relief, Simon heard once again the steady tramp of the Watch.

He explained to the constable, as best he could, the sequence of events leading up to his discovery of the dying man. 'It looks like one of the two young fellows you were seeking, though what he was doing on my doorstep, I've no idea. I can only think that he must have found sufficient strength to get to his feet, ask someone the way to the nearest surgeon, and then stagger off in my direction. It's not unknown for dying men to have a last burst of strength.'

'And there was no one else about when you found him?' enquired the constable.

Simon thought for a moment. 'I had a sense, no more, of someone making themselves scarce. Though whether it was his previous companion or his assailant, I've no way of knowing. On the other hand, it could simply have been some tired and innocent May Day reveller finally on their way home.'

The constable bent over the body, raising his lantern above it, as the rest of the Watch yawned and stood around. They were all tired, and sudden violent death in the street was hardly uncommon, especially where young men were concerned. 'Right, boys!' he said eventually. 'Matthew there, you go and fetch a hurdle from old Sam by the market – knock him up if you have to – then we'll take this fellow up and stow him away somewhere until the morning. There'll be a Crowner's 'Quest, of course,' he continued, 'and I'll have to give your name to the authorities.' Simon sighed. The last time he'd appeared at an Inquest had led to a chain of events that nearly ended in disaster.

As he waited for the hurdle to arrive, he examined the body of the young man again. It was definitely a sword that had given him his mortal wound, although he had also sustained cuts which suggested he had put up a fight before receiving the fatal thrust. Simon looked round to see if the man had dropped anything during the struggle that might help to identify him; he finally discovered, some feet away, a fine dagger with a chased hilt. Simon ran his finger down it. There was blood on the tip but not sufficient to suggest he had inflicted much damage on his killer if indeed it had belonged to him.

At this point, the men returned with the hurdle and Simon helped them lift the body on to it. 'Well,' he said after thanking the Watch, 'you know where I am if you want me again but, please God, not till morning. I'm going back to bed. Should they sound the Last Trump in the meantime, tell St Peter to leave me alone to sleep for the rest of Eternity!'

Now, after waking, he was content to lie in his bed for half an hour or more listening to the sounds of life returning to the empty house and the prattle of the Bradedges' little son. Finally, aware that it was well past his usual time for rising, he got up, pulled on his clothes and made his way to the kitchen. Anna had a fire burning merrily in the fireplace and was already busy with her pots and pans. The door to the yard was open and through it he could see his servant, John Bradedge, cleaning his master's boots – a routine and comforting domestic scene. Seeing Simon, John stopped what he was doing and came in.

'Was there a fight or trouble of some kind outside last night?' he enquired. 'There's what looks like a trail of blood leading to the gate and more beside it. When we saw it we were concerned it might be yours so I went upstairs in search of you but you were dead asleep.'

Simon thanked him for his concern. 'I was out to the world. I'd gone the best part of two days and nights without sleep. As to the blood – well, I finally got to bed only to be woken by a hammering on the door and went down to find some young fellow dying from a sword thrust. Who he was or what happened, I don't know. I sent for the Watch and they took him away. Maybe we'll hear more about it this morning. But now,' he said, firmly changing the subject, 'I'm going to wash under the pump. Find me something to eat and drink, will you, Anna? I must admit to being pleased you're back. I'm starving!'

Ten minutes later, his hair wet from the ablutions, Simon sat at the kitchen table hungrily attacking two pieces of fried bacon served with a hunk of bread. It seemed the Bradedges had enjoyed their brief May Day holiday to the full. First they had risen early to see the night revellers bring in the May, then watched the local May Queen's procession through the streets, and finally had gone on to a fair where John had bought his wife a knot of pretty ribbons and a piece of lace for her cap from a colourful pedlar, as well as a small wooden horse for the child. Simon explained how he had spent most of May eve in Oxleas Woods, returning home late in the morning only to be called out to Emma Ball who was half dead with childbed fever.

'Will she live?' asked Anna.

Simon sighed. 'I hope so. I've done all I can. She was at least improved by the time I left her, but she remains weak and poorly. As for the child . . . I can't see it surviving long. Fortunatus! Of all the names to bestow on it!' He stretched and yawned. 'When I've finished eating and dealt with some matters here, I must go and see how she does.'

'So you've no idea who the dead man was?' persisted John, giving his master a suspicious look. Once again, it seemed, no sooner was his master left alone without his servant's restraining presence, than he found trouble – or trouble found him.

'No. Well, not exactly,' Simon corrected himself, thus confirming John Bradedge's doubts. 'That is, I *had* seen him before, but only at a distance. I was looking out of Emma's window, keeping watch for her friend to return, when I saw him and another young fellow racing down the street pursued by a couple of others. I took it to be some May Day quarrel, probably over a woman, since they looked too well off to be thieves. Then, on my way home I met the Watch, and the constable asked if I'd seen any such fugitives. I told him what I've told you and we both agreed they were probably far away by that time.'

'And what did he want to know that for, unless they'd done something amiss?'

16

Simon shrugged. 'I don't know. He said merely that he'd been asked to look out for them.'

'You want to be careful,' returned his servant. 'Don't go getting yourself involved in anything you shouldn't. You know you've sworn you'll never do so again. You need a keeper, you do,' he muttered darkly as he prepared to return to the boots.

'You sound like an old nursemaid,' laughed Simon. He got up from the table. 'I'll go and tidy my papers in the study. Thank God it looks as though even the sick and the horoscope-seekers are too weary to come here today.'

He was as good as his word. He wrote up his casebook for the previous day, noting at length the various draughts he had given Emma Ball and the state in which he had found her, then added a few further lines on the results of the horoscopes he had cast for the two young girls. He was about to look up details of a new treatment he had recently learned of for the gout, when John Bradedge walked in without knocking. Simon looked up. His servant's face was grim.

'Seems my advice came too late,' he said grimly. 'You'd best come and see what I've found.'

They went out of the back door of the house and across the yard to the outhouse which was used both as a store and a workshop. Slumped in the corner in a state of exhaustion was the young red-headed man Simon had last seen racing down the street after his friend. Simon bent over him and shook him awake. The man groaned, opened his eyes and clutched his shoulder.

'Would you be so good as to tell me what in the Devil's name you're doing here?' Simon demanded. 'And how you got in?'

The young man tried and failed to rise to his feet. 'I climbed over your neighbour's wall at the back,' he managed eventually. 'As to what I'm doing here . . . it's a long story.' Like his dead companion he, too, spoke with a strange accent.

'Are you Flemish?' asked Simon.

'No, that he isn't,' broke in John, before the man could reply. 'He's not from the Low Countries.' He peered at the man again. 'You're a Scot, aren't you?'

The man nodded. 'I'm from the Borders.' He tried again to stand, winced and went white. 'I have a sword cut on the shoulder,' he gasped. 'I tied it up as best I could. I came looking for ye – we were told ye're a doctor. Is that so?'

Simon nodded. 'Let me look at that wound then. Help him to his feet, John, and bring him into the house. I can see to him more easily in the kitchen.'

Back inside he helped the man ease himself out of his doublet and then opened his shirt to examine the wound. Having probed round it gently, he patted his patient on his good shoulder. 'It's nasty and it'll pain you, but it's not fatal. You're lucky – it missed all the vital organs. I'll bathe it for you and put a salve on it and give you a draught for any fever, then you'd best be on your way.'

'Davie!' said the man suddenly, pushing Simon away. 'What's happened to Davie? Is he here too?'

'A young man with black hair in a blue velvet doublet, much of your height?'

'That's right. Ye do have him here then?' He looked around as if expecting to see his friend hidden in a corner somewhere then saw the expression on Simon's face. 'What is it? Where is he?'

'I'm afraid your friend's dead,' Simon told him gravely. 'I was woken in the night to find him lying on the path almost gone.'

'Dear God!' The young man stared at him. 'How?'

'Run through just below the heart,' responded Simon, firmly pushing him back in the chair and beginning to clean the cut. 'When I opened the door he was lying on the pathway. I turned him over and it was clear he was bleeding heavily. As I examined him to see if there was anything I could do, he died. That's all I can tell you. Did you leave him in such case?'

'Nae willingly. He'd a gash on his thigh then, but certainly nae thrust to the body. As I said, we were told of ye an' the last thing I recall clearly is hauling him towards your door – wounded, yes, but nae fatally. Then . . .' he paused for a moment as if struggling to remember . . . 'that's right! I heard footsteps and turned, and some limmer went for me wi'a dagger. He chased me into an alleyway and then I canna remember a thing . . . Ouch!' he exclaimed, as Simon probed the wound.

'I came to a while later tae find there was no one about. I dragged mysel' round to the front of yer house but saw nae sign of

Davie. I did nae ken what to do but thought it best I should hide mysel' until morning. Then I stumbled round again into the alleyway at the back of yer house and hauled mysel' over a wall into a garden and then through a gap in a hedge. By that time I could hardly stand. I tried the door to yer outhouse, found it open, and must have fainted again. The rest ye ken.'

'It looks as if your pursuers killed your friend then,' Simon responded. 'He must have received the second and fatal hit at their hands. Now, sit still while I apply this. I'm warning you, it'll hurt!'

His patient agreed it did, gripping the arms of the chair until his knuckles turned white. 'In the De'il's name, what is it?' he complained.

'A lotion made from the plant commonly known as "one blade" because it only bears a single leaf on its stalk; it's good for healing wounds and suchlike gashes. And this is a calendula salve – that's marigold – which is also good for healing. I'll put this pad against the wound and bind it tightly, and you should be all right at least for a day or two. Now,' he demanded, as he finished his bandaging, 'perhaps you'll be so good as to tell me who you are and what's behind all this? Quite by chance I saw you and your companion being pursued towards Rose Alley yesterday afternoon, and later on the local constable asked me if I'd seen the pair of you.'

'Well, sir, ye can have my name though I'd be glad if ye'll keep it to yerself,' the young man replied in his unfamiliar speech. 'I'm Alun Armstrong, of the Border Armstrongs. Davie is – was – my cousin, poor fellow. As to telling ye anything else . . .' He looked thoughtful for a few minutes, then continued: 'There's enough put in jeopardy by this business as it is.'

'Are you fleeing the law then,' Simon persisted, 'or being pursued by enemies?'

'As to the law, nae – so far as I understand yer English laws. We were here on private business to seek out Henry Carey, Lord Hunsdon – he who was Warden of the West March – on behalf of the Keeper of Liddesdale.'

Simon looked at him blankly. He might as well have been talking of the Kingdom of the Great Cham or the Islands of the Bemoothes as of the West March and Liddesdale. Yet hadn't the dying man tried

19

to gasp out something about Carey? The thought of my Lord Hunsdon, England's Lord Chamberlain, provoked a wry smile, for it was that very lord's mistress with whom he'd enjoyed a dalliance the previous autumn.

'See you,' continued Armstrong, 'His Lordship's son, Robert, is to be the next Warden of the West March. Did ye ken?'

'I know Robert Carey – that is, we've met several times. I saw to his wounds when we were both in the Low Countries and later advised him as to the outcome of an argosy in which he was a venturer, but as to the politics of England and Scotland, and the role played by the Careys, if any, I'm thankful to say I know nothing. Nor wish to.'

Armstrong sighed. 'All I'd have ye ken is that neither mysel' nor poor Davie are felons or masterless men. We were to have seen my Lord Hunsdon this very day, but hardly had we set foot in London when we were attacked. I've ma own ideas as to why, but if so . . .' He broke off abruptly. 'Let's just say if I'm right, it is indeed best ye ken nae more. What ye dinna ken, ye canna be made to tell,' he added grimly.

Simon was at a loss to know what to make of it all. Was he being told the truth, little though it was, or did Armstrong have something more sinister to hide? So far he had kept Davie's dying words to himself, but it had sounded as if he were saying Carey must *not* be told of something, rather than that he should. Simon opened his mouth to put this conundrum to Alun Armstrong, then decided against it. It would surely only complicate matters.

Then there was Davie's final whispered, 'Hermitage!' The word's religious connotation had caused Simon to wonder later if the dead man had been an illegal Mass priest, though admittedly he had not looked much like a man of the cloth; but then such a one would have had to be in disguise. If, as the red-headed man said, he and his cousin hailed from the Scots' side of the Borders, then were such priests tolerated there and allowed the freedom to roam unhindered?

That was most definitely no longer the case in England. For a long time Queen Elizabeth had been determined to allow religious differences, so long as recusants paid their fines and behaved themselves, for she was still haunted by the memory of the fires of

Smithfield kindled by her half-sister Queen Mary, when good men and women had gone to the stake for their beliefs. But since the series of plots centred round Mary Stuart, not to mention the Spanish Armada, times had changed and immigrant Catholic priests were hunted down without mercy; their fate, if caught, was the dreadful death reserved for traitors.

Simon shook himself. Whatever the truth, young Armstrong was right: the less he knew the better. 'So,' he said as he regarded his handiwork, 'what do you intend to do now?'

'Leave London and return to Scotland without delay,' Armstrong replied, 'not least for fear I draw the hounds on to ye as well. As for Davie . . .' He gave Simon a bleak look. 'What happens now? I can scarcely claim his body wi'out giving mysel' up, an' there's little point in that. Though I swear one day I'll avenge this. On the Borders we vow a life for a life!'

No, thought Simon to himself, I quite definitely don't want to become mixed up in any of this. 'There'll be an Inquest,' he replied, 'and I'm likely to be called to give evidence, seeing it was I who found your cousin dying. Since I've no wish to seek out trouble, so far as I'm concerned he's still an unknown stranger and as such I've no idea who he was and not the slightest knowledge as to why he was killed. If asked, I shall say what I thought was originally the case: that most likely he was the victim of a hot-blooded May Day quarrel – probably over some young woman. As for his burial, he'll be put in a pauper's grave unless there's money for a proper funeral.'

'Here.' Armstrong pulled a purse from his pocket. 'English guineas. Take what ye need to see him take a decent grave,' he begged. 'Tell them ye found his purse close by, if need be. Then, perhaps, one day we can bring him back home where he belongs.'

Simon nodded and took the money. 'You'd best stay close in my outhouse until it's dark and then seek to make your way out of London. If you still fear pursuit, you must decide whether to cross by London Bridge or ferry, though I'd advise the former. Then lose yourself in the City while making your way north. As to your pursuers, if you're unlucky they might well have stayed close by, assuming you would return to discover what happened to your cousin. On the other hand, they might be waiting for you elsewhere to prevent your seeing Carey.' He smiled. 'I can cast horoscopes too, but in your situation I would be terrified of making a mistake!'

Armstrong thanked him and they returned again to the outhouse. John Bradedge was despatched for an old mattress and a blanket and when he returned with them, Simon asked him to send Anna out with some food and drink, then swore him to silence. The look his servant gave him spoke volumes.

'And now I must leave you,' Simon told Armstrong. 'I've a sick woman to see to. I may well not return until dark, by which time I trust you'll be gone.'

Armstrong grasped him by the hand. 'My grateful thanks, sir. May I know your name? I've given ye mine.'

'Forman. Dr Simon Forman.'

'Well, Dr Forman, should ye ever be in need of a friend on the Borders – or elsewhere – ye can call on the Armstrongs for assistance. We are deeply in your debt. Tell any who might ask that Alun Armstrong's your friend till time stops.'

Much to his relief, Emma showed a definite improvement. She still looked weak but she was no longer flushed with fever. Her friend of the previous night was sitting on the end of her bed suckling the baby and all seemed to be well. He checked that Emma had taken the draughts he'd prescribed, and advised her to keep taking them until all were used up. She thanked him profusely.

'There's no need for that,' he told her. 'Be quiet and concentrate on getting well again.'

'There's just one thing,' she said, clutching at his hand. 'Do you think you could seek out Robin and ask him to come and see me? He trusts you. Tell him I near died of the child and that he has a son. It *is* his son. Look at his head against the light. See how the down on it is red like his father's hair. Say I beg him to come and acknowledge the boy after all we've been to each other, and that he must give Fortunatus his name.'

Simon said he'd do his best but privately doubted he would be able to persuade Greene to comply. Ever extravagant in his feelings, Greene had protested loudly and publicly that the child was none of his but was the result of some commercial coupling. In that he might

22

well have had a strictly legal point, but given the way Emma had cared for him over the years, letting him live in her own house and whoring to get the wherewithal to keep her drunken and philandering lover in funds, it seemed grossly unfair. Reluctantly Simon agreed and Emma gave him her errant lover's direction.

'It's quite close to St Paul's Church. He lodges with a shoemaker and his wife. Good people, they say. It's to be hoped he pays them for what they do.' She clutched Simon's hand again. 'I'm told he's mortal sick. Will you do what you can for him?'

As Simon set off on his errand of mercy he pondered again about the curious and violent events of the night. Alun Armstrong had seemed honest enough, yet . . . What was all that about 'hermitage'? If the dead man had been an illicit Jesuit priest then surely it would have been more likely for him to have gasped out 'abbey' or 'seminary' than 'hermitage'. It was a puzzle but not one he wished to unravel. Whether he had unwittingly harboured a Catholic priest or a Scots' traitor, it was best forgotten as soon as possible.

He found Greene at home and it was clear that Emma had been right when she said he was now a very sick man. While living with her on the Bankside, Greene had regularly called on Simon's services, whether he could pay for them or not. Over the years Simon had prescribed for a whole pharmacopoeia of diseases, from the clap to the various fevers brought on by an over-excess of drink. He had warned him continually that if he did not modify his style of life he would be unlikely to see his middle years, let alone old age. But Greene was incorrigible.

He was lying in his bed, his face dark and flushed, a swollen foot outside on the coverlet. He greeted Simon with a grunt. 'Come to gloat, have you? Come to see all your dire warnings proved right?'

'What brought it on this time?' demanded Simon, ignoring this.

'Four days' hard drinking with Kit Marlowe. You know what he's like when the black mood's on him. He paid for the drink,' Robert added, 'or at least I suppose his lover, Tom Walsingham, did indirectly. Since I woke up from it, I've been like this.' But in spite of his excesses his bed was clean and he had obviously been cared for.

'Who's looking after you?' Simon asked, feeling for his pulse.

'The shoemaker's wife. They've been very good to me,' he added, somewhat shamefaced.

'Then it's to be hoped you're paying them properly,' returned Simon. 'You're full of bile – the blood's racing through your veins. God's bones, man, you're poisoning yourself!'

'I *will* pay them properly. I'm going to write to my wife in Norwich and ask her for money for my care, though I haven't seen her since a year after the wedding, nor the child. Pretty bitch, though. Flaxen-haired.' Then a thought struck him. 'Why are you here? I don't recall asking these good people to send for you.'

'Emma asked me to come.'

Greene swore and turned his face to the wall. Simon leant over and forcibly turned him back. 'Sit up, will you, you're not yet at death's door! And at least hear what I've got to say. Yesterday Emma was near death of the childbed fever. It's taken all my skill to bring her round. She swears the child is yours and begs you to visit her and give the child your name.'

'It's a bastard!'

'It's a bastard all right, but very likely *your* bastard. At least please her in that after all she's done for you.'

Greene slumped down in the bed again. 'The child of a whore like Emma could be anyone's child.'

'The child is frail and unlikely to live long. The way you're going on, it will be a race to the grave between the pair of you. What possible harm can it do to recognise the boy for the short time he's on this earth?'

But Greene was adamant. 'I've the family name to consider,' he said, outrageously. 'The Greenes are well thought of and respected in Norwich.'

'So they might be,' fumed Simon, 'but not here. You've done everything in your power to drag their name through the mud.'

Greene sat up again and waved his arm in a grand gesture. 'Leave me, will you. I am, after all, a poet. I'll go further than that. A *great* poet. And a dramatist. Who cares for these fly-by-night peasants who arrive here from the country? My name will be remembered long after they've been forgotten, along with that of a meddling country doctor. Sneck off!'

Simon did as he was bid, but took the opportunity to have a word with the shoemaker to the effect that if Greene's illness took a turn for the worse and they wanted to send for him, he would come even though he was not supposed to practise north of the river.

The afternoon was still fine and he decided to take a boat across the river rather than walk across London Bridge. The rotting heads on pikes which usually decorated the entrance to it from the north side had struck an extra chill in him earlier as he considered again the penalties for giving succour to the Queen's enemies. But taken at face value, there was nothing in Alun Armstrong's story to suggest he was a traitor, especially if it was indeed true he was to have seen the Lord Chamberlain. There was little wind and although the tide was flowing up from the sea, the wherryman soon had Simon over the river to the steps close to his house. He felt in his purse for coins, paid his fare and then jumped out of the boat.

'You seem to have friends waiting for you,' said the wherryman as he bit on a coin to see if it was true. 'Up there!' He motioned up the steps. Simon turned to see a ring of faces looking down on him.

'No friends of mine,' he said with a laugh and began to ascend the steps. The men let him reach the top.

'Dr Simon Forman?' asked one, who seemed to be in charge.

'Yes. Can I do anything for you?' Simon enquired.

'Hold him, men!' ordered the speaker. 'Tie his hands behind his back.'

'What's the meaning of this?' shouted Simon, struggling to keep his hands free.

'I ask the questions here, not you.' The man in charge went to the top of the steps and whistled, and a sizeable boat, which had been stationary a few yards off, pulled in with no fewer than three men at the oars. Simon was hustled down the steps and almost thrown into it, his reception party following behind.

'Where are you taking me? Who are you?' Simon demanded. One fellow made as if to cuff him but their leader motioned him to stop. 'Leave all that – for now,' he added ominously. Then he turned to Simon. 'As for you, you'll know the answers to your questions soon. Let it suffice you that we're on the Queen's business.'

The oarsmen pulled away and the boat turned upriver, assisted by the incoming tide. They soon left behind the alleyways of the Bankside on the one side and the houses of the wealthy on the other, and in no time were passing the great houses of the nobility, set in their fine gardens, on the north bank.

After a short time it was clear they were making for Whitehall. Finally the boat arrived at a flight of steps close to the Palace of Westminster and Simon was roughly urged to his feet and pushed upwards. Then he was marched towards a small side door where the leader of the men dismissed his followers and, drawing a dagger which he held at Simon's back, told him to walk ahead without stopping or making any trouble or he would not be answerable for the consequences.

They climbed in silence up two flights of stone steps (this was obviously some unobtrusive rear entrance) until they suddenly emerged on to a carpeted corridor, off which led several heavily panelled doors. Still pushing Simon before him the man made directly for one of them and knocked on it. It was opened to him by a pale-faced fellow who, from his ink-stained fingers, would appear to be some kind of clerk. The two men conferred in whispers.

'Wait here a moment,' said the clerk, and shut the door again.

'Are you going to tell me what in God's name this is all about?' demanded Simon again, but the man merely gave him an unpleasant smile. The door re-opened and the clerk returned.

'You're to bring him in,' he said. The room was an austere one but furnished with wealth and taste. A polished wooden desk stood at one end of it, on which were set several neat piles of papers. Through a door he could glimpse a more modest chamber with a table where, presumably, a clerk or secretary worked. The dying light of the afternoon came in from a glazed window with diamond-shaped panes which overlooked the river. There was a movement from behind him and he turned as another man entered the room.

'You can go,' the newcomer said curtly to the guard. 'If I need assistance I'll call for you.' He was of average height but broad in the shoulder and with a face more suited to a tradesman than to the person of authority his clothes suggested, for his doublet was of dun velvet and he wore several fine rings on his fingers. Simon wondered who he was. The man seemed in no hurry to engage Simon in conversation but eventually, having walked up and down the room a few times, he went over to the desk, riffled self-importantly through some papers, then came round and sat on the front of it.

'So,' he stated, 'you are the necromancer, Simon Forman.'

'I am Dr Simon Forman, sir, physician and astrologer – but no necromancer. And who, may I ask, are you?'

'Edward Rowe, secretary to Sir Robert Cecil, son to the Lord of Burleigh. I am here on his behalf.'

Simon was appalled. Cecil was Acting Secretary to the Privy Council, 'Acting' Secretary because the Queen had so far refused to ratify his appointment to the position which had become vacant on the death of the great Sir Francis Walsingham. Rumour had it that Cecil had been so eager to assume the post that he was carrying out his duties without any financial reward whatsoever, to ensure that so coveted a place would finally be his; for it was one of great power. It also carried with it another responsibility, that of spymaster, overseeing and organising the network of intelligencers originally set up by Sir Francis. Sir Robert was considered by all to be a formidable man.

Sir Robert's secretary gave this time to sink in then asked: 'Do you know why you have been brought here?'

Simon shook his head. 'I have absolutely no idea.'

'Come now,' responded his interrogator. 'Surely you can do better than that?'

'Truly, it is a mystery to me,' Simon reiterated. 'I was on my way back from seeing a patient when I found your men waiting for me by the steps close to my house. They gave me no reason for bringing me here and I can think of none.'

Rowe smiled unpleasantly and clasped his fingers together. 'Then how does "treason" strike you? Treason against Her Majesty. Consorting with her enemies. And you know what happens to traitors, don't you, Dr Forman?'

Chapter 3

The Devil's Bargain

Sweet Jesu, thought Simon, going cold. This must be to do with the two young Scots but, like a drowning man whose life flashes before him in an instant, he realised it was essential he stick by his original simple story. He had been awoken in the middle of the night to find a young man dying on his doorstep; he had then called the Watch like any good citizen – and that was all he knew. Then a further frightening thought struck him. Sir Robert Cecil was known to be a fanatical anti-Catholic. Anti-Catholic! Perhaps his first surmise was correct after all and Davie *had* been a disguised Jesuit priest.

'You seem to have been struck dumb, Dr Forman,' Rowe commented.

Simon took a deep breath. 'That is because I'm quite astounded. There must be some mistake. I'm a loyal subject of Her Majesty and have never involved myself in anything remotely treasonable.'

The secretary smiled unpleasantly. 'So why then did a Scots spy make straight for your house last night?'

Simon gave what he hoped was the appearance of being completely nonplussed. '*What* Scots spy? Please will you explain to me what I'm supposed to have done.'

Rowe began to pace up and down once again. 'We have been given to understand that last night a young man, already under suspicion as an intelligencer, was found dying outside your house and you beside him.'

'Certainly I was woken by a hammering on my door when I'd been long abed and answered it to find a dying man outside. As I told the Watch *when I sent for them*,' he emphasised, 'I examined the

29

man to see if there was anything I could do, but he died almost at once. He had been run through with a sword and it occurred to me that he might well be the victim of a jealous lover who suspected him of taking liberties with the object of his affections on May Eve. The constable arranged for the body to be taken away and told me I might be called to the Inquest since I had discovered him. And that, truly, is all I know. I have no idea who the man was.'

Rowe stopped his pacing. 'Really? Then why did he come to your house?'

Simon shrugged. 'The only reason I can think of is that somehow he had managed to ask someone the way to the nearest doctor and had been given my direction. As I told the Watch, it's not all that uncommon for dying men to have a last burst of strength. I saw it myself on a number of occasion when I was soldiering.'

'Did he tell you his name? Ask about a companion? Indeed, say anything at all?'

Simon shook his head. 'As I've just told you, he died even before I could properly examine him.'

Rowe regarded him coldly. 'I do not know if I believe you, Dr Forman.'

'Then I'm sorry, Master Rowe, but it's the truth.'

Rowe came nearer. 'I wonder. I very much wonder. I ask myself, if I had you taken to Bridewell and put to the rack or, indeed, removed to the cellars beneath this building and handed over to Topcliffe to hang from his pillar, whether you might find that after all you had a great deal more to tell me.'

Simon was beginning to feel as if he was experiencing one of the nightmares to which he was prone – except that there would be no waking from this bad dream. He had no doubt the man would not hesitate to carry out his threat.

'All I can say to you, sir, is that I've seen men and even women put to the torture before I became a doctor and know how pain can be inflicted and its results. I know most will say anything to stop it. I also know my own limitations for, like many physicians, I do not bear pain well. I am quite sure that if you racked me or handed me over to the Queen's torturer, as you threaten, then I would say anything, *anything*, you wished, but since I know nothing of this dead man it wouldn't be real information because I have none. I don't see therefore how this could help you.'

'A fair point, Dr Forman,' came a soft voice from behind. Simon turned round in surprise to see a man standing behind him who had obviously entered silently through a door of which he had been unaware. He was of small stature, his dark hair swept back from a high forehead, and with a neatly trimmed beard. His doublet was of rich dark blue velvet, almost black, over which he wore a fine black gown while his ruff was of the most exquisite lace. His most striking feature however, was his left shoulder – which was quite definitely higher than the other, giving him something of a humped-back look. Born like it, thought Simon, who had seen several such. He knew at once with whom he now had to deal: Sir Robert Cecil himself.

Cecil looked across to his secretary. 'I cannot see that there was any need for this, Rowe. Dr Forman deserves better from us. Go now, I'll send for you when Dr Forman and I have spoken together.' He went over to his desk and sat behind it. 'You may pull up a chair,' he said to Simon, 'for I have a suggestion to make to you.'

Simon did as he asked, unable to imagine what possible suggestion so powerful a man could make to him. Cecil, however, seemed relaxed and at ease. 'When I took over my position from my esteemed predecessor, Sir Francis Walsingham,' he began, 'I thought it necessary to look into just who had been employed by him in his intelligence service. I was aware he had made great efforts to improve the calibre of his intelligencers from the days when such people were drawn from the ranks of the disaffected, those who spy only for money and those who are blunt tools and as such are easily expendable. Indeed, he made use of his nephew, Thomas, to recruit among the bright undergraduates at Cambridge – a truly novel idea, you must admit.'

Simon wondered where this was leading and it was with a jolt that he heard Cecil's next words. 'Which is where I found your name, Dr Forman.'

'But I never went to Cambridge, Sir Robert. Although the University recognises my qualifications.'

'I did not claim that you had, only that your name was on Sir Francis's files. It seems you sent or brought him intelligence during

31

your time on the Continent, first when you were a soldier and later as you studied medicine.'

Oh God, thought Simon, I hoped I'd put all that behind me. 'It was only on a handful of occasions, Sir Robert, and that many years ago. It came about because I was approached to do so, the first time by a senior officer. Then later by the secretary to Sir Antony Bacon who asked for any information that might come my way on the comings and goings of seminary priests from either Rome or the college in Rheims. He felt I was in a good place to pick up such gossip, being as I was studying in Italy and had contacts in France. He gave me money, for which I was grateful, to help me in my studies.'

A thought struck him. 'I trust the man *was* Sir Antony's secretary; he certainly showed me a document to that effect. But since I set up as a physician, I've had no such dealings with that world and want none.'

'Maybe not, but it seems Sir Francis thought highly of you. Highly enough to intervene on your behalf the first time you quarrelled with the College of Physicians. Oh yes, Dr Forman, I'm well aware of the position in which you find yourself now. Still without your licence to practise medicine, I understand?'

Simon wondered how long this was going to go on and whether or not, at the end of it, he would still be dispatched to the cellars to the tender mercies of Topcliffe, the state's official torturer, who openly boasted that he could get any information required out of a man whether he knew it or not. He became aware that Cecil was still speaking. 'The young man who died on your doorstep and his companion – whom we have not yet apprehended – are Scots from the Border country, here, we think, on a spying mission.'

Once again Simon was assailed by doubt. Was Armstrong's story of the message being taken to Lord Hunsdon untrue, and had they actually intended him some harm? Or was Cecil deliberately trying to trap him into incriminating himself? Why, oh why, he thought desperately, had some fool pointed the wounded man in his direction?

Cecil continued. 'The Queen is getting old, Dr Forman. Even Gloriana will die one day, and so it becomes ever more of a certainty that James of Scotland, Mary Stuart's son, will then ascend the throne. Indeed, it is the only possible resolution unless we want to see ourselves plunged into the kind of civil war that racked this realm throughout the last century – and I do not intend that should happen. There will, therefore, have to be delicate and careful negotiations to this end during the coming years. In the meantime, however, there are those who are not prepared to wait.

'I am well aware that there is a steady stream of men, or their emissaries, going north to Edinburgh to see how the land lies and, where possible, to ingratiate themselves with King James to ensure his favour on the death of the Queen. They range from cheap opportunists who can be easily dealt with to those who already have power in this land and want more of it when James comes to the throne. The more intelligence I can glean as to who is secretly negotiating with James, the better I can guard against later . . . mishaps.'

He rocked back in his chair. 'It occurs to me therefore, Dr Forman, that you can do me a service. I am told there are excellent physicians and doctors in Edinburgh. What more natural then that you should visit them to enquire as to their treatments and physics, and any new knowledge they might have? You have, after all, a reputation for acquiring and making use of such – to the obvious annoyance and irritation of the College of Physicians. What I am putting to you is this: you will go to Edinburgh to talk to your colleagues, and while you are there you will keep your eyes and ears open on my behalf.'

Simon swallowed. 'And what if I decline, sir?'

Cecil sadly shook his head. 'I am already taking a risk. There are those on the Privy Council who, I can assure you, are only too willing to believe that anyone linked to a possible Scots spy, even if he is now dead, is a threat to the realm. If I can reassure them that you are now engaged on my own personal business then I can save you from being handed over to Topcliffe to discover for them why you are alleged to have harboured the Queen's enemies. Speaking of which, I must apologise for my secretary; he tends to be over-zealous on my behalf.'

It *was* a nightmare, thought Simon, and he wasn't going to wake up. Whilst Cecil's attitude was eminently reasonable, the bargain was no bargain at all. Simon's choice lay between the dangers of undertaking a deeply hazardous and unwanted enterprise to Edinburgh on behalf of Sir Robert Cecil, or hours of agony followed by certain death on the orders of other unknown but equally powerful members of the Queen's government.

'It seems you leave me no alternative but to do as you ask, Sir Robert,' he said finally.

Cecil smiled. 'Come now, it's not as desperate as that. So,' he continued in practical tones, 'take a week or so to put your affairs in order here before you leave for Edinburgh. I shall send to the College of Physicians this very day commanding they restore your licence to practise immediately, and I will see that you are given sufficient funds to ensure your needs while you are away. I reckon it will take you at least ten days to reach Edinburgh, given the terrain through which you will have to travel. Let's hope that you will find out all I need to know within two or three weeks of arriving. That would mean you'll be back in London by the end of June or beginning of July.'

'May I take my manservant with me?' asked Simon.

'I see no reason why not. I presume he's trustworthy?'

'Most trustworthy. Last year he saved my life when I was set on by . . . er . . . assailants.'

'Very well. Now I will also make arrangements for you to see my good friend, Lord Hunsdon, the Lord Chamberlain.' It was all Simon could do not to show surprise. So Hunsdon *was* involved! 'Have you met His Lordship?' asked Cecil.

Simon admitted that he had not, but that he was an acquaintance of His Lordship's son, Robert Carey. Since Cecil was said to have his spies everywhere, he wondered if the question had a hidden meaning and that somehow he had found out about his brief affair with Hunsdon's black-haired mistress.

But if that was the case, Cecil gave no sign of it. 'Carey was once Warden of the English side of the West March and, as such, is probably the most knowledgeable man there is on the problems that can beset travellers crossing the Border – and on how information passes through it in both directions. It is not yet common knowledge but Robert Carey is soon to take up the same position when the present incumbent leaves. Sir Henry will give you any advice you might need, not least the best route to Edinburgh from Carlisle . . .'

'Carlisle?' Simon broke in. 'Why Carlisle? Surely it's quicker and easier to travel north on the eastern side of the country?'

'In strictly practical terms yes,' agreed Cecil, 'but there's trouble on the East March and you will be safer going through Carlisle. It might also be helpful for the castle governor there to know your whereabouts. You might well find that, compared to crossing the Border without trouble, discovering for me who is plotting in Edinburgh will be the easiest of your tasks! Unfortunately, for many miles on the Scots side lie what are known as the Debatable Lands where the rule of law, such as it is, lies in the hands of dangerous and ruthless brigands.'

Cecil stood up. The audience was obviously at an end. 'So, go home now, Dr Forman, and prepare to go north. I'm aware of the misgivings you must have and the dangers you might face but be assured, you are on a vital mission. And it is an honour, is it not, so to serve our Queen? You may take one of my boats to your home.' He got up and opened the door to his secretary's room. Inside Simon could see the clerk, Rowe and another man who had his back to the door.

'Take Dr Forman down the steps and find him a boat, will you?' said Cecil to the clerk, then turned back to Simon. 'I will send for you again in a few days' time to give you final instructions. In the meantime I'll despatch a messenger to the Lord Chamberlain asking him to see you.'

After Simon and the clerk had left the room Cecil resumed his seat at his desk and pulled one of the pile of papers towards him. Rowe, after saying something quietly to the other man in the clerk's office (who then shrugged and shook his head), came back into Cecil's room and went over to his master. Cecil looked up at him with impatience. 'Well?' he snapped. 'What now?'

'Do you think what you've done is wise, sir?' Rowe asked. 'After all, you know very little about the man.'

Cecil gave him a steely look. 'I think Dr Forman will do very well. He will do very well indeed. Now get back to your work.'

* * *

Simon arrived home to be greeted by his servants with obvious relief but a relief clouded with apprehension.

'One of the wherrymen came and told us they'd seen you hustled away in a boat by a group of men who looked as if an officer of some kind was in charge,' John Bradedge told him as soon as he got through the door. 'When he saw your party making upriver he feared you were being taken to the Star Chamber – and so were we!'

'I didn't quite get that far,' Simon responded, 'but it was a close thing. I nearly ended up hanging from Topcliffe's pillar!'

Anna gave a cry of alarm which was echoed by a snort from her husband. 'I wager you a crown it's to do with the man that died on our doorstep and he who hid in our outhouse – don't worry, he's not there any more. When we heard the news I told him immediately and we were able to hustle him out the side way, wrapped in an old cloak, during a heavy shower of rain. I *told* you you shouldn't have had anything to do with it.'

'And I told you there was no alternative presented with a dying man,' Simon said patiently.

John looked unconvinced. 'So now what? I don't imagine that's all there is and that we can now forget about it.'

Simon sighed. 'I'm afraid not. I was taken to the office of Sir Robert Cecil. Yes, you might well look like that,' he added, seeing the expression of dismay on his servant's face. 'I stuck to my story, that I knew nothing of the man who died, and whether or not I finally convinced him I don't know, but he persuaded me that my duty lay in going to Edinburgh on a special mission for him.'

'Why you? Surely you told him that as a doctor you've plenty to do here?'

Simon grimaced. 'It wasn't quite such a straight choice. Sir Robert gave me two options: to go up to Scotland on his behalf and with his protection, or to take my chance with his colleagues and possibly be put to the torture to extract any information I might be withholding from them.'

John turned to his wife. 'I knew we shouldn't have gone away. Look what happens when we leave the house for so much as a night! Just see what you've got yourself into,' he continued, turning back to Simon.

'I've not "got myself" into anything,' Simon replied testily. 'Circumstances have brought this about. The only part I played in finding myself in this predicament so far as I can see is my being a physician. Anyway, there appears to be no alternative. Cecil has given me a week to put my affairs in order and then I must leave for Carlisle then Edinburgh. It seems I must cross the Border on the west side because it's the safest place to do so, although from what Cecil said, "safe" is a somewhat relative concept. He has also told me I must seek advice from the Lord Chamberlain since he was once Warden of the West March. So it does look as if the Careys are involved in all this in one way or another but how, God alone knows!'

He felt suddenly very weary. 'Oh, and there's one more thing, John. I asked Cecil if you might accompany me and he agreed. It will mean your being away a month or six weeks but not, I hope, much longer. You're free not to come, of course,' he added, 'but I'd be relieved if you would.'

'Try and stop me,' replied his servant. 'Though what the end of all this will be, I can't imagine.'

The next morning a messenger arrived from the Royal College of Physicians bearing an official document reinstating Simon's licence to practise in the City. Eagerly awaited for so long, the circumstances in which the College had finally carried out what they had so long promised failed to rouse in Simon, as he read the accompanying letter, the feelings of relief and pleasure he had expected. Had they wished, he thought dismally, they could have done this months earlier and without the intervention of so mighty a politician. Not long afterwards he received a second messenger, this one bearing a missive fastened with the seal of the Lord Chamberlain of England and summoning him to a meeting with His Lordship the following day at his townhouse over the river.

So, after a brief breakfast, Simon took himself off across London Bridge in search of His Lordship. It was a fine spring day and the Bridge was crowded with shoppers and sightseers. As he crossed under the archway on the north side, Simon averted his eyes from the decaying heads of those convicted of treason which were regularly displayed there, wondering gloomily if his would join them should he fail in his mission.

As he sat in an antechamber in Sir Henry Carey's house waiting to be shown in to see the great man, he tried to recall what he knew of him. Henry Carey, Lord Hunsdon, was both in build and personality very different to Cecil. Although now well into his sixties he looked considerably younger. He was still handsome, tall and broad-shouldered with a soldier's bearing. He was cousin to the Queen, the eldest son of Mary Boleyn, the late Queen Anne's sister, but it was widely rumoured that he was more than that, for Mary had been mistress to King Henry VIII before her sister's disastrous marriage to that monarch, and her own marriage to one of the Carey family had been a hasty one.

Looking at the fine surroundings and obvious trappings of wealth and power, Simon hoped sincerely that no breath had ever reached the Lord Chamberlain that they had shared his official mistress, if only for a few weeks. The woman in question, Emilia Bassano, dark, predatory and sensationally attractive, had made an overt set at him and he had found it both flattering and exciting, even though he loved elsewhere. But he had seen nothing of her since the previous autumn and had been told she was now married to a court musician, one Alfonso Lanier, and was the mother of a son called Henry after his real father. Like father, like son, he thought, considering His Lordship's own probable father. How easily the great ones can palm their offspring on to others.

He was woken from his reverie by the entry of a servant who informed him that Lord Hunsdon would see him in the library. He found His Lordship looking out of the window, his great bulk blocking the light. The face he turned on Simon was not a particularly friendly one and his tone was positively chilly. 'I do not know why Sir Robert Cecil has asked for my assistance in helping you reach Edinburgh in safety, Dr Forman, though no doubt he has a reason. I doubt it is his urgency to learn new ways of curing the clap. Nor does it take a fortuneteller to divine that the honour does not sit happily on you. Indeed, if it was thought worthwhile one might speculate on what means were used to convince a man such as you to do as he has asked.'

Simon's mouth went dry. A man such as you? Was that intended as an insult? Would my Lord's next remark refer to Emilia? Suppose he was harbouring a mad jealousy and would either refuse to help Simon or, even worse, give him false information which would lead to his death. The biblical tale of David and Bathsheba provided just such an example.

'You seem far away, Dr Forman,' Carey broke in loudly, causing Simon to jump. 'However,' he continued, 'since you will go, I must do my best to help you.' He went over to a table in the corner of the room and came back with several sheets of paper. The first was a map. 'This is the part of the Border where you will cross from Carlisle, part of the West March where, for a short while, you will have to pass through the Debatable Lands. You see I have marked for you two suggested routes, one straight up north through Moffat and then north-east to Edinburgh, the second up through Liddesdale to Hawick and thence to Edinburgh. The latter looks the rougher and more difficult but the Keeper of Liddesdale, John Carmichael, is a fair and just man and we have had many dealings with each other. I have written a letter for you to give him if you meet up with him.'

'And will that keep me safe?' enquired Simon, wondering why the name John Carmichael struck a chord.

'Safe!' Hunsdon gave a grim laugh. 'No one and nothing is safe on the Borders. Do you know anything of those that live there?' Simon shook his head. 'Then I'll tell you. Many are little better than savages. The clans or tribes stretch across both sides of the Border. Sometimes they fight each other, sometimes those on the Scots' side fight those on the English, but both are quite capable of ignoring local enmities to unite against soldiers sent by either government – and many claim they have no allegiance to the English Queen or the Scottish King but only to themselves. To the frightened folk of the lowlands they're known as the Reivers – thieves and murderers who descend on helpless farmsteads and villages in the dead of night, carry off their cattle and kill any who stand in their way. They have their own laws and their own codes of honour, if such a word can be used of them.'

For the next quarter of an hour he expanded on his theme. How the English and Scots Wardens of the Marches were supposed to keep the peace and how difficult it was, particularly as not all those charged with the task were fair or impartial in their behaviour. Also that the lawless Border provided great cover for intelligencers from both sides to cross into each other's countries and return bringing information back to their respective rulers. As he listened, Simon's spirits sank lower and lower. From what Hunsdon said and Cecil had hinted, it looked as if he'd be lucky even to reach Edinburgh alive.

'But surely as a doctor,' he suggested, 'I'll not be considered a danger to anyone?'

Hunsdon laughed cynically. 'In 1582 a man was arrested by Sir John Forster on the English side of the Border. He claimed to be a barber-surgeon – and when they searched his baggage they did indeed find a set of instruments for pulling teeth and cauterising wounds. They kept his goods, including a handsome looking-glass – Forster was never nice in his conduct and thought it would please his wife – then sent him on his way. Days later, when the man had long disappeared, Forster discovered letters hidden between the glass and its wooden back, letters written in code. Walsingham's code-breakers were set to work and found various references to an unknown "Enterprise of England". Thus we discovered the plans for the great Armada. Since then, I doubt whether your being a physician would save your skin.'

He spent a little while longer going through various documents and letters he had written which might be of use, then he made it clear the interview was at an end. 'That's all I can do for you, Dr Forman,' he said brusquely. 'I trust you'll find it of use.' Simon thanked him and was about to leave when the door opened and a younger man entered whose features bore a close resemblance to those of the Lord Chamberlain. He looked at Simon in amazement.

'Simon Forman!' he exclaimed. 'What in thunder are *you* doing here?'

'You know my son, Robert?' asked His Lordship in some surprise.

Robert Carey smiled broadly. 'We met first in the Low Countries, Father, before Simon took up either doctoring or casting horoscopes professionally. Since when, I've availed myself of his services under both hats. He has dosed me with his medicines and promised I'd be cured, and also reassured me the stars foretold my argosy would bring me good fortune. He was right on both counts. So what brings you here, Simon?'

'I'm to go to Edinburgh and your father has been giving me his advice,' Simon replied.

'It seems your friend here is to pay a visit to discover what new wonders of medicine are favoured by Scots doctors. And that no lesser person than Sir Robert Cecil is mindful of his safety,' added Sir Henry with evident disbelief. He turned to Simon. 'I do not know if Cecil told you, Dr Forman, but Robert here is soon to be Warden of the West March.'

Robert Carey clapped Simon on the back. 'Now you're here, come and have a cup of wine with me and let us reminisce about old times.'

So Simon took his leave and Robert led the way down a corridor to a small sitting room, calling to a servant to bring them a bottle of canary and two wine cups. 'Now we're alone, Simon,' he said, 'perhaps you can tell me exactly how you've come to find yourself travelling to Edinburgh and what Cecil has to do with it?'

Simon felt he did not know whom to trust. Davie Armstrong's dying words had seemed to imply there was something the Careys must on no account be told, yet Alun had said they were actually on their way to see the Lord Chamberlain with a message when they were set upon. Until now he had never had cause to distrust Robert Carey and he was desperately in need of help and advice.

He came to a decision. He would tell Robert some of the truth, leaving out anything he thought it unwise to divulge. So he explained that on the night of May Day he had been awoken to find a man almost dead at his door and that later that day he had treated another who had been wounded. 'The second man told me he was Alun Armstrong and he who'd died, Davie, his cousin. He also said they had been bringing a message to your father from the Keeper of Liddesdale who I now know to be Sir John Carmichael, who's known to your father. Somehow news of the first man's death outside my house reached high places, as a result of which I was taken to Whitehall and threatened with torture until no lesser person than Sir Robert Cecil himself intervened to save me. I told the man who questioned me that I knew nothing of the dying man and had not seen his companion and had no idea who they were.'

'And you said the same to Cecil?'

Simon said he had, 'But I don't know if he believed me. Were you expecting these men then? Or know what their business was?'

Robert shook his head. 'I know nothing of it. But if, as you say, they were Armstrongs from the Border country then I can only imagine it must have something to do with the West March. Possibly Carmichael thinks there is trouble brewing and has sent word to my father, knowing that I am to become Warden there.'

'Cecil said it's thought the men were spies.'

'Then he must know little of the Border clans in general and the Armstrongs in particular,' Robert commented. 'I imagine the Armstrongs would be the last people King James would trust as intelligencers! But I still don't understand why you must go to Edinburgh.'

Simon had to admit his reasons sounded somewhat thin. 'It's as I told your father. I'm going to talk with Scots doctors and, while I'm there, I'm to pick up any gossip I might think useful,' he finished lamely.

Robert heard him with growing incredulity. 'And that's all? You were so easily persuaded on so hazardous a venture merely to discuss physic receipts and listen to tittle-tattle?'

Simon was beginning to feel desperate. 'When Cecil saved me from the rack, or worse, he told me that there are those in high places – he didn't name them – who believe I'm in league with Scots intelligencers since one they suspect as such was found outside my door. They would have handed me over to Topcliffe for him to extract what they think I know.' Simon shuddered. 'He said the only sure way to save myself and prove them wrong was to go to Edinburgh under his protection in my professional capacity, and while there to serve the Queen by keeping my eyes and ears open for any information that might be of use to him. Then, on my return, he'll ensure I'm left in peace.'

Robert threw up his hands. 'But you could have told my father all this! He would have understood. And Cecil sent you to him?'

'He called your father "my good friend". '

'Father would be unlikely to reciprocate the compliment. His view of Cecil is lower even than mine. He's a man who plays a deep game. Which reminds me, have you heard the latest Court jest? They say that when Cecil pisses, his urine turns to ice!'

Simon smiled bleakly. 'What do you think I should do then?'

'Well, it seems you now have little alternative but to do as he asks. Our task must be to keep you as safe as possible.'

'Are you going to tell your father what I've said?'

'Oh, I think I must,' said Robert, 'not least because the Armstrongs were bringing him word from Carmichael.'

But if that really *was* the case, what was it they should not or could not be told, thought Simon, once more assailed by doubt. Robert too looked thoughtful and he suddenly exclaimed, 'That's it! What we must do is ensure you have someone completely trustworthy to go with you. I've a distant cousin, Richard Wilmore, who'll do very well – and Father trusts him. You'll like him. He'll be a pleasant companion, for he's bright and lively and he can also handle himself well in trouble if necessary. No,' he continued as Simon seemed disposed to object, 'I insist. You'll need all the help you can get. Don't look so glum,' he added kindly. 'Between us all we should bring you off in one piece. And now, let's drink to the success of your mission in a bottle of good canary wine. Possibly in more than one bottle! You obviously need both cheering and fortifying.'

Chapter 4

The Road to the North

Time raced away during the few days left to Simon to sort out his affairs, but in spite of all he had to do he called on Emma to see how she was faring. Albeit frail, she was up and about, complaining that she was still unable to make her recalcitrant lover accept her son as his. The baby, now suckled by her friend, was also improving, though Simon could not believe it would survive long past infancy.

He also paid a last visit to the father of the said Fortunatus. He found Robin Greene in a strange mood, propped up in his bed with pillows, covering sheets and sheets of paper with an almost unreadable scrawl.

'What's this? A new play, a satirical pamphlet?' Simon asked as he attempted to examine his reluctant patient.

Greene fixed him with a glittering eye. 'It's my deathbed repentance. And this,' he held up a small heap of closely written sheets, 'is my "Groat'sworth of Wit"!'

'Deathbed repentance, you old reprobate,' exclaimed Simon. 'The Devil hasn't yet stoked the fires hot enough to receive you!' and smiled even though he considered it all too likely that Greene, although dramatising himself as usual, might well be speaking the truth. He had deteriorated even in the course of a week. There was nothing left of the upper part of his body, while his legs and feet were grotesquely swollen.

'I've brought you some medicine made from the ash of the juniper to help relieve the dropsy. Here, take it. It's a gift.' Greene thanked him gruffly. 'I'll leave hearing your confession but I need cheering so give me some shafts from your Groat'sworth of Wit.'

'You can read it when it's published,' retorted Greene with some of his old spirit. 'As to my confession as you call it.' His face took on a haunted look. 'Do you believe in an afterlife, Simon? *Really* believe, that is.'

'The best minds have told us there is one.'

'Damn you, I don't want a sermon! Do you really believe that at our death we go before the Great Judge, and that those who have sinned are sent to burn in the Everlasting Fire?'

'I find it hard to believe in a God Who would condemn ordinary folk who have committed ordinary sins to spending Eternity in torment. It would mean that, say, the man who killed in passion after discovering his wife in the arms of her lover is no better than the tyrant who puts thousands to the sword, while a poor thief who steals out of need becomes the equal of he who defrauds hundreds of their savings. If God exists, as we must believe, then surely He must also have compassion for poor weak sinners.'

Greene looked thoughtful. 'Kit Marlowe says there is no God.'

'Kit Marlowe is a law until himself,' Simon shrugged. 'But enough of this glum talk. Tell me what you're writing, I haven't got all day. I go on a long journey at the end of the week. I have business up north.'

Greene raised an eyebrow at this but without more ado read him snatches from his work. His Groat'sworth of Wit appeared to be levelled at any other writer who might dare to consider himself remotely as good as he, most especially Richard Burbage's rising star of the Lord Chamberlain's Men, William Shakespeare from Stratford-upon-Avon. In his scenario Greene, in the persona of 'Roberto', a man of brilliant wit, splendid appearance and with a gift for exquisite prose and verse, rounds on Shakespeare, the 'upstart crow' from Warwickshire with 'a Tiger's heart wrapped in a player's hide who supposes he is as well able to bombast out blank verse as the best of you, being an absolute Johannes Factotum and in his own conceit the only Shakescene in the country!'

Simon laughed and left him. Nearing death or not, Greene remained incorrigible, but the poet's very real fear of it and what might come after continued to haunt him for some time as he himself had experienced not dissimilar concerns since the death of Davie

Armstrong and the events that followed it. It might even be, he thought wryly, that both he and Greene would know the answer to his questions before the year was out.

He also had to face parting from Avisa and trying to explain to her why it was necessary for him to leave just as it looked as if she was finally going to consummate their relationship. Getting a message to her asking for a meeting was difficult, as he knew her husband was at home but finally, desperate to see her before he left, he sent Anna Bradedge round to her house with a note to the effect that Dr Forman had made up the salve Mistress Allen had asked for and needed to explain its use to her himself since he was shortly having to leave London.

Avisa arrived later that same afternoon. Her husband, she told him, was busy in the City and not expected back until a little later. Then she gave him a searching look. 'What is it? You look very grim. Have you called me here to tell me you no longer wish to see me, or have you other bad news to break?'

'I wish to see you every minute of every day of my life, dear heart,' he told her, taking her hand and kissing it. 'But yes, I do have something unpleasant to say to you. I must go north on business.'

'But why? Just as we . . .' she stopped. It had taken him months of patient persuasion to make her commit herself this far and now, it seemed, their growing love was to be postponed yet again.

He did not know what to tell her. He could not imagine she would ever betray him, but he was aware that if he told her everything he might well put her too in jeopardy, not least because her husband was a known Recusant and all such households were suspect in the present climate. Fear struck him. Possibly even now there were people watching his every move, set on by those Cecil had warned him against. He reined in his imagination. He was, after all, a physician and people were constantly coming to his house.

'You say nothing,' she commented.

He took both her hands in his. 'There are things I cannot tell you without putting you at risk. Suffice it to say that I am sent north on the Queen's own business and that I have no choice in the matter.' She gave a stifled exclamation. 'I hope to be back again safely by early July.'

She returned the pressure of his hands. 'I'm no astrologer but I fear there is great risk involved. Is that so?'

'It might well be. Let's hope not.'

Avisa's eyes filled with tears and she put her arms round his neck. 'I will think of you – and pray for you – every day then until you return, and when you do I promise that from then on I will be to you whatever you want me to be.'

A few minutes later he saw her to the door. He insisted she heaped her basket with herbs as well as a pot of salve, adding a large and noticeable bottle containing only coloured water. 'I fear I may be spied on,' he told her. 'It's fortunate that I have many calls for advice, for even . . .' he stopped short of mentioning his fears, 'for even those who might be showing too much interest in my affairs can hardly suspect *all* my patients.'

Exactly a week after his first interview with Cecil, Simon rode out of London accompanied by Robert Carey's distant cousin, Richard Wilmore, and the faithful John Bradedge. He had been called before Cecil briefly once more, mainly to negotiate the financial side of the matter. The Secretary of State appeared pleased when Simon told him that Sir Henry Carey had been most helpful with his advice, had explained the situation on the Borders to him and, at his son's request, had even gone so far as to arrange for a member of his own family to accompany him to Edinburgh, prompting Cecil to remark that this seemed an excellent idea. It struck Simon that whatever Carey's attitude to Cecil might be, it did not seem to be reciprocated.

As for Richard Wilmore, he was a pleasant and intelligent man a little younger than Simon and the two had found much in common when Robert Carey introduced them to each other. Now, a few days later, Simon, Richard and John, their saddlebags bulging, picked their way carefully through the busy streets and suburbs until they reached the open road and were able to give their horses their heads. After several days of warm sunshine, the weather had turned grey and there was a light drizzle which did nothing to lift Simon's spirits, daunted as he was not least at the prospect of the length of the journey before them.

For the first two or three days he was on almost familiar ground as the route took them through Coventry where, some six months previously, he had caught up with a clever murderer. How simple that piece of a villainy seemed, he thought, compared to the world in which he now found himself. But gradually he became more cheerful, and most grateful to Robert Carey for sending him such a sympathetic companion as Richard Wilmore to whom he felt more drawn with every day that passed, not to mention long evenings spent in strange inns.

Simon was still not entirely sure how much Richard was in the confidence of either of the Careys or if he knew the real purpose of this mission. He would have liked to confide in him, and ask his advice, but for the time being decided it was probably best that he remained wary until he was more sure of his ground. He was also unable to make up his mind what the Lord Chamberlain's attitude to his venture really was: cynicism certainly, but what else?

For only after he had left Robert Carey that day did he ponder on his friend's remark that 'he was playing a deep game'; had he been referring to Sir Robert Cecil – or his own father? But in the meantime he and Richard shared enough interests to avoid venturing on sensitive or doubtful topics.

From Coventry they turned northwest towards Preston, a long and tedious journey. As they neared the town John Bradedge, who had remained morose and unusually silent for most of the trip, volunteered to ride on ahead to see if there was a hostelry on the roadside that could accommodate them and also provide a change of horses as they still had many miles to go. He returned half an hour later to inform them he'd found an inn of sorts which also had a stable, and that they'd best make do with it as there was precious little else in the vicinity unless they went into Preston itself. 'And,' he added with relish, 'the landlord says if you think the road's bad here, just wait till you go further north. It gets worse and worse!'

The inn proved to be a gaunt, stone-built building. A faded sign over the door informed them they had reached the Lancaster Arms. They dismounted from their horses in the inn yard, handing them over to an elderly and surly ostler, and went into the taproom where a small fire smouldered in the grate. The weather was distinctly colder this far north, and it seemed the bright sunshine of London's

May Day had yet to reach this corner of Lancashire. The taproom was empty except for a neatly dressed man of about forty who sat eating at a wooden table opposite a second who, from his dress and demeanour, Simon took to be his servant. The man looked up as they entered and acknowledged them with a nod.

The landlord, whose manner was no more welcoming than that of his ostler, greeted them without a smile. 'There's mutton stew,' he growled. 'If tha' wants owt else then tha's out o' luck!' Tired and hungry as they were they informed him it would suit very well and then asked for ale. 'Sit down then,' the landlord replied, still without a flicker of interest, 'and I'll send t'lad over to thee with it. Ben!' he bellowed. A tousled youth appeared reluctantly from the kitchen quarters at the back. 'These three gents are wanting ale. Tek it to them, then tell your Mam there's three more bowls of stew wanted.'

The ale turned out to be better than expected and the mutton stew, when it arrived, truly worthy of praise. Their response to it appeared to mollify their host somewhat.

'Going far?' he enquired as he watched them eat.

'Only to Carlisle,' replied Richard quickly as he munched on a hunk of bread. 'I've business with the castle governor and my friend here's come along to keep me company.'

'Then tha's a weary road ahead of thee,' the landlord returned. 'Not least t'long drag up to Penrith. And never trust t'weather over t'moors, it's fair one minute, foul t'next. Mist and fog can come down like that!' He banged his fist on the table, making the bowls rattle. 'Like an old wife dropping down a bedsheet. As to horses, tha's in luck for I've three. That gent over there,' he motioned to the man they had seen when they entered, who had now finished his supper, 'changed his'n not long back. Mine are none so pretty to look at and hard in t'mouth, but they'll see thee all right as far as t'Border.'

They continued eating in comparative silence, finished their supper, and were about to make for their beds when the inn's other guest rose and came over to them.

'Forgive the intrusion,' he said, 'but I heard you telling our host you were bound for Carlisle. So am I. I wondered therefore if we might travel together, for the road is fraught with hazards both because of the terrain and also from footpads and highwaymen who prey on lonely travellers.'

'I see no reason why not,' replied Simon, looking at Richard to see if he was in agreement.

'It seems a sensible idea,' he responded.

The man held out his hand. 'Then may I introduce myself? James Ford, wool buyer out of London. I've been north looking at fleeces and woven cloth and am now travelling on to Carlisle to visit my sister who is married to a soldier stationed there with our Border force.'

'Simon Forman,' responded Simon, shaking the proffered hand and deciding at the last minute to omit his profession. 'This is my friend, Richard Wilmore, and my servant, John Bradedge.'

'Then we are well met,' smiled Ford. 'Will you take a last drink with me, or are you all too weary?'

They agreed to do so and chatted together for half an hour or more, but all were tired and soon made for their beds. 'We'll meet here in the morning then,' Ford suggested. 'I reckon, if our luck holds, we might even reach Penrith within the day, and Carlisle almost certainly the day after. I've undertaken this journey several times, you see,' he explained.

The next morning all five set out together but the weather was poor and, as the landlord had gloomily predicted, it soon became considerably worse. The damp drizzle turned to a thick mist while the road became rougher with every mile they went; by mid-afternoon it was clear they would have to put up for the night sooner than they had hoped. But the following morning the weather changed again, the sun shone, and they made good progress as they climbed up towards Penrith. Over to the west a range of purple hills rose from out of an extraordinary landscape, their peaks contorted into strange shapes.

'Mountains!' exclaimed Simon, reining in his horse for a better look. 'I had not expected to see any such in this country.'

'You've seen mountains elsewhere then?' enquired James Ford, picking up the inference. 'Where was that?'

'When I visited Italy some years back,' Simon told him. 'Higher than these and capped always with snow, even in the summertime.

But certainly not more fantastically shaped.'

'Around and between these lie lakes of water,' James informed him, 'big enough to be inland seas. But it's an inhospitable country except in high summer, as I've found when my trade's taken me there.'

With the better weather, the light lasted longer and it was still only dusk when they reached Penrith. Behind, before and all around them lay mile upon mile of empty moorland, a bleak landscape which made Simon, a true city man at heart, feel as if he had been stranded on the moon.

The inn in Penrith was busy but the landlord was able to offer one room to Simon and Richard and a smaller one to Ford, while the two servants would have to make do as best they could in the loft along with several other men.

'If you ask me, that's a funny fellow we've fallen in with,' John Bradedge commented as he helped his master and Richard lug their saddlebags up to their chamber. 'Leastways, his servant is. You can hardly get a word out of him! I've spent two whole days riding beside him, without knowing much more than that he's called Saul and comes from London.'

'It could be he just wants to keep himself to himself,' said Simon, more interested in feeling the mattress to see if it was likely to provide any comfort. 'God's Breath, but I'm saddlesore! And stiff!' He yawned. 'Some people prefer to say nothing to strangers and after all, I've hardly been forthcoming myself. Apart from telling Ford I live on the Bankside when in London, I've done my best to maintain the role of a gentleman of leisure accompanying my friend to Carlisle to see something of northern parts.'

John was unconvinced. 'Well, if he turns out to be other than he is, don't say I didn't warn you. What do *you* reckon to Ford, Master Wilmore?'

Richard shrugged. 'He's affable enough, though I can't say I've learned all that much about him. But as Simon says, he's gained precious little knowledge of us either.'

John shook his head. 'Well, I've been thinking about it. All we know is that he's a wool buyer going to Carlisle to see his sister. I've noticed it's mostly been him asking you questions. I asked that Saul whereabouts they lived in London and he said "near Finsbury Fields" – which could be anywhere. Have you asked Master Ford if he's a wife and children or if he works for himself or another?'

'I think you're refining too much on his reticence,' said Richard. 'No doubt he feels as we do: that as strangers together on a lonely road it's best to be cautious.'

'Shall I see what I can do, Doctor?' John suggested. 'I'm sure I can talk surly Saul into sinking a few quarts of ale and that might well loosen his tongue.'

'And yours also, I fear,' commented Richard.

John looked aggrieved. 'You know you can trust me, master, don't you? Tell Master Wilmore how I've done it for you before.'

'Certainly John's been invaluable at finding things out for me,' Simon agreed. 'I've yet to meet the man who can drink him under the table – he seems to have a head of teak.'

They went back down to the taproom, where a number of other travellers had taken refuge for the night. James Ford was sitting by the fire puffing on a long pipe, a quart of ale at his side. He certainly looked harmless enough. 'I trust your beds are comfortable,' he said, making room for them beside him. 'So far as I can tell, mine's the softest I've slept in since I left home.' He groaned and stretched. 'I fear I must be getting old – I'm as stiff as a coffin board.'

'Likewise,' replied Simon, sitting down gingerly on the wooden bench.

They dined on excellent capons, served with turnips and beans, followed by a custard pudding – the whole washed down with strong ale. The room was warm and the talk noisy, and Simon found himself nodding off where he sat. He was shaken awake by Richard. 'If you're happy to make your way to our chamber I think it's time we talked,' he said in a low voice. 'We have a good enough excuse for an early night, considering the way we have come.'

Once back in their room Richard looked around to see that all was as they had left it then he bolted the door. 'It could well be that Ford is everything he says he is, and I'm inclined to believe him, but the doubts raised this afternoon make me think it best we now put our cards on the table and be frank with each other. So I will tell you straight away that Robert Carey has explained your plight and your real reason for going to Edinburgh, though I do not think his father is fully aware of the situation. But Robert felt it best I should know as much as possible, to enable me to help you in any way I can. One of the reasons he chose me to go with you was because as a boy I spent some time in the north with Sir Henry when he was Warden, and so know something of the ways of the Border country and its people. And I too have a letter from His Lordship to Sir John Carmichael which I'm hoping to deliver.'

'And what other reason did Robert give for his choice of you?' asked Simon, with a smile.

'That he and I are not only related but are fast friends and, that being the case, I would never betray you.'

It would, thought Simon, be churlish to harbour any more doubts and he said so. Richard walked over to the window, where final streaks of light could still be seen in the sky. 'Not at all. You were right to be careful. Possibly I too should have said something before this, and I'm sure Robert intended it that way. But I felt I had to be sure of you too. It seemed to me most odd that a busy London physician should be sent to Edinburgh on so potentially dangerous a mission. But I rather gather you had little choice.'

Simon nodded then sat on his bed and told Richard how it had come about that he now found himself in an inn in a godforsaken northern outpost on a venture he had no wish to undertake. Richard heard him almost in silence, merely asking the odd question from time to time.

'Well, I promise I'll do my best to see you don't come to any harm. It might also serve us well if we can catch up again with the young man, Alun Armstrong. The Armstrongs are desperate enemies but can be good allies, and if you treated his injuries then you'll be much in their debt even if his companion was not so fortunate. Speaking of which, who do you think set on them?'

Simon sighed. 'I've thought about it a good deal without coming to any conclusion. Alun Armstrong spoke vaguely of shadowy enemies for whom they had been unprepared, but went no further. Then it's been suggested to me that he and his cousin were suspected of being spies, and I wondered if orders were given in high places to kill them before they could do any damage.'

Richard looked doubtful. 'But surely if it was thought they were intelligencers, then the last thing anyone in authority would want would be their deaths – their *immediate* deaths, that is – before they'd been interrogated as to the reason for their presence in London. I'm sure every effort would have been made to extract such information from them, after which what better than a public trial and death at Tyburn?'

Simon shuddered. 'It's a mystery. Perhaps if we catch up with Alun Armstrong he might enlighten us further.'

Richard agreed. 'You say he left over a week before we did?'

'The very day I was taken to Whitehall. John Bradedge, very sensibly, was fearful the house would be searched and so sent him on his way.'

Wilmore counted on his fingers. 'That means he had an eight-day start and we've taken, let's see, the best part of eight days to reach here. How bad were his injuries?'

'A nasty flesh wound on the shoulder, but it touched no vital spot. I cleaned it and treated it with a salve then bound it up. And I gave him a draught against fever. He's young and fit and should soon make up the loss of blood and heal well. Unless his pursuers have caught up with him, then I'd say he'd every chance of having reached Scotland days ago.'

'Well,' Richard responded, 'we must hope he has. But I'm for my bed now. I'm not made for these long journeys.' The two men stripped off their boots and outer clothes and fell in under the blankets. 'I trust you're right about your servant,' yawned Richard as he snuffed out the candle set between them.

'Never fret,' replied Simon. 'As I told you, I'd back John against any comer in a competition of tankards. He's proved it again and again.'

But there is a first time for everything. As they went downstairs to their breakfast they were joined by James Ford. He smiled and wished them good morrow, adding, 'I had no idea I was in such distinguished company. I trust you slept well, *Dr* Forman!'

Chapter 5

The Bolted Room

Simon caught up with his servant in the corridor which led to the taproom.

'God's Death, man! What have you been about?' he roared, grabbing John by the collar of his doublet. Then, recalling that there might well be other interested listeners, he sank his voice and hissed: 'So you were going to loosen his tongue, were you? Sweet Jesus, he certainly loosened yours!'

There was no doubt that John Bradedge had made a night of it, but he put on a brave face. 'What do you mean?' he asked with an injured air.

'You know very well what I mean,' continued Simon as Richard looked on with interest and a certain amount of superiority. 'What *you* have found out – if anything – remains to be seen, but Master James Ford has just addressed me as *Dr* Forman. You were fully aware that I'd said nothing of it myself.'

'I suppose it slipped out somehow,' said John unhappily. 'I don't remember telling him. Does it really matter?'

'It matters because the less anyone knows of us, the better. And what do you recall from your night of carousing, since you boasted of your ability to make men tell all? What more do you know of Saul and his master?'

But John had nothing to add. He had to admit he knew no more than he had the previous day. 'And that's strange, Doctor, because so far as I can recollect we didn't drink all that much, even though I've a mortal bad head. I've drunk far more and felt much better than this. I could swear I emptied only a tankard or two then went to my bed. When I woke this morning I found I hadn't even taken my boots off.'

'I hate to say I told you so,' said Richard with a cynical smile as they took their places for breakfast. Ford, it seemed, had already finished his, said the servant who brought them their bread and cheese, and was waiting outside for them in the inn yard.

Simon shook his head. 'I can't understand it. I really can't. On my oath, it's never happened before.'

'Well, there's no point crying over spilt milk,' Richard responded, applying himself to his breakfast. 'It probably doesn't matter. It might well be anyway that your name rang a bell – he is, after all, from London – and that he remembered you were a doctor of his own accord and was just showing you how clever he was!'

They did not linger over their food; having thanked the landlord and settled their reckoning, they went out to their horses. John was already there, busy attaching their saddlebags while Ford paced up and down, obviously impatient to depart. As he saw Simon he hailed him. 'I wish I'd realised you were a physician before,' he said, 'for I'd have asked your advice on a small matter.'

'Tell me now, by all means,' replied Simon, somewhat embarrassed, 'and if I can help I will.'

Ford came over to him and brushed aside his hair, wincing. 'My pesky barber clipped my ear when he was cutting my hair. It bled profusely as such small wounds do, but I thought it had healed, yet now it seems quite sore.'

Simon took a look. The cut extended from just above the earlobe to about halfway across it and had sliced right through the flesh. It did seem to be healing but the area around the bottom of the cut was inflamed and angry. 'Very nasty,' he commented. 'I fear your barber must have been very careless to cut you like that. One wonders what might have happened had you asked him to shave you!'

'He was drunk,' responded Ford shortly. 'After he'd blundered, I could smell it on his breath.'

Simon went over to his saddlebag. 'I have very little on me in the way of salves,' he said, 'but I think I can lay my hands on some calendula ointment.' He rooted in his bag and finally brought out a jar. 'I'll put some of this on for you and I'll also give you a note to take to an apothecary in Carlisle so he can make up a stronger salve for you.' He applied the ointment as best he could and Ford thanked him warmly.

Once again the day was fine and they made good speed, arriving in Carlisle before the end of the afternoon. Here they parted company with James Ford. 'I shall now go and find my sister,' he told them. 'I sent her word I was coming but my letter might well have gone astray. Possibly I'll see you over the next few days.' He paused. 'When do you return? I plan to be here about a week then ride back to London. Perhaps we might travel together again.'

'It rather depends on how my business goes,' responded Richard smoothly. 'We're not too sure of our plans as yet. But no doubt, as you say, we shall meet up with each other and by then I should have a better idea.'

'I'll look out for you then,' said Ford. 'And many thanks, Dr Forman. My ear feels much easier and as soon as I've seen my sister I'll find an apothecary and have your receipt made up.'

Carlisle Castle was at the far northern end of the city, built up against one of the walls, but its imposing height was immediately visible above the roofs and streets through which the trio wended their way. At the entrance Richard Wilmore produced a document, secured with the Carey seal, which the officer on duty at the gatehouse scrutinised carefully; then he smiled.

'From Lord Hunsdon himself, I see. Times were better when he was Warden of the West March, Master Wilmore.'

'His son Robert is set soon to follow in his father's footsteps.'

'Well, it can't come soon enough. Our present Warden is merely passing the time until he returns home. Now, if you wouldn't mind waiting in here,' he continued, ushering them into a plain room with wooden forms set against the wall, 'I'll tell the Governor of your arrival. I'm sure he'll want his guests to stay here in the castle, and we now have fine new provision for visitors.'

He reappeared a short while later. 'The Governor says you must certainly enjoy our hospitality while you are here, sirs,' he told them. 'He's busy at present but asks that you dine with him tonight.' He put his head through the door of an adjoining room. 'Sergeant Taylor! Take these gentlemen over to the Queen's Row, will you?'

A burly man, with greying hair, appeared in the doorway. He surveyed the three men then burst out, 'John Bradedge, as I live and breathe! What brings *you* up here, you old rogue? Sorry, sir,' he added, addressing the captain, 'but John and I soldiered together in the Low Countries.'

'I see,' said the captain with a smile. 'Then no doubt you'll find much to recollect when you go off duty. In the meantime, do as I ask.'

Sergeant Taylor led them through the gatehouse archway and out into the courtyard beyond. 'You're to be quartered over there beside the keep,' he told them, 'in the new row Lord Scrope had built some fifteen years back. You'll find it very comfortable, sirs. But John here would be most welcome in my own home.'

'You don't live in the castle then?' asked Simon.

'Those of us who've been stationed up here a long time and have families are allowed to live outside, although we are obviously always on call,' Taylor explained. 'If you can spare John of an evening, I'd be most grateful for it so happens I'm not on duty these next two nights and, as my captain said, we'll have much to say to each other after so long. We went through a great deal together.'

'Very well,' said Simon, giving his servant a hard look. 'I trust he'll behave himself. He'll answer to me if he doesn't! But will he be able to come and go at will, or will he need a pass of some kind?'

The sergeant shook his head. 'Things are pretty peaceful here just now,' he said, 'and while we obviously can't let in every Tom, Dick or Harry who'd like to look around, there are few problems for those with legitimate business, so long as they come in and out during daylight hours. Soldiers come and go all the time, of course, and we know most of the regular visitors such as the carters and provision merchants and garrison wives, and not all the servants sleep in. Ordinary visitors are mostly restricted to the courtyard though. Of course, if there is any trouble locally, then no one other than members of the garrison are allowed through the gate unless by permission of the Governor himself.'

By this time they had reached a fine row of new brick-built buildings and Taylor showed them through an imposing doorway over which was set the royal coat of arms with the letters E and R each side of it and the date 1577 underneath. Immediately a man, who was obviously a steward, appeared and the sergeant explained who they were and that the Governor had offered them his hospitality.

The steward bowed. 'Then come with me, gentlemen, and I'll show you to a suitable chamber. And what of your servant?'

'He's to stay with me. We're old campaigners,' replied Sergeant Taylor. Then he left them with a salute, and made his way back to the gatehouse.

Simon and Richard followed the steward along a corridor and up a flight of stairs into a fine chamber with a window looking out on to the inner courtyard. The man looked round to make sure all was as it should be. 'The beds are made up and I will bring you towels and a ewer of water and a bowl. You must be tired and dusty after your journey. If there's anything else you need, let me know. I'll be back shortly.'

Simon was pleased to note that there were two separate beds. This had rarely been the case on their way north, the inn outside Penrith being an exception, as most roadside innkeepers expected those travelling together to share a bed; indeed, lone travellers often found themselves sleeping beside complete strangers. It was a practice he intensely disliked – unless his bed companion happened to be female! The Governor certainly did his guests proud. With its rugs on the floor, a small table and chairs and even a fireplace, the accommodation was positively luxurious.

'I hope Bradedge heeds your words,' said Richard as he stripped off his doublet and began searching through his saddlebag for a clean shirt, muttering that he hoped the castle ran to a laundress who could wash their dirty clothes before they travelled any further.

'I truly believe he will,' said Simon. 'Believe me or not, I've never known him taken at a disadvantage before. You can be sure he'll take care this time, though since the Governor is now well aware who we are and that we are on business here on our way to Edinburgh, no doubt that will get about without any help from John. But I'll be on the safe side and ram it home once again. Faugh!' he exclaimed as he, too, rooted in his bag, 'I trust you're right about the laundress. I'm badly in need of clean shirts, hose and smallclothes.'

At this a thought struck him. 'How long do you propose we stay here?'

'Tonight and tomorrow night,' returned Richard. 'We deserve a day's rest. I'll see if the Governor knows the whereabouts of Carmichael, for that could save some time.' He reached once more into his saddlebag and brought out a rough map. 'Come and see here,' he said, spreading it out on the table.

The map showed the length of the Border and Scotland some miles to the north of Edinburgh. Simon noted, with a sinking heart, that immediately before them lay the Debatable Lands.

'This line here,' said Richard, pointing along it, 'is the great wall built by the Emperor Hadrian to keep out the Scots. There were forts along every mile of it. Unfortunately, however, it didn't succeed! Further on lie the remains of another, which also failed. Now as Carey probably told you, there are two main routes to Edinburgh, both old Roman roads, one running north along the eastern side of the country, the other from the west. However, I propose to take neither, at least not to begin with.

'There are two other ways we could go: one through Langholm here, up to the town of Hawick through Ewesdale and thence on to Edinburgh, or the second along Liddesdale which also leads to Hawick. I favour the second, which not only takes us off the main road and so raises less curiosity but Robert Carey told me he thought Alun Armstrong was one of the Mangerton Armstrongs and so could be found in Liddesdale. Now, if it turns out that Carmichael is also there, which he might well be, seeing he is the Keeper of the Dale, then by taking that route I can kill two birds with one stone.

'I'll make discreet enquiries and if that does not turn out to be the case and Carmichael is from home, then we'll make for Langholm, a stronghold of the Armstrongs. It might even be that we will find young Alun there. Either way, once we reach Hawick we can pick up the old eastern Roman road to Edinburgh they call the Dere Street. I must warn you though that it's risky whichever way we cross the Debatable Lands, for there are many lawless men on the Borders. However, given ordinary luck, we should cross safely.'

Simon looked completely bewildered. 'What in the world would I have done, had you not been sent to guide me?' he wondered.

'Gone straight up to Edinburgh using the main road and keeping your fingers crossed you didn't encounter a band of Reivers going about their business. Having me with you though does have its disadvantages, for I must see to my business as well as helping you safely through yours.'

'That seems a small price to pay for your knowledge and companionship,' Simon assured him. He felt Richard had become a true friend during the past fortnight.

'I think we can be reasonably frank with the Governor,' said Richard finally, rolling up his map, 'apart from telling him the real reason behind your mission.'

The steward returned at that point with towels, bowls and a ewer of hot water. He assured them that the castle employed a number of laundresses. He then left them again, returning after a few minutes with a servant who collected their dirty linen and took it away. The steward looked round the chamber once more. 'You have everything you need now, gentlemen? Very good. The Governor has asked me to tell you he dines at eight and will see you then in his quarters.' His eyes fell on the door. 'The castle is secure enough, but as you see there is a bolt here that you can draw if you wish.' He paused and coughed delicately. 'The *garderobe* is at the end of this corridor to the left, should you require it, though there are chamber pots under the beds for your regular needs.'

A little before eight o'clock Simon and Richard, washed, brushed and wearing their last remaining clean shirts, presented themselves before the Governor and were ushered into a fine large dining room. The Governor chatted affably about the castle and its often blood-stained history.

'You see it in peaceful case now,' he told them, 'but in the past it has withstood many a siege and bloody episode – and not only from the Scots.' He explained how it had changed hands during the last century's Wars of the Roses. 'In fact, at one time the Yorkists held it against a combined force of Scots *and* the army of Lancaster. After that we were given siege weapons by no other than King Richard the Third – him they call the Crookback. Indeed, tomorrow I'll get one of my men to show you the carvings on the walls made by prisoners of that time, if you're interested. Then, of course, it's not all that long since we were a prison for Marie Stuart when she fled Scotland.'

'Speaking of Border troubles, do you happen to know the whereabouts of Sir John Carmichael?' asked Richard. 'The Lord Chamberlain wishes me to have a word with him.'

The Governor shook his head. 'I know only where he is not – and that is safe home in Liddesdale. He rode out a week or so back to investigate some fracas on the Border and so far as I'm aware has still not returned. As I say, the West March is relatively peaceful at present but there is trouble constantly breaking out on the Middle March, the mischief coming from both sides. I fear more bloody incidents before long.' He turned to Simon. 'But I expect you find all this talk of war and Border battles wearisome, Dr Forman, being a physician.'

'But I wasn't always a doctor,' returned Simon. 'There was no money for me to train to become one and so I went for a soldier in the Low Countries and learned at least some of my skills on the field. From there I went on to study in Italy, though now I am recognised both by the University of Cambridge and the Royal College of Physicians.'

'If you studied in Europe I'm surprised you feel the need to visit Edinburgh. I find it hard to credit that the Scots doctors will have much to teach you.'

Before he could answer Richard did so for him. 'Oh, that's easily explained. When I told Simon that Lord Hunsdon wanted an assessment of the position on the West March before his son takes over as Warden and that, since we had journeyed so far I might as well also gauge the political mood in Edinburgh, he wanted to know if the doctors in Edinburgh really are as clever as is rumoured. So I invited him to come with me to find out for himself. I admit too that it will be interesting to see what passes at King James' Court in view of what the future is likely to hold for all of us.'

Once again Simon was grateful for Richard's quick wit and wondered again however he would have managed, had Robert Carey not been so thoughtful as to provide him with such an intelligent companion. He came out of his reverie to realise that the Governor was asking them how long they intended to remain in Carlisle.

'We would like to leave the day after tomorrow,' Richard told

him, 'if you are happy to extend your hospitality that far. We both
need a rest after such a long journey.'

'And it will also give your laundresses a chance to wash and dry
our clothes,' Simon added, 'for they have not improved by our being
so long on the road!'

The Governor poured wine into three cups. 'Then let us drink to
your forthcoming journey and a safe return home. And you are more
than welcome to stay here on your way back too, although if matters
are shortly settled on the East March, where there has lately been an
incursion, then no doubt you'd wish to return to London by the
shorter route. Now,' he said, settling back in his seat, 'what news do
you bring from London? And how go the playhouses? I hear they're
as popular now as the bear pits . . .'

The next day passed pleasantly enough, both men having enjoyed
a good night's sleep, while John Bradedge had arrived promptly at
the castle that morning, quick to assure Simon that he had said
nothing out of turn.

'We talked the night away, but it was of old campaigns and the
wars and what we had done since. We sank far more ale than I did
the other night, of that I'm sure, yet I have no problem recollecting
all we spoke of. I'd thought Harry Taylor was cast off like me without
a shilling after our last campaign, but it seems he'd once done a
service to a Captain Forster which put him in the man's debt and so
he took Harry back home with him, for the Forsters are plentiful
hereabouts and well thought of. It was the captain who recommended
him for service with the garrison.'

'Did he never want to go back south?' enquired Simon.

'He hankers after it still. But he's now married to a local girl and
has a son and a daughter and a third child on the way, and says there
are many worse places to be than Carlisle Castle.' John paused. 'I
did ask if he knew of a sergeant married to the sister of a London
wool merchant but since I didn't know the man's name, Harry
couldn't help me. He says that as well as the garrison in Carlisle
there are numerous small forces stationed all along the border and
the man might well be with any one of them.'

The Governor was as good as his word, detailing a young officer
from his household to show Simon and Richard around the whole

castle and its many buildings, including the great keep in which were the rooms with the carvings on the walls made by prisoners a century earlier: St George and the Dragon, two fighting men, the coats of arms of great families of both York and Lancaster, two dolphins leaping – 'This man must have been to sea or at least near the coast,' remarked Richard on viewing these.

'And here's the white boar of Crookback Richard,' said Simon, pointing to it. 'Along with some saucy pictures of naked women!' His friend came over to see and both men laughed.

They came out of the dark keep into sunshine unusually warm for the time of year, according to their guide. In spite of the castle housing a military garrison the scene before them was both busy and domestic. A group of men sat polishing swords and cleaning guns, joking with a couple of cooks who had taken advantage of the fine weather to sit outside to peel their turnips. Laundresses passed bearing washing to hang out on a higher level and a group of lads shouted noisily as they kicked a ball about in the corner of the courtyard.

'It seems peaceful enough now,' commented Simon, surveying the scene.

'It's deceptive, though,' said the young officer. 'It can change any time. If you want a reminder, you should pay a visit to Gallows Hill where men are still hanged, drawn and quartered for treason.' Simon shivered. 'But you must visit the town as well now you've come so far,' he added. 'It's surprisingly civilised.'

A little while later they did so, taking John Bradedge with him. They looked out for their travelling companion, the wool merchant, or his servant but saw neither which was hardly surprising as it was market day and the streets were crowded. They did indeed find Carlisle surprisingly pleasant, admittedly helped by seeing it bathed in sunshine, commenting on the fact that so many of the neat rows of houses, unlike their counterparts in London, had their own sizeable gardens. There was also a fine church in the centre of the town.

Simon sighed. 'I think I could happily spend a week here. Would that I could do that, then return home and invent some news to keep Cecil happy, but I fear he'd realise my deception quickly enough. I only hope I can fulfil his expectations of me. What exercises me most is that I might be being watched by other nameless persons, bent on seeing what I'm about. Though perhaps I'm being unduly nervous.'

'There's only one thing of which you can be certain where the game of politics is concerned,' replied Richard, 'and that is that there are many players – Cecil included – and that some are honest, some hold their cards close to their chests and others cheat.'

After a little while, feeling thirsty, they sought out an inn for some ale. It was full to bursting with market people, townsfolk, off-duty soldiers and a number of women of obviously doubtful virtue assisting the soldiers to spend their pay. The pair had to squeeze themselves through a thick press of people before they could find space enough to stand. Tapsters, rushed off their feet, pushed their way through the crush slopping ale on to the customers from their trays.

John nudged Simon. 'Isn't that our friend Ford over there, Doctor?' They both looked and saw it was indeed the wool merchant, at which point he turned and also saw them.

'Let me buy you a drink,' he called out. 'I can see the landlord standing in the doorway. You'll never get heard otherwise in this bear pit!' So saying, he pushed his way towards the door and, within minutes, a tapster appeared bearing four quarts of ale and Ford came over to join them.

'I trust you found your sister well?' said Richard politely as they thirstily drank their ale.

'I did, and she was most pleased to see me, not least because her husband is from home. She finds it hard here, being so far from the family and she's often on her own. And as to my ear, Dr Forman, I found an apothecary last evening and applied his salve. It stung mightily but this morning it was nearly healed.' He brushed away his hair again to show that the inflammation had almost disappeared. 'And you,' he added, 'your business goes well?'

'Well enough,' Richard replied, 'though we may be here somewhat longer than I thought.'

'You are actually staying in the castle then?' continued Ford. 'Isn't that somewhat uncomfortable?'

'Not at all,' Simon assured him, 'for we're housed in the fine new apartments built for guests. It's more like staying in a great house than in a fortress. Governor Musgrave has been most civil to us. And John here lodges with an old companion from his soldiering days who he discovered is a member of the castle garrison.'

Ford smiled. 'It seems you're lucky in your accommodation. I'd imagined such guests rooms as there might be in such a fortress would be dark and dank. And presumably you can come and go as you please?'

'More or less,' Richard told him. 'It seems that when the West March is quiet as at present, visitors have more or less free access until the gate is shut at ten o'clock.'

They continued chatting on general matters and then Ford excused himself. 'I've promised my sister I'll go back and dine with her. Oh, one more thing – I, too, will be here for another few days. As I suggested before, if it suits us all and you have concluded your affairs, then might we not journey home together?'

'Very possibly,' replied Richard smoothly, and left it at that.

That evening they dined in the great hall of the castle. John Bradedge had spent the rest of the day with the Taylors and wanted his friends to meet the London doctor for whom he worked, so they had arranged to go to the house after supper.

'You'd best come armed then,' John had warned them. 'You heard what they told us, that it looks peaceful enough here but that you never know. Make sure you buckle on your swords and have your daggers with you. Remember what happened the last time you didn't take my advice,' he persisted as Simon looked as if he might object, referring to an occasion the previous year when Simon, unarmed, had been attacked in an alleyway.

They did as he had asked and walked through the warm summer evening to the Taylors' house. Though now nearly nine o'clock it was still almost broad daylight. Sergeant Taylor greeted them warmly, as did his wife, now obviously well forward with child and blooming with it. Then, mindful that the castle gates would be locked at ten, they made to leave.

'Be sure to be at the castle at first light,' Simon told John as they rose to go, 'for we must be on our way.'

'I'll see he is,' laughed Taylor, 'for I'm on duty myself at six o'clock.'

There were still plenty of people about the streets as the weather was so warm. Noise rose from the open doors of taverns as they passed by. Suddenly Richard stopped and looked behind him, frowning, his hand on his sword hilt.

'What is it?' asked Simon.

'I've the oddest feeling we're being followed. But I can see no one who looks suspicious. Can you?'

That part of the street was relatively empty of people except for a family making their way homewards coming in the opposite direction and a pair of lovers, oblivious to all but themselves. The two men walked back a little, but there were a number of narrow lanes and alleys running off both sides of the road, and there seemed little chance of finding their pursuer if indeed there was one.

'Well, thanks to John, we are both armed,' said Simon, 'and can give a good account of ourselves should we be attacked by some lonely villain. Do you really think we might be being watched?'

Richard shrugged. 'Anything's possible here on the Border. Everyone's suspicious of everyone else, especially strangers. As for the authorities, both sides, English and Scots, send their intelligencers to see what the other's up to and who's coming and going, while the Border clans, the Reivers, keep watch for rich pickings. And all towns have their cutpurses. It might be any of them or no one at all, but just my fancy.'

They continued on their way with no further alarms. It was now nearly sunset and they would need to hurry to pass through the castle gate. Having done so they climbed wearily up the stairs to their room, where they found a candle already burning in its candlestick and their clean clothing lying on their beds, fresh from the laundresses.

'I'll pack in the morning,' yawned Simon. 'It shouldn't take long, though I'd intended to do so tonight.'

There was a knock on the door and a lad entered bearing two foaming tankards.

'What's this?' asked Richard. 'We sent for no ale.'

The boy shrugged. 'The soldier asked me to bring them.'

'Well, let's not look a gift horse in the mouth,' said Richard. 'Set them down by our beds, will you?' The boy did so and left.

'I see you're considered of far greater quality than a poor physician,' joked Simon as he went over and picked his up. 'Mine is but plain pewter while yours is of fine chased work. What it is to be a scion of a great family!'

In answer Richard, who was sitting on the end of his bed, heaved a pillow at him. They drank their ale then made ready for bed.

'Should I bother to bolt the door, do you think?' Simon asked.

'Perhaps it might be wise,' yawned Richard. 'Though we're probably safer here than anywhere else we're likely to be on our travels. I'll do it.'

He went over and slid the heavy bolt back into place then returned to blow out the candle, but before doing so he looked at his hand. 'There seems to be some grease on the bolt,' he said. 'I've got it on my fingers.'

'Perhaps the steward greased it yesterday,' commented Simon. 'He did make a point of showing us how everything was in the most excellent order, if you remember.'

'That must be it. Dear God, I'm tired. I hope I feel livelier than this in the morning.' And with that Richard blew out the candle and got into bed.

In spite of being so tired it took Simon some time to get off to sleep, his mind full of uneasy thoughts. In common with many astrologers, he rarely cast his own horoscope and had not done so before setting out for fear of what he might learn, but he now determined to do so at the first opportunity. Forewarned was forearmed and he was grateful he'd decided to bring at least some of his charts with him. It then occurred to him that this second skill might well prove useful in Edinburgh as a means of ascertaining the motives of others. Having settled that he fell asleep, aware from his companion's rhythmic breathing that Richard had long preceded him.

But he slept only to be haunted by dreams, awaking suddenly from one in which he was lying in a dark forest with a serpent coiled around him, squeezing him painfully. Fully awake, he realised that it wasn't a serpent but his bowels that were giving him pain. Obviously he had eaten or drunk something that disagreed with him. He rose from his bed and felt for his bedgown. Richard was still peacefully asleep. Now what had the steward said about the *garderobe*? Down the corridor and off at the end of it? But left or right?

He staggered out of bed and made for the door. The bolt ran easily in its track and he stumbled out into the corridor. It was pitch dark. He decided it must be to the right and made his way in that direction until he saw a soldier standing at the end, obviously a sentry of some kind.

'For God's sake tell me where I can find the *garderobe*,' he begged. 'I'm *in extremis*!'

The soldier said nothing but turned him round and pointed to the other end of the corridor. He got there just in time. Drenched in cold sweat and clutching his stomach against the cramps, Simon had no idea how long he sat there. Finally the spasms ceased and, shivering from head to foot, he went out and felt his way along the corridor and so back to his room. Richard was still asleep. Bolting the door behind him he fell into bed and into oblivion.

He was wakened the next morning by a knocking on the door. 'Masters, your servant's here,' said the steward.

'Draw back your bolt and let him me in,' called the voice of John Bradedge. 'You did say you wanted an early start, Doctor.'

Simon sat up and called out that he was coming. It all seemed like a bad dream now. Did he really arise in the night consumed with stomach pains, or had he dreamed it? Richard was still asleep and the bolt on the door securely fastened. Simon stood up and swayed slightly on his feet. He felt quite weak and dizzy; it must have been true.

He went over to the door, slid back the bolt, apologised to the steward and let John Bradedge in.

'You look the worse for wear, Doctor,' commented John, eyeing his master critically.

'It's hardly surprising. I spent half the night in the *garderobe* consumed by gripes in my bowels.' He began to pull on his clothes, calling over to Richard that it was time and more they were up and away. There was no response.

'What a slugabed!' Simon commented to John with a smile. 'He'd sleep through the Last Trump.'

He put on his shoes and went over to his friend and shook him by the shoulder. Nothing happened. A chill went through him. 'Richard!' he called urgently. 'Are you all right? What is it?' There was still no response.

Thoroughly concerned, he flung back the coverlet and turned the man over, then drew back with an exclamation of horror at the sight of the empurpled face, the bulging eyes.

'Sweet Jesus! What have we got here?' he whispered.

John came over and joined him, and together they looked down at the dead man.

'Has he suffered an apoplexy?' queried John.

Simon bent over Richard's body then slowly shook his head. 'Look here,' he said, pulling the nightrobe gently away from his poor friend's neck. Around it was a thin line, but so deep that it had drawn blood in some places.

'It's the mark of a garotte,' he whispered appalled.

A slight sound caused him to look up. Standing in the doorway was the steward, his face frozen in shock. 'You had best stay right there, Dr Forman,' he said. 'I must fetch the Governor.'

Chapter 6

The Borderers

'What are you doing?' asked Simon as the steward left them.

'Looking in his saddlebag,' responded John brusquely. 'Here, you'd better take these,' and he handed Simon the rolled map and several documents including a sealed letter addressed to Sir John Carmichael.

Simon was scandalised. 'We can't do that! What will happen if anyone finds out?'

'Why should they? And it's better you have them than the Governor here or anyone else. Take them, put them somewhere safe,' he urged. 'One's a map and we'll need that to know where we're going.'

Reluctantly accepting the sense of this, Simon put the map in his own saddlebag and hid the documents inside his doublet. Then they sat and waited for Musgrave.

The Governor entered the room briskly and went straight over to the bed and looked at the body. Simon joined him.

'As you see, sir,' he said, once again pointing out the thin deep mark, 'his killer used a garotte.'

The Governor looked at him coldly. 'My steward tells me the door was firmly bolted when he brought your servant up here this morning. They had to knock loudly and call until you opened it.' Simon agreed that was indeed the case.

'You locked it last night when you went to bed?'

'We did, although neither of us felt it was really necessary. It was habit, I suppose.'

'So this murderer passed through a bolted door; meanwhile you slept through it all.'

Simon saw only too well where this was leading. 'But there was some time when I was out of the room,' he said, and explained briefly what had happened.

'And how long were you away?'

'I don't really know,' said Simon miserably. 'Some little while, I think. I didn't dare return here until I . . . until I was sure the spasms were abating.'

'You're suggesting therefore that someone came into the room while you were gone and killed him then? Someone who had the foresight to know the room would be empty for a brief while? Or perhaps you're trying to say that this unknown person murdered Richard Wilmore on impulse?'

'I don't know. Please believe me – *I don't know*.' Then a thought struck him. 'There was one strange thing, now I remember. It was Richard who locked the door last night and he came back rubbing his hand and saying there appeared to be grease on the bolt.' Simon crossed over to the door and examined the bolt. 'Yes – see? The knob on the bolt still feels sticky,' he peered down into its mechanism, 'and there's certainly a deposit of something here. Look for yourselves.'

The Governor and the steward both examined the bolt. 'Do you know anything about this?' Musgrave asked the steward. 'Have you greased the bolts of late?'

The steward shook his head. 'There's been no need. No one has complained that they did not work properly.'

'It would mean the bolt could be opened and closed very quietly,' said Simon. 'It might even have been possible, since the door doesn't fit tightly, that the bolt could have been moved from outside by the use of, say, a dagger-blade by someone determined to get in.'

The Governor still looked unconvinced. 'Well, there's no question of your leaving the castle now. You and your servant will move into my own quarters immediately. I must set enquiries going into this business. I'll see you in my office within half an hour, Dr Forman, to continue this conversation. Pack your things and my steward will show you to my apartments. In the meantime this poor fellow here must be safely bestowed. I shall have to write at once to the Careys informing them what has happened, of course.'

'I would like to send a letter to them as well,' said Simon. 'Richard was my friend!'

Within the half hour he was seated in the Governor's office and it was plain that Musgrave was even more suspicious. He repeated the fact that when his steward had come to rouse him the door had been bolted on the inside; he reminded Simon there was no proof he'd ever left the room. As to the grease on the bolt, it might well be that some servant while cleaning the rooms had thought it required some attention; the Governor was making enquiries to that effect.

'Are you really trying to say that you think *I* killed Richard?' demanded Simon, now thoroughly aroused. 'Putting aside why, in God's name, I should want to kill my good friend and travelling companion, the very person who was going to guide me through this godforsaken Border country and bring me safe to Edinburgh, then why now? There would have been ample opportunity during our journey, such as nights in isolated wayside inns, not to mention the hundreds of miles of lonely roads out of sight of even a house, let alone a town or village. I could have murdered him at any time, had such been my intention. So tell me why, sir, that being the case, I should wait until we reach a fortress such as Carlisle Castle, fully garrisoned with soldiers, and kill him here?'

The Governor looked at him sternly. 'I have no answer to that. But since you first arrived I've been certain there are matters concerning this visit to Scotland of which I'm unaware.'

'Richard explained the purpose of our going to Edinburgh when we arrived.'

'And I told you I found your reason for accompanying him on his mission a strange one.'

'If you're suggesting I'm not even a doctor, then by all means send to London to seek confirmation of it,' retorted Simon in exasperation. 'You'll discover that I also cast horoscopes as well, though God knows I didn't foresee anything like this!'

He was beginning to feel that the more he protested, the further he sank in the mire. But if he was ever to leave the castle, he had to try and dampen the Governor's obvious suspicions. 'Can we not go over the events of last night once again?' he asked. 'It could be something's been missed or forgotten.'

The Governor shrugged. 'Very well, though I can't see where this is leading us. Though if that's to be the case, then I think it best what you have to say is recorded. For future reference,' he added grimly. 'I'll call for my clerk.'

With the clerk sitting at the desk with quill and paper, they went through the whole story yet again. But this time as Simon answered the Governor's questions, other recollections began to return, not least details of the events of the previous evening – but Musgrave was obviously beginning to find it all wearisome and a waste of time. 'So you say now that Wilmore told you he thought you were being followed when you were in the town last night?'

'That's right. We'd left John, my servant, at the house of Sergeant Taylor and were on our way back. When Richard told me of his suspicion we stopped and looked back down the street, but there was no one there apart from townsfolk going about their business. We even retraced our steps a little but there were alleyways off both sides and it would have been easy enough for a pursuer to conceal himself.'

'And after that?'

'We came in through the castle gate, went straight to bed and fell asleep without more ado.'

'You spoke to no one, took no refreshment before doing so?'

'No, as I said . . . God's Blood!' Simon exclaimed, smiting himself on the forehead at the recollection. 'What a dunderhead I am. That must have been it!'

'I don't follow you,' said the Governor.

'The drinks. *There was something in the ale!*'

'What ale?' demanded Musgrave exasperatedly. 'What new riddle is this?'

'The ale the lad brought to us in our room. We were surprised as we'd not asked for any, but having been offered it we drank it gratefully. *Of course!* And now I think of it, there was a difference too. I joked with him that he was obviously considered of more worth than I as he had the finer tankard. That would ensure we each drank what was intended for us.

'I know this sounds far-fetched,' he continued, seeing the Governor's face, 'but hear me out. Once he was in his bed, Richard slept so deeply that he didn't even stir when I left the room, although I know from sharing rooms with him on our travels that he was usually a very light sleeper. I think we were both drugged, but with different substances – Richard most likely with poppy syrup.

'As to me – well, the symptoms could well have been caused by a minute amount of one of the mineral poisons or with a herbal mixture of the kind given to those who have problems with their bowels. That would be sufficient. Neither poppy syrup nor a non-fatal amount of a mineral or herbal poison would taste in a quart of strong ale. The first would soon put the drinker into a heavy sleep – and I have personal experience of knowing how effective that is, for someone once tried to do away with me in such a fashion. The second draught – the one I drank – would make the person ill with the vomiting or the flux or both. It would certainly ensure they had to rise from their bed.'

'Have you the slightest hope of proving this?' responded the Governor in a tone of obvious disbelief.

'If Richard was given poppy syrup, then the pupils of his eyes will be dark and contracted even in death. I admit I didn't think to look closely since the state of his face was . . . well, you saw for yourself and it was plainly obvious how he died.'

Musgrave rose. 'Then let us take another look. I ordered that he be taken to a room in the keep and decently laid out.'

Together they walked over to the keep and through into an inner chamber where two servants were finishing laying out Richard's body.

'Now stay where you are, Dr Forman, and tell me again exactly what it is I should see.'

The dead man's eyes had already been closed and covered with two coins; Musgrave removed these as Simon explained again what he might expect to find. The Governor opened first one eye and then the other. 'Certainly the pupils are as pinpoints and dark as you say, but might not that be because of the manner of his death?'

'The whites of his eyes could well be bloodshot because of it but no, it would not produce that effect on the pupils. May I look now?'

The Governor nodded and they both examined the eyes again.

'You see,' said Simon, 'it is exactly as I described to you.' Gently he closed the eyes again and replaced the coins. 'There's another thing too,' he continued triumphantly. 'I do have proof that I left the room last night, for when I struggled out into the corridor trying to find the *garderobe*, I turned the wrong way and had to ask its direction of the soldier on duty. Sweet Jesus, I must have been drugged to forget that!'

The Governor looked astonished. 'What soldier on duty?'

'He who was standing at the end of the corridor by the bedchambers.'

'But there would be no soldier on guard duty within the building. It's quite unnecessary to have a man there. There is a full guard in the castle with an officer in charge throughout the night and sentries posted on all the vantage points. You're sure it was a soldier that you saw?'

'He was dressed like one of your men, certainly. Come to think of it, he didn't speak. He merely pointed me in the right direction.'

The Governor snorted with exasperation. 'We'll soon settle this,' he said and strode out of the room, Simon following at his heels. He went straight to the guardroom and demanded to know who had been on duty the previous evening. When told that the officer in charge was sleeping, he ordered the man to be woken and sent immediately to his office. He then went to the hall used by soldiers when they were off duty, discovered who had been the most senior man there the night before and had him sent for as well.

A few minutes later a sleepy lieutenant arrived along with a sergeant who said he had been one of about twenty men in the hall at the time. First the Governor asked the sergeant if he or anyone else had sent tankards of ale to the two visitors during the evening. The sergeant shook his head. 'Then go and see if you can find out who did,' Musgrave ordered, and turned his attention to the lieutenant. 'Did you set a man to guard our guests last night?'

The lieutenant looked mystified. 'Why should I do that, sir? How was I to know they wouldn't be safe in your very own guest lodgings? My men were at their usual posts, I can swear to that, for I went the rounds myself on a number of occasions.'

'Is there any way someone could have entered the castle during the day without your knowing,' enquired Simon, 'and having done so, hidden himself away undetected?'

'There certainly ought not to be,' snapped the Governor.

The lieutenant cleared his throat. 'There *ought* not to be but, to put no finer point upon it, sir, there's been much coming and going of late. Since everything is so peaceful at present, perhaps we have become a little slack.' He gulped at the expression on Musgrave's face. 'Outside servants often arrive in groups, then there are tradesmen bringing in goods, some on foot with lads to help them, others in carts which are brought into the courtyard to be unloaded. Over the last months there's been little need to take extreme precautions for fear of attack, nor have we any prisoners here at present who might try to escape.' His voice faltered. 'So I couldn't say on oath that it was beyond the bounds of possibility that someone determined enough might have got in undiscovered, and out again this morning, although that would be more difficult.'

'I see,' said the Governor icily. 'So what you're telling me is that there is a chance, however remote, that a man could have secretly entered the castle yesterday and then lain concealed until nightfall?' He rose and banged his fist on his desk. 'I shall make it my personal business to ensure that if indeed that proves to be the case, it can never happen again. Never! In the meantime call out the present guard and add to them any others that are necessary. I want the entire castle and its grounds searched from top to bottom and end to end. Tell them should it transpire that a stranger did get into the castle, I'll have every man who was on guard duty yesterday flogged! Jump to it, man!

'It seems you might have a point, Dr Forman,' he continued, resuming his seat as the lieutenant scurried off, 'though I can't pretend I'm convinced. It is all so far-fetched. Even if you're right and some malignant stranger managed to conceal himself here, disguise himself as one of our men, drug your drinks and murder Wilmore, then to what end? For what purpose was he killed?'

'I cannot imagine, sir,' replied Simon honestly. 'The only idea that comes to mind is that someone did not want him to reach

Edinburgh, but as to the reason . . .' He shook his head.

Musgrave considered this. 'I will allow you've given me pause for thought, but unless you can convince me otherwise, I see no course but to keep you here in Carlisle for the future while further enquiries are made. Surely there's no longer any reason for you to travel to Edinburgh if, as you say, you were merely accompanying Wilmore in friendship? It can hardly be worth crossing the Debatable Lands and facing the hazards that lie between here and Edinburgh merely to seek possible new medical knowledge. So give me time to assure myself you did not kill Wilmore and then you can go back to London without further delay.'

It seemed to Simon that there could now be not one, but three, fatal outcomes to his mission: the Governor could decide after all that he was guilty and hang him in Carlisle, or he could insist he return to London and take measures to see he did which would mean he'd failed in his duty to Sir Robert Cecil and so would fall into the hands of those who believed he was in league with Scots spies. They would, no doubt, be convinced of it once news of Richard's death reached them. It occurred to Simon that even if the Lord Chamberlain had not been one of their party before (and he was by no means sure he wasn't), he'd show little mercy towards a man who was thought to have murdered one of his relations. The third, and almost equally dangerous alternative, was to press on to Edinburgh regardless through a countryside full of violent villains and risk being murdered on the way.

It was beginning to look as though his only hope of avoiding any of them was to continue to Edinburgh and attempt to do what Cecil had asked of him under his protection. He ought too, in justice to his murdered friend, try to meet Sir John Carmichael and deliver Richard's letter into his hands, and also if possible seek out Alun Armstrong. In view of all that had happened, perhaps Alun would now tell him the burden of the message he was taking to Carey which had triggered off so disastrous a sequence of events. But in order to do any of this he had to persuade the Governor not only that he was innocent but that he had a valid reason for continuing his journey.

'It would seem, sir,' he ventured, 'that I must tell you something more of the purpose of our journey – at least so far as I can, for there was much I did not know.'

The Governor settled back in his chair. 'Pray enlighten me then, Dr Forman.'

So, as carefully as he could, Simon embarked on yet another version of his tale. He told the Governor how a man had died on his doorstep and that later he had learned that he and a colleague were members of the Armstrong clan bringing a message of some kind from Sir John Carmichael to the Lord Chamberlain.

'And what was that?' enquired Musgrave.

'No one knows, sir, for after the one man died the other, so far as we know, returned to Scotland leaving it undelivered. But Robert Carey thinks it must have been to do with Sir John's assessment of the present situation on the Borders and wished Lord Hunsdon to know of it before his son takes up the post of Warden. That being the case, His Lordship decided to send one of his most trusted men north to see Sir John and, since he was to journey so far, decided he should go on to Edinburgh to observe at first hand what is happening in that city. More than that I do not know, for while we became good friends on our journey, Richard naturally did not discuss His Lordship's private affairs with me.'

The Governor looked thoughtful. 'I wonder what it was Carmichael considered serious enough to send word of it to Lord Hunsdon? For, as you know, the West March is quiet at present. As to Wilmore visiting Edinburgh, I imagine it would be useful for His Lordship to have an assessment of the present situation which obtains there, but I still wonder at your own role in this affair.'

'I can assure you, sir, it was as Richard himself told you: no more and no less. He wanted companionship on a long and hazardous a journey, I had time available and thought it most likely my only opportunity to visit colleagues in Edinburgh, and also I felt some extra interest since it was outside my door the young man, Armstrong, died.'

'Wasn't that somewhat strange?' asked Musgrave.

'Why? I am, after all, a physician. People frequently turn to me in dire need.'

The Governor rose to his feet. 'You have answered at least some of my suspicions, Dr Forman,' he said. 'I will continue making enquiries, sleep on it overnight and if I think I can trust you, then I will send you on your way to Edinburgh. You may go now. Remain within the castle.'

'But I would like to make some enquiries of my own,' urged Simon, 'since I am so nearly concerned. It could be that I might also be able to throw some light on this matter. I'd like to seek out the wool buyer we encountered on our journey. He seemed harmless enough but my man was suspicious of him.' Musgrave looked doubtful. 'Where could I run to? If you wish, by all means send one of your men with me to see neither I nor my man escape.'

'Very well,' returned Musgrave. 'Take your man with you but I'll give orders you're not to pass out of the town gate. And be back here by six this evening.'

'I told you from the first I distrusted that man Ford,' grumbled John as they left the castle some ten minutes later.

'Richard was shrewd enough and he thought him harmless,' said Simon. 'And why on earth should he want to kill Richard?'

John shrugged. 'Perhaps he didn't, perhaps he stayed safe outside and sent his servant in to do it for him. But think about it, doctor – he claimed to be a wool buyer yet he'd no wool or fleeces with him that I saw.'

'That's easily explained,' said Simon as they reached the tavern in which they had met up with Ford the day before. 'He said he could hardly go on to Carlisle laden with goods and that he'd arranged for a carrier to take his purchases back to London for him.'

The landlord of the tavern proved unhelpful. He did not even recollect Simon and Richard being in his establishment the previous day, let alone an unknown wool buyer. The taproom had been full and traders of all kinds regularly drank there from both sides of the Border. They then visited the house of John's friends, the Taylors, and Simon asked Mistress Taylor if she knew of any woman among her neighbours who had a brother visiting her from London, but she shook her head. There was none such among her immediate friends, but then she did not know all the garrison families as some lived outside the town. They tried other taverns, were directed to spinners and weavers of wool but all to no avail.

Finally Simon decided they were wasting their time.

'I think we're refining too much on this man Ford because he's the only person we can think of. Richard himself warned me that Carlisle was full of intelligencers and doubtful men from both sides of the Border. Why shouldn't it be a Scot who decided Richard journey no further?' Then a further thought struck him. 'God's Breath, John!' he exclaimed. 'Has it occurred to you that Richard and I might have drunk the wrong drinks? And that it was I, not Richard, who should have died? Now there's a thought.'

He repeated his suggestion that Richard's death could have been engineered from Scotland to the Governor when he returned as promised, and Musgrave admitted he might well have a point. By the end of the evening he seemed to have come round to the belief that had Simon indeed wanted to murder Richard, then he'd had ample opportunity to do so earlier on the journey north. Further confirmation that Simon might be telling the truth came very early the next morning when the body of an off-duty soldier, stripped of his uniform, was found by a farm labourer lying in a field outside the town. He too had been garotted.

So it was that by nine o'clock the following day Simon and John, profoundly relieved, found themselves on the road to Edinburgh. For the first few miles they took the road north which would lead through Moffat and then northeast towards the Scottish capital but some five miles out from Carlisle Simon stopped and pulled up his horse.

'We'll dismount for a moment and look at the map,' he told John.

'Whatever for?' queried his servant. 'The road's clear enough.'

'Richard was to have taken us up through a place called Langholm in the hope he might learn the whereabouts both of Sir John Carmichael and Alun Armstrong,' Simon replied. 'I feel I owe it to him to deliver his letter to Sir John if I can. And it might also serve us well to catch up with young Armstrong.'

'You're moon mad,' John exploded. 'Crazed, that's what you are! Haven't we enough hazards to fear even on a decent old Roman road like this without careering off into the wilds? These lands are infested with wild men who care for nothing. I spent last evening with castle servants who enjoyed nothing better than regaling me with tales of rape, pillage, burning and murder, of strange and dangerous customs and summary justice at the rope's end.

'These Reivers, as they are known,' he continued, warming to his theme, 'dress in black; they even paint their armour black so they can pass unseen in the dark. Some call them the blackmailers because of it. They ride into villages and demand money to keep the inhabitants safe from other gangs of villains, and if they won't pay up, then they burn their houses and put them to the sword. And you want to ride head on into the midst of them?'

Simon refused to answer, dismounted from his horse, undid his saddlebag and took out Richard's map which he unrolled. 'See, we must be about here,' he said, pointing to a place on the map. 'If that's so, then in about half a mile we should find the road divides, the left fork going on to Moffat, the right to Langholm and thence up to Hawick and on to another road to Edinburgh. It might even be shorter that way.' He paused. 'If you don't want to come with me, John, I shall quite understand. There's no reason why you should put your life at risk; this business has nothing to do with you and the danger we are undoubtedly in is none of your making. And you have a wife and child waiting for you at home.'

In answer John too got down off his horse and looked at the map. 'I've no intention of leaving you behind to almost certain death,' he growled. 'There's got to be one of us with some common sense.'

The town of Langholm was shown clearly on the map in the valley of the River Esk and John estimated it was at least twenty miles further on. 'It will be into the afternoon before we reach it,' he said, 'that is, if the road is not too rough. I think once there we should not venture further until tomorrow, as the last thing we want is to be caught out on the road miles from anywhere with dusk falling. Presumably Langholm has an inn of some kind.'

They remounted and when they reached the fork in the road, took the right-hand way to Langholm although John looked far from happy at the decision. At first they rode through flat and marshy countryside. The road was surprisingly good, possibly another stretch of Roman road made to service the great wall, and so they made considerable progress, passing through the village of Longtown where they stopped at a poor and dilapidated inn for some bread and cheese. The landlord was surly, eyeing the English strangers with so much suspicion that they were thankful to pay their reckoning and leave.

But soon the road rapidly deteriorated until, as they began to climb steadily towards Langholm, it was little more than a well-beaten track running beside the River Esk. At one point, as they looked across the river, they could see a strange, round stone castle rising to a considerable height but there appeared to be no one about. The sun shone and it became very hot; the only sounds were those of their own hoofbeats and the noise of the swift-flowing river.

Then a stone rattled down in front of them. They pulled up but could see nothing. Another stone rolled down the bank to their left and into the road. Ahead of them was a sharp bend and it was with an increasing feeling of unease that they continued slowly on their way. As they rounded the bend three horsemen rode out from a cluster of stunted bushes and lined up across the road in front of them.

Simon and John stopped in their tracks. The horsemen said nothing. They were dressed entirely in black which made the flash of sun gleaming on their strange steel helmets seem somewhat sinister. Simon looked wildly over his shoulder with a view to trying to escape, but even as he did so a larger group of men appeared silently on the road behind them, apparently out of nowhere, calling to those in front in an incomprehensible tongue.

'God have mercy on us!' John exclaimed. 'I fear we've fallen among thieves.'

The middle man of those barring their way rode forward until he was level with Simon. 'An' wha' brings ye here, strangers?' he asked, modifying his speech somewhat.

'We are travellers bound for Edinburgh,' Simon replied. 'We intend no harm.'

'Why d'ye ride this road then?'

Simon shrugged. 'We have a map and it seemed the quickest way.'

The man laughed unpleasantly and the fellow on his left leant over and said something to him, still in the same thick speech. Simon could make little of it except that it seemed to bode no good.

'Jamie here wants to knae if we maun cut yer throats,' replied the first man, who seemed to be the leader of the band. 'That's wha' we do wi' spies.'

'We are no spies, I promise you,' said Simon desperately. 'I am a doctor from London on my way to Edinburgh to visit colleagues and this is my servant. We're honest men and have no other purpose.'

There was a murmur of disbelief from behind him and several of the men rode round to join those in front. They went a little apart and it was clear that an intense discussion was taking place. Soon it was obvious there was disagreement, for voices were raised in argument and time and again they all looked over towards Simon and John.

Eventually the leader returned and raked Simon with a piercing look. 'A doctor, is it? We'll see what the chief has to say to that, though some of my men think we shouldna take any chances an' kill ye here and now and ha' done wi' it. But dinna look fer lang life or think o' trying to escape; ye'd be dead afore ye struck the ground.'

With no more ado the whole party moved off. The sun was now unpleasantly hot and Simon was desperately thirsty. Around him the men chattered to each other in their own tongue.

'Are you Scots or English?' asked Simon of their leader as the man fell back for a moment to ride beside him.

'Did ye hear that?' he shouted to his men. 'Are we Scots or English, he asks!' He laughed loudly, dug his spurs into his horse, and rode to the front of his men, turning to Simon as he went. 'Man, we're the Borderers!' he said, and laughed again.

86

Chapter 7

Hermitage

From where Simon and John were taken prisoner the road ran beside the River Esk for several miles and then began to climb upwards towards the town of Langholm. They reached it sooner than they had expected because of the speed at which their captors rode, stopping for nothing. As they entered the town Simon mused on what would happen if he shouted for help, but decided it wasn't worth the risk. Those going about their business in the main street stared at them silently as they passed by, while faces peered out from behind shutters. The Reiver band rode on and out of the town without slackening its pace then began climbing upwards again. High bleak hills rose steeply on either side of the road while above them in the unusual heat, the disc of the sun blazed from out of a sky of brass.

'How much longer?' gasped Simon, as the leader of the band once more reined in beside him. 'We're parched with thirst.'

'Ye've a way to go yet.' He looked at them critically and then apparently relented. 'Halt!' he called out, and the horsemen stopped. 'Gi'e the prisoners some water. An' ye tak some yersen.' The men pulled out leather bottles and drank, then two of those guarding Simon and John handed them each one. They drank greedily although the water was warm and brackish. Within minutes they were on their way again.

'Where do you think we're bound?' John asked Simon wearily.

Simon shook his head. 'The milestones say this road leads to Hawick. Surely we can't be going as far as that though.'

The mad ride continued until the end of the afternoon then, without warning, the horsemen stopped at a place where a track led into the road at a right angle from the east. Their leader looked back at Simon and John and motioned his men up it before returning to his captives.

'Twa hours should see us hame,' he told them.

'Two hours!' exclaimed Simon. 'But our horses are tired out. And so are we.'

'Aye, ye've soft English steeds,' the man replied critically. 'Ours are nane sae bonny but when needed they'll tak us fifty or sixty mile.'

If they had found the first part of their journey unpleasant it was as nothing to the last. For what seemed like days they wound up and down across endless rolling miles of hills, sometimes descending deep into a valley bottom, next clambering steeply up to yet another high point only to see nothing but a waste of moorland ahead, their horses labouring and sweating and obviously distressed. Eventually they reached a place where the track began to run beside a fast-flowing brook or small river. In front of them was a bend falling away downhill.

As they rounded it the sun finally began to sink in the west, a brilliant scarlet disc set against a metallic sky splashed with great blotches of bright orange. Having looked behind at the sunset, it took Simon some time to focus on what was ahead of him.

'God preserve and keep us! What in Satan's name is that?' exclaimed John as Simon blinked to clear his eyes from the blazing light at his back. Rising before them was an enormous, brutal black shape, a massive fortified keep, from which was reflected the lurid red glow of the setting sun.

The leader of the band, hearing John's question, turned round to them. 'Welcome tae Hermitage!' he said and drove his party down the hill, across the drawbridge and into the dark beyond.

Hermitage! Simon rocked back in his saddle. So that was the meaning of Davie Armstrong's last word – this grim fortress, and the message they were bringing to Sir Henry Carey must, therefore, have some connection with it. He tried once again to make sense of the boy's dying words. 'Hermitage' – well, he knew what that meant now; 'Carmichael' – that was Sir John whom he had set out to seek; the Careys yes, but he was still at a loss to know what it was that must not be told and to whom. To the Careys? Yet if that was the case, why risk life and limb trying to reach them?

He had no time for further surmise for the prisoners were led into an inner courtyard and roughly told to dismount. From there they were marched into a bleak guardroom in the main keep itself, where a substantial number of grim-looking men sat around busily cleaning weapons. The leader of the captors exchanged greetings with them, then ordered one to fetch the captain.

'What now?' queried Simon, almost beyond caring.

'We'll see wha' Captain Elliot has tae say.'

They were soon to find out. Captain Elliot, a stocky man with a grim and weatherbeaten face, said little at first beyond asking them their names and business. Then he took their captor over into a corner for what became a prolonged and sometimes heated discussion. Finally it looked as if the two men had reached some kind of agreement and both came back over to them.

'Willie here tells me ye've been spying,' stated Captain Elliot.

'We most certainly have not,' responded Simon determinedly. 'I told your men the truth. I am a doctor on my way to Edinburgh and this is my servant. By all means search my saddlebags if you want confirmation. You'll find in them only clothes and necessities for my journey, a few draughts and salves and some horoscope charts.'

Captain Elliot motioned to Willie who left the guardroom, returning within a few minutes with Simon's saddlebag, the contents of which he proceeded to pull out on the floor. It was as Simon had said.

The Captain was unimpressed. 'Nae, I havna time ta bother wi' all this. Hang them, Willie. Ye should a kilt them on the road and saved the trouble.'

'Now what?' muttered John in Simon's ear.

Simon played his only card. 'Then before you do so, hear this. I told you the truth when I said I was a doctor bound for Edinburgh. What I did *not* say was that I was also bringing with me letters to Sir John Carmichael from Sir Henry Carey, Lord Hunsdon, he who was Warden of the West March and is cousin to Queen Elizabeth.' Saying which, he took the letters from his doublet and flourished them in front of the captain. 'I know nothing of their content,' he added as

Willie made to wrench them from him, 'but you will see they're sealed with the Great Seal of the Lord Chamberlain of England and I intend to put them into Sir John's own hands – and only into his hands – unless you kill me first, which of course you can easily do. But in the circumstances, that might not be the wisest course of action to take.'

He knew he must keep talking at all costs. 'If you know where he is, either send to him and tell him I am here with letters for him from Sir Henry Carey or, if you prefer, take us to him – though in the name of all that's holy, give us food and drink and a rest first.' Simon was suddenly aware that the noise in the room had subsided and that Elliot's men, aware that something of moment was occurring, were now watching with interest.

Elliot looked round at them. 'Well, ye've made yer point,' he conceded, 'and I reckon ye canna run from Hermitage. Carmichael's been awa' aftae' a hot trod on the Border but I've word he's even now on his way home. Did ye ken he were the Keeper of Liddesdale?' Simon said he had been told as much. 'Well, ye're now in Liddesdale.' He finally made up his mind. 'Verra weel. Ye can keep yer letters till Carmichael comes. If ye're lying, ye're deid and Carmichael won't save ye. Put them in one of the storerooms,' he said to Willie, 'and gi' them somethin' tae eat and drink.'

'Willie who?' enquired Simon as they limped after their captor.

'Elliot, wha' else?' he replied.

'Are you the captain's brother then?'

The man looked blank then for the first time his face relaxed in a grin. 'Nae, man, we're near all Elliots here. Down the valley and in Eskdale 'tis Armstrongs.' He led them into a small dark room piled with sacks of provisions. 'I'll lock ye in,' he told them, 'but I'll see ye're sent supper.' He looked round, found a candlestick with a half-burned candle in it and felt in his pocket for his tinderbox. He carefully lit the candle. 'I'll send a man tae ye,' he said, and left them to themselves.

As soon as he had gone Simon flattened a place on top of one of the sacks and sat down, wincing as he did so.

'You did well, Doctor,' said John. 'I thought we were sped!'

'Well, the best that can be said is that we've survived so far,' replied Simon cautiously. 'Sweet Jesus, what a crew! And if you say "I told you so", exhausted and weak as I am I'll wring your neck!'

John smiled to himself. 'Let's just hope that this Keeper of Liddesdale really does come soon then, and that there's nothing in that letter that'll harm us. Supposing it's warning him against you as a spy sent to Scotland by the Secretary of State himself. You say he promised to protect you, but I can't see how he can do it if he's in London and we're here.'

'That's a risk we'll have to take since we have no choice.' Simon pulled a wry face. 'But I can't believe Richard would have knowingly brought me up here with him, when he had what could amount to my death warrant in his possession.'

A few minutes later the door was unlocked and a young man entered with a tray on which were two steaming bowls, some bread and two tankards of ale. Behind him came another man dragging two straw mattresses. These he dropped on the floor and then went back for two blankets which he threw in after them. The young man thanked him and as he left, set the tray down before John and Simon along with another candle.

'Ye'll be weary,' he said. 'Riding wi' Willie Elliot's no joy!'

'I ache all over,' Simon agreed. 'I've ridden as long in the past, but that was years ago when I was soldiering and over better ground. And I was younger and harder too.'

The young man handed them the bowls of stew. 'A soldier? Willie says ye're a doctor.'

'So I am now. And I suppose you're an Elliot too?' he asked, applying himself to his food with a will.

'I'm a Kerr, Jamie Kerr. My mother's an Elliot though.' He sat down on one of the sacks, obviously finding the captives of interest.

'This is a grim place,' commented John, polishing his bowl with his bread.

Jamie concurred. 'Aye, 'tis wild country hereabouts an' Hermitage Castle's a bloody history. Two hundred years ago or more it was kept by William de Soulis. They say he practised black magic and drank the blood of virgins. What is sure is that one day he invited all the Armstrongs from Mangerton to a great feast to make peace after a feud. When they rode in they were greeted by de Soulis and his folk,

91

very grand and dressed in their best, and shown into the great hall decked with greenery in their honour. Each Armstrong was sat at table with a de Soulis man to his left and right and so the feast began with food and drink of the finest. Then a huge silver salver was brought in, the lid was taken off and there lay the head of a black bull. All knew what it meant.'

'What was that?' asked John, horribly fascinated in spite of his tiredness.

'Blood on the Borders! And at that, each de Soulis man drew his dagger and stabbed to death the Armstrong seated on his left. But de Soulis paid for it in the end,' he concluded cheerfully.

'He was tried for the deed and rightly condemned?' suggested Simon.

'No, they didna bother with anything like that in those days. The people down the valley in Newcastleton dragged him from his castle and boiled him alive!'

Merciful God, what people have we come among, thought Simon.

'Then we'd Queen Marie Stuart herself here in my father's day, when she was playing whore to the Earl of Bothwell.' He stood up. 'But I'd best not linger, they'll wonder what keeps me.'

'You don't speak like the others,' Simon commented.

Jamie smiled. 'I can if I wish. But I was away to Edinburgh to the university.' He went to the door and paused. 'I hope it goes well for you. Carmichael's a fair man.'

Simon stood up. 'Before you go, do you know a young man by the name of Alun Armstrong? About your age, red-haired and also much of your height.'

'Aye,' replied Jamie slowly. 'That is, I know *an* Alun Armstrong. He's one of the Mangerton Armstrongs. Why do you ask?'

'Because I met a young man of that name in London and was able to do him a service. It might be that he could speak for me.'

'If it's the same man, then no doubt he would. But the one I know's been away these many weeks. I'll see if anyone knows where he might be. In the meanwhile, sleep now if you can.'

In spite of their aches and pains and the straw mattress on a stone floor, both men fell into an uneasy slumber from which they were awoken some hours later by the sound of hooves clattering into the yard outside. The candle had long guttered out and it was pitch dark in the room since it was not yet dawn. They were both wondering what would happen next when they heard the sound of footsteps outside their door and Willie Elliot entered, carrying a flaming torch. 'Ye're to get up and come wi' me,' he ordered.

Simon and John looked at each other. 'What now?' asked Simon. 'Are we then to be hanged after all?'

'Mebbe. But it's nought to do wi' me. The Keeper of Liddesdale has ridden in and is asking for ye. Ye can tell yer tale to Carmichael and see if he'll believe ye.'

They followed him out of the room, still stiff from the previous day's ride. Dawn was only just breaking and through an open doorway they could see fires burning in the courtyard which was now bristling with men. Willie led them across the great hall and up towards a flight of stone steps leading to the floor above. Another large fire burned below and there were torches stuck in sconces all round the walls. A group of men stood below the staircase, one in the process of taking off his steel helmet, and as the three men ascended the stairs he threw back his head and looked up.

'God's Blood!' he shouted out. 'Dr Forman! What in the world brings ye here?'

Willie Elliot stopped in his tracks. 'Who's that?' he called down.

'Alun Armstrong of Mangerton,' the young man responded. 'I've but now ridden in wi' Carmichael,' and with no more ado he leapt up the stairs. 'Where are ye takin' them?'

'To the Keeper. We found them on the Langholm road. Some o' the men reckoned they maun be kilt and I'm nae convinced mysen they're nae English spies.'

'Spies!' roared Alun. 'Dr Forman saved my life!' He pushed his way in front to stand level with Elliot. 'I'll come with ye to Carmichael, Willie. If it wasna for Dr Forman I'd be deid. Not only did he bind up my wounds, he had me hid me in his ain house to save me from my enemies. I told him then that if he was ever in need of aid from the Armstrongs then he'd have it. An' I meant it!' he concluded triumphantly. 'He's had my word.'

The small party made its way through an arched door and into the main living quarters used by the Keeper when he was at Hermitage.

Here some effort had been made at comfort, for there were rugs on the floor and a polished table, chairs and some benches. An open door led off to a bedchamber with a curtained bed. Sir John Carmichael was sitting at a table reading some papers when Elliot led the party in, but he stopped what he was doing and looked up.

'So, these are the men, Willie,' he said, then frowned. 'And what are you doing here, Alun?'

'I've come to speak for them,' the young man replied. 'This is Dr Forman. He I told you of, who saved my life and kept me safe from pursuit. Before I left his house his servant there told me he'd been taken away by officers of the Queen. He was fearful he'd nae come back.'

'It would seem he is what he says he is then,' Carmichael commented to Willie Elliot.

'Aye, mebbe. We'll soon know. He says he's letters for you.'

Carmichael looked thoughtfully at Simon. 'Willie here tells me you were found on the road to Langholm and brought here by his men.'

'And nearly killed there and then,' said Simon. 'Though we'd done nothing to merit it. Then, after it was decided our throats weren't immediately going to be slit we were dragged here, riding for hours without food or drink, threatened with hanging and then locked in a dark storeroom for the night. If this is Border hospitality then I'll settle for a cell in Newgate!'

In spite of himself Carmichael smiled. 'Have you breakfasted?' he asked.

Simon and John shook their heads. 'Willie, take Dr Forman's servant down to my own kitchen and see he's given food and drink – and tell them down there if he's not treated with courtesy, they'll answer for it to me personally. And also ask one of the servants to bring us up some breakfast. I'm sorry you were so roughly treated,' he continued as the two men left the room, 'but these are hard and dangerous times. We can take no risks.'

'The Governor of Carlisle Castle told me the West March was relatively untroubled at present.'

'That may be so but there's fighting on the Middle March which could spill over west, and we've just now had the hot trod raised for a party of English who'd come thieving over the Border. I'd to see that didn't get out of hand for fear it might set the West March ablaze.'

Simon was totally mystified at this latter piece of information but decided there were more pressing matters than to ask what a 'hot trod' might be. He felt in his doublet and produced the two letters, the one Lord Hunsdon had given him and the other which had been in Richard's saddlebag. 'I've no idea what they say,' he told Carmichael as he handed them to him. 'This first was written by Sir Henry Carey on my behalf and the second was to have been given you by my companion, Richard Wilmore, a relation of the Careys.'

'And why is he not here to do it in person?'

'Because he was killed in Carlisle.'

Carmichael looked up in astonishment. 'How was that?'

'Someone entered the room in which we slept and murdered him in his bed. He used a garotte. It's thought the murderer must have entered the castle secretly during the day and then waited until night fell. The officer on guard that night admitted to the Governor afterwards that there were often insufficient checks on those coming in and out.'

Carmichael stood up and went over to the window. It was now full daylight. 'I warned the Governor last time I visited him that I found discipline at the castle too lax, but he'd have none of it coming as it did from the Keeper of Liddesdale. Things have grown altogether too slack there. Is it known why this man was killed?'

Simon shook his head. 'It might be that he had a private enemy unknown to us, but it has occurred to me since that the most likely explanation is that someone did not want him to reach Scotland alive.'

Carmichael considered this. 'And what was your role in this venture, Dr Forman?'

'I was to have accompanied Richard to Edinburgh. Having heard of the excellence of my colleagues there I have long been interested in seeing if this is indeed so and discussing with them our common problems.' This did not go down so well for Carmichael looked frankly unconvinced.

'It seems those who've crossed your path of late suffer grave ill fortune,' he commented dryly, 'for two of them have now met their deaths.'

'He'd no hand in what happened to us,' broke in Alun. 'Davie died before Dr Forman could do anything for him and it was entirely by chance we were directed to his door.'

'By which time there was nothing I could do for the lad,' Simon confirmed, 'but one mystery at least is solved. He muttered a few words before he died though they did not seem to make sense, the last of which was "Hermitage". That puzzled me greatly but I now know what he meant if not what he was trying to say. I thought at first he must be a religious of some kind, possibly even an unlawful Mass priest.'

'Davie, a Mass priest!' exclaimed Alun, 'He'd but one notion – that after we'd done wi' our mission to Lord Hunsdon we'd gae after the lasses!'

There was a knock at the door and a servant entered with food and drink which he set down before them. Carmichael motioned them to it and then opened the two letters from the Lord Chamberlain. He read both through with great care then addressed Simon.

'Your letter from Carey is discretion itself, Dr Forman. It merely confirms who you are and informs me you are Edinburgh-bound to discuss medical affairs with doctors in the city, but that from Hunsdon is more interesting.' For one awful moment Simon considered the possibility that the letter Richard was carrying to Carmichael damned him in some way, but he saw Carmichael did not seem greatly perturbed.

'Well, Carey supports at least the first part of your tale,' he continued. 'It's clear you knew nothing of what brought the Armstrongs to London, indeed had no knowledge of either of them until Davie died at your door.' He gave Simon a keen look. 'I presume you did not tell him of the assistance you gave Alun, for he says he only learned of it later from his son. No doubt you had your reasons. He also writes that it was at the urging of Robert that he was persuaded this man Wilmore should go with you to Edinburgh and that on his way he was to have delivered this letter and also learned from me the burden of the message I attempted to send to His

Lordship. But all this makes me think the reason you give for visiting Edinburgh cannot be the one.'

He paused. 'Carey states that the Acting Secretary to the Privy Council, Sir Robert Cecil, has a particular interest in you. Is that so?'

Simon did not know how to respond. 'Ye can trust Sir John,' urged Alan. 'It might well help ye more than ye know, and after what ye did for me I'll swear ye're safe wi' us.'

'It occurs to me, Dr Forman,' Carmichael added gently, 'in view of what Alun says, that you were taken away by the Queen's officers the day after Davie died, that this was done on the orders of Sir Robert Cecil. Am I right?'

Simon felt on firmer ground. 'The day after Davie died I was indeed taken to Whitehall though I do not know on whose orders, and accused of being in league with spies from Scotland. I held to my story: that I knew nothing of the man who died outside my house and said nothing of Alun, but I don't know how much longer I'd have been able to hold out had Sir Robert Cecil himself not intervened for, when he arrived, I was being threatened with torture. It was he who saved me, saying he thought I was speaking the truth.

'To put it briefly he convinced me there were those in high places however, who would not believe me and his solution was that I go to Edinburgh using the pretext of exchanging knowledge with doctors in the city, but in reality to keep my eyes and ears open as to who is there from England making overtures to King James. Such a mission under his protection, he said, would prove my loyalty to Queen and Country, otherwise even he might not be able to save me. I might hardly add that so dangerous a venture was no wish of mine. I've not knowledge of such intrigue and did not know who to trust, which is why I told Sir Henry Carey very little. It was different where Robert Carey was concerned for we were already acquainted and I was grateful for Richard Wilmore's company – indeed, I was relying on him not only to bring me safe to Edinburgh and home again but to assist me while there.'

Carmichael nodded. 'What you say makes sense. And now your guide and companion is dead. What did Governor Musgrave make of that?'

'At first he thought I'd killed him since we were sharing the same bedchamber. Later I hope I was able to convince him otherwise.'

'Perhaps you'd best tell me in detail what did happen in Carlisle,' said Carmichael and so Simon did. At the end of the story Carmichael sat for a while in silence then commented, 'This has the mark of devilry on it and makes me wonder indeed if the two deaths are connected. I send a messenger to Carey and he dies. Carey sends a messenger to me and he dies too. You have given me a great deal to think about and I must take time to do so.' He stood up. 'You're friend to Robert Carey, you say? Well, it will be a good day for the West March when he takes up his father's place. The Careys I can trust to the death, which is more than I am prepared to say of others. So what are your plans now, Dr Forman?'

'I must press on but I fear attempting to reach Edinburgh on my own,' Simon admitted. 'Suppose you let me go and I leave here, and ten miles further on run into another band of men who take me somewhere else or, this time, kill me on the roadside?'

'I'll take ye safe to Edinburgh,' broke in Alun, 'though I'll not stay long within its bounds – there's many there wi' no love for Armstrongs – then we'll agree a way of seeing you safe back across the Border to your home when ye've done what ye have to do. But now let the two of ye come home with me to Mangerton and rest for a day or so. There's folk there who'll want to shake the hand of the man who saved my life. What d'ye think, Keeper?'

'It sounds sensible,' Carmichael agreed. 'It will give me time to consider the best way to move forward.' He took Simon's hand. 'We'll talk again in two days' time, Dr Forman, meanwhile Alun will see you safe bestowed. Send the Captain to me before you go.'

'How far away is Mangerton?' Simon asked in some trepidation as he followed Alun down the stairs to the hall below.

'Seven or eight mile down Liddesdale, no more. Are ye saddle sore?'

'Painfully,' replied Simon with feeling. 'Your men stopped for nothing.'

'That's the way of the Reivers,' smiled Alun. 'We think southerners soft.'

Half an hour later they rode out of Hermitage, accompanied by

John, on small tough horses while their own were rested at the castle. Simon was both surprised and relieved to discover that Hermitage stood only a brief distance from another road which also ran north to Hawick but Alun turned them in the opposite direction. After a little while he drew rein beside a river and pointed across it to a tall grey tower similar to the one they had seen on the road to Langholm. 'That's Mangerton,' he told them. 'And *that*,' he continued, motioning towards a gaunt stone cross ahead of them on the roadside, 'is where they rested the coffin of Alexander Armstrong of Mangerton after the massacre at Hermitage by de Soulis.' It was clear two hundred years was quite insufficient to have wiped away the memory of that black event.

At that Alun turned off towards the river, explaining that it was fordable at that point, and within minutes they reached the complex of buildings that was Mangerton. A servant appeared at once to take Alun's horse, casting a surprised and suspicious glance at his companions. 'Tell my mother we have guests,' Alun told him. 'Most particular guests, for it was Dr Forman here who saved my life in London.'

The men dismounted and as their horses were led away, a woman of middle years, finely dressed in a dark velvet gown, appeared from the doorway and greeted her son with a kiss on his cheek. Quickly he explained the situation to her then without more ado introduced Simon to her.

'So,' she said as he bowed to her, 'it seems we owe you a great debt indeed, Dr Forman. Come away in. Be welcome in our house.'

Chapter 8

Kate

As Simon discovered, the bleak fortified tower at Mangerton was only occupied by the family when danger threatened. He was shown into the sturdy stone house beside it which looked of recent date – and was, its predecessor having been razed to the ground during an internecine feud some ten years earlier. Inside, the furnishings if not grand were comfortable, but what did surprise him was how finely both his hostess and her female relatives were dressed, their gowns cut after the French fashion. It was clear that however rough the lives of the menfolk might be, their women did not run short of velvet and damask.

Alun's father was still away from home on the hot trod, although expected back at any time, bringing with him his cousin 'Kinmont Willie' who had business with Carmichael at Hermitage. Kinmont Willie Armstrong, Alun told Simon, was already the stuff of legend, one of the most famous and daring men on the Border, notorious from end to end of it.

As John went to stow his master's possessions away in the room that had been put at their disposal, Alun finally explained to his puzzled guest the meaning of the words 'the hot trod'.

'It works across the Border both ways,' he told Simon. 'At least it should! The aim of the Wardens on each side is to try and prevent cattle raids or affrays of any kind that might upset the peace. One way is by means of good intelligence so that there is some warning of those crossing the Border with thievery in mind in the hope that they can be prevented before there's serious trouble. But if that doesn't happen and a band of Reivers from either side rides off with

101

cattle and loot, then those who have suffered have the right to follow them and try to fetch their goods back.'

In the old days, he continued, all that was necessary was to raise a sufficient number of men who, armed to the teeth, would chase after the raiders and if they caught up with them, administer summary justice on the spot. 'To alert the neighbourhood that a pursuit was on, they'd snatch up a burning peat from their hearths and gallop off, holding it above their heads – hence the "hot trod", the hot track.'

But of late it was no longer so easy. Nowadays a representative of a family or hamlet that had suffered had to lodge his complaint with a man of good fame and sound judgement and declare his cause, stating what property he had lost, and asking that person to come in person to witness the trod. Apparently there had been a serious incursion at the lower end of Liddesdale, which was why the Keeper himself was out of Liddesdale as he had been called as witness.

Simon shook his head at such primitive justice and the ambiguity with which Alun developed his theme, for it seemed reiving raids were still justified by both sides, a point he made to his host as they were summoned in to dinner.

'It's a hard country, Simon, with hard ways. We've lived for centuries as a battleground between the two sides so it's not surprising we've had to devise ways of our own. Cattle raids and the seizing of booty's still a way of life.'

'And what of the women?' Simon asked, as Mistress Armstrong motioned them to the table.

'They're loyal to their menfolk and they too have their own customs. It's not unknown in a household where meat is running short for a wife to give her man a covered dish at breakfast-time. When he lifts the lid he finds inside a single spur – that means the larder's nearly empty and it's time he did something about it. And it's not so long ago that when a child was christened, the priest left the right hand unhallowed so that it might deal a more deadly blow to the enemy.'

There seemed little to say in answer to this and Simon sat down at table wondering what might be served up, but the fare set before them was simple and good, and he was relieved to see that the large covered dishes contained only meat, turnips and other vegetables with neither a black bull's head nor a spur in sight. During the course of the meal Simon answered the questions put to him by his hostess as to his reasons for visiting Scotland, as courteously as he could, along with several on medical matters for it soon became apparent that Mistress Armstrong had no small skill in doctoring herself, something of a necessity in a territory where there were few physicians.

Afterwards Alun took Simon outside and from a low hill near by showed him the extent of the Mangerton lands. As they stood looking down at the river below them there was a sudden glint of metal on the road the other side of the valley and within minutes a band of armed men had come into sight.

'That'll be Father,' said Alun, to Simon's relief. After everything he had heard in recent days he would not have been surprised to learn that it was a band of enemy Reivers from the south with mayhem in mind coming to retrieve their property and that they should take to the tower at once! 'And now you'll also meet Kinmont Willie. No doubt he's brought some of his family to ride with him as usual; they're bonny fighters.'

They stood awhile in the warm afternoon sun watching the band of horsemen as they forded the river before turning to ride briskly up the track towards Mangerton. 'That's Father riding in front, Willie's just behind him,' Alun pointed out. 'Let's go down and meet them.' By the time they arrived back at the house the courtyard was full of men, dismounting and tying up their horses. Alun wasted no time in introducing Simon to his father and his famous companion, and explaining who he was.

The former looked at Simon shrewdly. 'Whatever reason brings ye here, then I'm glad to meet ye,' he said. 'In the meantime, I trust my wife has seen to all your needs?' Simon assured him that she had. 'Good. I'll see these lads have a drink and then Willie here can get off to Hermitage and we can talk further. There's nae need to look sae black, Willie,' he continued, looking at his cousin's face. 'Dr Forman's no' likely to have saved Alun's life then ridden to Scotland to bring harm on us all.'

Simon agreed, adding, 'I only wish I could have saved the other lad, too.'

'Aye.' Armstrong's face darkened. 'That was a bad business. An' if we ever find out who did it and who set it up then we'll no rest until he's avenged whoever and wherever they might be.'

Two servants appeared bearing trays of tankards which they handed round to the men who had taken the opportunity to unbuckle their arms, as the sun was strong, and take off their strange steel helmets. Nearest to Simon was a slender youth who had ridden in close to Kinmont Willie and was presumably, from his fine smooth skin, the baby of the family. As he watched idly the boy pulled off his helmet to reveal to Simon's astonishment two long plaits of dark red hair.

Alun saw Simon's astounded expression and laughed out loud. 'Ye've left my friend here fairly winded, Kate,' he called out to her. 'Come over here, Simon, and meet my Cousin Kate.' The girl turned, looked up and grinned. There was a definite family likeness between her and Alun.

'Is it usual for women to ride out with the Reivers?' enquired Simon.

The girl shook her head as Alun put his arm round her shoulders. 'Nae, ye can rest easy, we have no bands of Amazons roving the Border. Kate here is a law unto herself and rides with her father's agreement if not his blessing.'

'I've nae wish to stay home while my brothers have all the excitement,' Kate confirmed. 'I can ride as hard and am as quick with a sword as any of them.'

Alun turned his eyes heavenwards. 'Her father prays she'll settle down soon and find herself a good man. Though heaven help him if he's looking for domestic bliss!' He tightened his grip on the girl, at which she flinched away from him. 'Are you hurt, lass?' he asked, suddenly concerned.

'I'd a cut on the arm,' she admitted. 'It's nothing. It's just a wee bit angry, that's all.'

'Then let Simon look at it for ye,' said Alun. 'It's the first time we've ever had a doctor from London here at Mangerton.' Together they went into the kitchen of the house and Alun explained the problem to his mother who was overseeing the dinner while Kate stripped off her doublet and rolled up the sleeve of her shirt as far as she could. The cut, however, was obviously higher up, a none-too-clean dressing showing below the sleeve-edge from under which an angry red was spreading downwards on the pale flesh.

'I must see what's under the dressing,' Simon told her. 'Can you ease your shirt down over your shoulder so that I can take it off?'

The girl flushed and looked at Mistress Armstrong. 'Come into my own room,' said the older woman. 'Alun, go and see if there's anything you can do for your father while Dr Forman takes a look at Kate. There's no need to look so coy, girl,' she continued, pushing her firmly ahead of her. 'The man's a doctor. He's seen worse things than a woman's bare shoulder.'

Once in her small sitting room she helped Kate slip her arm out of her shirt then held up the shoulder of her shift. Simon began carefully unwrapping the dressing which had stuck fast in places. 'Can you bring me some water?' he asked Mistress Armstrong. 'I'll need to dampen this to loosen it.'

She went back to the kitchen returning almost at once with a jug of hot water and a bowl. Simon carefully sponged the dressing, unwrapping it as he did so. He finally removed it entirely to reveal an angry wound about three inches long. 'Hm, that's nasty. It must be quite painful.'

Kate shrugged. 'It's no' so bad. Wrap it up again, it'll do. I pay it no mind.'

'It needs more than that,' said Simon. 'If nothing's done, the poison will give you at best a sore arm and at worst a bad fever. If you'll be patient a few minutes I'll fetch a salve from my room.' He went in search of it and as he took the pot out of his baggage he was reminded of the last time he'd used it on James Ford's ear. He wondered how the wool buyer was faring and if he'd heard of the trouble at the castle. Presumably he was on his way back to London by now.

He returned to the small sitting room and showed the salve to Mistress Armstrong. 'I know you keep herbs and salves of your own. Have you betony and comfrey? Dried, if not fresh? Excellent! Then we'll make an infusion and clean the wound with it. Both have powerful properties, being under the influence of Jupiter and Saturn respectively. Then I'll apply my own salve and we'll put on a clean dressing. But it will need watching. If you find you begin to run a fever then you must take feverfew in wine – I'm sure Mistress Armstrong also has feverfew as she keeps such an excellent still room.'

The older woman left them to fetch the herbs for which he had asked and Simon began to wash the cut. 'So, you find a woman's life not to your liking?'

Kate grinned again. 'Aye, I do. Household duties and spinning and sewing and thinking what meat we should have for supper and dancing attendance on a man and getting up ten times a night to a screaming baby! Though I'm nae such a fool as to think I'll never come to it one day,' she sighed. 'For a woman at the end of the road there's always a man and weans.'

'Aren't you fearful you might be killed before then?'

'Ye can be killed on the Borders just as well sitting home at the spinning wheel,' she retorted. 'The raiders coming up from the south will steal your cattle, spike your man through the heart and cut your throat without another thought.' Then of a sudden she changed the subject. 'If ye're a doctor, do ye also study the stars and cast horoscopes?'

Simon smiled. 'I do. Though I only have a few of my books and charts with me.'

'Will ye cast one for me?' she asked eagerly.

'I'll try my best if that's what you wish. But only if you agree to my treating your arm properly and your looking after it!'

Mistress Armstrong returned with the herbs and Simon asked for hot water to be poured onto them in the kitchen while he probed the cut, and also for some clean strips of cloth. Kate bore his examination with fortitude although she gripped her lip between her teeth throughout.

'Well, there doesn't seem to be anything else amiss,' he said finally, 'so we'll clean up this pus with the infusion then I'll put my salve on it and we'll bind it up again. I'll take another look before I leave.'

'And my horoscope?' she insisted.

'Horoscope!' echoed Mistress Armstrong. 'What nonsense is this?'

'Dr Forman casts horoscopes too,' Kate told her, 'and I've asked him to cast mine.'

Mistress Armstrong shook her head. 'Well, I don't hold with it, but doubtless it's a waste of breath saying so if you're set on it. Let's hope it'll tell you it's time you stopped all this gallivanting about the countryside and asked your father to find you a good husband. And now if you've wit enough to do as the doctor says and mind that arm, leave your father to ride up to Hermitage with your brothers without you. You're welcome here until it's time to go home. And I'll find you a gown so you look less like a heathen!'

A little later a neatly dressed young woman in a blue stuff gown, her hair now coiled round her head, presented herself to Simon demanding he keep his promise and cast her horoscope.

'You realise this cannot be as full a one as I could have cast for you at home?' he said as he spread out some charts on a small table. She nodded but gave him her eager smile and rubbed her hands in anticipation as he asked her for the information he needed to know. She was, she told him, eighteen and born under the sign of Gemini at her father's castle at Kinmont.

'And do you know the time of day?'

'My mother told me once I was born very quick, being the youngest, and that I came with the rising of the sun.' He noted that down then asked what it was in particular that she wanted to know.

'Oh, everything! What lies ahead of me? What will I do, what kind of a husband will I get me, will I have children, will I see old age?'

'Sweet Jesus, is there anything you *don't* want to know?' he laughed. 'If I'm to tell you a fraction of this then I need time. We'll meet again before supper – meanwhile I'll do my best.'

He watched her as she went lightly out of the door feeling, yet again, the familiar stirrings of attraction and desire. She was not conventionally pretty, certainly not as exotic as the Lord Chamberlain's Emilia, nor as beautiful as Olivia (a young woman with whom he was once involved – with nearly fatal consequences), nor did she have the special qualities of his Avisa. But she had fine features and the lovely bloom of youth. A mental procession of the ladies he had taken to bed in recent years passed briefly before his eyes, not least those patients of a coming-on disposition who had made it only too clear what they had in mind.

Kate was quite unlike any of them: a desirable wildcat with all the wiles of a young girl but one who was quite literally capable of killing her man if necessary when out on a raid with her brothers. Dalliance with her would be extremely pleasant (that is, if he could persuade her to agree) but he balked at the prospect of what might come next if it were discovered he had abused the Armstrongs' hospitality by seducing one of their marriagable girls: he had a vision of being chased across Scotland by half a hundred steel-bonneted Reivers out to avenge family honour. He shook his head, laughed at his own weakness where a pretty woman was concerned, and applied himself to his task. He also decided, since he had charts and books to hand, to see what, if anything, might be immediately in store for himself.

The latter was a mistake as it so often was when personal answers were demanded of the planets. Kate's horoscope was even more obscure and he found it hard to interpret. Alun, coming in search of him some time later, found him in a thoughtful mood.

'Are ye still asking the stars what they've in mind for Cousin Kate?' he asked with a laugh, then handed Simon a sealed note. 'This came for you just now – I presume it's from Carmichael himself.' The letter was brief and to the point. The Keeper had sent a messenger to Carlisle Castle the previous day asking the Governor for his account of the murder and he was now awaiting a reply. He therefore requested Simon's patience a little while longer. Simon read on:

Unless you are lying to me, which I doubt, wrote Carmichael, *then I fear you are in grave danger while you are from home. It seems obvious that your wisest course would be to return to London without delay, but I realise that you are unwilling or, more likely, unable to do so. My feeling is that you are between the devil and the deep blue sea, for there are too many factions in the boiling cauldron of the King's Court in Edinburgh and that of your Queen in London, and you will be lucky if you can escape being sucked into it. However, we will talk more of this anon.*

Simon put the letter into his pocket, chilled to the heart, as it so accurately reflected what he had learned from his own hasty horoscope casting, wherein he had seen before him nothing but a tangle of ways, many of them leading nowhere, coupled with a sense of approaching disaster whether for himself or another he could not tell. As to Kate, he wondered quite what he should tell her. He had rarely cast for anyone previously where so much remained unclear. Her immediate future was bright, her health was good and she was much sought-after in marriage. It was like looking into a fog.

'Bad news?' queried Alun eventually as Simon still said nothing.

'I've to wait awhile as he's sent to Carlisle to know more. As to bad news, he tells me only what I know already – that I'm set on a hazardous path.'

'Well, if ye're to stay another day or so let us make the most of it. Tomorrow we'll ride out and I'll show ye some of the countryside. For now ye'd best find Kate and tell her fortune for her.'

He found her sitting outside in the sun with the other women, her menfolk having ridden off to Hermitage. Mistress Armstrong made her disapproval clear as the girl leapt up and ran towards him.

'Well? What've ye seen for me, Dr Forman?' asked Kate, her face brimming with mischief.

He put on a brave smile. 'An old, old man for a husband and a life of piety and prayer.'

She looked aghast. 'Are ye serious? Is that *all* ye can see?'

'Ye asked for it yersel', Kate,' commented Alun, coming up behind Simon. 'It sounds most suitable to me. An' 'tis right, Simon, is it not, that when the old fellow dies she'll be away to France and turn nun?'

Kate looked from one to the other then began to pummel Alun. 'Ye're joking with me, surely?' she said, looking from one to the other. 'Tell me that's not true!'

Simon smiled broadly. 'No, Kate. It's not true. Not so far as I can see, but then I must admit I could not see very far ahead. Much would seem to depend upon you and the choices you will soon have to make. But I foresee this way of life of yours hasn't much further to run – but then you hardly needed a reader of the stars to tell you that, being the age you are and of good family. You'll be pleased to know you'll have many suitors from which to choose.'

'And long life?' she asked.

He hesitated. 'I see no reason why not. But while you continue wilfully to put yourself in hazard, no one can be sure of anything. The path of your life disappears into a mist where I could not follow, possibly because I am tired and have few of my charts and books to hand. My own feeling is that your future now rests with you, my dear.'

He left her to ponder on it and went in search of John Bradedge to tell him it would be another day at least before they left for Edinburgh. He found him sitting with some of Master Armstrong's men in their guardroom. He received the news of yet further delay with a weary sigh, grumbling that at this rate they'd be lucky to be back home before Christmas, let alone by July as had been demanded of Simon.

'There's precious little I can do,' Simon told him. 'If we're to have any chance of coming off with whole skins then we need all the help we can get and Carmichael is a power in the land and, most rarely, trusted by both sides or at least by the Careys. I have no idea whether Cecil trusts him. I'm sure Robert Carey has been straight with me but as to his father, I still can't decide. Cecil obviously thinks highly of him while the Careys frankly dislike Cecil.' He groaned. 'Who knows what these great ones are about? God's Blood, what am I *doing* here? Why in the name of all that's holy did that poor wretched boy have to die outside my door instead of that of any one of the other London physicians?'

'Because you won't keep your nose out of other people's affairs,' responded John dourly. 'I'm past telling you what you should do. Let's hope this mad trip will teach you a lesson – that is, if we live long enough for you to learn it.' Simon departed, aware that no sooner had he left the room than John would regale his companions with tales of his mad master's previous exploits. At least he seemed to have lost his dark suspicions of every fighting man on the Border and even, like himself, was finding it easier to understand what was said to him. The Border tongue no longer sounded so much like a foreign language.

The next morning with the weather still fine, Simon rode out with Alun and also with Kate, who had been determined to accompany them. They set their horses up a track until they reached the top of the hill behind Mangerton. From there the land swept away before them into the far distance without a sign of human habitation, crossed only by paths made by cattle or sheep. Alun and Kate set off at once at a gallop, racing each other across the moorland, while Simon picked his way more soberly behind.

'How long will it take us to reach Edinburgh from here?' asked Simon when Alun and Kate returned breathless to his side.

'A good day, so long as we keep going, the nights being as light as they are. Don't look so downcast! The sooner ye get there the sooner ye'll come back, though I wouldn't want to be in your shoes hanging round the fringes of Jamie's Court. Though at least ye're no' the sort for him to want to make ye one o' his favourites – ye're no pretty enough. So that's one risk ye'll no' have to take!'

Simon opened his eyes wide. 'Is he inclined that way then?'

'Aye, so they say – though he'll do his duty to the Stuart line. But it's something of a scandal how he favours the good-looking young callants.'

'Are ye shocked, Simon?' asked Kate with a grin.

'Not shocked at his fancy. Though it's said to be against the laws of God and man, there's a fair few of that persuasion in London too and some of them, so it's rumoured, in high places, but that it should be so openly known and spoken of . . . and he King of Scotland and likely soon to be King of England too.'

'Well, it's best ye know,' Alun continued, 'for as well as all those Scots and English seeking favours and to feather their nests when the old Queen dies, there's also those prepared to go both ways between the sheets if there's hope of a fortune at the end of it.'

They returned home to find a message awaiting Simon from Carmichael bidding him come to Hermitage that afternoon though he noted, to his relief, that Carmichael assumed he would be staying at Mangerton before setting off for Edinburgh. Simon had no desire to pass another night in the Keeper's grim fortress, even if this time he was unlikely to be hanged in the morning. So, after dining on an excellent game pie, Simon and Alun rode back once more up the valley.

As they rode together their conversation turned again to Wilmore's murder, who might have carried it out and why. It had exercised Simon throughout the previous days and he had begun to form a conclusion. 'You know I told Sir John that the reason for it might be that someone did not want Richard to reach Edinburgh? Well, even if we don't know exactly who, I've been thinking I might know why. Both he and I were set on to see who from London was in Edinburgh and what they were about. In his letter Sir John likened the situation there to a boiling cauldron. Is it not possible, therefore, that some young blood from England got wind of our coming and decided to take measures to prevent his activities being discovered?'

Alun agreed that was a possibility. 'But if that was the case, surely they would have murdered you as well?'

'I've thought of that, but quite possibly it was actually believed that I was visiting Edinburgh only to speak with medical men and merely accompanying a man known to be close to Lord Hunsdon. If that was the case they'd reckon that if I wasn't myself suspected of the murder then I'd almost certainly return to London.'

Alun nodded. 'It makes sense. And, of course, it would mean some young nobleman wouldn't have to dirty his own hands with the business. He'd easily find someone to kill for him, for a price.'

By this time they were in sight of Hermitage. The looming fortress still made Simon shudder even in the sunshine, and even though the busy activity in its courtyard gave at least some appearance of normality. Among those sitting outside in the sunshine he saw Kate's brothers who, bored with inactivity, were playing dice with several other young men. As Simon was asking that they be shown up to the Keeper's chamber, they met with Kinmont Willie himself.

'Is my lassie behaving herself?' he asked Alun.

'Aye. And Dr Forman here's seen to her wounded arm.'

Kinmont Willie seemed surprised at this but looked at Simon and thanked him. 'She said nothing of a bad arm to me.' He sighed. 'The Lord sent me seven tall sons and but the one daughter, and she the last of the brood. She was always determined to keep up wi' her brothers and play the boy from when she could first walk. And once she was sixteen there was no holding her but she must ride with us.'

'And what does her mother say to that?' enquired Simon.

'Her mother died when she was ten years old. And I admit to being soft with her and letting her have her way. But, as everyone's telling me, it's time and more she'd a husband and I'll see to it before

112

the year's out, that I swear, whether she will or nay. So what of her arm, Dr Forman?'

'A sword cut, much inflamed. She's lucky it didn't give her a fever. I've cleaned it for her and put on a salve and if she takes care it should heal quickly as young flesh does.'

Kinmont Willie thanked him. 'Tell her we'll be back for her tomorrow and then we ride for home.'

'Where's that?' enquired Simon as one of Carmichael's men led the way to the upper storey.

'Over to the east, almost to Solway Moss,' Alun told him. 'He's a grand tower there and much land. He's a wealthy man, is Kinmont Willie. Whoever takes Kate will have a good dowry with her to sweeten the bargain.'

Carmichael was reading a letter when they entered the room. As they did so he threw it down then came straight to the point. 'The castle Governor confirms much of what you told me of the happenings in Carlisle, Dr Forman, though I think it only fair to tell you that he still appears to harbour some doubts as to your role in the man's death.'

'I thought I'd convinced him otherwise; that he'd accepted that a determined intruder secreted himself in the castle and killed Richard, particularly after they found an off-duty soldier dead as well. And I could hardly have murdered both of them.'

'It's suggested that task might have fallen to your servant.'

'The Governor knows very well that couldn't have been the case, for not only was John out of the castle that night, he was actually lodging with one of the garrison sergeants. It's preposterous!'

Carmichael seemed to agree. 'No doubt once you had left, there were those only too happy to persuade him it had to have been you, not least those likely to suffer for their laxity in checking who'd gone in and out that day.'

'And what do you think, sir?' asked Simon.

'I think you're an honest man in a damnable position. Tell me, since you've had some time to consider it, have you any more notion now who might have killed your friend and why?'

So Simon repeated what he had told Alun: that someone unknown had decided Richard must not reach Scotland, the reason being that he could cause serious trouble by informing Lord Hunsdon about who was currying favour at the Scots Court and what they might be up to, and Carmichael agreed it was all too likely. Then he spoke again.

'Now, Dr Forman, I'll tell you what I have decided. If you are still set on going on to Edinburgh then I must warn you I have little influence either within the city or at Court. But there are still those who owe me favours and I'll see if there's anything I can do. What I will say is that if you need my protection on your way back, then that I can certainly afford you, even if you decide it best to cross the Border on the Middle or East Marches, for that too could be arranged.'

'I'll see he gets to the Border afterwards come what may,' promised Alun.

'Meanwhile,' continued Carmichael, 'I will try yet again to send word of what I fear to Sir Henry Carey, but this time by a different route. And this time I'll try to seek a meeting with him or, if he cannot come north himself, then with his son.'

'Can you not trust Simon with it then? If not now, then on his way back.'

Carmichael paused. 'I would rather not wait that long, but even if that wasn't the case there are good reasons why I think it best Dr Forman knows nothing of it. Not least for his own safety.'

'Then I won't press you, sir,' said Simon, 'but I would beg, if you are sending word to the Careys, that you tell them of my deep distress at the death of Richard Wilmore, for I know he was most dear to them, and how I'll do my best to discover his murderer. Perhaps you could say what I think happened and why.'

Carmichael sighed. 'All I will tell you is this. When I agreed to Alun and Davie going to London, since they wanted so much to see the wonders of your city, the information I proposed to give Carey was mainly speculation. Now, after two violent deaths, I am convinced otherwise so this time my messenger will be discreet and secret. As to the death of Wilmore, I shall do as you say and advise Sir Henry that I accept your version of events in Carlisle and that I agree with your suspicions. So, go on your way now with my good wishes and keep your wits about you!'

As the two men were leaving his room, Carmichael suddenly called Simon back, motioning Alun to go on ahead. 'One more word of warning, Dr Forman. My fear is that you are in double jeopardy, from enemies in London as much as from those you are set to watch. It was black mischance Davie Armstrong died at your door.'

'So I've never ceased to appreciate,' Simon agreed, chilled by his words.

Carmichael looked hard at him. 'Do you know anything of a man called Rivers?'

Simon shook his head. 'No. Should I?'

The Keeper paused for a moment. 'Not necessarily. It's but a thought I've had. He's one who brings trouble in his wake and I've heard it said he's been seen of late on the Borders. If that is true, then it doesn't bode well. Well, no matter, let's hope we meet safely soon with all this behind us.'

Simon was silent throughout the ride back to Mangerton and Alun, realising he had much on his mind, said little until they dismounted. 'So,' he declared 'tomorrow it is. We must be away by six. We'll need good horses and that I'll see to now,' and he went off with a wave of his hand in the direction of the stables.

Simon's last evening at Mangerton was a pleasant one. There was good food and wine and a ballad singer who told of bloody Border raids and deeds of daring, of love and betrayal. Leaving the dining table for a little while halfway through the evening to clear his head, Simon found Kate had stolen outside behind him. He had examined her wound again on his return from Hermitage and was pleased to see that it looked a great deal less angry.

'I'll give you some more of the salve,' he'd told her as he applied a clean bandage. 'Then have your maid or someone dress it again in two days' time and from then on until it is quite clean. Once it's dry you'll have no need for the salve but keep it bound up until it's properly healed to avoid the mischance of opening it up again. And promise me you will avoid doing anything to spoil my good work,' he added, giving her a friendly pat. She'd looked at him with her dancing eyes and asked what dreadful punishment he would inflict if she failed to heed his advice. But now she looked serious.

'So you must go tomorrow?'

'Indeed I must. I've tarried here long enough already.'

'I do not know what business carries you to Edinburgh,' she stated, giving him a keen look.

He wondered how much she had guessed. 'I thought you knew, Kate. I visit my colleagues in the city to see if I can learn from them.'

'I don't think I believe that,' she replied.

He said nothing. He found it difficult to lie to her.

'Tell me, Simon,' she continued, 'have you a wife back home there in London? And if so, what does she think of your venture north?'

'I have no wife. I've never had a wife.'

'Never? I wouldn't think you one that disliked women.'

'Very definitely not. I'm drawn to them too much for my own good. That I have no wife is because the first woman I would have married died before I was able to do so, and the second . . . well, the second is already wife to someone else.'

She gave him a long look and seemed about to say something then, of a sudden, she reached up and kissed him full on the mouth. Shaken, he found himself beginning to respond then he stopped and put her gently from him.

'No, Kate,' he said gently. 'This won't do. I'm a guest of your family and will not dishonour their trust, though believe me I am sorely tempted. You're a desirable young woman with your life in front of you. I told you true when I said I had difficulty seeing your future in the stars, but one thing I can promise you – and that is that there's no part in it for me.'

She looked at him gravely. 'Simon, I have no skills with charts and books and magic symbols, but sometimes I have the Sight, as did my mother and grandmother before me. I will tell ye now that our paths will cross again before you return home, though how or why I do not know. Only that it will be a dark meeting.' And with that she turned away.

They returned to the hall and sat side by side listening to the wild poetry of the Border. He thought he would remember that evening to the end of his days, the stone-flagged hall, the men in their fine dark doublets, their leather jerkins and armour laid aside, the women in their velvets and lace and the candlelight flickering on them all. And beside him the desirable and lovely girl who rode recklessly with her brothers holding aloft the burning fiery peat as they vanished into the night.

Chapter 9

Edinburgh

It was a relief to Simon that the weather was still fine as they prepared to set off early the next morning, but it was soon made clear to him that the ride to Edinburgh was going to be a hard one. There would be no stopping off at inns for refreshment and a rest, it would be bread and cheese and leather flasks of water packed into their saddlebags for sustenance, while breaks by the wayside would be brief and only to rest the horses. Asked what road they would be taking to Edinburgh, Alun told them it would be that which was quickest and least observed. There was no alternative to their going north to Hawick, but once they had skirted the town they would ride cross-country, picking up the Roman road halfway to their destination.

Simon thanked Alun's parents for their hospitality and both wished him well, Master Armstrong shaking his hand warmly and assuring him he was welcome to stay at Mangerton on his return if he wished, and that he was sure his son would see him safe back over the Border. To Alun he said merely that he expected him back the following day and that he must take no foolish risks. Simon looked for Kate but there was no sign of her. She had left him feeling deeply uneasy. He did not discount her strange prophesy for he did not doubt that there were those, often women, who had the Second Sight, and after his brief stay on the Borders he could believe anything of its people.

They rode down the track from Mangerton, crossed the river then turned their horses northward up the valley. As they did so Kate appeared on her sturdy pony from behind a clump of stunted trees, dressed once again in breeches and blackened breastplate, her steel bonnet on her head.

'I thought I'd ride with you as far as Hermitage,' she told them. 'I might as well go partway to Hawick with you and it will save Father coming for me later in the day.' She smiled at Simon but said little as they trotted along the road. The apprehension that had gripped him as he left Carlisle Castle returned in full force now he had left the comparative safety of Mangerton, and again he realised how much he had been relying on Richard Wilmore to help him when he reached Edinburgh. He did not even know where he should stay, what was expected of a visiting doctor from London. Should he choose an inn and thus find himself a continuing object of interest and curiosity to the landlord and other fellow-travellers, or seek lodgings?

'Do you wish you were coming with us?' he asked Kate some time later, aware that he had said nothing to her for half an hour or more.

'Aye, and I'd like fine to go to London too and see Queen Elizabeth and all the great wonders there, but I've nae wish to find mysel' wi' a sword through me like Davie or a string round my neck like yon fellow Alun tells me ye were travelling with! As to Edinburgh, we Armstrongs have little cause to trust the Stuarts any more than Queen Bess. Sixty years back this King Jamie's grandfather declared amnesty on the Borders and invited Johnny Armstrong of Gilnockie and his family to come hunt the deer with him as a sign of goodwill. When they arrived ready for a day's hunting they found themselves taken away and hanged, twelve in Edinburgh and the rest at Carlenrig so I think I'll stay where I am!'

They continued up the valley until they reached the track leading to Hermitage where they made their brief farewells. Kate made no reference to any of the events of the previous evening, merely touching her helmet with her whip as she left before cantering off towards the castle without a backward glance. They rode on until the sun was high in the sky before halting for a short while off the road for refreshment. 'Is it always as hot as this in Scotland in May?' enquired Simon.

Alun grinned. 'It's not. It's rare enough even later in the year. Ye're in luck. Next thing ye know it'll rain for a week.'

Eventually they reached the main road, still riding with hardly a pause until Simon, feeling as if he had spent his entire life on horseback, mentally promised himself that when he returned to London (*if* he returned to London), he'd restrict himself entirely to visits he could make on foot. With a shock he realised it was less than a month since he had ridden back in the dawn with the happy band of May Day revellers. It seemed like years ago and in another life.

Finally they began a long descent, the road passing through an increasing number of hamlets and villages, before suddenly straightening and flattening out, and almost without warning they reached the city itself. They stopped as Simon gasped in astonishment. In front of them the land levelled off with here and there a scatter of houses, but rising sheer from out of it was an enormous outcrop of rock on the top of which stood a great castle.

'I had not thought to see anything so grand,' commented Simon.

'Aye, it's a fine sight, is it not?' Alun agreed.

'And the King lives there?'

Alun shook his head. 'He was born in the castle but goes there only to hold special court in the Great Hall. He stays over yonder at Holyrood Palace. Ye should climb up though – there's a fine view from Castle Rock over to the Forth and the sea.' He led them across the flat ground then on to a street with houses each side which climbed steeply up towards the castle; a warren of other streets branched off it. Halfway up he finally reined in outside an inn. 'We'll stay here tonight and I'll enquire as to lodgings for ye tomorrow. Then, when I've seen ye settled I'll away home after we've agreed when I should come back and look for ye again.'

Simon slept little that night, tired as he was. The long ride made his limbs ache and he was so saddlesore he was unable to get comfortable in his bed. John Bradedge, snoring away at the other end of the room, only added to his irritation as his mind raced round and round like a rat in a trap. Finally he rose, lit his candle, rooted in his saddlebag for some salve, and did the best he could to soothe his aches and pains.

Alun was as good as his word. The next morning he found them lodgings in the house of a decent widow a few minutes away from the inn and arranged with the landlord that the distinguished London doctor and his servant should stable their horses there while visiting the capital.

Simon thanked him. 'I wish the rest was so easy. Richard was going to make introductions for me, find out the physicians I should talk to. Now here I am and I don't know what to do.'

Alun clapped him on the shoulder. 'Be of good cheer. Ye'll find yer way around and see what ye have to see. At worst go home and make it up; they'll know nae different back there in London!'

Simon doubted it. Time was running out. Cecil had allowed only two weeks at most for him to reach Edinburgh and he was already behindhand. So far as he could see it would be July before he and John could expect to be back in London, and he wondered how Anna was managing without them. She must be sorely worried. Finally he arranged with Alun that they would meet at the inn in the evening three weeks to the day from the present and quite possibly ride out as far as they could that same night when few folk were abroad.

Perhaps, thought Simon, his young friend's half-joking remark was not so foolish after all; perhaps he could invent what he was unable to find out. Before he left for Mangerton Alun went with them to see them safe to their lodgings in a tall and narrow house squeezed in between its neighbours. The widow, an elderly body, was pleasant enough and seemed most content when Simon paid her sufficient to cover their stay for three weeks, promising her more if he found his business detained him further. Then Simon and John went outside to say goodbye to Alun. Simon had become increasingly fond of the young man and, to his own surprise, found he had acquired a grudging respect for the hard life of the Borderers in spite of their savage and blood-drenched history, and he took great comfort in the knowledge that there were those from whom he could seek aid should the need arise.

After Alun had ridden off, Simon and John set out to explore the narrow streets and alleyways close to their lodgings, finding them teeming with life and as crowded as those of the Bankside. 'No doubt with the same sort of cutpurses, thieves and coney-catchers as we have at home,' commented John dourly, 'and now, Doctor, would you mind telling me what you've learned from yon Carmichael and what you propose we do here without Master Wilmore?'

Simon told him what he could and admitted the prospect was a daunting one. 'I must discover the names and directions of the most respected physicians and introduce myself, while at the same time trying to find out who is here from England without arousing suspicion.'

'And what am I supposed to do while you're about all this?'

'Go to the taverns and public places, make friends with whom you will, and find out what is said or known about any of the Englishmen visiting the city and note it for me. But there's something else you might mark as well. I believe Richard was killed by someone here, or on the orders of someone here, to prevent his reaching Edinburgh. Possibly the same hand was behind the death of Davie Armstrong as well. See if there's any gossip to that effect. Two sets of eyes and ears are better than one, and you may well hear and see things I don't. My fear is that there will be those here set on to watch *me*. There's been plenty of time now for a message to have reached here from London to that effect.' They had stopped outside a tavern. 'Let's try some of their ale. I'm still thirsty from yesterday and stiff,' he grumbled, rubbing his back.

The tavern was dark and low-ceilinged, and coming in as they did from bright sunlight it took a while for their eyes to adjust and enable them to take in their surroundings. A scattering of drinkers either stood together or sat on benches close to the hatchway from which the host served ale, while over in a corner a man sat on a bench, a cup of wine in front of him, apparently absorbed in a book.

'God's Breath!' exclaimed Simon: 'Is it possible we have our first piece of luck? But what on earth is *he* doing here in Edinburgh?'

'Who? Where?' John looked round the dark room but could see nothing by way of explanation.

'Over there – Kit Marlowe. You know, the Rose Theatre poet, he who wrote the play of *Tamburlaine*. Robin Greene's great drinking companion,' he prompted as John remained silent. 'You surely must have seen him often enough about the Bankside.'

John blinked, focused his eyes on the man in the corner, and gave him a look of withering disapproval. 'That I have – and often drunk and blaspheming. I heard he killed a man in Hog Lane sometime last year, or at least he and a friend of his did and that the friend went to prison for weeks but he was let out after a few days. But then they say he lives like a lord and has friends in high places.'

'Thomas Walsingham's his patron, that I do know,' Simon agreed, 'though how much of the rest is true or mere taproom gossip I wouldn't like to say. But he might prove very useful – indeed, he could be my salvation. Tell the tapster to bring ale to us over there while I go and speak to him.'

The man who raised his head from his book when Simon bade him good-day had striking good looks, his pale face dominated by large eyes so dark they were almost black. His hair was also dark and worn long, nearly down to his shoulders. He was well and neatly dressed in a dark velvet doublet with a fine white shirt beneath. He looked more the picture of a poet than a violent street-fighter, but Simon knew that his reputation for losing his temper and reaching for his sword to solve a quarrel, particularly when in drink, was most likely justified.

Marlowe looked up from his reading in some surprise at the greeting, but to Simon's relief, given his known mercurial temperament, he seemed positively pleased to see a familiar face. In the past they had only ever exchanged pleasantries, for their paths had never crossed professionally since Marlowe had the ministrations of Thomas Walsingham's personal physician at his disposal should he fall ill. But the reputation of each was known to the other, and Marlowe told Simon how he had heard much about him from the actors at the Rose, not least how he had tracked down the murderer of a man who had been found stabbed to death inside the theatre the previous year.

'Have you seen anything of Robin Greene?' he asked as the tapster brought their ale and John joined them. 'He was not well when I left London six weeks ago.'

Simon sighed. 'I fear his illness might well be mortal this time. When I last saw him two or three weeks back he was busy writing what he called his "repentance" – though much of it seemed to be devoted to telling his friends what *they* should be repenting of!'

Marlowe laughed. 'He showed some of it to me. I told him I didn't mind what he said about my attraction to "unnatural vice" –

after all, it seems perfectly natural to me – but that I took exception to being described as a "scheming Machiavel", though personally I happen to think Machiavelli was a clever fellow who is much maligned.' Then he gave Simon a shrewd look. 'Now, Simon Forman, what brings you to Edinburgh?'

Simon stayed silent for a moment wondering how far he could go in trusting Marlowe, when the poet answered for him. 'Could it be that you're here on business? Intelligence business? I can think of no other reason, though how you've come to be caught up in it, I can't imagine.'

'What would you say if I told you I was here merely to exchange views on medical matters with Edinburgh doctors?'

Marlowe smiled broadly. 'That you were lying in your teeth.'

Shaken, Simon looked swiftly round but no one seemed to be paying any heed to them and the drinkers at the other end of the taproom seemed sufficiently involved in their own affairs and, he hoped, were making enough noise to drown out this bizarre conversation. 'And you?' he managed finally.

'Oh, I'm here spying,' replied the poet without more ado, then added, 'don't look so shocked.'

'How can you risk saying such a thing?' Simon whispered.

Marlowe shrugged. 'Everything's a risk, life most of all. And I can't see you posing any threat or turning me over to the authorities, so I might as well be honest. Now tell me, am I right? *Are* you here on similar business? You can trust me, I promise you, and you can't have many friends in this city.'

Simon and John exchanged looks, that which John gave Simon speaking volumes. It was obvious that, left to him, they would have got up and made for the door at once, but Simon motioned him to remain where he was. Explaining his dilemma to someone from his own world in London who, whatever his faults, was admired for his bright mind and quick wit could hardly make his position any worse.

'I have *no* friends in this city,' he said and, as briefly as he could, he explained to Marlowe the sequence of events which had brought him to Edinburgh, and how Cecil had told him his only hope of clearing his name lay in undertaking the task he had been set.

'So we're bent on the same task,' Marlowe commented. 'Seeing who is here and what they hope to achieve.'

'Then why has Sir Robert Cecil also sent me?' asked Simon.

'Because the members of our most esteemed Privy Council trust no man, certainly not each other, and therefore not only send out spies, but spies to watch each other. Did Cecil mention my name at all?'

'No, he said very little. He sent me to Sir Henry Carey, asking him to give me what assistance he could, but that too I found alarming since he was the very person the two young Scots were on their way to see when they were waylaid with such dreadful consequences. And something the dying boy said made me think there was some matter of which His Lordship must not be told . . . but I can't even be sure of that. Though I was fortunate in one respect – I was already acquainted with his son, Robert.'

Marlowe looked up. There was still no sign of interest among the rest of the drinkers. 'Finish your ale,' he said, 'and let us discuss this matter further outside. We'll walk up towards the castle and I'll show you the view. And what do *you* make of this business?' he asked John Bradedge as they left the tavern.

'It's all too deep for me,' was the grumbling response. 'All I know is that somehow I must get the doctor here back to London in one piece at the end of this mad venture. I'm tired of telling him to keep his nose out of other people's affairs. If I and my family hadn't been from home that night, I don't believe any of this would have happened.'

They continued walking steeply uphill until they had almost reached the outer fortifications of the castle. As Alun had said, the view from the top was magnificent, with the sea stretching out into the distance like a sheet of silver. 'And you, an innocent in these matters, was actually sent here alone?' Marlowe persisted.

'The Careys arranged for Richard Wilmore, a member of their own household, to accompany me to Edinburgh to help in any way he could. During our journey we became good friends.'

'And what did Cecil say to your taking with you so useful a guide, or didn't you tell him?'

'I did tell him and he thought it a good idea.'

'And where is this Richard Wilmore now?'

'Dead. Murdered.'

'Jesus Christ!'

This did bring Marlowe up short, though his exclamation caused John to shudder at such a blasphemy and tell himself that as soon as it was practicable he'd point out to his master that what he'd heard about the poet was obviously only too true and that he should have no more to do with him. John was not a religious man, going regularly to church of a Sunday only because he would be fined if he did not, but he was deeply superstitious and saw no point in tempting Providence.

Simon continued: 'When we reached the Border we stayed in Carlisle Castle as Sir Henry had sent a letter requesting the Governor should accommodate us. His son, by the way, is soon to be the next Warden of the West March on the English side. Richard also planned to meet Sir John Carmichael, the Keeper of Liddesdale, to discover what it was that was so urgent he found it necessary to send the two young Armstrongs to London. Once he had done so then he was to stay with me until we returned, but the morning we were due to set off I found him dead in his bed, strangled.'

Marlowe looked at him in amazement. 'The devil you did!'

Simon heaved a sigh. 'I thought I'd convinced the Governor I'd nothing to do with it but it seems he still has doubts, or rather has resurrected them after my departure. Though why I should kill the very person who was so invaluable to me and wait until I was inside an army garrison to do so, I can't imagine.'

'And what do you think? I know you have wit in such matters.'

'That someone, very likely one of those we are both set on to watch, felt it best he never reached here.'

Marlowe looked grim. 'It could be, I suppose. If that's the case then whoever did it either thought you'd turn tail and run, or that if you did press on then it would be better for you to be here without Wilmore. Simon Forman, you are indeed in deep trouble!'

'Can you help me then?' pleaded Simon.

'I'll do my best over the next day or two, but I must return to London soon, not only to report what I've discovered so far – it's not of all that much import – but because I've written a new play for the Rose and the players will expect me to be there while they work on it. That matters to me a great deal more than all this nonsense.'

If that was the case Simon wondered why the poet had bothered to come to Edinburgh at all. 'Oh, I was restless,' Marlowe explained, 'and in a sour temper because I'd quarrelled with Tom Walsingham. However, I can at least introduce you to people who might prove useful to you, and point out those of our fellow-countrymen you should watch. I can also take you to Court. As to finding you suitable doctors, then we must needs enquire around if you are determined to go through with that farce.'

'So how did you get involved in this business then?' asked Simon, as they retraced their steps back into the town.

'Me? Oh, I was approached at Cambridge. Sir Francis Walsingham, the great spymaster himself, asked his nephew Tom to look for likely people with real intelligence who wished to serve their country in such a fashion, and since we were already involved as lovers and I'd a reputation for wit, he introduced me to Sir Francis.

'Oddly enough I was up at Cambridge at the same time as our present spymaster, though he was some years ahead of me. We never took to each other though; he couldn't bear the thought of a mere cobbler's son acquiring a university education. Anyway, to cut a long story short I rather fancied the idea of pitting my wits against foreign foes with the added spice that it was dangerous and I'd need to be always one step ahead of the game. Do you know, I even managed to pass myself off as a recusant would-be student priest at the seminary in Rheims, and utterly convinced them I'd return to England to prepare the people to revolt? I had to have a special dispensation from the Privy Council to be allowed to take my degree as I'd been so long away "on the Queen's most secret business".'

'And now?'

Marlowe's face darkened. 'From time to time they pull the strings that attach us to the spider and haul us back to the centre of the web. No, the work of an intelligencer no longer excites me.'

'How do you pass yourself off here then?' Simon persisted.

'As a mad, reckless poet looking for subjects for the playhouse and with a taste, like the King, for pretty young men. There's many such at Court and I was immediately invited into their circle. Of course, I don't trust any of them.'

He clapped Simon on the shoulder. 'Now we must work out the best way to proceed and see what can be done to ensure you have something to take back home and tell Cecil. The death of your colleague is sinister indeed.' He paused. 'Do you know a man called Rivers?'

Simon shook his head. 'No, but strangely enough, Sir John Carmichael asked the same question. Who is he?'

'A master intelligencer.'

'Is he also in Edinburgh then?'

'I trust not, for he's a bird of ill omen. He's also a true craftsman. He can kill in many ways and without a qualm, disguise himself so his own mother wouldn't recognise him, and above all has an air of sincerity about him that deceives almost anybody. If I didn't agree that the most likely explanation for the murder of your friend is that it's the work of someone here, I'd be tempted to see his hand in it. It's his style.'

Simon shuddered. 'Would I know this man if I saw him?'

'I doubt it. He's ordinary enough to look at but a gifted player of parts.'

'Would *you* recognise him then?' asked Simon.

Marlowe thought for a minute. 'I think I might! Do you know what an actor finds most difficult when playing a role? Not altering his face or his voice but changing the way he walks. I don't mean he that limps around the stage as Crookback Richard, that's easy, but he perhaps who plays two parts in one play.'

They had almost reached the street where Simon lodged. 'Let's meet again in the tavern at, say, six this evening,' said Marlowe, 'and I'll take you with me to a supper party to which I've been invited.'

'Where's that?' enquired Simon.

'At the house of a man called Edward Seton. I know very little of him except that he is a bachelor who keeps open house and seems to know everyone who is anyone – indeed, his hallway often seems to resemble the middle aisle of St Paul's great church in London. But there can be no shortage of money there, for the food and wine at his supper parties are renowned.'

'And does he favour one of the many factions who vie for power at the King's Court?'

Marlowe thought for a moment. 'Not openly. Though there'll be plenty of others present who have reasons for being here, not least young bloods who are part of the faction of that rash fool, the Earl of Essex. You'd think the role of the Queen's first favourite would be sufficient for him. Mark my words, he'll overreach himself one of these days. Perhaps I'll write a play about it – *The Tragical Rise and Fall of the Earl of Essex*. I can see it now. But enough of this. You'll see for yourself presently.' His eyes rested on John with his burly build and scarred face. 'And I should bring your man with you. You need someone to watch your back as you walk the streets.'

Just before they parted Simon asked Marlowe the nature of the play he had written which was of such pressing importance to him. The poet gave him an evil grin. 'Well,' he said, 'so far I've given the penny stinkards and their wealthy betters a terrible tyrant, a Jew who shows up the Christians as hypocrites and liars and a King who, let's say, shares my own amorous tendencies. So what now but a man who challenges God and makes covenant with the Devil! Do you know the *Faust Book*?'

'Have nothing to do with him!' warned John as they entered their lodgings. 'Didn't you hear what he said? Writing such wicked things and to put on the stage, too! No good will come of having any truck with him; as well as go the whole way and deal with Satan direct.'

Simon laughed out loud. For the first time since Richard's death he felt he'd an ally of his own kind and his spirits rose accordingly. 'Oh come now! The *Faust Book* is a mere tale and Dr Faustus gets his just deserts and is dragged down to Hell. Don't worry, your soul is safe enough!'

Chapter 10

A Surfeit of Sucking Pig

Marlowe was as good as his word and arrived at the tavern promptly at six o'clock, commenting on the fact that such punctuality would astound his friends and acquaintances in London, where he was notorious for either arriving late or failing to arrive at all. That was, he said, because there was a good deal less in Edinburgh to distract him, no Robert Greene or Thomas Nash to lure him into a tavern for just one more drink and to bandy wit and compete in verse with him, no players waylaying him to discuss their roles in his latest play nor any pretty young man to seduce into a love affair. 'Why look on the likes of a poor poet when there's a chance of becoming the King's first favourite?' he enquired of a scandalised John Bradedge.

The house they were to visit was near to the Palace of Holyrood, and while walking to it he told Simon that he had returned to his lodgings to find a letter awaiting him from Thomas Walsingham, the only person who knew his whereabouts and what he was doing. 'Though we had not entirely made up our falling out, I felt it as well someone was acquainted with my business in the event I should disappear! According to Tom, the number of Plague cases in London is increasing by the day and so the authorities have, yet again, ordered the playhouses to close at least for the next few weeks.

'So my loss is your gain. I'll stay here for another week or so, and between us we'll try to find sufficient matter to enable you to make your peace with Cecil. With two of us working on it, you should be able to leave shortly after I do. I would suggest our travelling together but it will obviously look better if we arrive home separately.'

Simon agreed but added that he wondered if Cecil might consider

131

he'd not spent long enough in Edinburgh in view of the time he had taken on his journey, but Marlowe dismissed his fears, saying that the Secretary of State was unlikely to know exactly when he had arrived in the city.

'What about you? Won't you be expected back earlier?'

Marlowe smiled. 'You forget, I'm here as a free agent. I'm under no such duress as you and it will amuse me to help you escape the clutches of those in London who would have your head. This has been dreary work so far.' As they reached their destination, however, he stopped and pulled Simon to one side. 'But I must admit I am uneasy about you, and not only because of the way you were forced into coming here and undertaking a task for which you are, to put it bluntly, so unsuited. There is something which does not fit.'

'What makes you say that?'

Marlowe looked round to make sure they were alone. 'For a start take our host, Edward Seton. When I called on him earlier to ask if I might bring you with me tonight, he said at once, "Ah, the English doctor, Carey's man", as if he already knew of you and that you were in Edinburgh. I was somewhat surprised even though, as I told you, this town is known as a meeting place where all and sundry peddle gossip.'

The comfortable feeling Simon had been experiencing all day began rapidly to drain away. 'What do you propose I should do then?'

'Nothing for now except be vigilant. And whatever you do, hold fast to your story that you're here purely to meet with fellow physicians. Not everyone is as cynical as I am.'

He rang the bell outside the house and it was opened to them by a well-dressed servant who showed them into a long room which seemed to be entirely filled with young men dressed in the height of fashion. Puffed trunk hose in colourful silks and satins were topped by slashed and pinked doublets, some cut in the extravagant French manner, making Simon even more aware of his shabby, travel-stained clothes. This was a society in which wealth, or the appearance of it, was openly displayed. He wondered, as he regarded the exotic assembly, if he was now in the same room as the man who had either killed Richard himself or arranged for him to die; if so, which of these peacocks would be capable of such a thing, and what had they to hide?

He also noticed there were few women present and they obviously of doubtful virtue. The Edinburgh women he had seen so far had been soberly dressed and most circumspect in their behaviour. These were quite obviously neither, a fact on which Simon remarked to Marlowe, after they had been greeted by their host and John despatched to the servants' quarters with the message that he be given hospitality while his master dined above stairs. Marlowe then formally introduced Simon to Seton. 'And what do you do in Edinburgh, Dr Forman?' he asked.

'I'm told your doctors here are held in high regard,' replied Simon, 'and therefore I wish to meet with some of them to discuss their views on various medical matters, particularly the new knowledge that is coming to us from Europe.'

He was then introduced to a bewildering array of fellow guests, Scots and English, all of whom on the face of it at least seemed content to accept his reason for visiting Scotland; none of them seemed in the least sinister. After a little while they were called in to supper. 'You must meet my own physician, Dr Richie,' Simon's host suggested as they went in. 'He's a man of much skill, especially when it comes to the pox and he's a deal of interest in new ideas. We'll talk later and I'll give you his direction.'

'It will only confuse you if I try to tell you who's who and what they're about now,' said Marlowe in a low voice as they were shown to the supper table, 'but the man to your left is young Jack Dudley and quite sound, apart from his being one of Essex's men, while the ugly florid-faced fellow opposite with the glazed eyes is Sir Harry Danvers, here in Edinburgh on his own account having run through the family money. Dear me, he's even more repellent in drink than I am, and that's saying a good deal!'

The meal was an elaborate one with many courses and the wine flowed freely – too freely, Simon felt as he tried to keep a clear head. No sooner had he drained his glass than a servant refilled it. After several weeks of plain fare he was also finding the richness of the food daunting. To his surprise in view of such warm weather there were oysters followed, along with an array of fowls of various kinds, by roast sucking pig. It was a rich mixture. The noise was almost unbearable as some twenty gentlemen all raised their voices in order to make themselves heard, and Simon pitied the poor musicians and a singer who had been hired to entertain them while they ate.

He found his neighbour, Jack Dudley, to be a pleasant fellow with a keen interest in astrology and the new sciences; Dudley told him they must certainly meet again to discuss these fascinating matters further. 'As to the study of the stars,' he continued, 'it's hard to know whether you should make your expert knowledge known at Court or not, for King James has strange notions. Mind you, if you can convince him you have a way of keeping him safe from witches you'll be made for life!' Simon's head was beginning to reel. Offered a further portion of sucking pig, he declined.

'What's wrong with you then?' bellowed the man, Danvers, opposite. 'Can't stand a fellow who doesn't like his food.' At which he leant over the table and helped himself to more sucking pig from the tray being held out for Simon, dripping grease and gravy liberally over Simon's only reasonably decent doublet. He then rammed a huge portion into his mouth commenting, as Simon sought to wipe the worst of the grease off himself, that such stains scarce mattered given the cut of the doublet and the quality of the cloth. This prompted Marlowe, who always became acid-tongued in drink, to congratulate Danvers on his knowledge of the clothing trade and ask if he kept a stall on the Cheapside back home in London.

Danvers gave him a look of intense loathing and seemed about to respond in kind, then changed his mind and after champing his way noisily through yet another piece of sucking pig, belched, and regarded Simon again. 'Do you consider yourself a gentleman?' he enquired next.

Simon inclined his head. 'I am Dr Simon Forman, a member of the Royal College of Physicians and acknowledged by the University of Cambridge. And yes, I consider I have the right to the title "gentleman".'

'Only by reason of your profession,' sneered Danvers. 'Not a *born* gentleman. I thought as much. When at home I do not dine with my doctor. Should he be in the house at suppertime he eats with the servants and considers himself fortunate.' There seemed nothing to say in answer to this and so Simon turned back to his companions in an obvious manner.

'A gross and disgusting fellow,' remarked Marlowe. 'He reminded me once that my father's but a Canterbury shoemaker and I offered to call him out but he declined. Such fat bullies are always cowards. Take no notice. He's not worth your trouble,' he continued with added significance, 'certainly not worth risking drawing attention to yourself. He'll continue slopping at the trough until he falls over. How he imagines his behaviour will further his suit with the King is beyond me, and since this is one of the few places where English and Scots meet in relatively friendly fashion, there's little doubt that what we English do and say swiftly reaches the Court. Make a note of him, however,' he whispered in Simon's ear. 'He's all grist to your mill.'

To Simon's relief Danvers turned his attention to one of his neighbours as a procession of servants appeared bearing puddings, marchpane sweetmeats and fruit. Simon waved them away, wanting only to be out in the fresh air and away from the heat and noise to clear his head. Danvers, he noted, helped himself liberally to marchpane and to something that looked like a syllabub but was apparently called 'athelbrose'; it consisted mostly of cream whipped up with oatmeal and a spirit of a more fiery nature even than brandy. Pressed to try some, Simon took a spoonful from one of the small dishes in which it was served and found it too sweet and rich after the shellfish and pork, while the spirit which was liberally added to it burned his mouth.

It was then one of the young women provided for their entertainment came over to them. She was quite striking, for her hair – which she wore long down her back – was of an even brighter red than Kate's, though her features were considerably more coarse and she had the slightly pitted skin that goes with a constant recourse to the wine cup or sack bottle. She was dressed in tawdry finery, a purple dress cut low beyond the bounds of decency, across which was draped a tarnished gold scarf. At first she turned her attention to Marlowe but when all she could draw from him was a chilling stare, she sat herself on Danvers' knee and began spooning the athelbrose into his mouth for him, making eyes at Simon while she did so. He

135

felt too bloated with food and drink to respond and after a little while she grew tired of Danvers and wandered away.

Finally the evening's entertainment drew to an end and Simon could decently take his leave. As he waited for John to join him, his host reiterated that he should meet Dr Richie who would no doubt suggest other physicians who might be of use to him; to that end, Simon should return the following morning whereupon Seton would send one of his servants to accompany him to the doctor's residence.

Simon and John walked back to their lodgings having declined Marlowe's offer to accompany them since he seemed set to stay the night and Simon had no wish to spoil his enjoyment. According to John the servants were mostly a dour lot with a deep suspicion, not to say dislike, of England and all things English and he had had much ado to elicit a civil word from some of them. However, once he had made a remark about his service in the army in the Low Countries he had found himself more favourably regarded by two or three of the men who had also served abroad and with whom he could exchange experiences. It had been difficult to learn much without rousing suspicion but he had arranged to meet two of the ex-soldiers for a few stoups of ale in a tavern the next day – or rather this day, since it was now well after midnight.

'There was one thing though, Doctor,' he mused. 'Among them was a fellow I could've sworn I'd seen before, but try as I would I couldn't place him. He said very little for himself and I was told he had but recently been taken on. Only in the last day or so, in fact.'

'Was he Scots?' asked Simon. 'Is it possible you saw him at Hermitage or Mangerton? Or even Carlisle Castle?'

John shook his head. 'Not at Mangerton certainly. He was definitely Scots though he did not sound as foreign as the Border men nor as refined as some of these Edinburgh lords, though as he'd little to say for himself, I hardly heard him speak.'

'What did he look like then?'

John shrugged. 'Like no one you'd notice. Much of your height and beardless, with mouse-coloured hair.' He shook his head. 'I was probably imagining it. He looked like any number of people I know and I've drunk a fair amount of ale. The servants do well in that house.' As both were weary, neither felt inclined to discuss the matter further and so went thankfully to their beds.

After breakfasting and taking a good walk to clear his head, Simon returned to his lodgings to find the servant who had let them into Seton's house the previous evening waiting for him in the hall in something of a state of alarm. One of Master Seton's guests who had stayed overnight had been taken seriously ill, and although Master Seton's physician, Dr Richie, had been sent for at first light, he was from home. Would it be possible, therefore, for Dr Forman to come back with him to see the sick man?

'Of course,' Simon answered. 'I'll come immediately.' In normal circumstances he would immediately have gone for his bag and some basic remedies, but he decided against it for the present, for no doubt the missing Dr Richie would soon arrive. So, leaving word as to his whereabouts with John, he set off at a brisk pace.

Seton thanked him for his prompt attendance. 'I must apologise for imposing on you, Dr Forman, but my guest wasn't prepared to wait until Dr Richie returned.'

'Have you then no other physician near by?' enquired Simon.

'None that could be fetched quickly,' replied Seton, somewhat shortly. 'It was one of my servants who reminded me of your profession. As to your patient, it's Danvers, Sir Harry Danvers. Did you meet him last night?'

'Indeed I did,' said Simon. 'A man of huge appetite, as I recall.'

'Aye. Harry does tend to indulge himself, yet his sickness seems far more severe than might be expected by mere over-eating. Since its onset he's been taken with the most severe stomach cramps coupled with much vomiting.'

'And when was that?'

'Some time in the early hours. Probably about three o'clock.'

'Have any of your other guests been similarly afflicted?' asked Simon as they climbed a handsome staircase to the bedchambers above. 'For it did occur to me – and I trust you'll take no offence at this – that both oysters and sucking pig could be thought risky in such unseasonably hot weather.'

His companion looked somewhat offended at this suggestion, informing Simon at some length that though the dinner menu had been planned well beforehand when the weather was cooler, both shellfish and sucking pig were fresh in on the day they were cooked.

'With oysters, of course, there's always the possibility of a bad one however careful they might be in the kitchen,' commented Simon as they reached the bedroom door. 'I've been called to prescribe for the results of such on numerous occasions back home in London.'

A sour and foetid smell greeted him as he went into the room. The bed curtains had been drawn back and Danvers, now clad in a nightshirt, was tossing and turning against his pillows, his face drawn and grey and running with sweat. There was no doubt he was truly ill. He opened his eyes as Simon bent over him.

'The physician that calls himself a gentleman,' he managed through gritted teeth. He reminded Simon strongly of some of the less flattering portraits of the Queen's late father, Henry VIII, in his latter days.

'It has been impossible to find Dr Richie,' Seton told him, 'and since Dr Forman was here and you have continually told us that you're *in extremis* then it seemed sensible to have him see what he can do for you.'

Simon prodded Danvers' huge belly, causing him to shriek and demand he take his hands off him at once, then submitted but only with great impatience to Simon peering into his eyes, listening to his heart and feeling his brow.

'How long after supper did this come on?' asked Simon.

'I don't know,' grumbled Danvers pettishly. 'I'd gone to bed. Suppose it must've been several hours – aargh!' he groaned as he suffered another spasm.

'Have you also a running of the bowels?'

Danvers shook his head. Simon stood back, regarded him then turned to Seton as Danvers again doubled up in pain.

'He is obviously suffering from severe inflammation of the stomach and bowels, most likely caused, as I suggested, by his having eaten a bad oyster or lamprey, followed by a surfeit of sucking pig. This, in turn, has brought about a fever. You have a good apothecary near by?'

He was informed that there was.

'Then send to him for some masterwort which, taken in wine, is the very finest remedy for a sick stomach and also sorrel and red sage, these latter to be boiled and made into a posset-drink. You must drink this as hot as you can,' he continued, turning to Danvers, 'for it is essential we sweat these bad humours out of you. To this end too you must wrap your head in a thick cloth to encourage the sweating.' He thought for a moment then added, 'And also, if he has it, some root of *convolvulus turpethum*. Be sure whoever you send gives the right name. We don't want *turbith* or *turpeth* – that is, salts of mercury – by mistake. Perhaps I'd better write it down. If there is no quick result then we must consider other remedies.'

'Aren't you going to bleed me?' asked Danvers.

Simon thought for a moment. 'I am not one that turns easily to blood-letting for I'm of the opinion that in many instances it makes matters worse, not better. However, in this case it might be advisable.' He turned to the host. 'Naturally I have only brought the bare essentials of my trade to Scotland with me, but if you will be so good, send a servant to my lodgings to ask my man, John Bradedge, if he'll come at once bringing with him my case of instruments. Now, if you'll give me pen and paper I'll write a note to the apothecary.'

That being done Simon was left to keep Danvers company. In reality he was less than sanguine about the outcome of the sickness, for even as he sat there the spasms appeared to be getting closer together and more severe, although the vomiting had ceased, presumably because there was now nothing for the sick man to bring up. Certainly, he mused, it was possible a bad oyster could cause severe sickness and spasms of pain – indeed, he'd known some die of it – but he could not help but think this illness was of an altogether more drastic nature.

Within a short while John Bradedge arrived with his master's bag and Simon immediately bled his patient, which did at least seem to provide some relief. He then left John to sit with him while he went downstairs to see to the proper preparation of the apothecary's herbs. He was obviously a bright fellow for he had sent the masterwort already distilled, with a note to the effect that he had taken it both from the root and leaves as he understood the patient to be gravely ill.

Simon took a small quantity and asked one of the maidservants to mix it with honey and add a little white wine to alleviate the bitter taste. He then opened up a small package of a yellowish powder and carefully checked that it was the *turpethum* not *turpeth*. Of this he measured out sufficient to lie upon a shilling and added the same quantity of sugar to it. The sorrel and red sage he put to steep in boiling water.

Seton, who had followed him into the kitchen, watched him preparing the remedies with interest and was intrigued to know the difference between the two almost identical-sounding substances.

'The *turpethum*,' Simon informed him, 'is a plant medicine and can be used as freely as the patient is willing to take it, for it has a bitter taste even with sugar, whereas the other is a mineral compound. It, too, can be used in grave cases when all else has failed but it is very difficult to gauge the correct amount, and if you give a patient too much then it might well make matters worse or even prove fatal! I myself therefore hardly ever use it because of the risk.'

'Is it possible to mix them up? Are they at all alike? I saw you look carefully at the powder you are using.'

'They are much of the same yellow hue,' Simon admitted, 'but their texture and smell is quite different. Such prescribing is not for novices or for the home physician, but it's easy for an experienced practitioner to tell the difference or an apothecary such as your own.'

Returning to his patient, who seemed a little quieter, he made him take the *turpethum* and sugar direct from a spoon, followed by the draught of masterwort. Danvers continued to grumble between spasms but took the medicine. Simon then ordered the patient's head to be wrapped in warm cloths and sat down again to await the results of his treatment, informing his patient he would shortly give him a posset to drink to aid the sweat.

He was wondering when he would be able to get away to meet Marlowe, when Seton entered the room accompanied by a distinguished-looking gentleman in a long gown whom he introduced as Dr Richie. The doctor quickly took in the scene and apologised, explaining that he had unexpectedly been called out of town.

'I feel it's I who should be apologising to you,' said Simon, 'since you are physician to this house. But as the matter seemed so urgent, I felt I had to offer my services.'

'You were quite right. Your duty as a physician surely overrules every other consideration and I'm not one of those who would prefer to see a patient succumb rather than receive treatment from a potential rival!' Dr Richie reassured him. 'Now, can you tell me the nature of the problem?'

So Simon explained the symptoms and what he had done in an attempt to alleviate them. Whether because of the medicines or through sheer exhaustion, Danvers appeared to have fallen into something of a doze, although he still moaned and clutched his stomach from time to time. Dr Richie opened his nightshirt and listened to his heart and felt his stomach.

'You say he ate to excess last night?' Simon nodded.

'That's by no means uncommon,' broke in Seton, 'but as I told Dr Forman, he's never been taken in such a way before.'

'Then he's been fortunate,' commented Dr Richie dryly, 'for a man of his weight and choleric humour is inviting a seizure of some kind.' He then checked with Simon the treatment the patient had received and, having been advised of the blood-letting and medicines, declared himself highly satisfied. 'I could have done no more myself,' he told them as a maidservant appeared bearing a steaming cup. 'And you have arranged a posset? Excellent, excellent. Well, Dr Forman, I think we can safely leave the patient now and I'll look in again myself later on. I'm told you are visiting Edinburgh with a view to meeting members of our profession, so may I suggest you come home and dine with me? We can discuss other medical men it might be useful for you to see.'

Simon was delighted, not least because the doctor had given him an opportunity to leave the house; he willingly accepted the invitation, telling John he was free for the afternoon but to tell Marlowe what had happened if he saw him.

The meal was a pleasant one and Dr Richie an interesting host with whom Simon found he had much in common. Like himself, he had studied abroad and was open-minded to new ideas and Simon, emboldened by his interest, told him of his own problems with the College of Physicians in London and how they had attacked him for his admiration for the teachings of Paracelsus and how they still believed in the old orthodoxy of Galen in the field of anatomy.

'It would seem your elderly physicians are far behind the times,' commented Dr Richie, 'and must have been overtaken by almost all European doctors, many of whom now turn to Vesalius on the subject of anatomy.' Time passed pleasantly enough as they considered the merits and demerits of blood-letting, the testing of urine, the use of specific remedies for certain conditions and, finally, the influence of the planets on the treatment and outcome of disease.

In view of what had happened during the last few weeks, Simon found it both comforting and stimulating to sit and discuss medical matters with a fellow physician, and his interest in Richie's views was quite genuine. On his return to London he would, he decided, write to the College of Physicians pointing out that even in Edinburgh his beliefs found more acceptance than their own. He finally left after Dr Richie had promised to introduce him to several of his colleagues over the next few days. On returning to his lodgings he found a note awaiting him from Marlowe suggesting they meet for supper in a tavern chosen, for discretion's sake, some distance away and which offered a good pigeon pie. After learning from John that all was well and there were no further surprises, he made his way to the rendezvous at the appointed hour to find the poet already there before him.

'I hear you were called in to treat Danvers,' commented Marlowe after calling to the tapster for a bottle of wine. 'Don't concern yourself, it didn't take spies to tell me that. I called round at the house this morning and was told by a servant you were even then closeted with the patient so I didn't disturb you. Does he mend well?'

'I trust so,' replied Simon cautiously, 'but the attack, whatever caused it, was very severe.'

'And what do you think did cause it?'

Simon frowned. 'I'm not sure. Most likely a bad oyster or even simply the sucking pig, though if that had been tainted then there would surely have been many more taken sick. Dr Richie, when he arrived, seemed to think that Danvers' gluttony and excess might well have brought on such a seizure without any other factor.'

'Come then,' said Marlowe, 'let's put that hog and his sickness behind us and discuss pleasanter matters, for tomorrow I am to take you to see the King in state at the castle and the following day to the Court at Holyrood.'

'How have you achieved that?' asked Simon in surprise.

'By dint of pulling a few strings. The visit to the castle was not too hard to arrange, for the King is receiving the new French Ambassador in the Great Hall there tomorrow and wishes to appear before him surrounded by hordes of admirers and in the greatest state. So many people have been invited to attend that it was not difficult to acquire invitations for two more. Holyrood Palace, where we will be guests at a banquet, was rather more difficult but I have managed that too. We shall be on an obscure table with obscure people, but both occasions should give you a splendid opportunity to see who is present and what standing they have. And you can add it to your list of what you'll tell Cecil with my goodwill.'

The rest of the evening passed pleasantly enough and Simon was again surprised at how moderately Marlowe conducted himself in view of his notoriety on the Bankside, finally coming to the opinion that the poet had sufficient sense of self-preservation to avoid his usual wildness while in a strange place. It was just before midnight when they left the tavern, and as they were still deep in conversation Marlowe walked to Simon's lodgings with him. Simon knocked on the door, hoping he would not disturb his landlady, to find it opened immediately by a grim-faced John Bradedge.

'There you are at last!' he exclaimed. 'I've tried looking for you everywhere.'

'Why, what's wrong?' asked Simon, a chill feeling beginning to spread through him.

'They sent for you from the household where the sick man lies. It seems your patient's taken a turn for the worse.'

'You'd best go home,' Simon said to Marlowe. 'I'll get my bag and go there straight away.'

'Certainly not,' the poet replied. 'I wouldn't miss this for anything. I insist I come with you to offer my support in case they behave like the potentates of old and decide to punish the doctor if the patient dies!'

Simon looked appalled. 'Sweet Jesus, I trust the case is not as bad as that!'

They hurried through the dark and now quiet streets. Simon was obviously awaited, for the door was opened to him at once by the distraught housekeeper. 'You're to go up straight away, sir,' she told him. 'Dr Richie's with him now but it seems he's mortal bad, not likely to last the night out.'

Simon ran up the stairs, followed at a more leisurely place by Marlowe, to discover what looked like the great deathbed scene as set up on the stage of a playhouse. Numerous candles had been lit to lighten the gloom, throwing a lurid glow on the sick man who was propped up on pillows and gasping for breath. Dr Richie was standing by the bedside while Seton, and a couple of companions, stood looking on in silence. It was immediately clear that the situation was indeed as the housekeeper had said. The two doctors greeted each other without words.

'When did this relapse occur?' asked Simon quietly.

'Some two hours ago, or so I'm told,' whispered Dr Richie in reply. 'I was sent for a little while later and, unable to fathom the reason for it, sent then for you.'

'I've but now had your message, having dined out,' Simon told him. 'I came as soon as I could.'

Dr Richie sighed. 'I doubt it would have made any difference. I fear the poor fellow is beyond any mortal help now.'

There was a moan from the bed and the sick man opened his eyes and began looking round as if in search of someone or something. He narrowed his eyes as if his sight was failing before finally fixing his gaze on Simon.

'Oh, it's you, is it, gentleman doctor?' he croaked. Even as he spoke he suffered another acute spasm of pain. 'God's Blood, you've poisoned me, you bastard!'

There was a long silence punctuated only by the dying man's laboured breathing. It lasted until he was dead.

Chapter 11

The God in the Machine

'Poisoned! Of course I didn't poison him. He was already a sick man before ever I saw him.'

Simon was facing Seton in a downstairs chamber. They had left the corpse to the women servants to see to, Dr Richie having pronounced life extinct. Seton and his companions appeared unconvinced. Simon looked round the circle of faces. It was Carlisle Castle all over again. Then he pulled himself together. The circumstances were completely different.

'When I saw Danvers he was already gripped by spasms of the stomach, had a fever and was vomiting. There was no obvious cause for his distemper and I explained that it could be due to a number of things – over-indulgence in rich food, tainted pork, though I imagine that would have affected others, or, most likely of all, a single bad oyster. So I prescribed what I thought best and bled him to allay the fever.'

'And I agree that Dr Forman did exactly as I would if presented with the same symptoms,' Dr Richie concurred. 'You refine too much on this. The man was raving in his death throes.'

'I watched you preparing the remedies, Dr Forman,' Seton said heavily, 'and remember your saying then, and indeed beforehand when you asked me to send to the apothecary for the ingredients, not to confuse – what was it, turpeth, turbethith . . .?'

'*Convolvulus turpethum* with *turpith* or, as it is sometimes called, *turbeth*.'

'You said yourself it could be dangerous and that both were yellow

145

powders and not unalike. Couldn't you or the apothecary have made a mistake?'

'Most certainly not. I explained to you as I measured it out that one was a fine powder and the other gritty with a distinctive smell. I also told you I virtually never used the latter as it was difficult to judge the dosage.'

'How much of the mixture did you use, Dr Forman?' asked Dr Richie.

'Sufficient to cover a shilling coin and no more.'

'Then,' Dr Richie stated, 'if a mistake had been made and *turpith* mistaken for *turpethum* then it might even have helped the sick man rather than killed him, for it too can also be used, though with extreme care, for severe distempers of the stomach. I myself have prescribed it over the years though I agree with my colleague that it can be dangerous in unskilled hands or if the dose is too great. You do not favour it yourself then, Dr Forman?'

Relieved to find an ally, Simon said that he did not unless he was at home with his own books and remedies, knew the patient well and had followed the course of the disease since its onset – and even then, he had prescribed it but three or four times. 'But surely we can test this for ourselves now,' he said. 'I left all the medicaments in the kitchen where I prepared them, the phial of distilled masterwort, the dried sorrel and red sage, and the package of *turpethum*.' He then led the way without more ado to the kitchen quarters, the rest following at his heels.

The bench at the side of the room on which he had prepared the medicines was bare and clean. Obviously the herbs had been cleared away. A girl was stirring something in a pot over the fire while a fellow servant sat in a dark corner apparently absorbed in polishing a heap of spoons and knives.

'The herbs,' began Simon, 'the ones I left here after making up the medicines. Where are they?'

The girl shrugged. 'What herbs, sir?'

'The herbs I had for the sick man upstairs,' responded Simon, almost shouting in his exasperation.

'I know of none, sir. There were none left down here,' the girl returned.

Simon appealed to Seton. 'You saw me here making the medicines up, you've just said so yourself.'

'Where's Cook?' enquired Seton. Cook was long abed, he was told.

'You couldn't have missed them,' Simon insisted. 'There was a glass phial from which I'd taken about a third of its contents, a fine cloth bag containing red leaves and a small parchment package of yellow powder.'

The girl shook her head. 'No, sir. There's nothing like that here.'

The kitchen was dark, lit only by some tallow candles, but in spite of that Simon pushed past her and began to look along the shelves and open cupboards, moving jars and pots and lifting up clouts and cloths. However, the kitchen was large and cluttered and the missing herbs could have been anywhere.

'I suggest we all go home for the night,' broke in Dr Richie. 'Possibly your cook has put them somewhere for safety,' he said to Seton, 'and will be able to lay her hands on them first thing in the morning. It's very late and since there's nothing more to be done for Danvers there seems little point in our spending any more time on a fruitless search.'

It was at this point that a servant, who had been standing quietly in the shadows in the far corner of the kitchen made his presence known. 'Begging yer pardon, sirs,' he said in a quiet Scots voice, 'but surely Dr Forman took the herbs away wi' him after he had seen to the making of the posset? I was standing over there at the time' – he pointed to the door of a stillroom or closet which opened off the kitchen – 'an' I'm certain I recall his putting them in a wee bag and taking them away wi' him.'

'I had no bag, man, nor could I carry them away since I had a glass of medicine in one hand and a dose of a powder and a spoon in the other,' replied Simon angrily.

'Not *then*,' the man insisted. 'Later. Ye came in wi' yer doctor's bag and put them into it and went out. I thought ye were away home to yer dinner.'

Seton looked grave. 'Well, Dr Forman?'

'I did no such thing,' said Simon wildly. 'Dr Richie asked me to dine with him and we left together. We were never out of each other's sight from when he came into the bedchamber until we went out through your front door.'

'That's certainly true,' Dr Richie agreed. 'You're mistaken, fellow.' The servant looked at him, shrugged, but said no more. As Simon watched, he walked over to a door leading to the back yard and disappeared through it. There being no more to be said, they all left the kitchen. Marlowe was lounging outside in the hallway, a glass of wine in his hand. Simon explained to him what had happened, including the apparently mischievous intervention of the serving man.

Marlowe squinted at them through his glass. 'Well, this has been a fascinating interlude,' he commented with a slightly drunken smile, 'and might well furnish a plot for the playhouse. I'd rate it almost equal in likelihood to poisoning by kissing pictures or secret cavities in rings, the kind of thing the groundlings love. Just the stuff for a thrilling afternoon at the Rose. But since the night is half over, this is not a playhouse and we are but mortals in the ordinary world, I intend taking Dr Forman away and walking with him back to his lodgings. If you want my opinion for what it's worth, the world's well rid of Harry Danvers!'

'You don't need to come out of your way for me,' said Simon as they made their way across town.

'It makes little difference,' Marlowe replied, 'and I feel it might be safer if there are two of us. How's your swordplay?'

Simon glanced at him. 'Not too rusty. I've taken fairly regular practice since someone tried to kill me in a Bankside alley a while back. Why? Do you think we might be attacked?'

'I don't know.' Marlowe looked suddenly both serious and sober. 'But this whole business is beginning to stink like rotting fish. Just consider the facts. You journey to Carlisle with a scion of the Careys and he dies in your bedchamber. You arrive here and, strangely, it's already known in a household notorious as a hotbed of Scots-English intrigue, that you are in town. At which point a man is taken sick, you treat him and he dies. So now there are two deaths which might be laid at your door.'

'But I don't see how they could be linked,' replied Simon desperately. 'If, as I suspect, Richard was killed to prevent his coming to Scotland, then surely had it been thought I'd also be best out of the way, I too would have met my death in Carlisle. Why let me reach Edinburgh and then poison a man in the hope I might be suspected of having done it? It doesn't make sense.'

Marlowe stopped. 'I wonder. I wonder if we might have been looking at this whole matter the wrong way around. Are you familiar with the term *deus ex machina*?'

'The God in the Machine?' said Simon impatiently.

'A device of the ancients used in their drama where a god descends from Olympus to preside over a series of events which he controls and brings either to a good or bad conclusion. I wonder if we have encountered such a one.'

Simon yawned. 'I don't know what you're talking about. Please let me go to bed!'

Marlowe let it pass. 'Fortunately, thanks to your friend the Scots doctor, it's unlikely this matter will be pursued further unless he's put under severe pressure to make him change his mind, but we can hardly fool ourselves the story of Danvers' death won't get out and be widely disseminated, growing in colour each time it's passed on. The other matter I consider most strange is the part played by the serving man. I ask myself why he chose to try and stir up trouble in the way he did.'

They continued their walk in silence until they reached Simon's door. 'Could the man have been poisoned?' asked Marlowe, as he was about to leave. 'Not by you, of course, but during the meal?'

'Heaven alone knows. As you are aware, we all ate from the same dishes. The shellfish were in those large bowls in the middle of the tables, while the sucking pig was sliced and brought round on the platters. If you recall, Danvers was so greedy he reached over the table to take more from the servant standing between myself and Jack Dudley and in so doing, spilled gravy and grease all down my doublet.' This jogged his memory. 'Sweet Jesus, I must ask John if he can clean it sufficiently for me to avoid being refused entry to the castle tomorrow after being mistaken for a beggar! I'll also send him over to talk with Seton's servants for he told me of a fellow, newly taken on, who he thought he knew but could not place. It might be our man. But now, *I must get some sleep!*'

John was snoring away in the corner of the room as Simon stumbled wearily towards his bed and fell at once into a deep sleep. But as was often the case when he had much on his mind, he awoke two or three hours later, wide-eyed and staring at the dark ceiling. Yes, it was possible Danvers had been poisoned, he conceded, but how – and when? In his wine? But again the bottles, like the food, had passed freely around the revellers sitting at the tables. The food . . . He sat up suddenly. Could that be it? The strangely named athelbrose had been served in separate dishes so it might have been possible to tamper with one of them. Simon had a sudden vision of the red-haired whore, sitting on Danvers' knee feeding him, her purple gown falling down off one shoulder. I wonder . . . he thought, but before he could pursue it further, he was overtaken by sleep.

Marlowe arrived the next morning bringing with him one of his own doublets. 'Try this, as we're much of a size. If it fits then you can borrow it while your landlady takes yours to a laundress for you. Have you thought further of the events of last night?' he added as Simon thanked him.

'Almost constantly. You asked me if Danvers could indeed have been poisoned. Yes, it's possible. Did you have any of that cream dish called athelbrose?'

'A little. I didn't care much for it.'

'Nor did I. It was sweet with honey, rich in cream and, I was told, had oatmeal mixed with it as well as a fiery spirit that burned the mouth. But almost alone of the dishes we were offered it was served in separate bowls. It depends which poison was used, but it could either have been stirred in with the oatmeal, if it was a powder or, more likely if it was a draught, added with the fiery spirit. So it would have been possible to ensure only Danvers was poisoned. And what's more, I know how it could have been achieved.' Before he could continue Marlowe said it for him.

'By the redhead who sat on his knee feeding him with the stuff. Of course! So, we have established how we think Danvers was made ill. Next, it would be necessary to ensure you treated him. Why did Seton send for you, rather than Dr Richie or another local physician?'

'I was told Dr Richie had been called from home and when I asked Seton why he hadn't sent for another Edinburgh doctor, he said they were unable to find one quickly and that a servant had reminded him of me. I suppose it makes sense and of course, Richie did arrive not long after.'

'By which time you'd already treated the man. So the further poison, if such was the case, must have been administered in one of your medicines?'

'The only possible one was the sage and sorrel posset, which I left to steep in the kitchen. Seton watched me mix the others myself and carry them straight up to Danvers. The posset, on the other hand, was brought up later by one of the maids. But again we're back to the fact that no one could have foreseen I'd be there to treat Danvers.'

'Unless Dr Richie had been called out on a false errand. I suppose it's possible that some unknown enemy of Danvers present at the feast wanted rid of him and so put something nasty in his pudding. Your intervention would then give them a heavensent opportunity to finish him off, with the added attraction of throwing suspicion on you for his death. That's the most comfortable explanation.'

'Comfortable!' exclaimed Simon.

'Oh yes. For the other is that Danvers' death was merely a device to implicate you in a death, any death, and if that's the case then again I hear machinery and the whirring of cogs and wheels.'

Simon sighed. 'And might explain why that servant was so determined to make matters worse, for perhaps he was paid to do so – which reminds me. I must send John to speak with Seton's servants since he is on drinking terms with some of them.'

He found John in the landlady's kitchen chatting to her maid. He greeted his master with a surly grunt for he was finding their stay in Edinburgh unbearably tedious and was becoming increasingly anxious as to how his wife and child were coping with his absence. Asked again about Seton's serving man he had little to add, and when Simon told him to come and tell his tale to Master Marlowe, he grumbled even more.

Pressed again to describe the servant, he spoke of a nondescript fellow in his middle years with no special features, no beard, no scars but yes, he supposed he could have been the same man Simon saw.

'You also said you thought you'd seen him before but couldn't place him. Why was that?' asked Marlowe.

John frowned. 'I've puzzled over it since but can't think why. I think it was something I saw,' he added cautiously.

'Do you know, I think there was something about him too, now I come to think of it,' Simon broke in. 'You know what you said to me about an actor's walk? I wasn't really taking much notice at the time but I've just remembered seeing him walk out after speaking to us and there was something in his gait . . . but I may be imagining it, having had the notion put into my mind.'

'So what do you want me to do?' John asked.

'Go back to the kitchen quarters. Make any excuse you like. Tell them your master's still concerned over the missing herbs and ask if they've been found. You made the acquaintance of some of the servants the other night. Offer to buy them ale, they must be allowed out of the house some time. But most particularly, seek out and talk to this particular man, see how he reacts to your questions, and try and loosen his tongue. Think of what it was you thought you recognised about him and note it.'

There was a considerable press of people outside the castle gate when they arrived, and soldiers were continually pushing them back to allow carriages through. They were informed that King James and the Queen were already in the royal apartments and that the French Ambassador was expected shortly. Armed with letters of authority to enter, they were directed onwards and upwards to Palace Yard, a helpful citizen pointing out, as he laboured up the steep slope beside them, that it had been constructed over vast vaults, a mighty task undertaken by hundreds of labourers. They arrived panting in the Yard itself, one side of which was a fine palace and beside that a door which they were told led into the Great Hall. They found it already almost filled with people all dressed in their best and talking noisily. At the far end of the Hall was a dais on which were set two thrones.

Within a short while trumpets sounded from outside and immediately attendants cleared a way through the waiting crowd, the great doors were thrown open and the King appeared accompanied by the Queen and followed by a large train of courtiers. The men immediately doffed their hats and bowed low, the ladies curtsied to the floor. The room fell silent as the royal procession made its way to the dais and the King and Queen sat down on the thrones. King James did not make an impressive figure, thought Simon, as the monarch had passed within feet of where he was standing. He had a somewhat shambling gait, his beard failed to disguise a weak chin and his complexion was florid. No one could call him a handsome man.

'As you see,' whispered Marlowe, 'he has nothing of his mother's great beauty. You'd think she'd played him false but for the fact he so closely resembles his murdered father. They say he constantly dribbles because his tongue's too big for his mouth. The Queen is hardly better looking, but what can you expect from out of Denmark?'

A close group of gentlemen stood behind the royal couple, notable among them half a dozen particularly good-looking young men with whom the King turned and joked from time to time. Marlowe craned his neck in order to have a better view. 'See those fellows at the front of the crowd near to the dais? There's Dudley and another of Essex's men along with a number of our fellow countrymen. They're making no effort to conceal that they stand on good terms with King James. You must tell Cecil that you saw them, of course, and where – I'll give you their names – though he must already be aware they're here and what they're about. Of more significance are those who do not make such a show of themselves.'

A single trumpet sounded again and this time the door opened to admit the French Ambassador, a grave man in a long dark velvet robe, accompanied by two attendants. He walked sedately up to the dais, hat in hand, and made an elaborate obeisance. He then turned to one of his attendants who passed him a parchment document bound in silk ribbon, presumably his letter of accreditation, which he then handed to one of the King's men who, in turn, passed it to the King. James read it and, after inclining his head to the Ambassador in a gesture of assent, motioned the Frenchman to join him. He then handed the letter back to the Ambassador, who handed it to one of his men, who read its contents to the assembly before him; after which one of the older noblemen standing beside the King made a short reply. When a few pleasantries had been exchanged, King James gave a signal, rose, and with the Ambassador following behind with the Queen, he led the way back to an inner chamber. Immediately attendants appeared, informing the people that they should now leave.

As Simon and Marlowe made slow progress down the steep path, crowded now with those who had been in the Great Hall, Jack Dudley caught up with them. 'Not much of a show, was it, compared to the Court of Queen Bess?'

'I've never been to Court,' Simon replied. 'I've only seen Her Majesty in progress through the streets but it was a brave sight. She looked magnificent.'

'Near to she's an old, wrinkled woman who paints her face an inch thick, with what there is of her hair concealed by a wig red enough for a whore,' remarked Marlowe. His earlier good humour seemed to have deserted him and he was evidently in a fretful and restless mood.

'I hear Danvers is dead,' commented Jack.

'And what else have you heard?' enquired Marlowe aggressively. 'Come on, there's no need to be coy. It's clear from your face that rumours abound. Let me guess now – Seton called in Simon here because his own physician could not be found, and he then proceeded to poison Danvers. Is that it? Or did Simon sprinkle a subtle poison on his supper and then prevent the Scots doctor from attending him in order to finish the job?'

In spite of himself, Dudley smiled. 'Something like that.'

'I wonder you're prepared to stand so close to so dangerous a fellow then,' mocked Marlowe.

'I find it hard to believe any of it,' Dudley responded, 'and anyway, that household's always awash with scandalous tales. As I sat beside Dr Forman throughout the meal and am certain he did not put powders or potions in Danvers' food, I've already made it clear I've no time for such foolish talk. And since he only treated the man by chance, I cannot credit the rest either.'

Simon gave a wry smile. 'I'm thankful someone believes me.'

'From the way Danvers was stuffing himself, gross as he was and the room so hot, it was hardly surprising he was taken ill,' Dudley continued. 'Now, friends, shall we dine together?'

At Marlowe's suggestion they walked to the tavern where he and Simon had met the previous evening and found themselves a table in the corner. There were several drinkers present who obviously knew Marlowe, and very soon he was drinking heavily, becoming ever more bitter and wayward in his talk and after a little while he went over to join them.

'What's the matter with him?' asked Dudley as they heard Marlowe call for yet another bottle of wine. 'We all know what he's like in London and how unpleasant he becomes in drink, but I've seen little sign of it here in Edinburgh.'

As if he had heard them Marlowe, who was now arguing heatedly with a burly man who had just come in, turned and then wove his way unsteadily back towards them. His face was flushed and his eyes over-brilliant. He banged the bottle down on the table, poured himself a glass and drank it in one gulp. 'Don't look at me like that,' he said to Simon. 'You've seen me only on my best behaviour. Now the black mood's on me and I'll drink, with or without your leave.

'That man over there,' he waved an arm towards the burly man, 'says he's a follower of John Knox come to turn us from our sinful lives. Knox the Puritan, Knox who sees the fires of Hell waiting for all of us. Why, this is Hell and we are part of it, hypocrite!' he shouted out. 'That's from my latest play. Do you believe this is Hell, Puritan?'

Drinkers and diners were beginning to look round and there was a murmur of disapproval. 'Remember where you are,' said Dudley, clutching the poet's doublet. 'This isn't the Bankside. These are people who take their religion seriously and if you carry on like this you'll find yourself in gaol.'

'It wouldn't be the first time,' sneered Kit.

'Then if you won't be quiet on your own account, for God's sake remember the predicament your friend is in. You surely don't want him taken for a blasphemer as well as a murderer?'

Marlowe gave him a mutinous look, seemed about to say something then thought better of it. He detached himself from Dudley's hold. 'Very well. I'll mind my manners – at least until you've gone.' He swayed a little then shook himself. 'I'll meet with you tomorrow, Simon, before the King's banquet. Do you go to it, Dudley?'

'I do. We can meet beforehand at my lodgings if you like,' Dudley suggested as he and Simon rose to go. Marlowe nodded and returned to his friends. 'He's a danger to himself and everyone else in this mood,' Dudley commented as they went outside.

Simon agreed. 'From what you said, I take it you also know him in London?'

'I've met him a few times in the company of Tom Walsingham and, on occasion, in taverns and at the Rose Theatre. He's quite brilliant, of course, and writes the most glorious verse but he's so reckless and doesn't seem to care how much he offends his friends or how many enemies he makes. He seems absolutely determined to tempt Providence.'

The rest of the day passed quietly enough. Simon found a note awaiting him from Dr Richie inviting him to meet several of his colleagues at his house the following morning and, after a brief walk around the town, he went back to await the return of John Bradedge.

'Well?' asked Simon, when his man finally appeared. 'Have you learned anything more?'

John gave him a significant look. 'The man I saw and the one you spoke to yesterday are one and the same. Of that I'm assured.'

'Did you speak to him? And have the medicaments been found?'

John shook his head. 'I couldn't speak with him for he's gone, left his new service without a word of warning. As for your herbs and such, no, there's no trace of them. Some below stairs, and I'm told also above, believe you've blamed the serving man for their loss to save your own skin, and that's why he's disappeared. There are others, though, who say—'

'What?'

'That it's strange he stayed so short a time and in such circumstances.'

Simon thanked him. 'Well, at least no one drank you under the table this time.'

John gave him a speaking look. 'Am I never to be allowed to forget the night with the wool-merchant's man, Doctor? It's never happened before and will never happen again.' Then he looked at Simon and slapped his thigh. 'That's it!' he roared. 'That's it! That's what I saw!'

Simon was exasperated. 'What's what, man? What did you see?'

'His ear. He'd a nick on the ear, exactly like that of James Ford!'

Chapter 12

Warnings of Danger

Simon lay awake half the night reviewing what John had told him. Could James Ford and Seton's servant be one and the same person? He tried to remember what the man looked like. It had been difficult to see his face in the dark kitchen, for he had lurked in the shadows. Ford had been bearded, of course, his hair long and his accent very definitely English. Simon had placed him as possibly hailing from Suffolk, which would also explain his interest in wool. But it would have been simple enough to shave off his beard, cut his hair and adopt a Scots accent if he had a flair in that direction. He pictured seeing him again walking out of the door. The shape of his body and his stance could be Ford's, but he was by no means certain.

But if it was him, what did it mean? If, as Simon was now convinced, Richard was killed on the orders of some intriguer in Edinburgh, then Ford or whoever he was could well have been the man hired to carry out the deed. And what better way to discover where Richard would be at any one time than by posing as another traveller on the road? Yes, he thought, it made sense. Possibly the original plan had been to kill them both that night but, failing that, it might well be assumed that Simon would either be hanged for Richard's murder or return at once to London; either way he would pose no threat. But in the event he had pressed on to Edinburgh.

So to Danvers. Whether or not Danvers was taken ill through natural causes, presumably Ford, still acting on the orders of his unknown master, had seized the opportunity to throw the blame for Danvers' death on Simon. Surely it followed therefore that the most likely suspect was Seton, in whose house Danvers had died and who

157

had harboured Ford in the guise of a servant, the man most likely to have killed Richard. Simon tossed uneasily and tried once again to sleep. He would look at it afresh in the morning.

But morning brought no further enlightenment and the theory no longer looked as attractive in the cold light of day, so Simon was only too pleased to be able to take himself off, as promised, to the house of Dr Richie. He was relieved to find that the good doctor had no wish to pursue the matter of Danvers' death and, from the reception Simon received from his colleagues, if they had heard word of the matter then they gave no sign of it.

They were soon in deep discussion regarding two of the great hazards of the age, the plague and the pox. Asked what he would prescribe, if anything, for the first Simon explained how during one recent epidemic he had caught the dread infection himself and survived it. 'The buboes appeared in my groin and the red plague spots on my feet.'

'And what reason do you give for your delivery?' asked one of the doctors.

'I have often lanced the buboes on patients or cut them out when I have had a chance to treat them as soon as they appeared,' he replied, 'and this is what I did for myself. As I understand it, there are two sorts of plague – the black, under the influence of Saturn, and the red, under that of Mars. Those of Mars often come to a head quickly and break themselves or can be cut, but one must be careful about dressing the wounds left from lancing since the sores themselves are dangerous and infective. It was the red plague that struck me down. Had it been the black plague and black spots had appeared on me, then all that would have been left to me would be to make my peace with God.'

'And you recovered fully?' Dr Richie enquired.

'Only slowly. It was some five months before I truly regained my health and strength. At the beginning of the recovery period I drank regular draughts of a distillation of groundsel, hops, wormwood and centaury, and another made of raisins and juniper berries.'

'You were indeed fortunate,' commented the doctor who had questioned him, 'and I intend making a note of your treatment.'

'Fortunate, yes – with God's help. But I can assure you it was by the use of these conventional medicines, *not* necromancy – which is what some claimed when they discovered I'd survived the dreaded disease!'

He then enquired as to the treatments they prescribed for the pox, and there followed a discussion during which the merits of applying lead plates to the body above the reins (or kidneys) was balanced against dosing with a mixture of pulp of the fruit of cassia mixed with that of tamarind, decoctions of sarsaparilla and *lignum vitae* – or even a preparation of the latter to which were added horse dung and frankincense.

Altogether Simon found it a fascinating morning and parted with his Scots colleagues on good terms. While there were one or two who had expressed the view that the old ways were always the best, the rest had been considerably more open-minded than the members of the committee of the Royal College of Physicians when they had demanded he come before them. Before they went their separate ways, Dr Richie suggested they might all meet again within a week and this was agreed.

Simon was relieved, for he was becoming concerned at how he could spin out the supposed reason for his visit to Edinburgh any longer than that. Certainly he might arrange to meet various physicians independently, and even discuss individual cases, but there was a limit to how many times he could impose on them in such a way, as these were busy men with their own affairs to which to attend. He was now regretting having told Alun so definitely that he would be in Edinburgh for two to three weeks, even though he could not have foreseen how soon he'd be plunged into trouble again.

He made up his mind. He would stay another ten days at the most and take full advantage of Marlowe's offer to give him sufficient information to satisfy Sir Robert Cecil, while also seeing if it was possible to discover who really was behind Richard's death. He was still considering how best to set about all this when he met up with Jack Dudley and Marlowe at the house the former had leased for his stay in Edinburgh. Marlowe was reticent about the outcome of the previous day's debauch but his red-rimmed eyes, skin even paler than usual, and general dishevelled air suggested he had made a hard night of it and for once he had little to say.

It was clear to them as soon as they arrived at the Palace of Holyrood that they were very much at the lower end of the social scale of guests invited to so grand an occasion. Simon and Marlowe had ribbed Jack Dudley on his fashionable attire, his russet velvet doublet slashed to show copper silk beneath, the whole trimmed with copper lace, his puffed trunk hose and elaborately clocked stockings, but his dress was positively sober compared with that of some of the other English guests, their extravagances of style and colour standing out against the more sombre hues of those of their Scots hosts. The latter's wives and daughters also displayed less showy attire than their English counterparts, though they favoured both fine cloth and lace.

The apartments at Holyrood were grand indeed and the banqueting hall into which they were guided was hung with fine tapestries, the tables set with silver plate and fine glassware. They were shown to a table at the lower end of the room where a number of men and women were already seated. Neither Dudley nor Marlowe appeared to know any of them, and it was clear the Scots regarded them with no little suspicion. They could hardly be blamed for that, thought Simon, if there really is so much intrigue going on in the Court.

'Close by are Marie Stuart's apartments,' Marlowe told Simon, 'where she dined with her secretary, Signor Rizzio, on the night Darnley and his friends arrived and murdered him before her eyes. They say he screamed and hid behind her skirts when they came for him,' leading Simon to enquire if there was a single place left in Scotland without its tale of blood.

The banquet was a long one, and with such a large number of courses and so many people to serve, it was hardly surprising that much of the food was cold and unpalatable by the time it reached them. The King and Queen and the French Ambassador were seated on the high table at the other end of the room along with a number of Scots lords and a handful of favourites. The Queen's progress up the room had been carefully watched, particularly by the women, to see if she was showing any signs that she might finally be with child, but that did not appear to be the case even though she had now been married to James for three years.

Simon looked across at the rows of crowded tables. Higher up the room he saw Seton sitting at a table with men Marlowe had previously pointed out as being of Essex's faction, and close by was another table of Englishmen. 'The man in the blue is a relative of Sir Francis Bacon,' Marlowe told him, 'Indeed, there are scions of most of our noble families present. But not, overtly, any Cecils or Careys. One of my tasks,' he continued confidentially, 'was to discover what the Careys might be up to, but so far the only person everyone considers to be of their camp is yourself, and you are working for Cecil!'

Course followed interminable course. The Scots sitting at their table unbent only slightly and Simon wished the whole event over. He found it almost impossible to keep track of who was supposed to be acting on behalf of whom, and was becoming, with every hour that passed, more certain than ever that he was far too ill equipped and lacking in political acumen for the task he had been set. The most obvious intriguer was the Earl of Essex; indeed, Jack Dudley made no secret of the fact in conversation, even going so far as to tell him that the Earl himself planned to make a secret visit in the not too distant future. But surely, thought Simon dismally, all this activity must be so well known to Cecil that it would hardly be worth the telling.

Finally it was over and the three companions were able to leave the table. The royal party had withdrawn to the private apartments but knots of people stood talking together in a long gallery outside the room in which the banquet had been held. Jack Dudley was hailed by a group of young men who invited him to go back to their lodgings and play dice with them which he agreed to do, leaving Marlowe and Simon alone.

As they turned to go they saw Seton ahead of them chatting with a group of people and, from the way he kept glancing at them, it was clear he was talking about Simon. In fact, it was so marked that Marlowe went over to them and asked outright what their interest was in Dr Forman.

'You know very well,' Seton retorted. 'A guest of mine has died claiming Dr Forman poisoned him.'

'But you know very well that can't be true,' declared Marlowe. 'Jack Dudley and I sat beside Simon throughout supper while

Danvers stuffed himself like a hog. Simon left early and then you sent for him yourself to treat the man the next day, a treatment which your own Dr Richie swears could not be faulted. So I suggest you stop spreading this farrago of nonsense any further.'

Seton gave Marlowe a look of intense dislike. 'Nonsense, is it? Possibly Dr Forman hasn't told you that this is not the only death with which he's recently been closely involved. While they were journeying here from London, his companion was found murdered in the chamber they shared together at Carlisle Castle – a chamber with a door bolted *from the inside*.'

'How did you hear of this?' Simon demanded.

'I have a relative in Carlisle. He has sent me word of it and also of how you set about trying to blame the guards for their laxity in letting the supposed murderer in.'

'The captain of the guard admitted himself that they had grown lax,' returned Simon. 'And as to the door being bolted, it was not so all night as I left the room for a considerable time due to sickness. Did you also learn that a soldier was later found dead and stripped of his uniform, suggesting that the murderer had used it as a disguise to enter the castle? Had the Governor not accepted my innocence I doubt he'd have let me proceed on my journey. Richard Wilmore was my dear friend; there's no reason on earth why I should have harmed him.'

It was clear from Seton's face and those of his companions that Simon was not believed. 'Come on,' said Marlowe, 'there's no point in bandying any more words with these . . . *gentlemen*.'

'Wait,' said Simon. 'There's one more thing. Was your informant a man called James Ford, by any chance?'

Seton gave every appearance of looking surprised at his question while Marlowe looked puzzled. 'No, it was not. I've never heard of this man Ford. Are you now trying to say *he* killed your friend?'

'Come on,' urged Marlowe, pulling Simon away. 'I've told you – there's no point in wasting your breath here.'

Seton looked at him with contempt. 'Go back to London, Marlowe, to your playwriting and your low companions. And if you value his safety, take Carey's man with you!'

'That was deeply unpleasant,' said Simon as they reached the open street. 'Do you think it's now widespread that I strangle and poison wherever I go, not to mention that I'm supposed to be "Carey's man"?'

Marlowe shrugged. 'Edinburgh's a hotbed of rumour as you must know by now. This one will run its course then let's hope some other tasty scandal succeeds it.' As he spoke they came to a tavern and Marlowe at once turned into it, saying he was in need of drink. 'Shall I call the tapster and have him open the wine in my presence? And pour it into the cups myself? That way I trust I might safely drink with you! Now,' he continued as the wine was brought, 'did your man find out anything more about Seton's servant? Was he able to speak to him?'

'As to your last question, no, for he's disappeared. But if you recall, I told you John thought he'd seen the man somewhere before. When he got back last night he suddenly remembered why. He said the servant had a nick or healed cut on his ear, across the lobe. I treated exactly such a one on the ear of a wool buyer called James Ford we met up with on our way to Carlisle. Ford had a beard, longish hair and an English countryman's way of speech, but I suppose if he shaved off his beard, cut his hair and changed his tongue then he and Seton's servant could be one and the same man.'

Marlowe's eyes widened and he poured himself another cup of wine. 'So how did you meet up with this man Ford?'

'At an inn near Preston. When he learned we were going to Carlisle he asked if he might join us since the way's lonely and hazardous. Neither Richard nor I saw any reason to deny him.'

'Did he say much about himself?'

'Only that he was buying fleeces and wool and that he often journeyed north on such business. He was civil and we passed the time quite pleasantly with him. He also told us he had a sister in Carlisle married to a sergeant and was going there on a visit. John took an instant dislike to both him and his servant and actually tried to loosen the servant's tongue with drink but without success.'

'If he was so ordinary, why did you think it necessary to have your man pump his servant?'

'To be honest I didn't think it was, nor did Richard. But there seemed no harm in it.'

'Did you see Ford again?'

'Yes, in a tavern in Carlisle. He drank with us, asked if we were comfortably lodged and said how pleased his sister was to see him. Nothing of import. He also suggested we might meet to discuss riding back to London together again as we'd led him to believe Carlisle was our only destination. Richard told him we'd think about it and so we parted. We didn't see him again.'

'And you see Seton's hand behind all this?'

Simon said that he did. 'You told me you knew little about him. What *do* you know?'

'I've been making some discreet enquiries,' said Marlowe, 'and I admit he seems something of an enigma. I'm told variously that he leans to one faction, then to another or that he favours Essex. He's a Scot, as his name suggests, but his father married an Englishwoman and he was born in London, only returning home some ten years ago. His family were impoverished but he has plenty of money. Oh yes, there's much that is mysterious about Edward Seton . . .'

'Then he must be our man!' interrupted Simon excitedly. 'He feared his activities would be reported to London and so had his man, this James Ford, kill Richard in Carlisle.'

'So why didn't he also kill you?' Marlowe wanted to know.

'I've thought of that. Perhaps he intended to but was unable to do so. But he must have thought that after Richard's murder I'd either be suspected of it and held in the castle, or worse, or that I'd take fright and go back to London. Yes,' he continued, warming to his theme, 'everything fits, don't you see? So his plan comes to nothing when, after all, I arrive in Edinburgh. You said he already knew I was here when you asked if you could bring me to supper.'

Marlowe looked extremely doubtful but urged him to continue.

'So he decides to find another means of destroying me. He or Ford poison one of the dishes of athelbrose and encourage the girl to feed it to Danvers. Then they ensure I'm called in to treat him and Ford poisons the posset which I make Danvers drink. And he dies! And my reputation is ruined and no one believes anything I say, not only here but when I return to London.'

Marlowe pushed his chair back and stood up. 'It's all far too elaborate. I admit you have a case but something about it doesn't seem right to me. Surely the easiest way would be for him to have you knifed in some dark alleyway.'

'But you spoke of a God in a Machine,' replied Simon, hurt. 'Can't you see how well Seton fits the role?'

Marlowe shook his head. 'No. No, I can't. Sweet Jesus, my head's still pounding from last night. I'll come to your lodgings tomorrow morning. Perhaps a night's sleep will help us both make more sense of this.'

But to Simon's amazement Marlowe arrived the next day while he was still at his breakfast, booted and spurred for a journey. 'I'm leaving for London,' he said, before Simon could ask the reason for it, 'and I think you and your servant should pack at once and come with me.'

'Why?' exclaimed Simon. 'Why now?'

'Because I believe you are in desperate hazard. When I returned last night I found another letter from Tom Walsingham urging me to come back to London at once. He says there's grave mischief afoot and I must stay no longer. He mentions the man called Rivers of whom I spoke.'

'The intelligencer?'

'God knows what Tom means or what it portends but I must heed his warning and return to London. He hints only that some desperate intrigue is afoot. My instinct is that it also involves you, which is why I beg you to come with me now.'

'But I can't,' said Simon. 'I must meet with the doctors as that's my supposed reason for being here, and I must satisfy myself that I know the hand behind Richard's murder even if I can do nothing about it.'

Marlowe gave an exasperated sigh. 'But what use is that if you die in the attempt?' He clutched Simon's arm. 'I've been thinking of it most of the night and, yes, I agree Seton's behaviour's suspicious, but I still don't think he's your real enemy.'

Marlowe's attitude was so unlike his usual cynical self that Simon had to admit himself shaken. 'Well,' he said, 'I'll give it two or three more days then send John to Liddesdale to ask Alun Armstrong to see me safe to Mangerton. Once there I should be secure enough.'

Marlowe closed his eyes and clutched his head. 'You're a fool!

But if you won't listen to reason then I suppose I'll have to accept it.' He pulled a paper out of his pocket. 'I'd already written you a list of those people you should tell Cecil are here, with a note of what you should say about them. It will cover much of the same ground that I'll be reporting too, but no matter. He could expect nothing more of you, quite likely not as much. And I'll also do what I can for you behind the scenes back in London.' He paused. 'So if I want to send you word, then you'll be here two or three days more? And after that this place called Mangerton?' Simon nodded. 'Don't leave it any later. I truly believe that if you do, the consequences might well be fatal. Remember what I said about the god in the machine. I meant it, Simon, it's not poetic licence!'

'And you?' asked Simon. 'Will you be safe? Apart from other hazards, aren't you concerned at crossing the Debatable Lands alone?'

'That's a risk I have to take and there are worse ones.' A strange look passed over his face. 'Indeed, I think the danger of meeting up with a band of Reivers on a raiding mission is the least of those I might soon have to face.'

'You've been very good,' said Simon.

Marlowe roared with laughter. 'If you say that kind of thing and it gets about back home it'll ruin my reputation! Don't you know I'm arrogant, adder-tongued, thoroughly evil and care for nothing and no man? Well, I'm for the Bankside, the taverns, the playhouses, friend Tom – and civilisation!'

Simon watched him ride off down the street with deepening apprehension. He had, yet again, lost a good ally. He was also soon to miss Kit as a companion, for the day was Sunday and he was about to experience the joys of a Scots Sabbath, during which from dawn until midnight no entertainment was allowed. 'A foretaste of Hell', Marlowe had called it.

On a Sunday there could be no dancing, no music, no play-acting or frequenting of alehouses or games. Men, he had been told, had been arraigned for fishing, grinding corn or plucking geese on a Sabbath, and women for selling candles and baking bread. Without exception everyone was expected to be in church, and that included visitors to the capital as well as residents. That being the case he suggested to John Bradedge that after they had done their duty, they should fetch their horses and ride out into the country. Even if they were unable to find an inn or an alehouse in which to pass the time at least they would be out of the city.

Somehow the interminable Sunday morning passed, during which Simon listened to the longest and most hideous sermon he had ever sat through, the minister only coming to life when he described the horrors awaiting miserable sinners once they had shuffled off their mortal coil. He relished every Satanic punishment, from boiling in oil and being prodded with pitchforks to roasting in the Everlasting bonfire. It was well after noon by the time the wretched man had finished and later still before Simon and John were able to ride out of town after eating a cold repast, their landlady apologising for not providing them with a hot dinner because she was not allowed to cook on a Sunday.

While in church Simon had craned his neck and endlessly looked around to see if there might be anyone there who seemed to be watching him or looked suspicious or might resemble someone they had seen elsewhere on their travels, but the building was crowded and he finally had to give up. Now as they left the centre of Edinburgh behind he once again kept looking round to see if they were being followed, but that did not seem to be the case.

Reaching open ground they let their horses gallop, enjoying the freedom and fresh air. After a little while they reined in and Simon told John that Marlowe had left that morning for London, having been advised to do so, but saying only that he had also urged them to do so as soon as was practicable.

'I suggest we give it two or three more days, and that you then make your way to Mangerton and tell Alun Armstrong how matters stand and that I wish to leave at once.'

John listened gravely. 'I'd rather not leave you here on your own, Doctor,' he said finally. 'Surely there'd be less suspicion if we stay here together, then, when you decide to leave, I'll pack our bags and take them quietly out of the lodgings while our landlady's from home. Our leaving early shouldn't cause any comment since we are fully paid up. And we can tell the landlord at the inn when we go for our horses that we're merely riding out for exercise as we did today.'

'Do you think we can find our way to Mangerton alone then?'

John sought to reassure him. 'I doubt I could pick our way across the moors and back lanes between here and Hawick as young Armstrong did, but the main road from here is marked clear enough and after that I reckon we'll know where we are. And since no one will know we're going, who's likely to come after us?'

Simon agreed. 'Very well, but promise me one thing. If for some reason matters go truly awry and anything happens to me or we need urgent help, then don't wait to be asked. Make for Mangerton at once and seek assistance from the Armstrongs.'

'Do you fear something of the sort then?' asked John, thoroughly alarmed.

'In view of what's occurred already, I think *anything* could happen,' replied Simon grimly, 'and Marlowe is sure I'm in real danger.'

Waking early the next day, Simon was considering how best to make use of the remaining time at his disposal when matters were unexpectedly taken out of his hands. First he found a letter awaiting him from Dr Richie asking if he would meet him that morning to discuss a particularly interesting case of his; then, no sooner had he breakfasted than Jack Dudley called on him with an invitation.

'I wondered whether or not you were engaged elsewhere this afternoon, Dr Forman? For I've been telling people that you cast horoscopes and a number of my friends, both Scots and English, have asked if you would be willing to cast for them.'

Simon was surprised but the request seemed harmless enough. 'I don't see why not. But you must tell them that I've only brought a few charts and books with me, and so would not want to commit myself to long or detailed forecasts.'

'Then come to my lodgings this afternoon and we'll look forward to your company if that's convenient.'

Simon was delighted. 'I've been invited this morning to go with Dr Richie to see one of his patients but after that I'll be quite free.'

'Excellent! Then let me make another suggestion. This evening I've invited these same friends and acquaintances to stay to supper and propose to provide them with a special entertainment. So why not join us? Are you acquainted with Master Thomas Grinston's work, *Certain Divers Recreations*? No? Well, I won't spoil your enjoyment. So come when you will and cast for us this afternoon while we all have clear heads, then later we can drink and dine. There's beds enough for you to stay the night if you wish; there's no need to have to stagger home in the small hours.'

Simon set off for Dr Richie's house feeling a good deal better. He didn't see how he could come to any harm by taking up Dudley's invitation to cast a few horoscopes and enjoy an evening's entertainment. Dudley at least seemed both straightforward and affable, and even Marlowe had harboured no doubts about him. It might also enable Simon to find out more about Seton, although he was beginning to come round to Marlowe's view that there was little point in his risking remaining much longer in the hope of proving Seton was involved in Richard's death.

Dr Richie met Simon at his door and took him on foot a matter of some ten minutes' walk away to a respectable-looking house in a street that largely housed members of the merchant class. The good doctor's patient was a pale and thin woman in her thirties who had been brought to bed eight times. All the children were living, but on the last occasion she had suffered severe bleeding, the aftermath of which was still troubling her, for the slightest effort tired her and she had been unable to suckle the child.

Nothing tried so far appeared to have had any effect. Some of his colleagues, Dr Richie told Simon, prescribed the letting of blood in such cases but he was doubtful since the woman was already so weak, a view with which Simon heartily concurred.

'Do you still suffer from a flux?' Simon asked her.

The woman nodded. 'Aye, Doctor, and it's now ten weeks since the birth of the child even though I've been taking Dr Richie's medicines.'

'What are they?' Simon asked Dr Richie.

'An infusion of senna leaves, rhubarb root and agaric which has improved her condition somewhat but not sufficiently. Is there anything more that you can recommend?'

'Possibly you could try an infusion of feverfew in white wine with a little cinnamon and nutmeg added. In London it's widely used by midwives to assist in expelling the afterbirth and to strengthen the womb. Do you think it possible that not all of the afterbirth came

169

away, and that is what is causing the trouble? If so, it would not hurt to have leaves of tansy applied as a poultice to her lower belly. What you also need, my dear,' he said, turning to the woman, 'is every nourishment to give you strength and most certainly not to fall with child again so soon.' The woman sighed and turned her head away.

'There's little to be done to prevent that if her husband insists she does her duty,' commented Richie wryly, as they left the woman after giving her maid instructions as to what to fetch from the apothecary and the application of the poultice. 'Poor woman, I fear another childbed will kill her.' They continued discussing the topic as they returned to the doctor's house. 'Have you wife and children?' Richie asked.

'No. For one reason or another I've never married. And since I've seen no woman in your house, I take it you haven't either or are a widower?'

'The last, I'm afraid,' Richie told him. 'My good wife died some ten years back of a cancerous swelling of the breast. Poor woman, she suffered much. In the end I was giving her ever-increasing doses of poppy syrup in an attempt to dull her pain. I have never wished to remarry. As to children,' he smiled, 'my son is presently studying to become a physician and my daughter's married to a merchant in Aberdeen.'

They parted in friendly fashion and Simon returned to make ready for his visit to Jack Dudley, putting together the charts and books he had brought with him. So long as he did not promise wonders he would no doubt do well enough. His preparations reminded him again of Kate's unsatisfactory horoscope, which had made him uneasy ever since. He left for Dudley's house after telling John he might well spend the night there. 'So go where you will. But keep an eye out in case of trouble, your ears open and your mouth shut!'

'And what do I do if you don't return safely in the morning?' grumbled his servant.

'God's Breath, man, I'll only be a couple of streets away and in good company. This, at least, is one occasion about which you *needn't* fret!' And with that Simon swung his bag over his shoulder and set off briskly in the direction of Jack Dudley's house.

Chapter 13

Divers Private Recreations

Dudley greeted him warmly and showed him upstairs to a pleasant chamber where a dozen or so men, both Scots and English, were drinking and chatting. Simon recognised one or two of them from the Holyrood banquet and others from Seton's fatal supper party. He was also somewhat alarmed to see Seton was also present but apart from greeting him coolly, he said nothing more. It crossed Simon's mind that even in so private a gathering there must be others, as well as himself, who were taking note of who else was there. He shivered slightly then told himself not to be so foolish or soon he would be imagining a spy behind every curtain and an assassin lurking in every dark corner.

'The Scotsmen present here don't consider the casting of horoscopes to be sinful then?' enquired Simon as he unpacked his bag. 'In view of your Sabbath I'd begun to think that such a practice would be considered a fast step on the road to hellfire!'

'The Scottish Sabbath and the power of the church may hold sway in public, but what happens in private is often altogether different,' Dudley assured him with a grin, 'as you will see this evening. I mentioned to you Grinston's *Divers Private Recreations*.' With that he introduced him to the company and Simon explained that away from his own study with all his books and papers he could not undertake a major horoscope casting for each person present, nor indeed would there be the time even if that were possible, but if the gentlemen would like to ask specific questions on matters of concern to them, he would do his best to answer them.

As he expected, the questions followed the familiar pattern. Would an ageing relative leave the enquirer his estate on his death since there was no immediate heir? Would the fair maiden to whom a young blade had sworn undying devotion repay him by allowing him the freedom of her person? Would a commercial venture succeed or fail? And, from one of the older men present, would he ever have a son? His wife had miscarried three times and they had but one sickly daughter. Simon made a mental note to talk to him later and ask if he would like him to call on his wife; perhaps there was something he could prescribe in the way of treatment – subject, of course, to his not offending her usual physician.

A bright young Scot of the name of Hamilton asked if he could simply be told what was immediately in store for him, good or bad. Having been given basic information as to his birth and its place and other relevant details, Simon made various calculations then frowned.

'Well, Dr Forman?' enquired Hamilton mockingly. 'Am I to come into a fortune, marry a beautiful wife, or preferably both?'

'I know nothing of that,' replied Simon, suddenly serious, 'but it seems from this that you should be wary, for there is one who is your enemy whom you least suspect.'

Hamilton looked startled then brushed it off. 'It seems I've been chosen to give the occasion a taste of drama.' Then he laughed. 'Now, I wonder which of you he's referring to?'

After the castings were over, several of the enquirers wished to press money on Simon but, in spite of the fact that he was now running somewhat low on funds, he refused. 'No, gentlemen. I'm not in my study and these are *not* proper consultations. While I've done my best to tell you the truth as I see it, I consider it to have been more in the way of entertainment rather than true foretelling.'

While Simon put away his charts, Dudley announced that there would now be a break in the proceedings until suppertime; he trusted his guests would be happy to amuse themselves until then with talk. In twos and threes some wandered out of the room, others sat where they were and discussed the affairs of the day, and Simon soon found himself accosted again by young Hamilton.

'Was it really true, what you said of my future, Dr Forman?' he asked. 'Or did you decide to use me to chill people's blood and show you have supernatural powers?'

'I would never do such a thing,' Simon assured him gravely. 'It would be quite wrong – immoral, in fact. I'm no common fortune-teller reading palms at a fair. Horoscope casting is part of my work as a physician and I use it most to foretell the course and outcome of an illness.'

'I see.' Hamilton frowned. 'Then I wonder what it meant? Why should one of my friends be a hidden enemy? So far as I know, I've not insulted or harmed any of them. But putting that aside, what really interests me are the new sciences which I know are much discussed in London. Your poet, Christopher Marlowe, tells me he belongs to a society called The School of the Night which meets to discuss such things. Do you also belong to it?'

Simon replied that he did not, although he knew of it. 'But such matters interest me too. Perhaps I should ask Marlowe to introduce me to it when I return to London.'

'You're one of Carey's men, aren't you?' asked Hamilton suddenly. 'He who's Lord Chamberlain and cousin to the Queen.' The room had suddenly gone quiet and to Simon the question appeared to hang in the air.

'I'm not sure what you mean,' he responded, playing for time.

'Well, all you English are here on behalf of some powerful faction or the other, aren't you?'

'I'm here purely in my professional capacity as a physician,' Simon returned, 'to discuss medical matters with your doctors which is what I'm doing and finding it very fascinating.'

Hamilton gave him a look of frank disbelief. 'Well, I suppose it's your business. But if you are Carey's man then there are far worse patrons. His reputation when he was Warden on the Borders was that of a fair and just man, and I know the Keeper of Liddesdale holds him in high esteem. I don't think he'd be one for underhand intrigue. But enough of politics, let's talk of other things.' It was a long time since Simon had had such an absorbing conversation. Hamilton's interests were wide, ranging over geography, the new mathematics and astronomy as well as literature and poetry. He was also fascinated by the effect all the new knowledge might have on the Christian faith.

'Surely from what we know now, Man's beginnings go back further than we are told in the Old Testament,' he asserted, 'and that being the case, we needs must query much else. Indeed, your Marlowe told me that he felt it most unlikely that Moses had spent all those years wandering in the wilderness when any ordinary practical fellow could have led the Jews into the Promised Land in a matter of weeks!'

'Marlowe has a great deal to say on many matters, and much of it considered dangerous even in London,' Simon warned him. 'Now he's promising us a play about a man who sells his soul to the Devil and so defies God!'

Hamilton appeared lost in admiration at such a prospect. 'I wonder if it is possible for me to go to London? I'd greatly love to see that. When do you return yourself?'

'In about a fortnight,' responded Simon quickly, not wishing to reveal the truth, 'but there would be little point in your coming with me then, much as I'd appreciate your company, as the playhouses are at present closed due to an onset of the plague. However, I'd be happy to offer you hospitality if you decide to visit London later. Perhaps we can persuade Marlowe to take you along to a meeting of the School of the Night.'

Involved as he was in the discussion of matters close to his heart and interest, the time passed quickly for Simon. Hamilton did not refer again to his being 'Carey's man'. Simon wondered how many of the others thought the same and if it really mattered. No one had talked to him of Sir Robert Cecil, which must mean that he took no part in what was going on in Edinburgh, apart from wanting to keep informed. No doubt as Acting Secretary to the Privy Council he had to report to its members. A sudden thought struck Simon. Cecil had offered him his protection and he had taken it to mean against his powerful but faceless enemies in England, but maybe it applied in Scotland too? If so, perhaps he could find some way of making it known without revealing the task he had been set. He wondered suddenly why Marlowe had not suggested it to him.

Shortly before suppertime a number of young women appeared and were introduced into the party; from their dress and demeanour they could scarcely be mistaken for the daughters of Edinburgh worthies. Among them Simon immediately recognised the red-headed girl who had sat on Danvers' knee at Seton's supper and plied him with athelbrose, possibly poisoned athelbrose. Her appearance in Dudley's house worried him and he questioned what part she was to play in the evening's proceedings. This time he must ensure he kept a careful eye on her. At that moment a servant announced that supper would be served in the dining room and the girls trooped in with the men and sat, laughing and joking, at table with them.

Determined that there would be no repetition of what had happened at Seton's party, Simon looked closely at every servant bringing in food, but none bore the slightest resemblance to Ford, for he was certain now that the wool merchant and the serving man were one and the same. Where his own safety was concerned, he was careful to take from dishes which it would be impossible to drug without half a dozen people becoming ill, and to drink only wine from bottles shared with his neighbours. Towards the end of the supper the girls suddenly disappeared, which surprised Simon for he had assumed they had been procured for the guests for the night.

As supper ended he wondered as to the nature of the entertainment his host had promised. He was soon to find out. Dudley, who was sitting at the head of the table, banged on it to silence conversation then suggested they should return to the other room where they were to see a Masque devised especially for the occasion. 'I trust we can all hold our tongues here?' he enquired with a smile.

'Are we to have a piece of a political nature then, and does our host wish us to keep silent about its content?' Simon asked Hamilton.

Hamilton grinned. 'I doubt that very much, knowing Jack Dudley. Well, we'll soon find out.' They went into the larger room in which chairs had now been set out in a semicircle, with a curtain looped over the door leading to the hall. As they did so, three musicians entered through it, two young men with fiddles and a third, grey-haired man with a recorder. They took their place by the door and immediately struck up a lively air. At once the curtain was flung side and a troupe of very scantily dressed young women danced in to much applause and vocal encouragement. When the music stopped the red-headed girl stepped forward and held up a board on which was scrawled *A Night in Elysium or Scenes from Greek Myths*.

What followed would have had John Knox spinning in his grave. In succession the highly appreciative and increasingly raucous company were treated to *Diana Surprised by Actaeon* (a plump blonde draped merely in a piece of blue cloth), *The Birth of Venus* (a dark young lady, covering herself somewhat unsuccessfully only with her own long hair), *The Abduction of Helen* (the two young fiddlers carrying off a girl wrapped in a small, silk sheet which she dropped just as she disappeared through the door), *Leda and the Swan* (a nubile contortionist partnered by a blushing servant with a pair of wings fastened to his jacket) until, after several more such items, the dénouement was reached.

One of the girls, rather more decorously garbed, appeared and informed the audience they were about to see *The Judgement of Paris*. She produced a gold-painted apple which she presented to Dudley and asked if he would play the part of Paris. To much mirth and jesting Dudley agreed and walked over to what passed for the stage area. The fiddlers, having returned from abducting Helen, joined their older colleague and began to play again, at which three figures, veiled from head to foot in white, walked sedately in. By gestures they indicated to Dudley that he must make his choice.

As he approached them, all three discarded their white veils and stood before him without a stitch of clothing. At this there was great applause and a number of loud remarks of a bawdy nature. Dudley walked up and down and round the goddesses and finally presented the apple to the dark young lady in her role as Venus.

Simon smiled. He had to admit to himself that he'd found the show highly enjoyable and all the more surprising considering this was Puritanical Edinburgh; he could well understand why the audience had been sworn to secrecy. He made a mental note to try to obtain a copy of Master Grinston's *Divers Private Recreations* immediately on his return to London. As for the girls, no doubt they had been well paid for their trouble and a little while later they appeared again, this time rather better clad, but making it obvious they were available later for entertainment of a more private nature should this be required.

'What weighty matters kept you and young Hamilton in such close conversation all afternoon?' asked Jack Dudley coming to sit beside Simon with a glass of wine. 'Affairs of State?'

'Hardly. Your young friend is fascinated by all aspects of new science and was looking for someone with whom to discuss his interest. Also he says Kit Marlowe was throwing doubts on the veracity of the Old Testament and that intrigued him too. He desires to visit London to see Marlowe's new play and asked if he could journey back with me, but I had to tell him our playhouses are shut at present for fear of plague, so there's little point in journeying so far until they open again.'

'You intend leaving soon then?'

'Shortly,' replied Simon warily, his attention straying across the room to the red-haired girl. As if aware of him she turned and gave him a look which left little doubt as to what she had in mind. Dudley followed his gaze then smiled broadly. 'I see you've more fascinating matters to discuss than the date of the Exodus and Marlowe's new play, so I won't detain you further.'

The rest of the evening passed with more talk and music and a great deal of drink. At first Simon told himself that he needed to keep the redhead at his side to prevent her from doing any possible mischief, but as time passed and he drank more and more wine, this no longer seemed the most important reason. He finally made his way to bed with her where she did indeed entertain him privately and with great diligence well into the small hours of the morning.

He awoke late to find the sun streaming in through the bedchamber window, unable at first to recollect where he was. When he remembered he felt for the girl but she had gone. A considerable amount of noise was coming from downstairs. It must be even later than he thought. He climbed out of bed clutching his aching head and searched for the clothes he had discarded in such haste the night before then, as a sudden thought struck him, looked for his purse. Yes, it was there, its contents still intact. He chided himself for suspecting her of one of the oldest tricks in the repertoire of coney-catching.

It was when he came to put on his breeches that he discovered his belt was missing. Cursing, he searched everywhere for it but without success. There was no possibility he could have taken it off before going to bed: its disappearance was a complete mystery. The noise downstairs showed no sign of abating, and he went in search of his host, holding his breeches up by one hand. Dudley would surely be prepared to lend him a belt until he discovered his own.

He emerged into the hallway to find half a dozen of the previous night's guests and Jack Dudley waiting at the bottom of the staircase. As he came towards them all turned and looked at him, suddenly silent.

'My apologies for being so late up,' he announced, 'and to cap it all, I can't find the belt to my breeches. Lord knows what I did with it last night. Do you think you can lend me one, Jack, while I continue to search for mine? It must be somewhere.' Still nobody spoke. 'What's the matter?' asked Simon, suddenly alarmed. 'What are you looking at me like that for?'

'You'd best come and see for yourself,' Dudley responded, and motioned Simon along the hallway at the end of which was a closet, its door open. 'Take a look in there,' he said. Inside lay the body of young Hamilton, his face congested, his eyes wide and staring, exactly as had been the case with Richard Wilmore.

'God's Blood!' exclaimed Simon, going white to the lips.

'You'll see he's a belt around his neck,' said Dudley. 'Is it yours?'

Simon bent to see. 'Yes,' he managed. 'Yes, it is.' Not a third death, he thought, not again. Nothing's going to save me now. He touched the belt with his finger and it moved relatively easily even though it had been buckled. He looked again then pulled it away slightly. Underneath was the same thin deep line that had been etched around Richard's neck.

'He wasn't strangled with my belt,' he said. 'Look, all of you,' he continued as they crowded round. 'See for yourselves. The mark under my belt is of the kind made by a thin piece of twine or a leather thong. Hamilton was garotted and whoever did it,' he went on, his voice rising in panic, 'looked to find some way to throw the blame on me. He must have come into the room early this morning when I was dead asleep, unless . . . where's the red-haired girl I took to bed? Perhaps she was in league with the murderer and he asked her to give him my belt. Even if she wasn't, at least she can vouch for the fact I never left my bed.'

'Who will take the word of a whore?' sneered one of the men.

Simon bent over the body again. 'He's scarce cold. He can't have been dead long. Who found him?'

'One of the servants, at about six o'clock. He came at once to me,' Dudley told him.

Simon stood up and faced them all. 'I did not kill him.'

'It seems passing strange then,' said another man, 'for I've heard that since you came to Edinburgh you attended a sick man and that he died swearing you'd poisoned him. And now you visit this house and someone else dies.'

'And,' chimed in a third, 'you spent much time with him in deep talk yesterday. Might one ask what matters you were discussing?'

'I already told Master Dudley the answer to that last night. Hamilton was fascinated by the new learning and new science. We spoke of geography and astronomy and the Old Testament.'

'And I heard him say last night that you were Carey's man,' persisted his interrogator.

'And *I* asked him what he meant by that,' retorted Simon, 'and told him I came to Edinburgh only to talk medicine with doctors – and that's what I've been doing. The man I attended who died was already ill and I prescribed nothing your esteemed Dr Richie would not have done in my place, as he says, pointing out the man was raving in his death throes. Yesterday he'd sufficient faith in me to ask me to visit one of his patients and give my advice.' He looked from one to the other. 'You can't *seriously* think I killed this young man? What could I possibly gain by it?'

Seton pushed his way to the front of the small group. 'You tell us.'

From outside came the noise of arrival. Jack Dudley walked over to Simon and put his hand on his shoulder. 'I'm sorry, Simon, word had to be sent to the authorities when Hamilton's body was discovered. I imagine these are the King's men.'

'Why was that necessary?' asked Simon desperately. 'What has this to do with the Court?'

Seton came and stood behind Dudley. 'Didn't you know?' he said with the smile of one who enjoys delivering bad news. 'Hamilton was a favourite of the King.'

There was a bang on the door and Dudley himself went to open it.

179

Simon heard him in close conversation with whoever was outside. Eventually he opened the door wider and ushered in a tall man with several burly fellows at his heels.

'Where's Hamilton?' asked the King's man without preamble and Dudley led him to the body.

'And there stands the English doctor whose belt you can clearly see around his neck,' said Seton officiously.

The King's man evidently knew Seton, for he greeted him with respect – which Simon found somewhat strange. Then he turned to Simon. 'So you're the English doctor? You admit this is your belt?'

'Yes, but I've no idea how it got there,' Simon insisted, then, as the King's man made no comment, he added desperately, 'Look for yourself. You can see it wasn't used to kill him, for beneath it is the mark of a garotte. I'd hardly kill a man in so anonymous a fashion then clumsily put my own belt around his neck to implicate myself!'

The King's man looked more closely. 'Aye,' he commented, 'that's true enough.' He paused. 'And I might well be inclined to believe you but for one thing. Word reached us some time ago that another man was killed in similar fashion in Carlisle Castle, and you in the very bedchamber with him.'

Simon again cursed his own naivety for not taking into account the fact that King James must have his spies on the Border like everyone else, no doubt even within the English garrison at Carlisle Castle. But even if that wasn't the case, obviously such a piece of news was bound to have reached the Scottish Court. The voices of those around him rose to an excited babble as they began to argue with each other as to his guilt.

One of the young Scots who had been particularly hostile then stepped forward. 'D'ye ken too that this English doctor's also accused of poisoning a man at Master Seton here's supper party?'

'Aye,' replied the King's man, 'that too, though Dr Richie's been spoken with and does not consider Dr Forman played any part in the man's death.'

'So what now?' Dudley asked him. 'I'll say here and now I don't believe Dr Forman killed young Hamilton.' There was a buzz of dissent. 'Hear what I have to say,' he said strongly. 'I know nothing of the events in Carlisle, but what I *do* know is that I sat next to Dr

Forman at the supper at which the man was taken ill, and there was no opportunity for him to have tampered with the food. There are also witnesses to his making up the medicines. As to last night, Dr Forman came here at my invitation to cast horoscopes for us and stayed on for supper, and as I recall Hamilton was still up after Dr Forman had gone to his bed.'

'Horoscopes!' The King's man seized on the word. 'Are you an alchemist then? Even, the Lord preserve us, a *necromancer*!'

'No, no,' Simon responded wearily. 'I'm a physician, a doctor of medicine – recognised by the University of Cambridge and licensed by the Royal College of Physicians. I also cast horoscopes as do most of my profession, mostly to learn the outcome of illnesses. Yesterday's horoscope castings were in a lighter vein and I swear no black arts were used.'

'That's odd,' broke in Dudley suddenly. 'Don't you remember! When Dr Forman cast Hamilton's horoscope he warned him of possible hazard from someone near at hand. He'd hardly give him such a warning if he intended to murder him!'

The King's man shook his head. 'That's as may be. All I know is that if it was true Hamilton had been killed and any among you suspected, then my orders were to take him not to gaol but straight to Holyrood, for Hamilton was close favourite to the King.'

'Are you arresting me?' asked Simon. 'Am I to be taken before a court of law?'

The King's man looked grim. 'That will be for the King to decide.'

'Then I must come with you. You don't need to set your fellows to bring me by force, though I'll swear on everything I hold sacred, the Bible if you'll find one for me here and now, that I know nothing of this matter.' He was still holding up his breeches. 'Could one of you lend me a belt so that I'm taken decently before the King?'

By mid-morning John Bradedge was beginning to get anxious. Surely even if his master had drunk deep and romped all night with a wench – for he knew the good doctor's proclivities only too well – he should have been stirring by this time? The landlady tapped on the door and asked if the two of them would be wanting some dinner. He put her off, saying they would be dining out.

Another hour passed. Thoroughly alarmed by now, John decided he would go and see if he could find his master. Taking his sword and hat, he set off in the direction of Dudley's lodgings. As he rounded a street corner he was horrified to see Simon being marched rapidly towards him on the other side of the road, an official-looking man at his side and several stout fellows walking behind. As he stood rooted to the spot, Simon, his face set, looked across at him but gave no sign of recognition.

Giving them just time enough to get by and to allay suspicion, John followed behind, grateful that the streets were busy and he was unlikely to be noticed. At first he had no idea where the party was going and it was not until it had almost reached the very gates of Holyrood Palace that he understood.

A small crowd outside watched the men disappear inside and John had to push his way through them. As he did so a man who was also watching with interest, detached himself from the crowd and made off down the street. John was vaguely aware of his going but any interest he might have had was overwhelmed by the enormity of the situation, for surely his master must be under arrest.

What on earth had happened? Without more ado he began to run as fast as he could back across the city to Dudley's lodgings, bent on discovering the truth. Why in God's name hadn't the doctor taken Marlowe's advice and left the city with him! When he reached the top of the street where Dudley resided he saw a knot of people standing outside his door talking animatedly. He stopped, straightened his clothes, did his best to stop panting for breath, then strolled past as if he were merely an onlooker. When he reached the doorway he halted and enquired in a mildly interested fashion what was to do.

'Black deeds,' replied a man with so ghoulish an expression that John realised it must be something very serious for he looked the kind of fellow that enjoyed hanging around a gallows.

John yawned. 'Really?' he asked in apparent disbelief. 'What then?'

'Murder, bloody murder – that's what! They say one of the King's favourites lies dead within, murdered by an English doctor!'

'God in Heaven!' gasped John.

'Aye, ye might well call on the Lord against such an iniquity,' responded the gallows'-watcher.

John thanked him and forced himself to walk slowly down to the end of the street. Then, turning the corner he ran for his life to their lodgings. God be praised, the landlady was out! He ran up to their room, and pocketed what money he could find and some small valuables of Simon's. He was going out of the front door on his way to the inn to fetch his horse just as a man who, from his clerical appearance was presumably in Holy Orders, arrived on the doorstep.

'Am I right in thinking this is where Dr Simon Forman resides?' he asked.

'Yes, yes,' John replied impatiently, 'but he's out visiting just now. I'm his man,' he explained.

The minister frowned. 'I've a letter for him from a young man I met on the Border – a Master Christopher Marlowe. When he learned I was making for Edinburgh he pleaded with me to carry the letter, even going so far as to say it was a matter of life and death. Ah well, I'll return later but he begged me to bring it here as a matter of the greatest urgency and to give it only into Dr Forman's own hands.'

'Then give it to me,' urged John. 'I'm even now going after him.'

At first the minister seemed unpersuaded but he was obviously very weary, and after being assured once again that John really *was* Dr Forman's servant, he handed the letter to him and went on his way leaving John wondering what to do with it. In normal circumstances he would not dream of opening a letter addressed to his master, but these were not normal circumstances, his master was under duress and it must have been something of real import for Marlowe to choose so unlikely a messenger.

Fearful that the next visitor might well be coming to arrest him, he left the house and went into an alleyway where he opened the letter. Its contents were brief. *Simon*, he read, *I've been almost as blind as you. Don't you see, FORD MUST BE RIVERS! But I was right that we saw this whole business the wrong way round – the deus ex machina exists. I daren't say more in case this falls into other hands but think, man, THINK! It's you who's the link in the chain and no one else. Go back to its beginning. But for God's sake, get out of Edinburgh!*

John shook his head. The words meant nothing to him; he even wondered if Marlowe was drunk when he wrote it, deranged or possibly both. He had no idea what on earth it meant, quoting fords and rivers and incomprehensible bits of Latin, along with links in chains. What was all too clear however, was that the last sentence and its warning had come too late.

He knew what he had to do. He continued on his way to the inn and asked for his horse, telling the innkeeper his master wanted him to ride out on an errand. Having mounted the mare, he trotted discreetly out towards the south of the city, ensuring he did not draw attention to himself. Then, having reached the top of the hill and the milestone to Hawick, he dug his heels into his mount, crouched low over the saddle, and set off hell-for-leather for the Border.

Chapter 14

Seven Days

Simon was marched round to the side door of the Palace, taken in through a well-guarded door, and then along a maze of corridors. He noted that once away from the splendours of the state apartments Holyrood Palace was, like many of the grand houses of the rich to which he had been called in London, dirty, rundown and even squalid. A glimpse into a kitchen made him shudder and wonder what Anna Bradedge, so clean a housewife, would have made of it.

Finally his captors opened the door to a small room and he was hustled inside. He heard the key turn in the lock then their footsteps receding and he was alone. He wondered what John Bradedge would do after seeing him being marched off in such a fashion. Knowing him, he was bound to enquire what it was all about. Would he then stay in Edinburgh to see what happened next, or set off at once for Mangerton and the Armstrongs? If he obeyed Simon's earlier instructions then it would be the latter, but how then was he going to be able to let anyone know where he was if John did return with aid?

The room was furnished with a chair and a table. He sat on the chair, his head in his hands, while his mind roved over the last few weeks. What a trail of disaster! Davie Armstrong, Richard Wilmore, the awful Danvers and now young Hamilton . . . Did they really have something in common, or was it merely the result of his overheated imagination?

Unwittingly he began to do what Marlowe had asked of him in the unseen letter that came too late, and went back over the chain of events. First, then, were the Armstrongs. Davie and Alun were quite legitimately on their way to Sir Henry Carey bearing a message from His Lordship's old Border acquaintance, Sir John Carmichael. England and Scotland were not at war and there was no reason why the Armstrongs should not have delivered their message without mishap. Yet someone, presumably because they guessed its content, decided they should never do so. But, thought Simon, since I've no idea what the message was about, it doesn't help me now.

Sir Robert Cecil had told Simon that powerful members of the government believed the young men to be Scots spies and he in league with them, which is how he had been persuaded to do what Cecil demanded of him but now, he asked himself, what exactly did Cecil himself think? He'd seemed to accept what Simon told him, but had remained deeply suspicious of the Armstrongs. From the first, Simon himself had found it hard to credit that Alun Armstrong was not speaking the truth, and he had every reason now to believe in his honesty. Yet if that was the case, why was Cecil, kept informed by what Marlowe had once described as his spider's web of intelligencers, convinced otherwise?

Then there were Davie's dying words. Up to now he'd been certain that the lad had been trying to say, 'must not tell Carey' – which had resulted in his mistrust of the Lord Chamberlain, which was only slightly lessened by the intervention of Robert Carey and his friendship with Richard Wilmore. But supposing he had been wrong, and what Davie had actually been trying to say was that he and Alun must not tell what they knew to anyone *other* than Sir Henry Carey, whatever the cost.

Which brought him to the death of Richard Wilmore, the man the Careys had chosen to assist him on his venture. Simon was still convinced that Wilmore was killed to prevent him going any further. Simon had assumed Richard's task was to find out from Sir John Carmichael what it was he wanted Carey to know, and then to help Simon in Edinburgh. But perhaps Richard was also on some other dangerous mission? He remembered how Robert Carey had insisted that he could have been frank and trusted his father, even though it was obvious Carey had no love for Cecil. For the first time Simon began to think it might have been wise for him to do so, even possibly to tell him of Davie's last words. Indeed, had he done so he could scarcely have been in a worse case than he found himself in now.

He got up and paced around the room. None of it made any sense! His head was spinning and in spite of the events of the day he was hungry, having eaten nothing since the previous evening. And what an evening. . . . In spite of himself he smiled at the remembrance of the naughty show presented by Dudley and that in turn made him recall the red-haired whore. Had she knowingly fed Danvers with poison? And gone to Simon's bed after the Masque so that some assassin could quietly murder Hamilton, even going so far as to steal his belt to put round the neck of the corpse? Which brought him back again to Seton, for he had been present on both occasions when men had died. If Seton was behind all that had happened then his object appeared to be to set up Simon as a murderer, but why? *Why?*

He was rudely interrupted from any further conjecture as the door was thrown open by a large man in a leather jerkin. 'Ye're to come wi' me,' he said, 'and don't think of trying to run away. Ye'd be spitted through the gut long before ye were out o' the building.'

They walked along a corridor, the guard's hand on his sword hilt, up a flight of stairs and along another passageway, this time carpeted. As his surroundings were becoming grander with every step they took, Simon realised they must now be in the royal apartments. They stopped at a door on their right at which his captor knocked discreetly. A grandly dressed equerry opened it to them. After a few quiet words had been exchanged, he let them into an ante-chamber with tapestried walls, fine rugs on the polished floor and an ornate carved fireplace. There was a further wait, at the end of which an inner door opened and the equerry entered, ordered Simon's guard to remain where he was, and ushered Simon through it; there, to his astonishment, he found himself in the presence of King James himself.

The King was informally dressed in a loose robe, and it was obvious he was upset for he stood staring sadly out of the window at the view of the hill opposite while sighing and wiping his eyes from time to time. He was alone except for a secretary assiduously working away at some papers at a desk in the corner, and a richly dressed much older man with an air of great authority who was standing beside the desk watching the door as Simon entered.

The King, hearing the door close, turned round. Simon bowed low and as he did so his eyes met those of James and he was

surprised to discover, in view of what he had heard from some of his
recent companions, that they were the eyes of an intelligent man,
though the face was old beyond his years. Hardly surprising, thought
Simon, considering that ever since his birth and his mother's flight
to England, the powerful Scottish lords had literally fought each
other to the death, first over who should hold the regency when
James was only a child, and later over who should have most
influence once he came of age. Again and again those in whom he
trusted had turned traitor.

The King looked at the older man who immediately came forward
and placed a chair for him to sit in before taking his place behind it.
Then the same man motioned Simon to come nearer. 'So you're the
English doctor of whom they speak,' he said. 'Your name?'

Simon bowed again. 'Simon Forman, sir, as no doubt you know.
And who might I have the honour of addressing?'

The man looked somewhat surprised at this but replied, 'I am
John Maitland, Lord Thurleston, Minister and adviser to the King.
And your business in Edinburgh, Dr Forman?'

'I imagine you must know of it too by now, for I've made no
secret of it. I came here to seek out your excellent physicians to
discuss medical matters of common interest.' He glanced uneasily at
the King who sat staring at him with little interest in what was being
said and still dabbing his eyes from time to time with a lace-edged
handkerchief.

'And what else?' enquired Maitland.

Simon looked at him as frankly as he could. 'I don't follow your
meaning, my lord.'

'Come, man, let's not play games,' barked Maitland. 'What's your
real reason for being here?'

'Only what I have told you,' Simon reiterated. 'What other
business should I have?'

'That's what I ask myself,' replied Maitland. 'What brings an
insignificant English doctor hundreds of miles merely to bandy
words with a handful of physicians?' Unknowingly, he echoed Sir
Henry Carey's disbelief at being given the same story. 'As to what
other business, you must know the King's besieged on all sides by
ambitious and calculating Englishmen determined to outwit each

other to gain his favour once he ascends the English throne. This Court seethes with intrigue as your great ones vie with each other for position. So tell me, Dr Forman, to which faction do you belong?'

'To none, my lord. I have no interest in such matters – how could I? I do not belong to the household of any great man. I am a simple physician whose time is spent ministering to the sick.'

'I don't doubt your credentials as a physician, but as to being simple . . . Tell me then, Sir Simple Physician, why death appears to stalk ever at your heels?'

'I do not know,' replied Simon desperately. 'Do you think I haven't asked myself the same question over and over? All I know, and will swear on oath, is that I've had no hand in any of this business.'

'What then of the laddie Hamilton?' The King had finally spoken. 'Can you tell us nothing of how he came to meet his end?' He was still choked for words and paused for a moment to collect himself before adding, 'And what business had you with him?'

'Why, none, sire,' Simon replied. 'I only made his acquaintance for the first time yesterday.'

'It is said you spent much time talking privately with him,' interrupted Maitland.

'We spoke only when others were about,' Simon said quietly, 'and nothing privately, nothing that couldn't have been said before anyone else. The young man was interested in matters of science and philosophy, and asked me my views on the New Learning and if I knew any of those in London who study such matters. He also expressed a wish to visit the city, not least its playhouses, having heard so much of them from one of our poets, Christopher Marlowe, who recently visited Edinburgh.'

The King looked at Simon suspiciously. 'What sciences, what philosophies?'

Aware of the King's aversion to anything smacking of witchcraft or necromancy, Simon replied carefully that Hamilton had expressed particular interest in mathematics and Biblical studies.

The King's eyes filled again with tears. 'And now the lad's dead and you can tell me nothing more?'

Simon shook his head. 'I promise I would if I could, sire. When I left him last night he was alive and well; when I awoke and

189

came downstairs this morning he was dead.'

The King turned to Maitland. 'What should we do now, John?'

'Charge him with murder and hang him,' Maitland responded briskly. 'The man's a walking menace!'

'But I didn't do it!' cried Simon. 'I'd no more hand in Hamilton's death than that of my friend Richard in Carlisle.' He looked round wildly. 'I'm telling you the truth, I swear it.'

'Aye, so you keep saying. I even think it possible, if unlikely, that you didn't,' said Maitland, 'but hanging you for Hamilton's murder will simplify matters nevertheless. It might well act as a deterrent to whoever is guilty and persuade him from further mischief.' A look of satisfaction crossed his face. 'And hanging an Englishman would go down very well with some of our people.' He came over to Simon, grabbed him roughly by the shoulder and turned him round. 'Look out of that window there at yon hill. That's Calton Hill, where we hang our felons.'

Simon, regardless of the presence of the King, wrenched himself free. 'I see only one thing, that it suits you very well to hang me. But have you considered that if you do so, far from stopping the murderer from striking again, it might encourage him, for he'll be convinced he's clever enough always to have another take the blame.'

The King seemed to accept his point but Maitland looked impatient. 'As well hang him and be done!' he growled.

Simon turned to the King and fell on his knees. 'I throw myself on your mercy, sire. Surely it would be better to discover who *did* kill Hamilton so that you can be sure the right man is brought to justice and there'll be an end to the matter. Of what possible value will it be to hang me, leaving the true murderer free? The next time he strikes it might be even nearer to you. I beseech you, allow me to see if I can discover the real culprit.'

The King motioned him to get up. 'Do you think then, Dr Forman, that you can find me the man who killed Willie Hamilton?'

'I can try, sire. I've had some small success previously in bringing such people to justice.'

The King turned to Maitland. 'What then, John?'

Maitland shrugged. 'I think it's a waste of time. But if you wish, let him see what he can do. But he must be guarded at all times.'

King James made up his mind. 'Very well, Dr Forman, I'll give you seven days from today. If you fail in your task then you know the consequences. I shall hand you over to Maitland here, and he will deal with you as he thinks fit.'

'And if you have any dreams of escaping to England, then banish them,' warned the older man, 'for one of my own men will accompany you wherever you go and stay with you in your chamber at night.'

'I may return to my lodgings then?' asked Simon, wondering if John Bradedge would still be there.

'You may not. New lodgings will be found for you and you'll be taken straight to them. A servant will be sent to collect your belongings.'

'Has anyone in authority spoken with Jack Dudley, in whose house this dreadful event took place?' asked Simon. 'For he, I know, believes in my innocence.'

Maitland gave another of his malicious smiles, seemed about to say something, then desisted. 'Dudley? Ah yes, a relation of your Earl of Essex, is he not? He is quite a hothead, your Earl. It's said he claims so great is his favour with your Queen, that she will make him her heir. Is it true?'

'I've no idea,' sighed Simon. 'As I said before, I've no interest in such things and know nothing of Court gossip.'

It was clear the audience was at an end, for King James waved his hand towards the door, whereupon Maitland ushered Simon out of the chamber and back into the small ante-room where his guard was still waiting.

'How am I to look properly into so serious a matter if I'm to be guarded day and night?' demanded Simon as soon as they were through the door.

'That,' replied Maitland, 'is your business, Dr Forman, not mine. Oh, and one more thing. Do not attempt anything untoward during your investigations, such as trying to seek help for we also have our intelligencers and they will watch your every move. Now, you will wait here in the Palace while arrangements are made to lodge you suitably and I will bring you your custodian.'

With that, Simon was taken back to the room in which he had been put on his arrival at Holyrood and left to his own devices. An hour or so later Maitland himself returned, followed by a thickset, unpleasant-looking fellow with a long scar running down the side of his face.

'This man,' Maitland told him, 'is Tam, a member of my own household. You will never be out of his sight. Neither wife nor mistress could stay closer to you than he will over the next seven days.'

'But how can I possibly go about the town accompanied all the time by a man such as he? He looks like a villain and,' he wrinkled his nose, 'he stinks like a sewer.' Maitland said nothing. 'I take it I *am* allowed out?'

'I have already told you, Dr Forman, that how you conduct your enquiries is no concern of mine. Mine is to ensure you present yourself again for judgement. It was you who persuaded the King to let you try to find a supposed other murderer, but I am under no obligation to assist you. You must manage as best you can. There's just one more thing I'd like to know.'

'And what's that?' Simon felt utterly weary.

'I'm told you're Carey's man. Is that so?' Then Maitland added, somewhat surprisingly, 'At least Carey's thought to have been an honest man when he was Border Warden.'

'I'm no one's man but my own,' Simon reiterated.

'I doubt that,' sneered Maitland. 'None of you English are your own men. Good day, Dr Forman.' He reached the door then stopped. 'I understand we're soon to have young Carey on the Border. And speaking of the Borders, don't look to the Armstrongs or any of the other bands of savages for assistance. It will help neither you nor them. The time is soon coming when the Borders will be cleaned of such.' And with that, he left Simon alone with Tam.

Tam jerked his head towards the open door and Simon went through it, his unwanted companion close at his side. They left the Palace and were soon walking through the narrow streets and alleys around St Giles Church until they stopped outside a tall, grim, grey house, one of a row. It had a heavy iron-studded front door and high windows more suited to a fortress than a dwelling place. Tam rapped on the door with the heavy iron knocker and Simon heard from within the sound of stout shoes clattering on a flagged floor. The woman who opened the house door to them was hardly more prepossessing than Tam. Of middle years, she was dressed in black from head to foot, apart from the plain white collar and cuffs that marked her as one of the Puritan tendency. Her hair was scraped back in a bun and her expression was dour.

She showed them upstairs to a bleak room with a high, barred window, furnished only with two pallet beds, a table and two uncomfortable-looking wooden chairs. A wooden bucket in a corner was, presumably, to accommodate their personal needs. Beside one of the beds was a pile of Simon's belongings and it was obvious from the way they had been thrown down that they had been subjected to close scrutiny. Looking round, Simon thought he would have preferred Hermitage, for during his brief imprisonment there he'd had the estimable John Bradedge to bear him company.

The woman left them, to reappear a few minutes later with a tray of rough fare. At least they're going to feed me, thought Simon, as he fell on the food. 'Have I leave to come and go as I please?' he asked his guard, for the man had hardly communicated so far.

'No wi'out me,' he grunted.

'I know that very well,' replied Simon testily, 'but I'm not likely to get far if I sit around here for the next week. I must go out and talk to people.' He found his purse among the scattered belongings on the floor and was relieved to discover that his small remaining amount of money had not been taken. He picked it up and put it in his pocket then looked for his rapier and dagger, but both were missing. Whoever had searched his goods had also left him unarmed. 'So,' he said, 'we'll go first to Jack Dudley's lodgings.'

Tam sat where he was and folded his arms. 'Ye've to go nowhere today. I've been told to keep ye here until morning.'

'But I only have seven days in which to complete my task!' shouted Simon. 'And this first one is already more than halfway over.'

But the man was obstinate: Simon was not allowed out until the next day. He had supper in his room and a candle for when it was dark. Tam, meanwhile, would be downstairs and when night came would take the other bed. Having made this announcement, he went out, locked the door and left Simon alone.

Simon paced up and down the small chamber, half mad with frustration. It was obvious that Maitland was going to do everything in his power to prevent him from succeeding in his task. Used as he was to being more or less in control of events, he now felt the trap closing in around him, unable to see any way out. He could not pretend to have lived a blameless life – who could? – but never in his worst nightmares had he imagined he would ever be threatened with the scaffold not once but twice within the same month. It seemed that he had temporarily escaped death in London only to find it waiting for him in Edinburgh – and he had thought himself unfortunate when he first fell into the hands of the Borderers!

Thoughts of those rough men made him wonder what Maitland's last remarks signified; presumably that he knew of his relationship with the Armstrongs. Did he also know of his meetings with Sir John Carmichael? As hour followed slow hour he became calmer and forced himself to think it all through again.

So, he had a definite suspect, Edward Seton – a man about whom no one seemed to know very much except that he was a good host and apparently tended towards favouring the Earl of Essex. He had been present on both occasions in Edinburgh when a man had died, and also common to both deaths was the appearance of the red-haired whore. Seton had spoken of hearing the news of Richard's death from a relative in Carlisle, but Simon was more and more inclined to think it likely that the details of the murder had been related to him at first-hand by its perpetrator, which now seemed likely to have been James Ford, who was really Seton's servant and had been in the kitchen of his house when Danvers died. That all seemed reasonably straightforward if difficult to prove.

As to motive, then he was sure he was right. Seton had his own reasons for not wanting them to come to Edinburgh, and by having Richard, who was actually known to be 'Carey's man', killed had assumed Simon would not continue his journey. When he did then every effort had to be made to remove him as well. He brushed aside Marlowe's argument that it would have been simpler to have had him dispatched in a dark alley. Thinking over their conversations about dark forces and Gods in the Machine he decided Marlowe, so subtle of mind and far more involved in the world of intelligencers, had let his imagination run riot. On one score, however, he had been right: staying in Edinburgh could yet prove fatal.

He passed a restless, almost sleepless night, unhelped by his companion who snored even louder than John Bradedge – but at least John kept himself clean and decent. When Simon protested to the landlady about having to share a room with a filthy fellow who stank, she told him he was lucky not to be sharing a bed! At long last the morning came, a tray of breakfast was brought up and finally Simon was allowed out.

He made at once for Dudley's house, his unpleasant guard trudging at his side, looking out for the red-haired whore. He must ask Dudley who she was and where he could find her. He gulped in the fresh air; it seemed like a week rather than hours since the previous morning. They arrived outside Dudley's house to a scene of great activity. Outside was a carriage, into which was being carried a growing pile of boxes, while a groom holding a separate horse stood a little to the side. It all had the appearance of an imminent departure.

'What's happening?' Simon asked a servant, full of foreboding.

'Better ask the master,' he replied.

The door stood open and Simon went in, Tam at his heels. A plump woman, looking flustered, came down the staircase and Simon recognised her as Dudley's housekeeper. 'Is Master Dudley at home?' asked Simon.

She nodded and looked behind her up the stairs. 'I'll see if he'll receive you,' she said, and retraced her steps. A few minutes later Dudley came down to them, dressed for a journey, with long boots, overcoat and whip. He shook Simon's hand and looked wonderingly at Tam.

'I'll explain later,' said Simon after they had exchanged greetings.

'I'm told you were taken before the King,' said Dudley.

'I was, and he's much distressed by Hamilton's death. I also saw Maitland, the Lord Thurleston, who appears to have much influence with His Majesty.'

Dudley whistled. 'Did you? A chilling man and one to avoid.'

'If you're lucky enough to be able to do so,' Simon agreed.

Dudley looked through the open door to the carriage. 'Well, Simon, I'm relieved to see you safe and sound but you must forgive me. As you see, I'm about to leave and must be off.'

Simon also looked at the carriage. His suspicion had been correct. 'Do you travel far?' he asked slowly. 'Will you be away for long?'

Dudley gave a hollow laugh. 'Oh, I'll be away for long, all right. I've been ordered out of the country.'

'God's Blood! On what grounds?'

'For presenting obscene and lascivious entertainments. It seems one of our number present the other night made it their business to go to the Palace and tell of what they had seen.'

Chapter 15

A Desperate Search

'Sweet Jesu!' exclaimed Simon. 'So that's why I wasn't allowed out last night.'

'If they'd had their way, I'd have been gone yesterday evening,' Dudley told him. 'It was all I could do to persuade them I must have twenty-four hours to settle my affairs and pack my baggage.' He stopped. 'I see from your face this is bad news.'

'Can you at least spare me a few minutes?' pleaded Simon. 'It's not too much to say it's a matter of life and death. I've been given just six days from now to discover who did kill Hamilton, or I'll share his fate.'

'God aid you then!'

'I'd rather hoped *you* might. This fellow here,' he gestured towards Tam, 'is one of Maitland's men set to guard me. I can neither eat, sleep nor, most likely, defecate without the fellow watching my every move and so I can never be alone, but even so I'd hoped we could talk. There are questions I need to ask.'

Dudley considered this for a moment, then he went to the door and told the groom with the horse and the coachmen to walk the horses and he would be with them in a little while. After which he turned back to Simon. 'Come and have a glass of wine to bid me good luck on my journey. And as for you,' he called over to Tam, 'keep your distance. You stink like a kennel.'

He took them through into the room in which the masque had taken place. 'Can that oaf read?' he whispered in Simon's ear. Simon said he didn't know but imagined not.

Dudley smiled then added quietly, 'We'll try him and see.' So saying, he took from a shelf an inkwell, quill and paper and placed them on a table, after which he went to the door and called to the housekeeper to bring him a bottle of wine and two glasses.

A sudden noise outside in the street caused Tam to look out of the window, whereupon Dudley scribbled away at what appeared to be a laundry list. Then he sat back. 'Now,' he said with obvious formality, 'how can I help you, Dr Forman?'

'Could you tell me the names of all those who were in your house throughout the night Hamilton died, including the servants?'

Dudley made great play of slowly dragging them out of his memory, meanwhile rapidly writing the names down on a piece of paper which he pushed over to Simon while Tam's back was still turned. Then he placed the laundry list in a prominent place.

'So eight of us stayed the night,' Simon noted, 'along with six of the girls?'

'That's right, and the rest of the party went home as did two girls. I saw them out of the front door myself. Then I locked and bolted the door behind them.'

'And what of the other girls? They were gone when I came downstairs.'

'They left very early, including your red-headed siren! One of the servants said he let them out near six o'clock. There was no one else about.'

'And the servants? How trustworthy are they?'

Dudley considered this. 'I can't pretend I know any of them well, as I hired them with the house, but they seem to be honest enough and I've had no cause to complain. There's Mary, that's the house-keeper; Agnes, the cook, two young maids and two men who help in the kitchen and do any heavy work. They were all here overnight and can vouch for each other, since Mary and Agnes share one attic, the two young maids the other and the men sleep in a room off the kitchen.'

At this point Tam lost interest in what was happening outside, turned round and saw the paper on Dudley's desk.

'Here,' he said, 'have ye writ down those names Forman asked for? If so, then let me see. I've to read everything that gets set down and then take it to His Lordship.'

'You can read then?' Dudley queried, making his disbelief obvious.

Tam hesitated. That was indeed what he had told his master, having learned to pick out the odd word here and there, but he had not reckoned on having to prove it. However, his mind worked slowly and he decided to say that he could.

'Here,' said Dudley, holding out the laundry list at arm's length. 'Read it out loud if you like. No, go back over there,' he added, putting his handkerchief to his nose. Tam squinted at the paper and frowned. After a minute or two Dudley banged the table. 'Well, get on with it! I've not got all day. It begins with the name William Gavin. It's clear enough, surely?'

Tam peered at the paper again. 'I know, I know. William Gavin,' he read, very slowly. It was obvious he could go no further. Then he folded it up and pushed it angrily into the purse he carried at his belt. 'I can read the rest without doing it for you so I'll take it to His Lordship in case it's important, and I'll have any other bits of writing ye might do, Master Dudley.' Simon and Dudley exchanged a speaking look and smiled as they thought what Maitland would say when Tam triumphantly presented him with a laundry list beginning with eight pairs of hose and two sets of linen underdrawers. But at least it had usefully proved the man was scarcely literate.

The housekeeper brought in a tray on which was set a bottle of wine and two glasses. She entered just after Simon had told Dudley of his meeting with the wool merchant, James Ford, and how he suspected that he and the man in Seton's kitchen who had made trouble for him, were one and the same. 'I suppose you had no such fellow about your place here?' he asked.

'Medium height, beardless you say when you saw him last, and with a healed wound on one ear.' Dudley turned to the housekeeper. 'Have you seen anyone of that description, Mary?'

She shook her head. 'No, sir.'

'There were no casual people especially hired for that night?' asked Simon.

Dudley smiled. 'Only the girls in the Masque, and they could hardly have smuggled a man in among their number, given the nature of the performance! And I explained to Dr Forman, Mary, that I personally locked and bolted the front door after the last folk left, and you can verify that the kitchen was made secure likewise, can you not?'

The housekeeper's face bore witness to her disapproval of what had gone on that night, but she agreed that the bolt on the kitchen door had been securely in place and that it was not opened again until the morning when 'those brazen lassies' had been let out. One of the male servants slept in the kitchen and would have heard anyone attempting to unlock it. Dudley thanked her. 'You can go now, Mary. I'll settle up for the wine before I leave.'

'Tell me,' asked Simon after she had gone, 'is there much friction between the young English and Scots here?'

'A little. There's bound to be, but no worse than between the Scots themselves – there's a long history of feuding there. But there's rarely more than a dozen or so English here at any one time, though it probably seems more to you because you've moved mostly in our own circle.'

'No simmering quarrel that you know of between young bloods? Quarrels over a woman when in drink, imagined slights, that kind of thing?'

'If that were the case I imagine at worst it would be either a sudden coming to blows or a duel. Certainly not a cord round the neck in the dark.'

'The Earl of Essex,' began Simon delicately, only too aware of Dudley's connections with the Earl, 'is there really a great deal of intrigue on his behalf?'

Dudley looked rueful. 'The Earl is a rash young man with mighty ambitions, and I say this as one who is related to him. I'll go further and be honest with you. He's quite capable of provoking trouble from a distance; intrigue is second nature to him but unfortunately, he's not very skilled at it. He's too impetuous, his temper is quick and when in a rage he says things that would be better left unsaid and so has made many enemies.' He paused for a moment. 'Intrigue? Obviously there is, but not more than on behalf of any others so far as I'm aware. Personally I think it all rather foolish.'

'I'm told Edward Seton is sympathetic towards him,' Simon continued.

'Maybe, but no one's quite sure where Seton's interests lie, he being half Scots, half English – though he seems generally to favour the English causes.' He frowned. 'Do you suspect him then?' So Simon briefly explained how he had come to that conclusion, but Dudley looked doubtful. 'Even if it is as you say and he wanted to prevent you finding out some hidden matter in Edinburgh, I can't understand his need to go to such lengths. I also ask myself what such a matter would be, since no doubt men like Sir Robert Cecil have their intelligencers here to tell them all they want to know. So far as I'm aware, there is nothing touching Essex which is of such moment.'

'All I know,' Simon told him, 'is that an important message was sent from Scotland to Sir Henry Carey, and that the man who took it was killed before he could reach him – which suggests there is some deeper matter here that someone does not want known in London. Do you think Seton capable of murder?' he persisted.

Dudley shrugged. 'Possibly. I suppose many men could be, given sufficient reason. As to Seton, I've only known him these last few months since coming to Edinburgh. He has money for, as you saw, he entertains lavishly and often. He enjoys gossip, being at the centre of things, possibly even a little intrigue, but murder . . .? I agree he provides a link of sorts between the deaths of Wilmore, Danvers and Hamilton, but that could as easily be chance. Consider, your own peril rests on those who believe the same of you for more or less the same reasons, yet I believe you to be innocent. I suppose it's possible Seton's playing some deep game. If he is, I trust it isn't on behalf of my own patron.'

'I assumed all you Essex men were of a single persuasion.'

Dudley sighed. 'You might well. But the Earl is given to telling one of us to do one thing and another something altogether different as the mood takes him. He is singularly inconstant.'

'Marlowe said no one in this city was to be trusted,' Simon commented.

'He wasn't far off the truth. I fear you've opened up a hornet's nest.'

There was a loud snore from the other side of the room. Tam, who had been sitting on the floor as he had become increasingly bored with the conversation, had fallen asleep. 'Look carefully at the list

I've given you,' whispered Dudley. 'Two of the men who were here for the masque and whose names I've underlined have never declared whose cause they support. It might be worth looking into. And all this while the Queen is still in good health and has all her faculties. I dread to think what it will be like when she is in decline.' He stood up. 'I'm sorry, but now I really must go.'

'The red-haired whore,' Simon remembered suddenly, 'she who I took to bed. Do you know her name and where she might be found?'

Dudley grinned. 'In spite of your dangers you haven't lost your taste for a tumble then?'

'The way I feel at the moment I'd probably refuse an offer from the real Helen of Troy,' groaned Simon, 'but there are matters on which I'd like to question her too.'

'All I know,' returned Dudley, aiming a kick at the dozing Tam as he went towards the door, 'is that she calls herself Jeannie and can usually be found in the alleyways close to St Giles.'

Simon thanked him profusely and Dudley shook him warmly by the hand. 'God's Speed, Simon. I wish you all possible luck in finding the real culprit, for I don't believe you murdered Hamilton or anyone else. I'll see if there's anything I can do when I get back home, but that won't be for about ten days.'

Simon sighed. 'By that time I might well be hanging on a gibbet!'

'Pray to God not!' They went outside, Tam grumbling along behind them.

'You travel by carriage then?' asked Simon.

'It's mainly full of baggage. I intend riding beside it most of the way, but it gets tedious and makes one saddle sore!'

'Then let's hope you don't encounter a band of Reivers looking for booty!' said Simon. Dudley grimaced as he mounted his horse then, touching his hat, trotted off behind the carriage.

'Am I allowed into a tavern?' enquired Simon of his unwanted shadow as Dudley disappeared.

Tam shrugged. 'I've nae been told ye canna,' he said and spat.

'Well, let's find one then. I'll buy you a quart of ale if you'll allow me some time to think. You can sit by the door while I take a far corner so that you can prevent me from trying to escape.'

Ten minutes later, Simon was sitting, pewter pot in hand, deep in thought. He had to admit he was disappointed at Dudley's reaction to his suspicions of Seton, but then he did not know the whole of the story. He sat in his corner so long that eventually Tam loomed up in front of him. 'Ye've had yer drink,' he grunted. 'We'll be away, back to the lodgings.'

Simon looked at him in amazement. 'But the morning's scarce over and there are many people yet to see. How can I do what I've been asked to do if I'm kept locked up most of the time?'

'The master said ye'd only to be let out once in the day,' returned Tam obstinately, 'and he didna say for how long. Now ye've been out.' He pulled a serviceable dagger out of its sheath. 'He also told me if ye try and get away I've to kill you, and that it wouldna count against me.'

It was obvious every possible obstacle was to be put in his way to ensure he failed in his task, thought Simon savagely. However, on his way back he insisted on being allowed to explore the narrow lanes and alleyways, Tam dragging along protesting at his heels and demanding to know what he was looking for.

'For a red-haired whore,' Simon told him. 'You keep your eyes open for her too.'

Like Dudley Tam misunderstood him. 'Whores, is it!' he exclaimed piously. 'Ye'd surely be better spending the time left to ye in this life on yer knees pleading with the Lord to spare ye from the everlasting fire than lusting after whores!'

Simon did not attempt to disillusion him but his search was in vain. There were plenty of girls about, though none he recognised from the Masque nor was there any shortage of offers for a wide variety of services, one or two young women hazarding the opinion that whatever it was 'Jeannie' could do for him, they could surpass it. Disillusioned and depressed he allowed himself to be led back to his prison. Again a tray of food was brought to him and Tam shuffled off after locking him in. Hours stretched ahead of him, crucial hours when he needed to be out and about seeing what he could discover about Seton and his movements. By the time he was let out again there would only be five days left.

Left alone he pulled Dudley's list out of his pocket. On it Dudley had written the names of the other guests who had been present at the Masque, with a mark against those who had left around midnight. This reminded him that Marlowe too had given him a list of names and information to tell Cecil. Where had he put it? Had Maitland's men found it among his belongings? Simon rummaged through them without success and in growing panic, until he remembered he had put it away in a small pocket on the inside of his doublet.

He unrolled the piece of paper and compared the names on that list with those on Dudley's. Yes, Seton's name was on both, as were a number of others. Some of those listed were known to him, some strange, but by combining the two he would have a reasonable document to give Cecil if he ever reached London.

Simon had another night of uneasy sleep with long periods of wakefulness, during which he planned how he was going to proceed the next day, finally deciding he would take the bull by the horns and actually call on Seton himself, being careful not to voice his suspicions. It was dangerous but with so short a time at his disposal, he had little to lose.

The city was wrapped in mist and a fine rain was falling as they set off the next morning. 'Where now?' grunted Tam.

'To the house of Master Seton and thence to that of Dr Richie.'

'I dinna know if ye can visit twa places in one day unless ye're quick about it,' Tam stated.

'You brought me home too soon yesterday,' raged Simon. 'I don't believe you were told how many calls I should make, and I'll take as long as I like. If I'm not to be allowed to go wherever's necessary, then kill me now and be done with it!'

For an awful moment he thought Tam might take him at his word, but in the end the man shrugged and let it pass and they walked together in silence until they reached Seton's house. The servant who answered the door looked at Tam with disgust, telling them in no uncertain terms to go round the back to the tradesmen's entrance and to be quick about it – to which Simon replied in his grandest manner that he had business with Master Seton and that he would wait where he was.

'I'll go see if Master Seton can see ye then,' replied the servant doubtfully. He returned a few minutes later and grudgingly ushered them inside the hall, telling them to wait by the door until the master came down to them. As the minutes passed, Simon began to feel that perhaps his visit was after all unwise, and he was just deliberating whether or not to leave when Seton appeared. He stopped short at the sight of Tam in obvious disgust and wrinkled his nose. 'Who's this filthy fellow, Forman?'

'The man Lord Thurleston has provided to guard me,' replied Simon, leaving it unclear in what capacity.

'Then wait outside in the yard, man!' ordered Seton.

'I'm to stay wi' the doctor wherever he is,' responded Tam.

'I'll see he doesn't leave by this door and you can guard the back,' Seton retorted. 'Anyway this matter, whatever it is, will not take long.' Reluctantly Tam did as he was told. If only the person he'd been left alone with wasn't also the man he suspected, thought Simon, he might even have tried to escape.

'Well, Dr Forman,' said Seton coldly, 'I can't imagine what you want of me. Indeed, I'm surprised you are free to go abroad at all in the circumstances.'

'I persuaded the King that it was better, since I did not kill Hamilton or anyone else, that I tried my best to discover who did. And that's my intention.'

Seton looked at him with derision. 'And are you succeeding?'

'I'm doing my best.'

Seton laughed unpleasantly. 'I doubt your best will be good enough. Whatever you discover is unlikely to be believed, coming as it does from one linked to so many deaths and few, I imagine, will want to assist you in your task.' Simon did his best to respond civilly, informing Seton that Jack Dudley had already given him much assistance. Seton seemed surprised. 'Dudley? I understood he'd already left Edinburgh. He took a risk with the Masque in this puritanical city. Someone must have spoken of it.'

'It seems somewhat savage to be sent from a country merely for putting on a show with a few scantily clad girls,' Simon commented.

'Had he been a Scot caught doing the same thing, the punishment would have been far harsher,' Seton responded. 'For less than that men have been set in the stocks or put on the penitents' stool in the marketplace, dressed in a sack and with a notice around their necks describing their sin, before being publicly whipped. But I agree it was harmless enough. Now, will you get to the point! I've many affairs needing my attention.'

Simon decided to plunge in. 'There was a servant working in your kitchen the day after Danvers died; he lied – said I had taken my herbs and medicines away with me when I had not. Who was he? When my man came to enquire about him the next day, it seems he'd disappeared.'

Seton looked blank. 'I have no idea. Servants come and go and I leave the hiring of them to my housekeeper. Why should I know his name? And why do you want to know?'

'My man recalled seeing that he had recently suffered a minor wound to his ear, which had resulted in a nick of flesh taken out of his earlobe. On our way to Carlisle, my companion and I met a man purporting to be a wool buyer, who went by the name of Ford; he too had just such a wound – I treated it myself. It seems strange to me that there should be two such men with similar wounds. Even more so that Ford, if that was his name, was in Carlisle when Wilmore died, and was your servant here when Danvers was taken ill.'

'I see,' exclaimed Seton, realisation dawning. 'You somehow want to implicate *me*. Are you seriously suggesting I set this man Ford on to murder your companion in Carlisle and had him here also when you came to supper – invited quite unexpectedly – ready to poison one of my guests, for the Devil knows what reason? Ah yes, no doubt you think I strangled Hamilton too or had this sinister associate of mine do it for me – disguised as a naked girl, perhaps?' So far from being enraged he seemed almost amused.

'It is as likely as that I did it,' said Simon, 'yet Lord Thurleston wants to hang me for it.'

'And hang you might well,' Seton agreed, looking at Simon with contempt, 'and with my blessing you, and all the rest of the troublemakers who come from over the Border. As to blaming it on me to save your own skin, you're crazed! If you try and spread this tale abroad, no one will believe you. Least of all Maitland, of that I can promise you. Now get out of my house before I have you thrown out.'

Sweet Jesu, thought Simon, as he and Tam trudged off towards Dr

Richie's house, his next port of call. What in God's good name prompted me to go to Seton and so give him warning of what I suspect? He was surprised how immediately Seton had realised the import of his questions. Obviously he was quicker-witted than he had thought. It could also be because, being guilty, he had immediately jumped to the right conclusion. But he felt uneasy all the same. Seton had been angry, but not in the way one might have suspected – and what did he mean when he said Maitland would believe him 'least of all'?

By the time they reached Dr Richie's however, Simon had convinced himself that Seton's reaction had been one of guilt.

Dr Richie, when applied to for help, was as courteous as ever though obviously both cautious and uneasy. He sympathised with Simon's predicament but made it clear that he kept himself strictly apart from political matters and was unhappy at the prospect of becoming involved in what he recognised as dangerous ground.

'I quite understand your feelings since I share them completely,' Simon pleaded. 'Which is why I find my present situation one out of a nightmare. For here I am in a strange place, accused of heaven knows what, and unable to convince people of my innocence. Could you at least send word to Lord Thurlestone on my behalf that you do not believe I had anything to do with Danvers' death? Your assistance in trying to counter at least that charge against me would be most helpful for, by the love of our Lord, I've no other friends in this benighted city!'

Dr Richie looked doubtful. 'I can, though whether my opinion will have any weight I do not know – though I've said ever since the sad event took place that I do not believe poison was involved and that you treated the man quite properly, said so indeed to one of the King's men who came to ask me about it, and it may be that he has already informed Lord Thurleston. As to the rest, I can make no judgement – although from your demeanour and the discussions we have held together I find it hard to believe that you would murder men in cold blood.'

'So you will help me?'

Dr Richie agreed that he would. 'I will write to Maitland now and tell him what I told the officer – that in my eyes you are innocent.' And with that Simon had to be content.

The drizzle had given place to heavy rain by the time they left the doctor's house, and people were hurrying along the streets, covering themselves as best they could against the wet. Tam had insisted they return to their lodgings in spite of Simon's protests, and they were halfway back when Simon's eyes met those of a young man, his head covered with a sack, who was staring at them from the other side of the street. Simon stopped in his tracks.

'What's the matter, why are ye stopping? Are ye after another whore?' grumbled Tam. 'D'ye want us to get soaked to the death?'

Surely, thought Simon, surely that's Alun Armstrong!

Tam pushed him from behind in a way that must have made it clear he was under duress. Simon's eyes held those of Alun for a second. 'Very well,' he said, raising his voice as loudly as he could. 'Since you give me no choice, take me back to my prison.'

'What d'ye mean prison? Ye're no in prison,' countered Tam, looking around to see who might be listening.

'It might as well be,' shouted Simon, 'since I've no way of getting out of it.'

Several people turned to look at them in spite of the rain. 'Shouting isn't going to help ye,' said Tam. 'Come away back now, or d'ye want me to drag ye?' They set off once again, this time Simon walking as slowly as he could, not daring to look behind him, until Tam caught him by the shoulder and hurried him along at a smart pace. His mind raced. Somehow he must communicate with Alun immediately, but how? Then he had an idea and stood still again, apparently getting his breath. 'I want paper and pen when we get back.'

'Ye're to have nothing except yer food,' Tam responded.

'Listen, blockhead,' fumed Simon, 'I need to write a letter to your master. *Now*. Since you claim you can read, then do so before you give it him. I don't care, I just want him to have it as soon as possible.' Tam said no more and when they arrived back he locked Simon in the room without another word, but shortly afterwards his landlady opened the door with a tray on which was not only his dinner but also an inkwell, pen, sand-pot and paper.

'Ye're to have these,' she told him without a smile. 'I'll be back by and by for your letter and I *can* read. Unlike yon loon downstairs.' The problem now was that, having used the excuse to write to Maitland as a means of acquiring ink and paper, he now had to think up something to say. Finally he decided he would use the missive to complain about the restrictions placed on him, along with hints that his investigations were beginning to bear fruit.

My Lord, he wrote, *I have been pursuing my enquiries with the utmost difficulty since your fellow informs me that I'm able to leave my lodgings only once a day, and that for a limited time. That was not what I understood to be the case when I was given so brief a span in which to conduct my investigations. I would ask, therefore, that you allow me to spend as much time as is necessary outside my room and not to place any restraint on my movements.*

However, in spite of this very real handicap, I have discovered a person here in Edinburgh who could well either himself, or through his agent, have carried out the murders of both Wilmore and Danvers, and very possibly Hamilton. No doubt he will deny his guilt, but I beg that you give me the freedom for which I ask to allow me to make out a convincing case against him. What would it profit you to hang me and leave him free to kill again?

Your obedient servant, Simon Forman, Physician, Member of the College of Physicians of London and of the University of Cambridge.

He read it through, sanded it carefully, and put it aside to wait for his landlady's return. She read it in front of him then nodded. 'I doubt it'll help you,' she said in her dour fashion, 'but I'll see he gets it,' and left the room, taking the tray and writing materials with her. As soon as she had gone, Simon lugged the table across the floor to beneath the high window, and climbed on to it. He could just see out into the street below. On the opposite side of it, still shrouded in his sack, stood Alun Armstrong deep in conversation with another man, also muffled against the weather but recognisable as John Bradedge.

At that moment they looked up and Simon waved, motioning them to stay still. Then he removed from his pocket the small piece of paper he had neatly cut from the end of the sheet given to him by his landlady, and on which he had written a brief note. After taking his purse and emptying out most of its contents, he pushed the paper inside and dropped it out of the window. The street was quiet and empty. John Bradedge detached himself from the wall against which he was leaning, looked up and down to see if anyone was about, then strolled casually across, picked up the purse, flourished it once in the air and put it into his pocket.

Chapter 16

The Red-haired Whore

Hoping his would-be rescuers understood the position he was in, Simon had scribbled on the note that he now had only four days to clear his name by finding out who really had killed Hamilton, and that everything was being done to ensure he did not succeed. His only hope therefore lay in flight, but if they were to spirit him away they had to get rid of his gaoler. Tam, he wrote, slept in his room all night and accompanied him everywhere he went, but did leave the house from time to time when Simon was securely locked and bolted into his room.

That night when he finally fell asleep he had a dream which stayed with him the next morning. He thought about it as he dressed, for he set much store by dreams. Years ago, in Italy, he had read an Italian tale – *Il Pecerone* – in which three suitors to a King's daughter had to make a crucial choice. They were presented with three caskets and they had to choose the right one to gain the lady. As he recalled it, the lady had assisted the man she wanted to make the right choice.

In his dream he stood alone before three caskets, and a woman who seemed at one time to be Avisa and at another the red-haired whore of the Masque, informed him that if he chose right it would bring good fortune; if wrong, disaster. She seemed to be guiding him in the right direction, but when the moment came, he turned away and opened the wrong one. Why on earth, he thought, did a tale read so many years ago come back now to haunt his dreams? If it had a meaning then he was unable to understand what it was.

He shook his head and after his meagre breakfast told Tam he was determined to go where he liked and when. He took out the list of names Dudley had given him, of those who had stayed the night at his house, against two of which he had put their direction; Simon decided to begin with them. At the time he took the red-haired whore to bed with him he'd thought himself fortunate to have a small chamber to himself, for he knew some of the others were sharing a room or even a bed. Possibly among them was Seton, which could mean that the other might have noticed, had he left the room for any length of time during the night.

It was still raining. This, Tam assured him, was more like what he might expect than the hot weather that had heralded his arrival. Simon could hardly bear to look at Tam; he made his skin crawl and Simon was beginning to feel that he would be joined for life to his malodorous companion. He looked round carefully once out in the street, but there was no obvious sign of either Alun or John; however, he took his time walking to his first destination in case either of them were watching out to see where he went. Once or twice he did feel as if he were being followed and turned to look, but there was no one behind him resembling either Alun or John.

The first visit was fruitless, for the man simply refused to see him in spite of his pleading with a servant that the matter was urgent. They had all been enthusiastic and friendly enough when they'd wanted their horoscopes cast for nothing, thought Simon as he was firmly turned away, but now he was in trouble no one wanted anything to do with him. He had more luck with the second man, who did allow him into his house, albeit at first with reluctance and yet again Simon rehearsed his predicament.

The young man heard him out but looked bewildered. 'I can't see how I'm supposed to be able to help you,' he said when Simon reached the end of his story. 'I trust you don't think *I'd* anything to do with Hamilton's death?'

'No,' soothed Simon. 'I'm merely trying to find out if anyone heard or saw anything untoward that night.'

His host looked a trifle sheepish. 'I can't say I did. I confess I'd drunk so deep I was even unable to avail myself of one of the girls, for I fell into a heavy sleep the moment my head hit the pillow. Indeed, I was hardly disturbed by the fellow in the other bed noisily taking his pleasure.'

'Was that Seton?' enquired Simon.

He shook his head. 'Seton was in the chamber across the passageway. I do just about recall seeing him going into it.'

Simon sighed and was preparing to leave since there seemed little more to be gained, when his host remembered something. 'I don't know why you're so interested in Seton, but I'm almost sure now I think of it that he shared his room with one of the Scots lads. I think his name's Fraser and I can tell you where he lodges – in the small court behind the inn nearest the castle, over a cobbler's. I'm sorry I can't help you more,' he added, 'but that's all I know. I fear this is no place for an Englishman in your circumstances. No doubt it would suit some of those close to the King to blame one of us, however innocent.' On which gloomy note Simon left.

In spite of Tam's protestations Simon insisted he continue following up the information he had just obtained. The streets were more crowded now and at one stage he thought he caught a glimpse of Alun some way behind, but could not be sure and did not want to risk drawing attention to him by stopping to see if he was right.

He found the cobbler without difficulty. Yes, he said, a young gentleman did lodge above him and had his own entrance at the rear of the premises, but when Simon knocked at the door he was told by a pert maidservant that Master Fraser was from home and not likely to be back until the next day as he had gone hawking with friends.

Thoroughly disheartened Simon debated what to do next. 'I'm going to have a drink,' he told Tam, 'whether you want me to or not. I'm damp to the bone after tramping backwards and forwards across Edinburgh, and thirsty. You'll have to drag me through the streets by main force if you want to prevent me doing so.'

'What do I tell my master? He said ye could go knocking on folks' doors, not lazing in taverns and chasing whores. He's already scolded me when I told him what ye'd been up to.'

So Tam reported regularly back to Maitland then. Every day? Twice a day? But since Tam made no move to prevent him, it looked as if the man's objections were becoming little more than a ritual – which could mean one of two things: either he was not prepared any longer to argue every point or that he knew none of it mattered as Simon's fate was a foregone conclusion. He pushed his way into the

213

first tavern they came to, half-hoping that miraculously either John or Alun would be in there but neither was.

As he drank deep he wondered what plans they might be making to try to rescue him and if so, with time so fast running out, when. Any optimism he might have felt, of definitely being able to prove Seton's guilt, was evaporating faced with the magnitude of the task. And even if he did, suppose Maitland refused to believe him? It might be that this whole business was nothing more than an elaborate charade so when he was brought to court, found guilty and hanged, it could be put abroad both in Scotland and England, that the murderous English doctor had been given every opportunity to clear his name but had manifestly failed to do so.

This, as he'd said to his friends in his note, left him a stark choice. If he delayed to the very last minute in the hope of finding convincing proof that Seton was the murderer and either did not succeed or Maitland did not accept it, then it was almost certain he would be hanged. Yet if he escaped before the time was up there would certainly be a hue and cry for him; if he was caught the outcome would be even more certain, for his running away could be held up as proof positive of his guilt.

He looked at the list Dudley had given him again. If he tried to see anyone else, it would mean having to discover where they lived, which could take hours, and the day was already well on. So finally he decided to make yet another attempt to find the red-haired whore. This time, in spite of Tam's rage, he was systematic, asking not only the street girls peddling their wares but the beggars, street vendors, doubtful characters lurking on street corners and the landlords of the less savoury taverns, but to no avail. She seemed to have vanished clean away.

Once he thought he was in luck when he saw the girl who had played Helen of Troy. She looked at him strangely when he asked after her friend. No, she said, she had not seen Jeannie since the night of the Masque – and was it true a man had been found dead in the morning after they had left?

'How many of you left the house early in the morning?' he asked in case Dudley's information had been inaccurate.

'All six of us,' she replied.

'And Jeannie?'

'Aye, of course.'

'And no one else?' he insisted.

She looked at him curiously. 'No. Why should there be?' Then, with growing agitation, 'What's all this about? Why d'ye want to know?'

Simon felt in his pocket and gave her some coins. 'Never mind, perhaps it's best I don't tell you.' Expecting him to demand her services for his money she was surprised when he began to walk away, and ran after him a little way. 'I'll tell ye one thing,' she said. 'You're not the only one asking after Jeannie. There's another man walking the streets trying to find her.'

Simon arrived back in his lodgings, his head pounding, and with the prospect of another long night stretching ahead of him. His mind returned to his dream. Did the choice of caskets represent the dilemma with which he was faced? To play for time or attempt to escape now? An hour's frantic thought brought no solution.

All of a sudden, he heard the door being unlocked.

'Ye're to come wi' me,' said Tam, indicating the way out.

Dear God, thought Simon, have I left it too late? Am I now to be thrown into prison or put to the torture without even being allowed to reach the end of my promised time? Steeling himself, he enquired where they were bound.

'To my master at Holyrood. He wants to see ye. Something to do with the letter ye sent.'

It seemed his ruse to acquire quill and paper had worked only too well, for it had resulted in Maitland sending for him. Presumably he had found Simon's letter convincing enough to demand the name of the man he suspected, he thought as he was hustled out of the house and along the now familiar route to Holyrood Palace. Bending down as if to adjust his boot, he managed to glance behind him and this time was almost sure Alun was following at a discreet distance. Surely, *surely* there must be some way of speaking to him! On their arrival at Holyrood he was shown straight into the room in which he had waited before, and within a short time Maitland entered, in his hand Simon's letter.

'So,' he began, 'you tell me of another man who was in all three places where these men died and you claim it's he who's guilty.'

'That's so,' replied Simon.

'Who is he?'

'I would rather not say at present.'

Maitland smiled his thin smile. 'How then do I know this man even exists?'

'What would be the point of my inventing him?' cried Simon. 'It would hardly help my cause. I don't want to tell you who he is until I have more certain proof, since if I do so now and he hears of it, then it will give him time to escape. As it is I foolishly gave him reason to think I suspect him.'

Maitland regarded him. 'What will it profit you to wait, seeing that you now have so little time?'

'Is that my fault?' raged Simon. 'You gave me seven days, the first of which I wasn't even allowed out of the room you have all but imprisoned me in. Next, I'm told when I do go out that it can only be for a little time. It's hard enough to be in my situation among strangers in a strange city and without friends, desperately trying to clear my name, without your doing your utmost to prevent me from being successful.'

'Why should I help you?' enquired Maitland. 'You know my own opinion. Who in London will be concerned at the hanging of an obscure English doctor? To what end is all this delay? So you claim another man murdered Hamilton, but refuse me his name.' He gave a snort of exasperation. 'I see no point in continuing with this farce.'

Simon's mouth went dry. At all costs he must continue to play for time. If Maitland had him thrown into prison now, then that would certainly end all hope. 'Give me just two more days then,' he pleaded, 'and let me spend all the time I can seeking the proof that will condemn this murderer. Your man's always with me, I'm never out of his sight and I have no means of escape. At the end of that time I promise I'll tell you who he is, whether I've proved it or not and you can do with me what you will. If you won't,' he continued as Maitland said nothing, 'then the King will have broken his word and I'll somehow find means of telling the King that I will make it known his word isn't to be trusted.' It was an empty threat, he knew, as he had no way of carrying it out but it was all he could think of in the circumstances.

For a dreadful moment he thought Maitland was going to refuse but he finally conceded. 'Very well, I will give you what you ask. As you say, the agreement was reached and agreed in the presence of His Majesty. You have until the evening of the day after tomorrow. Then I will send for you again, and unless you can satisfy me that you have found me Hamilton's murderer, then you will be tried. I yet expect to see you on the scaffold.' And with that he turned on his heel and left.

So now I have only two more days in which to entrap Seton, thought Simon, unless somehow Alun and John can rescue me. But how can they, when we can't even send messages to each other? As he and Tam went through the guards at the gate of the Palace, there was the usual crowd milling around outside and they had to push their way through it. As they did so a voice was heard loudly protesting that his purse had been stolen and there was an immediate disturbance as people looked around for the thief.

'Try that fellow there,' yelled the supposed victim, pointing at Tam. 'He's a villainous-looking oaf.' As Tam, enraged at the very suggestion, turned to face his accuser Simon saw that it was Alun, his red hair now covered by a large hat.

'What d'ye mean?' roared Tam, stopped for once in his tracks. The crowd swirled around them and Simon found himself rudely jostled by someone at his side. It was John Bradedge.

'We can't take you here, Doctor,' he whispered. 'There's too many folk to prevent it, but we think we can now see our way how best to do it.'

Simon looked at Tam who was still shouting that he had touched no man's purse, and that he was willing to be searched there and then. This proved to be a foolish gesture, for immediately half a dozen people in the crowd took him at his word.

'I've now only two days at most,' Simon whispered back, 'and I fear the next time I leave this building it will be to my death. You must get me away before that or I'm utterly lost.'

One of the searchers now held up the purse from Tam's pocket and asked Alun if it were his, whereupon Tam burst out with a string of oaths swearing it was his own. Alun shook his head and the excitement subsided, one of the searchers telling the crowd the man must live in a pigsty and never see water from one year's end to the next, and that he himself would now need to go and put his head and hands under the pump after handling so stinking a fellow. Immediately both Alun and John disappeared, but as Simon was locked back in his room for the night he felt at least a gleam of hope.

That night he had the dream again, or rather a variant. This time there were only two caskets and the woman was most definitely the red-haired whore dressed – or rather *un*dressed – as she had appeared at the Masque; she danced before him in a most lascivious manner to the music played by the same musicians who had accompanied her then. At which point a man standing in the shadows, whom Simon knew he ought to recognise, pointed directly to one of the caskets, yet again he made the wrong choice – whereupon the shadowy figure came over, laid an icy finger on him and insisted, 'Why didn't you listen to me?' Simon woke from the dream in a cold sweat. When did he make the wrong choice? When he tried to help Davie Armstrong? When he agreed to Cecil's bargain? By believing in Seton's guilt? So little time in which to search out the truth.

As soon as Tam unlocked his door in the morning Simon insisted on going straight out. He made at once for the lodgings of the man called Fraser, where he insisted to the maidservant that he *must* see her master without delay; the business was urgent and he would wait outside until he did so. He was there for some time, Tam watching him irritably the while, but finally he was shown in to find the young man seated at table tucking into a plate of cold beef. Simon recognised him at once as the ardent swain who had wanted to know whether or not his new love would soon let him into her bed. He greeted Simon in a friendly manner, motioned him to join him at table, then his eyes fell in horror on Tam.

'Your man can surely wait outside,' he said.

'I only wish he could,' replied Simon, 'but he's been put to guard me and sees it as his duty never to let me out of his sight. He can certainly go farther off though.'

'You – stay outside the door there,' ordered Fraser. 'There is no other way out. And now, Dr Forman, what is this urgent matter you wish to discuss with me?' Simon wondered however many more times he would have to limp through his tale coherently, but at least this time his listener seemed friendly.

'I see,' he said when Simon had finished. 'And now you ask if I shared a chamber with Seton that night? I did at first, but only for a short time.'

'How short?' asked Simon eagerly. 'When did he leave your room?'

'Oh, he was only there for a few minutes,' Fraser replied. 'One of the girls, the dark one, she who played Venus, had already agreed to come to bed, and when she came in search of me, Seton made to grab her but she told him he was too old for her and he went off in a huff. I was pleased for I've never liked the man. Nor, I will admit, three in a bed!'

'Why don't you like him?' persisted Simon.

Fraser shrugged. 'I don't know. There's something about him which is – oh, calculating as well as something not entirely straight. He claims to know people and to have done things which I find hard to believe, though one goes to his supper parties of course because one meets all one's friends there, Scots *and* English. I wish I could help more but he definitely didn't spend the night with me and could have prowled around the house all night for all I know. Have you asked any of the others?'

'One or two of those prepared to speak to me, but so far without any real success.'

Fraser gave this some thought. 'Do you recall a man called Campbell? A tall man with greying hair, older than the rest of us? He asked you if he was to inherit an estate or some money when you were casting our horoscopes. He knows Seton far better than I do and is coming to see me later today to discuss a horse sale we plan to attend. If you're prepared to wait, you're welcome to stay and we can ask him if he knows any more and can help us further.'

Remaining where he was would mean yet further delay, but having no better plans Simon thanked Fraser and accepted his invitation, saying that if necessary he would wait outside in the yard. Fraser would not hear of it; he could make himself comfortable for as long as was necessary, so long as Tam remained outside. The young man then excused himself as he had various affairs to which he had to attend. But hours passed without any sign of Campbell, hours during which Tam tried to drag Simon back to the lodgings and Simon steadfastly refused to go.

When Campbell finally did arrive Fraser insisted Simon eat with him, which he reluctantly agreed to do although by now he was almost sick with frustration. Finally, however, the subject turned to the matter in hand and it was clear Fraser had already broached the matter to Campbell.

'So you're after Seton, I hear?' Campbell began. 'What d'you know of him yourself?'

'Very little. When I first came here I was told he was a man who kept open house and possibly favoured the Earl of Essex's cause. I was taken to the supper after which the man Danvers died, by a friend from London. Seton appeared to me to live in some state and I wondered where his wealth came from.'

'Not from his family, that's certain,' responded Campbell, 'for his father was disinherited after his marriage, but certainly by the time he returned to Scotland he was able to set up in style. You aren't the only one to puzzle as to the source of his money. And you say it's rumoured among you English he favours Essex? Never! Though no doubt he has his reasons for letting you think so.'

'You don't believe it then?'

Campbell shook his head. 'None of us here, and I include Seton, really believe your Earl of Essex will have much influence with our King, even should he last so long without overreaching himself. Most of your schemers who send their men here are wasting their time. There are only a handful that matter to the King's advisers – such men of power as was your late Sir Francis Walsingham and his successor, Sir Robert Cecil. Cecil,' he continued, 'now there's a deep one, full of subtle plots they say and with a stable of intelligencers. I have friends who know about these things,' he explained, 'and they tell me one such has recently been seen here in Edinburgh.'

Simon waited for the blow to fall. Had his real purpose in the city been discovered after all? 'Who is that?' he managed eventually.

'A man called Rivers. Have you heard of him?'

'I've heard of him,' Simon replied with some relief, 'but not that

220

he was particularly associated with Sir Robert Cecil. I'm sure the friend who warned me of him would have told me had that been so.'

'Well, my authority is usually sound, but no matter. Now, to return to Seton – why so much urgency?'

'Because I have but until tomorrow night to convince your Lord Thurleston that I did not kill Hamilton,' replied Simon quietly, 'and the only way I can do that is to prove someone else did.'

'Do I take it you suspect Seton?' Simon said nothing. 'Then God help you, man. For I'm as certain as I am of the Day of Judgement that Seton is one of Maitland's intelligencers and that nothing takes place in his house which is not reported straight to Holyrood.'

Simon looked out of the door at Tam, wondering for one mad moment if he might make a run for it right now – but even as the thought passed through his head, Tam looked in. 'Are ye going to stop here all night?' he demanded. Then, even though all was lost and it now seemed pointless, Simon recalled what he had originally intended to ask. 'It hardly matters now, but did you share a room with Seton the other night?'

Campbell laughed. 'More than a room, a bed. He stalked in, saying he'd nowhere to sleep and how could I refuse, seeing it wasn't my house?'

'And was he there all night long until the body was found?'

'Aye, he was. And there's another that can vouch for it too, for we shared a girl, a blonde lassie, turn and turn about until it was light.'

This had to be the end. In his worst nightmares Simon had never even considered the possibility that Seton was not only actively on the side of the Scots but was actually an intelligencer for the very man who sought his own destruction. His only hope now lay in escape, and at once. His face grim, he thanked both the men for their help.

They, in turn, were sympathetic. 'I'll see if there's anything at all I can do for you,' Campbell told him, 'or whether there's anyone who might be found to take your part if you come to trial, but I must warn you I think it unlikely. Your last best hope, I'd say, is to try and break from that fellow and escape!'

It was with leaden steps that Simon made his way back towards his lodgings. So it seemed, at the end of the day, all his endeavours had come to nothing. They trudged on and once again Simon was convinced he was being followed, but he could see ño sign of Alun or John. He and Tam retraced their steps through the warren of narrow alleyways and it was as they did so that Simon stopped in his tracks. .

'What ye're stopping for?' grumbled Tam. 'Get on with ye now!'

Some way up an alley, leaning against a wall with her arms folded in front of her, was the red-haired whore.

'It's that girl!' he said. 'The whore who was at Dudley's house. I must speak with her.'

Regardless of any danger he might be in from Tam trying to prevent him, Simon raced towards her, Tam, showing a surprising turn of speed for one so large, close behind him while behind *him* came most quietly another man who then hid himself in a deep doorway. Hearing running footsteps the girl looked round, recognised Simon and immediately made off down another passageway. Desperation lent Simon speed and he caught up with her at the end of a blind alley where, with her skirts hauled up, she was trying to climb over a wall. Simon grasped her, twisted her wrists behind her back, and turned her round to face him.

'What d'ye want?' she bawled. 'Why d'ye chase after me? If your money's good ye could've had me up against the wall back there.'

'Why did you run away as soon as you saw me?' Simon demanded.

The girl looked at him sullenly. 'What was I to think, seeing ye coming for me in that fashion?'

'Was there any other reason?' he demanded. 'Has someone told you not to speak to me? Tell me, who arranged for you to take part in the Masque?'

She relaxed slightly at this. 'Why, yon man Dudley, of course. I'd been wi' him a number of times and he came looking for me and asked me to find some other girls willing to put on a show for some friends of his. I asked what kind of a show and he said he'd tell us what to do but that we'd have to agree to take all our clothes off. He said he'd pay us all well and he did. Taking our clothes off didna bother any of us. Some of the girls have weans to feed and we all need to live. That's all.'

'Did you go to his house to practise this show?'

'Aye, we went the day before. Dudley told us what he wanted us to do and how we should do it. It wasna difficult. Now if ye've done, leave me alone.'

'Look,' he said, pressing his remaining coins into her hand, 'there are things I've got to know. First, at the supper party given by the man called Seton, the one at which a man died supposedly of poison, you sat on that man's knee and fed him with pudding. Were you asked to do so?'

She looked mystified. 'Nae. What would anyone do that for? Anyway, he ate only a wee bit of the pudding and pushed the bowl away. I finished the rest myself. If he was poisoned, then it wasna that way.'

She could only be telling the truth. So the poison must have been put in the posset as he had suspected. It was all one now but he persisted nevertheless. 'Now to the other night. You came to bed with me, did Dudley pay for that?'

She shook her head. 'Nae. He left it t'us if we wanted to go wi' any of you, saying you men'd pay us.'

'But you never asked me for any payment,' Simon insisted, 'and yet you singled me out. Did you not want payment then?' She bent her head and tried to free herself. 'What is it?' he demanded. 'Are you frightened of something? Has someone told you not to speak to me?' In desperation he shook her. 'Tell me!' he shouted. 'Tell me, will you? Was it the man called Seton?'

She looked at him sullenly. Even in these circumstances he had to admit she was a very pretty girl, worthy of a better life. 'Nae,' she said at length. 'It was one of the musicians, the grey-haired old fellow with the wee pipe. Why he did it, I didna ken and didna ask, but I'll take money from anyone. He said I'd no to tell ye if ye asked but to say it was a free gift.'

Her face swam before his eyes as his world crashed at his feet. The musicians! Both he and Dudley had entirely forgotten the musicians. When recalling who had been in the house that night they had checked through all the guests, noted the servants, even counted in the girls, but had never even thought of the musicians who had played for the entertainment.

'The musicians, did they too stay the night?' he asked hoarsely.

Again she shook her head. 'They went straight off after the show saying they were wanted elsewhere. While we were downstairs putting our clothes back on, I heard them being let out through the kitchen door.'

'All of them? Did every one of them leave?'

She shrugged. 'I dinna ken, I wasna watching. I'd a mind they all left together but I canna be sure.'

'What was he like, this piper?' asked Simon.

She shrugged again. 'Just a man, that's all. About as big as you, perhaps a wee bit bigger.' But he felt she was not telling the whole truth.

'Please,' he begged. 'Please! Is there anything else you can tell me about him?'

She glanced uneasily around then said reluctantly, 'I mind I thought he was English. And he'd a wee piece out of one of his ears, like as if it'd been nicked by a knife or dagger. I saw him once afterwards in the street and heard him called Rivers. Now that's all I can tell ye.'

He pushed her aside and stumbled blindly away. As in his dream he had chosen the wrong casket. Marlowe had been right after all. There *was* a God in the Machine and to his horror, he finally realised who it might be.

The red-haired girl watched him go then began to retrace her steps. Simon's questions had unnerved her. She was no fool and she wondered what desperate matter was afoot. So lost was she in thought that she did not hear the footsteps behind her until the cord went round her neck. 'You bitch,' said the soft voice in her ear, 'and after being so well paid for your silence!' Then she knew no more.

After seeing to this unpleasant task James Rivers, master intelligencer, otherwise known as James Ford and also as wool merchant, kitchen man and player on the wee pipe, went back to the inn where he was staying and wrote an urgent letter to his master in London in which he said he had successfully accomplished his task and was therefore sending his man post haste with the news. He himself would follow at a more leisurely pace the following day. He felt justly pleased with himself, for he had dealt with every eventuality

224

with the utmost efficiency and had achieved everything he had been asked to do. He would have liked to have stayed and seen Dr Forman hanged, as he now most certainly would be, but he knew more pressing business awaited him back in England. He then sealed the letter, gave it to Saul and told him to ride with it at once to London.

Chapter 17

Flight

Simon stumbled unseeingly out of the alleyway beside Tam, but as they turned into the street another whore came from out of a dark doorway and accosted him, her hair and face half covered in a spangled scarf.

'Pleasure you, sir?' she enquired hopefully.

He was about to push her away, but she seemed curiously familiar and he stopped and looked at her more closely – whereupon he had a shock. It was Kate. Glancing sideways at Tam he clutched her to his chest, telling her loudly that he would be only too happy to accept her offer but that he was forced to leave at once. She appeared to protest and clung ever more closely around his neck, whispering for him to tell her what was happening.

'For God's sake,' he whispered back, 'tell them it's tonight or never. And if it's impossible then save yourselves. No, no, my good girl,' he added loudly, loosening her fingers. 'I've told you, I've no time for it now.'

'Will ye come away,' roared Tam. 'Will ye never stop chasing whores?'

Kate pulled away from Simon, shrugged her shoulders as if indifferent to her reluctant client and turned her attention to Tam. 'Who'd look at yon wee man,' she flattered, dropping her scarf and giving him a provocative smile, 'when there's a braw great fellow like you near by?'

Tam smirked. He looked uneasily up and down the street but obviously concluded sexual congress was impossible in the circumstances, since Simon would almost certainly take the opportunity to escape. 'I've to take this fellow back to where he's kept,' he said. 'Can I see ye later?'

Kate put her hand on his sleeve and peered up at him. 'Let's say in this same spot at about seven of that church clock?' And she turned away and disappeared whence she had come.

Between parting from her and reaching his prison, Simon's spirits swung wildly between hope and despair. Presumably his friends had been watching his lodgings and following his movements during the last few days, waiting for a further opportunity to speak to him. It seemed obvious what Kate had in mind: she would meet Tam at the appointed spot and somehow or other he would be got out of the way. But that still left them with the problem of rescuing him from a locked room, under the eyes of the watchful housekeeper and away to freedom. So far as he could tell, the woman rarely left the house – and it could be there were others on watch about whom he knew nothing.

Tam meanwhile was scurrying along at a great pace, smirking to himself and for once having little or nothing to say. Simon hoped for her sake that Kate would literally be able to keep her distance from his evil-smelling companion; as to any intimate contact, it didn't bear thinking of.

'I trust you'll clean yourself up before going with that lass,' Simon told him as he was locked once again in his room, 'for you give off the rankest compound of villainous smells that ever offended nostrils!'

As he paced up and down awaiting the turn of events, he struggled to come to terms with what he now knew. Firstly, if Seton had been responsible for the three murders and Simon had managed to prove it, then it would have availed him nothing if, as he now believed, Campbell was right and the man had all along been one of Maitland's intelligencers. No doubt Seton had already informed Maitland of Simon's suspicions, and it must have amused them both greatly, for he would have played right into Maitland's hands. Nor, he had to admit, was there any reason why either Maitland or Seton should have set him up in such a manner. It seemed a lot of trouble to go to, simply to hang an Englishman, any Englishman.

Then there was Rivers or Ford or whatever his real name was. 'A bird of ill omen', Sir John Carmichael had called him, while Marlowe had accorded him grudging respect as a master in his field, a cold-blooded killer who would have made a good actor. Simon had to agree. Each little cameo had been finely observed: the straightforward bearded wool buyer, the beardless servant most at home in the kitchen, the grey-haired old man (presumably achieved with flour and a slight stoop) who trilled away merrily on a pipe. So on whose orders had he been sent to Scotland? Who had organised so elaborate a sequence of events? And the crucial question; *who was the God in the Machine?*

It was at this point the housekeeper brought him his supper. He had no means of telling the time, but after a little while he heard the sound of conversation below his window. Tam was leaving and bidding farewell to the landlady. 'I'll be back within the hour,' Simon heard him tell her, 'then if all's well, I'll go to the tavern on the corner. You know he can't get out, and anyway you'll be rid of him for good tomorrow.'

Time passed on leaden feet; Simon felt like a rat in a trap. But in spite of this it seemed considerably less than an hour later when once again he heard Tam's heavy footsteps on the stairs. What had brought him back so soon? Had Kate balked at carrying out her part? He could hardly blame her. Or had they simply missed Tam at the rendezvous? The door crashed open and Tam lumbered over to him. He had certainly made no effort to clean or change his filthy clothes, but although inside the room, he still kept the hood of his coat pulled down over his head, and only his scarred cheek could be seen. However, he did not smell quite so foul as usual.

'Don't stand there gawping, Doctor,' hissed John Bradedge, 'we'd best be off. It's the only chance we've got and I don't know how long it'll be before someone finds yon stinkard.' Simon had to agree the disguise was excellent. Although John was not quite as tall as Tam, padded out with his clothes he could pass muster, particularly as both had scars on the same cheek.

'What are you going to say?' asked Simon. 'The woman below's bound to want to know why you're taking me out.'

'I've already told her I'd a message to take you back to Holyrood without delay. She seemed to accept it.'

Simon looked anxiously round his room to see what he could take with him, cursing those who'd deprived him of sword and dagger. He no longer had any money. There were some of his medical things and a saddlebag, but he could hardly carry those out of the door without causing comment. In the end he picked up his cloak and hat and stuffed what small things he could into his pocket.

They passed down the stairs, Simon protesting loudly that he had not been supposed to return to Holyrood before the next evening, John muttering inaudibly and pushing him ahead of him. The landlady opened the door of her room a crack and peered through.

'Seems ye'll have to wait a wee while for yer drink,' she said. John shrugged, nodded his head in acknowledgement, and hustled Simon out into the street.

'Where now?' Simon asked, as the door closed behind them.

'To an inn on the right side of town,' John told him.

'Isn't that risky? Won't the landlord be suspicious something's going on?'

'He's all right,' John assured him. 'He's married to an Armstrong lass and has no truck with much that goes on here in Edinburgh. He'll keep us safe until it's darker – the Devil take these long light nights! We daren't risk leaving until then but at least it's been a grey day and dusk will come earlier. We've taken four horses to a barn on the outskirts of town where an ostler from the inn's holding them for us. We'll make our way to them on foot, so we're less likely to be noticed. I warn you, it's going to be a long, hard ride with scarce a stop. Alun wants us safe in Liddesdale as soon after dawn as possible.'

'And what have you done with Tam?'

'Stripped him of his clothing, tied him up and dumped him in someone's back yard near where Kate met you this morning.' John sniffed his jacket and threw back his head in disgust. 'If that man ever takes a wash, which I doubt, then he must take it in horse piss!'

It was clear that John had learned his way about the city well, for within a remarkably short time they were entering the back door of a small tavern and went immediately upstairs to a bedroom where Alan and Kate were waiting for him. Kate, Simon saw, had changed out of her whore's tatty finery into the black leather breeches and doublet of

230

a Reiver. They greeted him with delight and relief, Kate throwing her arms round his neck and kissing him on both cheeks. 'I trust you didn't have to come close to the awful Tam?' enquired Simon.

She laughed as she released him. She had, she told him, met the hulking Scot as planned, then led him down a narrow alley to a passageway leading to the yard they had selected earlier in the day, suggesting a nearby wall was a suitable place against which the proposed transaction might take place. John and Alun were already there, hiding around the corner, and between them they dealt easily with the unprepared Tam as he struggled with his breeches in preparation of the treat in store.

'What if he's found sooner than you expect?' Simon asked.

'Then he'll think he's fallen victim to the oldest whore's trick in the world – being led on to allow her pimp or her villainous companions to rob him. Don't worry,' said Alun. 'He'll not be found till morning, by which time we'll be clear away.'

Simon nodded. 'I hope so.' Somehow it seemed all too easy. He put his sombre thoughts aside, turned to Kate and smiled. 'And what made you decide to come on this mad venture?' he asked, adding to Alun, 'Why did you let her take such a risk?'

'She'd have it no other way. She plagued the life out of me day and night until I agreed.'

'I thought you'd gone back to your home,' Simon told her.

She grinned. 'And so I did. But came again to Mangerton within a few days, wanting to know if they'd had word of you.'

'But why? We only met the once; I'm not worth the risk.'

She coloured slightly. 'Ah, but remember, ye've still to tell me my horoscope properly. I'm determined ye'll do so before ye leave for England.'

John took off Tam's outer clothing, rolled it in a ball and threw it into a corner of the room then, after putting on his own garments he went down to the taproom, soon returning with tankards of ale and some food. 'You'd best eat now, Doctor,' he said. 'We'll have little or no chance again until tomorrow.'

Simon, who had been unable to touch the food brought by the housekeeper, found his appetite again. 'Where are you taking me?' he asked.

'First to Hermitage,' said Alun. 'Carmichael's been told something of what's happened to ye and ye'll be safe enough there. Even King James is unlikely to waste men trying to take such a fortress for the sake o'one man, even if it were politic – which at present it is not. Then, when the hunt's died down, ye can come to us at Mangerton and from there it's over the Borders and to safety.'

'I wonder,' said Simon thoughtfully, 'just how safe that will be?' And he told them briefly of the events following John's flight to Liddesdale and the conclusions he had finally been forced to draw. 'I wasted most of what time I had chasing the wrong man,' he admitted. 'I built myself a castle of cards which collapsed in an instant.'

Alun's expression was sombre. 'So you reckon that fellow Ford was the intelligencer Rivers? And he also played the roles of servant and musician? Yes, it fits.'

'And that of a garrison soldier entering Carlise Castle unchecked so that he could murder Richard to prevent his going with me to Edinburgh. I now think Danvers was genuinely taken ill at supper, but Rivers had been hanging around the house sure I was almost bound to go there sooner or later, as everyone from England did. In the event it was almost at once. He's obviously clever with drugs and he was presented with an excellent opportunity when I was called in to look after Danvers. But that death wasn't enough for his purpose; there had to be another, more obvious one.'

'But why?' demanded Kate. 'Why did he do all this? And who set him on to it?'

Simon leaned back in his chair. 'I'm still not sure why. As to who, only a handful of people knew I was going to Scotland. I think we can set aside those faceless men of power of whom Cecil spoke. There was my immediate household, of course, but so far as my close acquaintances were concerned, I was merely going out of London on business. So there was Robert Carey, whom I completely discount, his father, Sir Henry – and why would he arrange the murder of his own trusted relation? – which leaves only my supposed protector, Sir Robert Cecil.'

It was noticeable that Alun did not seem surprised. 'Well, well – Cecil. When we're through with all this, Simon, I'll ask Sir John if you can be told what was in the message I was to have delivered to Sir Henry.'

Simon nodded. 'Cecil – the *deus ex machina* – the "God in the Machine" as Marlowe called him.'

This prompted John to remember the letter from Marlowe that had arrived too late, and he now brought it out of his pocket. Simon read it through. 'Had it only arrived a day earlier, had I only listened to him, we'd none of us be in this parlous position now. I think he probably realised that Cecil was behind it all along but did not know how best to tell me since I was so sure he meant me well.'

'Aye, Carmichael said it had the mark of Cecil on it from the start,' Alun commented, 'but then he loathes the man. But don't be blaming yourself for our being here, for this whole business's down tae us – to Davie and me. All that's befallen ye has come about because of what happened to us that day in London.'

'You were hardly to know,' said Simon. 'Where else would a wounded man go, except to a physician? And what could I do other than what I did?'

'And d'ye know something else?' said Alun. 'It was Davie made the cut in yon Rivers' ear that put you on to him. It must have been he who set on the men who tried to take us. I told you we were in a fight earlier that evening. We gave a good account of ourselves, so good that this man Rivers who'd been standing by until then joined in too and went for my back with a dagger. Davie wrenched it out of his hand and in so doing slashed his ear.'

Simon stood up and raised his tankard. 'Let's drink then to Davie and to the success of this mad venture and our safe arrival at Hermitage. And to no one finding Tam until tomorrow morning!'

'And to vengeance on our enemies!' added Alun, and drained his tankard in one.

It was two young thieves who found Tam. In the normal course of events he might well have stayed tied up behind an empty house for several days unless he managed to break loose from his bonds, but as luck would have it he was rescued within three hours of being put there. The two boys worked together, one distracting the attention of the victim while the other cut his purse, whereupon the first boy would pretend sympathy and apparently dash off in pursuit of the second.

But on this occasion they tried the ploy on a robust gentleman who saw through their trickery and chased after them himself with every intention of catching them and bringing them to justice. The lads fled down an alleyway and finding it to be a dead end, fear gave them the impetus to scale it, high as it was. The first boy dropped down and landed gratefully on something soft. He was surprised however, when whatever it was made a terrible noise. Getting to his feet, to more groans, he peered down and saw it was a large and dirty man, tightly bound and gagged.

'Will ye look at this, Willie,' he said as his companion joined him.

'Is he deid?' enquired the other.

'Dinna look like it. Ugh, he stinks!'

Tam made as much noise as breath allowed through his gag and thrashed wildly about.

'D'ye think we should untie him?' asked Willie.

Tam struggled even more. 'Verra well.' He took a knife from his belt. 'Keep still, man, or I'll cut ye. An' we want thanks for this.'

Five minutes later Tam was standing painfully on his feet rubbing himself down. All he'd been left with was a shirt full of holes and an unsavoury pair of drawers. 'I can hardly give ye anything can I, in this state,' he told them.

'What happened to ye?' asked Willie.

'A whore's trick. She made as if to go with me and then her men set about me and left me in this state. Can ye find me something to put over me while I go home?'

The boys looked at each other. One stood on the shoulders of the other and peered over the wall. Their pursuer had given up and disappeared. They then tried the back door of the empty house and found it broken open. 'There's some old sacks in here,' shouted one of them. 'Will they do for ye?'

'They'll have to,' grumbled Tam. 'There must be a way out the front for that's how I was brought in, through a door to a passageway beside the house.' The boys explored further and agreed that was so. 'Then I'll be off,' Tam told them, then gave them the address of the lodgings. 'If ye'll come in the morning I'll gi' ye something for yer trouble,' he promised, adding: 'What'll folk think when they see me like this?' As to what his master was going to say, he could imagine only too well.

At least one person saw him. James Rivers had dined and drunk well. He felt he deserved it and he was on his way back to his inn bent on a good night's sleep before starting his long journey in the morning. He had learned much of his trade from a real master, one Robert Poley, who was considered within the circles of secrecy to be unsurpassed. Rivers remembered Poley telling him never to relax and allow himself self-congratulation until he was sure – absolutely sure – that whatever mission he had ventured on was a success. He himself, he'd said, had once been so certain that everything would turn out well that he had allowed himself a few days' dalliance outside town with a married woman, only to discover on his return that everything had gone wrong. He had never forgotten it. Nor had Rivers until now, but he was a long way from home and all had seemed so secure. He'd had it on the best authority that Dr Forman would be taken straight to gaol in the morning, tried with the utmost celerity and despatched immediately after.

He had, of course, earlier considered the possibility of an escape, had even kept his eyes open for possible rescuers, but had seen no sign of any. Now, the sight of Tam, the man actually set to guard Forman, dressed in sacks and obviously having been attacked, appalled him. He did not consider for one moment that Tam had been set on by thieves or cutthroats – no, an attempt must be under way to save Forman. A chasm gaped before him. He could imagine all too clearly the scene when he was dragged before Cecil to explain his carelessness. Ten years of excellent, efficient – indeed superb – intelligence work would count as nothing set against one moment's carelessness. He must raise a hue and cry.

Meanwhile, wrapping himself as best he could in the sacks, Tam slunk through back ways doing his best to avoid the eyes of the curious. Arriving at his lodgings he battered on the door, demanding to be let in. 'Ye're soon back again,' commented the housekeeper as she opened the door, then stared at him as if she couldn't believe her eyes. 'The Lord preserve us! What's happened to ye? And where's the English doctor?'

'What d'ye mean I'm soon back again?' roared Tam. 'I was set on in the street, tied up and dumped for an hour or more, and ye ken well the English doctor wasna wi' me. I brought him back myself, you gave him his supper, he's up there in the room, ye daft witch!'

'Daft witch, is it?' screeched the housekeeper. 'Ye must've had a great bang on the heid too if ye think that! I'd nae put it at more than an hour or so since ye came back from wherever it was ye'd been and took the English doctor off wi'ye to Holyrood!'

'It's ye that's raving,' cried Tam. 'I went on my own. Ye *saw* me go, woman! The English doctor's awa' up in his room.'

'Are ye calling me a liar?' demanded the landlady, her eyes blazing. 'How many times do I have to say it? Ye took him awa' yersel' the noo to Holyrood Palace. An' he protesting all the way oot that he wasna due there until the morrow.'

Tam pushed past her and rushed up the stairs. Simon's clothes and effects lay on the floor as he'd left them, but of his prisoner there was no sign. 'You foolish auld besom,' he shouted back down the stairs. 'You mother of witches, who took him from here?'

The woman clutched her head and stamped her foot. 'Yersel', yer verminous stinking loon,' she yelled at the top of her voice.

'*But it wasna me!*' he responded in kind.

'Then it was yer double,' she yelled back, 'down tae the scar on yer cheek and yer stinking clothes.'

He looked at her as if she were indeed a witch, and at first seemed about to argue further; then the full implication of what had happened struck him. 'Find me something to wear, woman. Anything. I must awa' at once to the master or the villain'll be clean out the country.'

Simon and his companions waited restlessly in the upstairs room for the dusk which seemed long in coming. 'Just a little while longer,' said Alun, 'and we can go. It's worth being on the safe side.' He looked out of the window. 'It's scarce going to be dark enough all night, for the cloud's thinning and there's a good moon. But beggars can't be choosers and once out of the city we should be safe enough.'

At that moment there was a noise outside and then the sound of feet running up the stairs. The door burst open and the landlord came in. 'Ye'd best fly for yer lives,' he told them. 'There's a hue and cry out for ye. It seems the man ye left tied up has been found already.'

'How did ye hear of it?' asked Alun, pulling on his boots.

'One of my tapsters has just come in and told me. They say there's bands of armed men in the streets seeking ye. They'll be bound to try all the inns, and though we won't be searched first I've no way of hiding ye when they do come.'

'Of course not, ye've done more than enough as it is,' Alun agreed. 'We'll be off straight then.'

'What if they wait for ye on the road?' asked the landlord.

'They'll be looking for the doctor here and the one man who rescued him. Hopefully they'll search the city first before they set guards on the road and while they do, we should be able to get clear.'

The four of them left by the back door as unobtrusively as possible. It would take them at least twenty minutes, probably more, to walk to where their horses were waiting for them, Alun told Simon, 'But we mustn't draw attention to ourselves by racing through the streets. Walk steadily and quickly, don't run unless you have to. You two,' he nodded at John and Simon, 'go ahead and Kate and I will walk a little behind as if we are not with you.'

At first all went well and they passed through the streets without attracting any notice. Dusk was finally beginning to fall and the streets were emptying then, without warning, half a dozen stout fellows rounded the corner.

'Here, you,' shouted their leader, 'stop and answer for yerselves!'

'Why, what's to do?' enquired Alun, motioning Simon and John to continue on their way.

'Murder and treason, that's what's to do,' the man informed him, then seeing Simon and John disappear out of sight he bellowed, 'Where do they think they're going? Go after them and fetch them back. You two stay where you are.'

As one, Kate and Alun took to their heels and soon caught up with the other two, the posse of men in hot pursuit behind them. They rushed down a narrow street and then another and another. 'We'll be hopelessly lost,' John panted. 'They'll pick us up at their leisure.' Alun wasted no breath in answering him but pushed him down a narrow passageway, beside the entrance to which was a cart propped against a wall. As they fled down it he turned and jammed the cart across before following them. The passage was dark and seemed to lead to a dead end, but once they were nearer Simon could see it gave on to a lane running at right-angles to it.

'Take the left-hand way,' Alun told them. 'At least by the time they get down here they won't know which way we've gone and they'll have to split up.'

'You seem to know your way about,' said Simon breathlessly.

'Aye, I've spent the last few days making sure I do,' Alun replied. He slowed down slightly. There was no immediate noise of pursuit. 'As I remember, there's another narrow passageway soon which will lead us out towards the edge of town. No noise now.'

He was right. They crept down it as quietly as they could. Fresher air blew towards them from the end of it, but it was impossible to see what was outside for now dusk was falling rapidly. Alun stepped out and looked around and beckoned the others. 'We seem to have shaken them off,' he said. But he had hardly finished speaking before men appeared from out of the shadows. The party had indeed split up. 'We must finish this as soon as we can before they call for more support,' muttered Alun grimly, drawing his sword, and soon blade rang on blade. Simon, only too conscious that he was unarmed, looked on anxiously not knowing how best to aid his friends without either hampering or distracting them. Their pursuers were doughty fighters but so also were John and the two young Armstrongs, Kate being almost as skilled as her cousin. For a while, both sides were evenly matched.

Then one man was disarmed and wounded in the leg, and Simon promptly gagged him with his kerchief and hobbled him with his own belt, before tying his legs and arms together behind him. That left three to two and John had no compunction in coming up behind Kate's assailant as she fought him and knocking him hard on the head with his sword hilt so that he fell to the ground unconscious.

As the last of the men engaged Alun, Simon bent to pick up the sword of one of the wounded men, whereupon the man fighting Alun turned and hit out blindly at Simon, slashing him across the shoulder before running back into the darkness of the passageway.

Alun leant against the wall to get his breath back. 'How bad is it?' he asked Simon.

Simon examined the cut which was bleeding profusely. 'Bad enough, but so far as I can tell he's hit nothing vital. Can someone give me something to bind it up as tight as possible? I'm bleeding like a stuck pig and when these fellows are discovered my blood will lead them to us.'

Kate whipped off her kerchief, came over to him and, using his handkerchief as a pad, bound the wound as tightly as she could. 'That'll have to do,' she told him, 'but the sooner we get out of here now the better.'

John gave his own assailant another thump on the head to ensure he would not wake for some time, checked the gag and belt on the other man, then he and Alun lugged the two men into the shadows. 'Right then,' said Alun. 'Let's be off.'

It took them a good twenty minutes to find the barn on the roadside where their horses were waiting, and by the time he reached it Simon's head was already swimming from loss of blood. He wondered vaguely if he should give himself up now to save the others, but common sense told him that even if he did they might still be caught, and all that would happen was that they would then be hanged beside him. The ostler waiting with the horses took in the scene at once, but in answer to Alun's question said that he had seen no sign of soldiers on the road as yet, and so far as he knew, the way ahead was clear. Alun thanked him and they mounted at once, Simon needing considerable assistance. 'Where now?' he gasped as they reached the road.

'Up and out of town, then over open country avoiding the towns and villages until we reach Liddesdale. Once there we'll be safe enough even if there are bands of men out looking for us. But I must warn you, it'll be a rough ride.'

For Simon it was a matter of clinging on to his horse and hoping the animal was sure-footed enough to need little guidance. The night that followed was interminable as Alun led them as quickly as practicable through the Moorfoot Hills, skirting Galashiels and Selkirk before turning almost due south towards Hawick and Liddesdale. Finally as an early grey dawn broke, they rested briefly.

Alun came over to Simon and examined his shoulder, which was still bleeding. He looked grim. 'Drink this,' he said, passing Simon a flask. Simon took a swig and choked on the fiery spirit. 'And more,' Alun ordered.

'It burns the throat,' commented Simon weakly.

'Aye, but it'll help keep ye going.'

'I think you should leave me to take my chance,' said Simon. 'I'm holding you up. You'll easily make it without me.'

'Man, we've nae hung around Edinburgh for days and planned all this to gi' ye up!' his friend remonstrated. 'Set yer teeth and hang on and we'll get ye to Hermitage yet. Maitland can't know where we're heading; he can't have men on every road. He'd most likely think we'd make for the coast and take a boat.' He looked ahead, narrowing his eyes. A mist was curling towards them from the valley. He looked at it with satisfaction. It would help conceal them and from now on he knew every step of the way; and still, thank the Good Lord, there was no pursuit.

But he had underestimated their opponents. After Rivers had raised the hue and cry he had presented himself at the gate of Holyrood Palace demanding to see someone in authority at once as a notorious prisoner, one Dr Forman, had escaped aided by at least one man, possibly more. The news was taken at once to Maitland who immediately ordered not only a search of the town but that a detachment of soldiers be made ready for pursuit. Rivers stood and watched the preparations.

'I don't know who ye are and what's your interest, but ye seem to know a lot,' commented the captain of the troop as they made ready. 'So, since ye're so clever, perhaps ye can also tell us where you reckon they'll make for.'

Rivers had been thinking of that. He had learned something of Simon's progress from the Border and sojourn in Hermitage from sources of his own. If, as seemed likely, he had made friends with Carmichael as well as the Armstrongs, then surely that was where they would go. 'Almost certainly Liddesdale,' he answered with certainty. 'There's no time to explain but the man's in league with the Armstrong clan. If you go straight there now, surely you can cut them off before they actually reach Hermitage? If you'll give me a horse I'll come along with you. Whatever happens, Forman mustn't reach England alive.'

The mist was ever thicker as the fugitives rode on down Liddesdale, and Simon was now so faint John Bradedge had to ride beside him and lead his horse. 'Bear up,' Alun called out to them. 'We're nearly home.'

The soldiers camped out on the lower slopes of the hill heard their voices and smiled at each other with satisfaction. Two of them, leaving the rest with their mounts, walked with their muskets to a place from which they could easily look down on their quarry as they passed on the road below. All they had to do was wait. From a little apart, Rivers too stood watching to see what would happen next.

As the party came nearer Simon finally slumped unconscious over the neck of his horse. John, calling out to Alun and Kate who were riding behind them, left him and rode back to them. 'I don't know what's best to be done,' he said. 'Is there some way we can either tie him on to his horse, or should I try and take him up before me? Though the poor beast's been driven hard enough as it is.'

'Let me look,' said Kate. 'I'll see if there's anything I can do to revive him, we're so very near Hermitage now. If not, then I'll ride on ahead and seek help.' She rode over to where Simon, now oblivious, was almost slipping off his horse which, glad of a respite, was nibbling grass at the side of the narrow road. She reined in beside it and leant over Simon, hauling him back into the saddle then raising him as best she could to see if she could rouse him.

The musketeer above them raised his gun. No need to take the Englishman back alive, the orders had said. Much easier if he were dead. He took careful aim and fired. As he did so Simon fell forward again exposing Kate, who was still struggling to keep him on his horse, and so it was that the ball intended for Simon hit Kate full in the back.

The sound of the shot echoed from the hills around, followed by the cries of disturbed birds wheeling high in the air; after which there was silence. Then, as John and Alun sat on their horses frozen in horror, there came the noise of hoofbeats and jingling harness and the Reivers rode out of the mist.

Chapter 18

'On the Border was the Armstrongs, able men, somewhat unruly, and very ill to tame.'

Scott of Satchells

'Look to Kate,' shouted Alun to John after the first moment of shock, 'while I speak to these lads.' Briefly he explained the position to the leader of the Reiver band. 'Get two or three of your men there to help us take the wounded to Hermitage, will you?'

Three more shots whistled across from the two musketeers, after which they rejoined their comrades. Although their captain had heeded Rivers' advice he had also deployed troops on the road from Langholm to Hawick, since if it was true the prisoner was in league with the Armstrongs he might well make for the Armstrong strong-hold in Langholm. There were, therefore, only half a dozen soldiers in Liddesdale in the command of a sergeant. Suddenly faced by more than a score of men, and those notorious for their savagery, they turned and fled.

As the Reivers were about to spur after them, Alun's keen sight picked out another man on the side of the hill, one who was keeping close and not moving. Something in his stance jogged Alun's memory. He pointed him out to the leader of the band. 'Go after the others but leave that one for me. If he tries to get away up to Hawick then bring him back to Hermitage – alive. For he's mine.'

The man shouted the order and the Reivers galloped off up the road into the mist. 'What if he goes another way?' he asked Alun, as he turned to follow them.

'What other ways can he go?' Alun responded. 'If, as I suspect, he's ridden all night his horse will be tired. There are only two trackways from Liddesdale to the Langholm road – the one past Hermitage which he will most certainly not take and the lower one nearer to Mangerton. But I think he might well hope to ride down Liddesdale unsuspected after resting up for a while. If that's the case, tell your men not to touch him and allow him to ride down the dale without hindrance. I will tell them the same at Hermitage, but ask for spies to be posted along the river to watch his progress. Then he can be left to me: a life for a life.' The leader of the Reivers raised his hand in salute, dug his spurs into his horse, and galloped off after his men.

Alun looked again at the figure on the hill. He was now sitting beside his mount, his dun-coloured clothing making him hard to pick out. Alun prayed that he was right, that Rivers, for he was almost sure it was he, would take the road south down the dale. He walked over to where John had laid Kate on the ground and knelt beside her.

'Ye're safe now, Kate,' he told her, holding her hand. 'We're going to take ye to Hermitage.'

She tried feebly to shake her head. 'Tell him,' she said in a thread of a voice, 'tell him I know what the horoscope meant.' Two of the men came over and put a cloak under her and lifted her into the arms of one of the horsemen.

'I fear there's nae hope there,' said one, then turned to his companion. 'We'd best help get the other one down too.' As Alun watched them go, something sparkled and caught his eye. The spangled scarf Kate had worn in her role as a whore lay blood-stained on the trampled grass. He picked it up and put it inside his doublet, then, mounting his weary horse urged it towards the party making for Hermitage. He had never felt so bleak in his life.

Rivers' trade had taught him patience. Left alone he considered his position. Forman was badly hurt, possibly even dead or dying, but in case there was any doubt he must cross the Border as quickly as possible and make arrangements to ensure that even if the doctor did survive he never reached London.

He drew out of his doublet a rough map of the area and perused it carefully. It showed the two roads south from Hawick and the two trackways between them, with Hermitage Castle marked beside the nearer. He got up and walked to the top of the hill and looked across the valley. It was clearly impossible to try and ride to Langholm across a countryside of steep rough trackless moorland.

He looked at the map again. The second trackway would deliver him right into the middle of Langholm, almost opposite the Armstrongs' castle. It seemed his only choice therefore was to ride down Liddesdale and reach the Border that way. He came to a decision: he would wait as long as he thought necessary, preferably until after the Reivers had returned from their foray, then take to the road as an innocent traveller. Why should he be thought anything else? He carried nothing that would betray him.

A little over an hour later the Reiver band returned. From their demeanour it was obvious they had been successful – indeed, two of the men were brandishing muskets which they must have taken from the musketeers and they were laughing and joking among themselves. They looked neither to right nor left. They must be returning to Hermitage, thought Rivers.

He waited a judicious while longer, found a stream to water his horse, then began to pick his way gently down on to the road. The mist was finally blowing away and a watery sun shone down from above. It was very quiet, the only sounds those of his horse's hooves and the plaintive cries of the curlews and lapwings. He was still cursing himself for the last-minute carelessness that had allowed Forman to escape, though there was every chance it could be rectified. But he was not looking forward to his meeting with Sir Robert, nor to explaining why only half his mission had been accomplished.

The killings worried him little; there had been so many over the years. So far as the recent business was concerned, it had been necessary to prevent the young Scotsmen reaching Carey and he'd ensured it didn't happen, although he had not personally killed the one who died, merely stood by and watched it happen. His hand went to his ear. The other young man had paid for leaving his mark, he thought with a grim smile. Then Wilmore? He bore the man no ill, it was simply that he could not be allowed to accompany Forman to Scotland. Rivers was rather pleased with the way he had first ingratiated himself with his victims, then gained entrance to the castle so easily. That was by far the most complicated matter.

As for the other two, it was just a matter of tenacity, watching and waiting all the time until a suitable opportunity presented itself, in the one case Danvers genuinely being taken ill and Forman, at his suggestion, being called in to treat him, and on the other hearing from the red-haired whore, when he was availing himself of her services, of the coming Masque. Again he smiled. She hadn't even recognised him when he had presented himself in the guise of a pipe-player. As to her . . . well, she was always likely to end in such a way, given her trade. No, he lost no sleep over any of them. Killing was part of what he did.

Lost in thought he found himself coming to a place where a road forked north-east. A milestone informed him Castleton was in that direction while his own destination, Canonbie, lay twelve miles ahead. He continued on his way marvelling at the emptiness of the dale. He was certainly in luck. As he reached the first of the trackways over to the Langholm road he glanced uneasily to his right but if Hermitage Castle was astir, then there was no sign of it. A couple of miles further on he noticed a farmhand lazing on a bank, chewing a straw. The man called out a greeting and he replied in kind. As he then rounded a bend, he was unable to see the man leap to his feet, mount his horse (which was hidden behind some bushes), and canter off cross-country.

The mist had cleared completely now and it was becoming very hot; his lack of sleep was catching up with him and his eyes were heavy. To his left he saw a tower and beside it a substantial manor house with smoke coming from the chimney, but there was no sign of life. On his right a huge stone reared up in front of him and he wondered what it was and what it signified. Ahead, the road ran between scrubby copses, the branches of the trees making patterns on the road. He yawned and for a moment closed his eyes. As he opened them he saw the three horsemen appear almost silently from out of the woodland, fully armed. Wildly he turned his head to see if he could escape the way he had come, but as he did so half a dozen more men appeared from round the bend. All regarded him in silence.

He spoke first. 'What d'ye want of me, gentlemen?'

'You need not pretend to be a Scotsman, *Master Rivers*,' said Alun, and took off his helmet. His red hair glowed in the sun.

'I think you mistake me,' countered Rivers. 'My name is Ford and I'm returning to the Border to see to the fleeces and wool I bought and left there before visiting Hawick.'

Alun rode up to him and dismounted. 'Get him off his horse,' he ordered, and his companions grabbed Rivers and pulled him to the ground.

'This is no way to treat an honest traveller,' said Rivers, trying to free himself.

'But then you're no honest traveller, are ye?' said Alun.

Rivers looked round. He was now ringed with men. His mouth was dry and he had difficulty speaking. 'What are you going to do?' he managed.

'Prepare to meet yer God if ye have one. I'm going to kill ye,' Alun informed him. 'Let's see now – first there was Davie . . .'

'I didn't kill him,' Rivers interrupted.

'No,' agreed Alun, 'it was me ye tried to murder. But it was on yer orders and by yer men. Then Richard Wilmore, the two men in Edinburgh . . .'

Rivers looked again round the circle. 'You can't prove it.'

'Probably not,' Alun agreed.

Rivers was aware that all the time they were talking he was being pressed relentlessly back towards the huge stone by the roadside. Alun followed his gaze. 'D'ye ken what that is? It marks where they laid the body of Alexander Armstrong, chief of the Mangerton Armstrongs, murdered some two hundred years ago or more by an act of betrayal. We remember such things on the Borders.'

They had almost reached the foot of the stone. 'At least let me die in fair fight,' pleaded Rivers, trying to reach for his sword. His arm was immediately knocked aside and his sword taken from him.

'Fair fight?' Alun smiled again. 'A man so steeped in blood demanding fair fight? Ye who prefer the strangler's cord and the phial of poison to an honest weapon? Nae, nae, I think not.' Rivers was now almost up against the stone. 'I swore to avenge Davie's death but this is nae for him, nor for the others,' he continued almost conversationally. Then he stood back and looked Rivers full in the face. 'On the Borders we reckon a life for a life.' He drew his sword

247

arm back. 'This for my Cousin Kate!' he said – and thrust him through the heart.

Simon opened his eyes. At first he had no idea where he was as he looked round the whitewashed walls of the small chamber in which he lay. He raised himself slightly in his bed. His head swam and a pain stabbed through his shoulder; he lay back and closed his eyes again.

Slowly he tried to piece together events. They had left the inn in Edinburgh and were then attacked by armed men looking for him. Useless without a sword and seeking to take one from one of his assailants, he'd been wounded in the shoulder. He remembered that all right. There'd followed an interminable journey, his recollections of it becoming ever fainter from loss of blood, but he had little or no memory of what came after they reached the head of Liddesdale, except that he was almost sure John Bradedge was leading his horse and that he fainted, to be partially roused by Kate. Yes, that was right.

Then came another blank. He thought he recalled being lifted off his horse and carried somewhere, and that he had asked after the others, Alun, John and Kate and had been reassured. Kate. As soon as he could speak coherently he must ask if she was in the same place as himself, wherever that was, and if so, would she come and see him so that he could thank her properly. So they were all safe. He still didn't recognise his surroundings but he felt content and drifted back to sleep.

Some time later he woke again and was surprised to find Alun's mother bending over him holding a cup in her hand.

'Where am I?' he enquired weakly. He frowned, again trying to remember. Hermitage? 'Were we not making for Hermitage?'

'Aye, so ye were. But once our lads had seen the soldiers off it was thought better ye be brought to Mangerton where I could tend ye. Ye're safe enough here, there's men posted at both ends of Liddesdale and on the road over the moor from Langholm.'

Simon tried to raise himself, felt his shoulder and winced.

'It'll still be painful,' said Mistress Armstrong. 'It was a deep, long and nasty cut.'

248

Simon prodded it gently. 'Which you seem to have treated very well.'

'I told ye I'd some knowledge of doctoring. Ye were almost spent from blood loss when ye were brought in and then ran a high fever. So I gave ye masterwort and feverfew to help break it, and syrup of poppy for the pain, after which I took needle and thread and sewed up the cut. I trust ye'll forgive me such a rough practice.'

Simon looked at her in surprise. 'I've seen it done on the field of battle abroad,' he told her, 'but not I think since then.'

'Well, we've our own ways here and sword cuts are commonplace. Ye'll have a fine great scar but now it's healing well. Ye've healthy flesh.' She looked at him critically. 'I'll not keep from ye that at first we feared the worst, but ye improved fast once the fever broke. Now drink this brew of mine and then I'll look at your wound again.'

She held the cup to his lips and he drank, content to leave matters in her capable hands. Then she bent over him and unwound the bandage from around his shoulder and arm. Turning his head sharply to his left Simon could see the long cut snaking over the shoulder, pulled together now with thread. There was some inflammation along its length, but only a very little, and the wound smelled clean.

'What did you put on it?' he asked.

She hesitated as if having trouble finding the words. 'There were some of the salves left ye used for Kate. The naughty lass went off back to her home without taking them with her.'

He smiled. 'Dear Kate. Will you send her in to me? How does she feel now after such an adventure?'

The silence went on and on and then he saw her face. 'What's wrong?' he asked in a whisper. She did not reply. 'Something dreadful's happened, hasn't it?' he persisted. 'Tell me, I must know.' She looked at him, her eyes full of tears. A wave of sickness swept over him and he felt cold in the pit of his stomach. 'Tell me,' he urged. 'Please, tell me.'

'The lass was shot in the back by the soldiers when she went to yer aid. Don't you remember the soldiers above ye – the men with muskets?'

He shook his head.

'Five more minutes and our lads would have reached ye in time.'

Then she told him how, once the band of Reivers had arrived, Alun and John did what they could for Kate but that it was clear to both of them that she was past all human aid. 'It seems she hardly felt anything and that when Alun knelt beside her on the grass she said to tell ye she knew now what the horoscope meant. She died before they reached Hermitage. I'm told it made a grim sight when ye were both brought in, yerself unconscious and like to die and our lassie dead across her saddle, drenched in blood.'

Simon lay back and closed his eyes again. 'Dear God in Heaven!' he cried. 'It should have been me. Why wasn't it me?'

'Ye mustn't think like that,' Mistress Armstrong told him, sitting on the bed and taking his hand in hers. 'Nothing would do but she'd away to Edinburgh with Alun. Ye heard yerself how she was wild and hotheaded since she was a wee lass. If anyone's to blame it's Kinmont Willie for indulging her as he did and letting her ride with her brothers on the raids. We all told her it was not right behaviour and that it was time and more she settled down to breed sons with a good man, but she'd none of it. Within a week of ye leaving here she was back again wanting to know if we'd any news. Then when your man rode in to say you were in great danger and must be got away from Edinburgh without delay there was no holding her but she'd go too.' She gave him a sideways glance. 'I've a mind the lassie took a fancy to ye.'

She was right, thought Simon drearily. No wonder I couldn't see any future for her when I cast her horoscope. So lovely a girl, so brave a spirit, and now she was dead. Such a long, long trail of death which started with that of an Armstrong and ended with another. If this was indeed the end.

'Now, Dr Forman, ye must go back to sleep,' Mistress Armstrong told him firmly. 'Ye don't need me to tell you it's the best cure now the danger's passed.' She picked up a small phial. 'A little poppy syrup mixed with bettany in white wine. Then the next time you wake ye shall have something to eat and ye'll soon find yourself on the mend.'

She was right for the next morning, fortified by a bowl of broth, he felt greatly improved, so much so that he insisted on getting out of bed and sitting in a chair even though he felt as if his legs had

250

turned to water. His first visitor was John Bradedge, looking visibly worn, muttering that he had said all along no good would come of any of it and perhaps this would finally be a lesson to him. He was followed shortly afterwards by Alun.

He gave a smile of relief as he saw Simon. 'It's good to see ye sitting there, even if ye do still look like a wraith!'

'It should be Kate sitting here, not me,' he replied bitterly.

'That's not true. Kate took her own way as she always did. Ye know very well this wasn't the first time she'd put herself at such risk. Man, she was riding out wi' her brothers and playing the boy since she was fourteen years old! I truly believe that if I'd not agreed to take her with me to Edinburgh she'd have followed after me anyway.' He sighed. 'But I canna say she won't be sorely missed.'

'Did you want her for wife?' asked Simon.

Alun shook his head. 'Not that she wasn't a lovely lass, fit for any man's bed, but believe it or not when I'm home I'm one for a quiet life. There's enough danger and excitement out there without living with it in the house as well. And try as I might, I can't ever imagine Kate settled into a domestic life, seeing to the needs of her husband and presiding over a brood of children.'

He smiled at the thought then became more serious. 'Don't take it on yerself, Simon. Ye were trapped into this whole dirty business because of us. If you must blame anyone, then blame those who set the trap. And we did avenge her,' he continued. 'Did yer ken yon man Rivers followed along behind us with the soldiers? Nae, ye were too far gone. Well, when our men arrived to chase them out of Liddesdale I saw him there hiding out on the hill. There were but half a dozen soldiers and there were thirty or more in our band. While John and I took you and Kate to Hermitage, our men rode after your attackers. They killed three and the rest scattered and rode off back to Edinburgh without waiting for any more.'

'Won't that bring trouble on you? A bigger force perhaps?'

'King James isn't ready to move against us yet. It's too risky, we're almost impregnable here. It'll be a different matter when he sits in England and can bring in troops from both north and south – then I fear, there'll be no quarter given. But you're wanting to know about Rivers,' he continued, aware of Simon's growing impatience.

'I gave orders that no one was to touch him. I rightly suspected that he'd wait for everything to quieten down and then try and get down the dale to Canonbie, for his horse was tired and he wouldn't risk crossing the hills.

'So, after a while when he must have seen our men going back to Hermitage, he took to the road. He must have thought ye were either dead or badly hurt and so he wouldn't be recognised. I'd spies posted all along the road and we let him get as far as the stone marking the betrayal of Alexander Armstrong. It seemed suitable.' Alun looked unseeingly across the room. 'He showed no remorse. I ran him through the heart. Before I did so I told him it was for Kate.'

Simon clasped his hand. 'I'm grateful. What more can I say?'

Alun returned his clasp. 'He was vermin and deserved no better. Now then,' he said briskly, 'on a more cheerful note, who is this Avisa?'

'Avisa!' exclaimed Simon. 'What do you know of her?'

'Only that during your days of fever, when John Bradedge and I took turns by your side, you called out for her several times, beseeching her to come to you. I assumed she must be your mistress or, since ye're not wed, that you plan to make her yer wife.'

Avisa! It seemed a lifetime since he'd left her behind in London, since she'd promised him so much. 'I've great regard for her but I can't make her my wife for she's already that of another man. As to being my mistress . . . that's still unresolved.'

'Then the sooner we get ye back to her safe and sound the sooner ye can resolve it,' said Alun briskly. 'Mother says ye should now gain yer health and strength quickly and then we'll plan what's next to be done.'

Mistress Armstrong was proved right, for over the next few days Simon's condition improved steadily and his arm was healing well. He'd looked on with no small interest, though grimacing with pain, as Mistress Armstrong took her scissors and snipped out the thread which had held his wound together. Stitching a wound? It was an interesting notion and one he felt might be used with advantage in certain circumstances. When he had asked about it in Italy, he'd once been told, he recollected, that the Romans had sometimes practised it.

Two days later he was well enough to be up and dressed and

sitting outside. The weather was again fine and as he looked over to the road from Hawick he saw the glint of sun on steel as a small group of horsemen rode towards the ford, obviously bent on visiting Mangerton. As they drew nearer he saw Sir John Carmichael among them. After being warmly greeted by the Armstrongs, he was brought out to Simon and the two men shook hands.

'Well, Dr Forman,' said Carmichael, 'I'm glad to see you looking so well. When you were brought in to Hermitage I thought you might well be for the grave. I'm afraid your first visit to Scotland has been a sad one but now,' he continued, 'do you think you can tell me the truth as to what this whole business has been about? I realise it was hard for you when I saw you last, and that you had need to keep to your story that you were visiting Edinburgh to discuss medical matters, but it's obvious now that someone wanted your blood.'

Simon agreed there was nothing more to be gained from keeping up the pretence and so explained the circumstances which had resulted in so disastrous an adventure.

'Sir Robert Cecil convinced me that because Davie Armstrong came to me, there were powerful men who believed I was in league with Scots spies. God be thanked, he never knew I'd also cared for Alun. But what could I do? I was threatened with torture and certain death and he appeared to be sympathetic, offering me his protection in exchange for my visiting Edinburgh as his intelligencer.' Simon ran his hands through his hair in exasperation.

'How could I have been so foolish as to believe him? It was obvious to me once there that I was unlikely to be able to tell him anything he didn't already know, nor could I hope to equal those whose trade it is. I didn't even know the names of most of the Englishmen, let alone their business. It was a devilish trick to play.'

Carmichael did not seem surprised. 'I thought when we first met I saw the hand of Cecil in it, yet you seemed an honest man, no expert in secret matters.'

'At least I had one piece of good fortune for I met up with an acquaintance of mine from London who gave me much good advice. Some I took note of, but had I not been such a fool I would have taken it all.'

'And who was that?'

'A man called Marlowe, Christopher Marlowe. I wonder if you might have heard of him for he's a great poet and man of the playhouse.'

Carmichael said the name was not familiar to him. 'And what was such a one doing in Edinburgh?'

'He told me quite openly that he was on a spying mission and that he'd undertaken such a role on several occasions – in fact, ever since Sir Francis Walsingham recruited him years ago, but that he was under no such compulsion as I. In spite of that he was regretting having agreed to the mission and said when he was younger he'd seen it as a great game but that he no longer found it amusing. As well as trying to help me he warned me more than once that he thought the role I imagined I was playing was not that intended for me, and that I was there to serve another, darker purpose. He talked of a *deus ex machina*, being of a Classical turn of mind, and said he heard the sound of cogs and wheels. He was obviously right but I still don't understand *why*.'

A maid appeared bearing wine and two cups which she filled, then she curtsied to Sir John and left. Carmichael lifted his. 'Here's to your returning health,' he said. Then he looked more serious. 'I can't promise you I know all at the root of the matter but since you've been so frank with me, I will now be equally so with you. No doubt you must still wonder why I sent the two young Armstrongs to London?'

He paused, then marshalled his thoughts. 'Almost as soon as Walsingham died and Cecil took up the reins of power – albeit still, I understand, only as *Acting* Secretary of State – I became aware that he was making overtures to King James to assure his standing with him when your Queen dies. That in itself is not surprising since there is little doubt James will eventually be King of England, nor therefore that Cecil sees an opportunity for intrigue.' He sighed. 'Throughout our King's life, he has been surrounded by powerful men fighting over who should influence him most. At present it's Maitland, but Cecil, well aware that King James will always turn to the strongest and most powerful adviser, is determined to ensure that when he sits on the throne in London, there will be only one man holding that kind of power over him and that man Sir Robert Cecil.

'It soon became clear to me from what I saw for myself and what I learned from Edinburgh, that Cecil was already seeking to ensure he would have no rivals when the time came, and to this end he was doing his utmost to expose his competitors as untrustworthy, dishonest or unreliable. In the case of rash hotheads like your young Earl of Essex this is of little import, but when I learned that he was also denigrating your Lord Chamberlain, then I thought Sir Henry should know of it and sent to inform him – with the result you know. It seemed safe enough. Why shouldn't two young bloods want to visit your city and also pay a courtesy visit to the Careys on behalf of Sir Henry Carey's old Border colleague? Dear, dear.' Carmichael tutted sadly. 'Somehow Cecil must have got wind of it. He may not even have known my real intent; it was sufficient that Alun and Davie were proposing to visit Sir Henry. You have been caught up in devilish dealings.'

Simon looked at him thoughtfully. 'Devilish indeed, and I think I finally begin to see what was behind it. Cecil's intention from the first must have been to set me up as "Carey's man", for so I was addressed several times in Edinburgh and could not understand why. So, what better way to bring Sir Henry into total disrepute than to have Carey's man commit some dreadful crime, like murder, for which I'd be publicly tried and hanged! No wonder I felt all the time that events were slipping away from me, that I had no control. But what arrogance! Sir Henry is not only a man of power, he is the Queen's own blood relation. Surely Cecil will overreach himself?'

Carmichael looked doubtful. 'Sir Henry is an elderly man and Cecil a young one. He was in too much of a hurry and will realise he must learn to wait. After all, Sir Henry is older than the Queen and may not even be a rival when the time comes.'

'But what of me?' asked Simon sombrely. 'What will happen when I go back to London, though my heart misgives me that I might never reach it even now.'

'Wait a little longer until you've regained your health. I've already sent an official messenger along with four stout men with a message to the Careys. I've asked Sir Henry if he can send men of his own to see you safe home once you cross the Border. We'll ensure you come to no harm this side.'

Simon thanked him. 'You are a good man, Sir John.'

'I do my best,' returned Carmichael. 'I have no time for all this politicking. Sir Henry and I were always straight with each other and I trust it will be the same when his son Robert becomes Warden. When our countries have only one sovereign, then this enmity *must* end.'

Simon's health improved rapidly and he awaited the Careys' reply to Sir John with growing impatience. But what then? Since Cecil had obviously not reckoned on his survival, would he return only to find himself imprisoned – even executed – on some trumped-up charge? It was now July, over two months since he had left London, and full summer. One morning Alun asked Simon if he felt strong enough to venture on a short ride.

'Certainly. The more riding I do the better if I'm soon to make my way back to London,' he replied. 'I must go home now as soon as I can, whatever might be awaiting me back there. So where would you have me go? I know you and your short rides!'

Alun laughed. 'No great distance. But there's something I thought you might like to see.' They rode down from Mangerton to the ford and thence to the roadside monument to the betrayed and murdered Armstrong chief where Rivers met his end. As they reached the spot their horses became disturbed and Alun's shied away. 'They scent recent death,' he said. 'I've known it happen before.' There was a track beside the monument leading up the hill and to open country. As they turned their horses on to it, it rose steeply before them. Suddenly, to Simon's surprise, they found themselves at a graveyard.

'This is Millholm,' Alun told him, 'where we bury our dead.'

They dismounted and tethered their horses and Alun led him between graves marked by grey, weathered stone, some dating from the Hermitage massacre centuries before. In a corner, strewn with withered flowers, was a new and unmarked grave.

'Kate?' said Simon.

Alun nodded. 'Kinmont Willie was away on the Borders along with most of her brothers. We'd no way of telling him what had happened for some days, and so we thought it best she be buried here surrounded by other brave members of her clan. At first he wanted her taken home and raged that it was for he and her brothers to have avenged her not me, but in the end he saw reason. By the time he'd reached here Rivers would have been halfway to London.'

Simon looked round at the stones marking the resting-places of those who had died in centuries of Border bloodshed. 'So much blood,' he said. 'So much blood on the Borders.'

Yet in spite of its grim history, it was a peaceful spot. Across the valley Simon could see Mangerton with its stout tower and outbuildings. A farm lay a little below it and they were cutting the hay in its fields, the wind blowing its sweet smell towards the two men, while above them larks sang high in the sky. Simon went over to the grave, went down on his knees, and prayed for Kate's brave and restless spirit, that she had found peace at last.

Then they rode back to find a messenger awaiting them from Sir John Carmichael. Arrangements had now been made to take Simon over the Border to meet with Carey's men, who would be waiting for him on the East March in Hexham; Robert Carey himself would meet the party when it reached York. They were to set off the next day.

Sir John came himself to wish Simon godspeed. Alun was to ride with his men to Hexham and see Simon and John put safely into the charge of the Lord Chamberlain's men. Sir John also brought Simon a note from Robert Carey.

Sir John's letter to us made grim reading, he wrote, *but you no longer need fear for your life, for my father has made it plain that you are now under his personal protection, the personal protection of the Lord Chamberlain of England, cousin to the Queen – and to that end I'm taking no chances and will see you in York. My hearty wishes for a safe journey.*

All that remained was for Simon to thank Mistress Armstrong for nursing him back to health and Master Armstrong for his hospitality and for keeping him safe, but tears still came into his eyes when he tried to speak of Kate. They rode down Liddesdale in full sunshine to the road that would take them along great Hadrian's Wall to Hexham. A few miles along the way they met a band of steel-bonneted horseman led by Captain Willie Elliot, who had taken

Simon and John prisoner what now seemed like half a lifetime ago. He smiled in greeting, wished Simon well, and then they clattered away up the valley on business of their own.

Simon had no illusions as to the savagery of the lives of the Borderers, past and present, but their bravery was not in dispute, nor their loyalty to those they recognised as their friends. They had their own codes, their own concepts of honour and he knew he could never live long among them, but however severe, even barbaric, their way of life he was minded to think it infinitely preferable to the black political intrigue and betrayal in which he had unwittingly become caught up.

Chapter 19

Aftermath

Ten days later Simon and John, accompanied by one of their escort, rode back to the Bankside over London Bridge, the rest of the men having returned with Robert Carey to the Lord Chamberlain's house where Simon was expected shortly. Robert had been waiting for Simon by the time he reached York and they had spent the long journey south discussing the whole story and its implications.

The chain of events that began when Londoners were bringing in the May had ended in the heat and dust of summer. Along the City streets the flowersellers were now offering bunches of sops-in-wine, roses and Canterbury bells. Crossing the Thames, the travellers were assailed by London's familiar summer smells, of tidal water – for the river was high – the sweaty humanity through which they picked their way, the stink of the open kennels in the streets and, as the breeze was blowing from that direction, a faint breath of sweetness from the lavender fields on the hill behind Wandsworth. From the dust in the streets and the withered plants above the river foreshore, it was clear there had been little or no rain in recent weeks.

'A recipe for pestilence,' Simon remarked as they left the Bridge behind them.

Anna stared in amazement as she opened the front door to them, her little boy clinging to her skirts. Reticent as she usually was, she threw herself at her husband crying incoherently that she had begun to think they were both lost and that she would never see either of them again. Little Simon, who seemed to have grown inches while they had been away, looked warily at his father after so long an absence, but John swept his son and heir up into his arms and they all went into the house.

'Explanations will come later,' Simon said to Anna. 'I'm sure John will want to tell you everything himself. Go with her,' he said to his servant, 'and I'll see you in a little while, and take this good man who is with us through to the kitchen and give him some refreshment. I'm bidden to the Lord Chamberlain's house and he must escort me there,' he explained to Anna.

He stood in his hall and a wave of relief swept over him at things familiar. Cautiously he opened the door to his study. While he sometimes scolded Anna for dusting and cleaning his sanctum, preferring everything be left as it was, he was now only too pleased to see that she had done so, and that his books and jars and bottles were not lying under a carpet of dust. But in spite of that the room had an unlived-in air after an absence of two months or more. He gave a cursory look along his shelves of books and charts. He had left several of the latter behind him in Edinburgh after his precipitate departure, along with medicaments, clothes and his sword and dagger. All would now have to be replaced, and for that he needed money – for Cecil's had barely lasted out.

He would need a steady flow of patients and those wanting their horoscopes cast to make it up. Gloomily he wondered if there would even be any custom after so long an absence, but at least he now had his licence to practise back from the College of Physicians – the one good thing to come out of the whole sorry business – and that would enable him once again to ply his trade among the wealthy merchants of the City.

Simon left his study and went through the back door into his herb garden. Here there were definite signs of neglect. Anna had obviously remembered to water the plants from time to time, but many had grown lank and straggly from remaining unpicked, while others had withered away altogether; there was work here for many an hour. If the next few days failed to bring him custom then he would turn to it himself, but if they did he must seek out some fellow prepared to weed and tidy his garden for a few pence. Having let what he considered to be a sufficient time to pass for Anna to welcome John home properly, he re-entered the house and sought them out in the kitchen.

'If you have food for us all, then I'll eat with you,' he told Anna, 'and while I do so you can tell me what's passed while we've been away.'

'I have only some bread and cheese and a little salad,' she told him, 'for I had no knowledge you were coming home today. But as soon as I've served you, I shall go shopping for a good supper for you.'

'Did you have enough money to get by?' asked Simon, suddenly alarmed, 'for I'd expected to be back a month or more ago.'

'Oh yes,' replied Anna. 'I am very careful about such things.'

Simon called to his escort and they all sat down at table. 'Now,' said Simon as he broke his bread, 'what's been happening?'

Anna informed him that patients had continued to visit for some time, but as the weeks slipped by without word from him, enquiries grew fewer and fewer. 'But I'm sure they will soon be back, once they know you are here again,' she said confidently. Emma Ball had called on him twice shortly after he left, seeming most anxious and bringing with her a baby with a curious name – Fortunatus, was it?

'He's still with us then?' commented Simon.

Anna shrugged. 'He is, but I would not think for long. My little Simon here was half as big again at his age and much stronger.'

'And have you heard anything of Robin Greene?'

She shook her head. 'But his friend, that Master Christopher Marlowe, came last week to see if you were back and seemed worried when I told him that you were not. He might have news.'

'They were ever great drink-swiggers and gamesters together,' her husband agreed, 'but Marlowe's not long back from Edinburgh himself, for we met him up there – but that's a long story and I'll tell you all later.'

'Anyone else in particular?' asked Simon, trying to sound offhand.

Anna thought. 'Oh, Mistress Allen, the silk-merchant's wife – she came once or twice to see if you were home. She says she wants you to cast her horoscope for the success of a project she wishes to undertake, and that she would have you let her know when you are back again in London.' She looked critically at Simon. 'Your journey to Scotland has not improved you, Doctor,' she told him. 'You are thinner and have more lines on your face and there are more grey hairs on your head.'

He gave her a rueful smile. 'Maybe so, but as things turned out I'm lucky I still *have* a head!' He stood up. 'But now I must keep my appointment with the Careys, and perhaps on my way back I'll see if Emma Ball's at home and how she fares. She might also have news of Robin Greene.'

The Careys, father and son, greeted Simon warmly and with the greatest concern, expressing their relief at his safe arrival home. Robert had told his father the bones of the story, much to Simon's relief, so that he did not have to repeat it all yet again. Simon had spoken to Robert of Marlowe's part in it and they had decided, since they both had an admiration and affection for the infuriating poet, that it might be politic not to mention his name unless it was essential, so Simon told Sir Henry only that an acquaintance had warned him from the first that the reasons he was given to induce him to go to Edinburgh were not necessarily the real ones.

'Both he and Sir John Carmichael spoke of an intelligencer called James Rivers, skilled in the ways of disguise, secrecy and murder. Sir John told me there were rumours that he had been seen on the Borders, and my informant in Edinburgh later confirmed it. But at that time I still didn't connect him with Master Ford the wool buyer who travelled with us to Carlisle. To my cost,' he added bitterly, 'for had I realised, it might have been possible to prevent much mischief – not least Richard's murder. Worst of all was being suspected of that.

'It's obvious now that the murders of Danvers and Hamilton were designed to implicate me then have me publicly tried and hanged to discredit you, my Lord, and that Richard was killed to ensure he never reached Edinburgh – although Cecil seemed happy enough when I told him you were sending Richard with me.'

'In reality he must have been furious,' Robert commented, 'and decided there and then to ensure he never left Carlisle.'

'This whole business is almost beyond belief,' exclaimed the Lord Chamberlain, who was at heart a straightforward man who intensely disliked any kind of intrigue.

'A truly Machiavellian schemer, our friend Cecil,' said Robert, 'and you did well to come out of this alive, Simon. I have only one criticism of you, and that you already know. I told you when you first spoke to me on this matter that you could have trusted my father. Had you done so, he might have been able to intervene and stop it happening.'

Sir Henry agreed. 'So tell me, Dr Forman, why did you not?'

'There seemed to be good reasons. First, Cecil warned me of powerful enemies in high places from whom he was supposedly protecting me, though he refused to name names – although he did suggest I came to you for information about the position on the Borders.'

'Surely you did not think *I* was one of those "powerful enemies"?' demanded His Lordship, somewhat affronted.

'It wasn't only what Cecil said, my lord, but also Davie Armstrong's dying words. I told everyone he died having said nothing, but that wasn't strictly true. He was rambling, of course, and going fast but he repeated several times that there was something that must not be told. Then he spoke of you and finally of Hermitage. I had no idea what he meant by Hermitage – though I certainly do now – but I wrongly inferred that there was some life and death matter about which you must not be told, whereas of course it was quite the opposite: he had information that must not be told to anyone *other* than you! I was a fool.'

Sir Henry nodded. 'I see. That was most unfortunate.' Then he changed the subject. 'But how is my old colleague, Sir John Carmichael?'

'That I lived to tell the tale I owe in no small part to him, my lord. He's a good and worthy man and eagerly awaits your son's appointment as Warden of the West March. And for the rest, the Armstrongs kept faith with me to the end. In the case of one of them,' he continued, his voice faltering, 'even unto death.'

His Lordship smiled wryly. 'I'm glad to hear it. But you must remember that at worst the Armstrongs are untamed rogues whose Reiving bands terrorise not only the English south of the Borders but half their neighbours in the north! I agree though that they can be most loyal to their friends, while their courage is not in question.'

'They claim simply that they are the Borderers and so owe

allegiance to neither side,' said Simon.

'Of that, also, I'm quite aware,' returned His Lordship, 'but the days of the Reivers are numbered, for when both realms have but one sovereign all that will pass.'

Simon left with the praise of the Careys ringing in his ears, along with assurances as to his safety and a fat purse of money the Lord Chamberlain had insisted on pressing on him to assist him to survive until his patients returned again. Outside the Lord Chamberlain's house, he considered what to do next. Yes, he would call on Emma, but first he had a more pressing need, and so made his way through Blackfriars to the house of Master William Allen, silk-merchant. The door was opened to him by a servant, who informed him that Master Allen was away out of the country and that the mistress had been in Kent visiting her family but was expected back that very night.

'Then tell her Dr Simon Forman called,' he told her, 'with regard to the horoscope she wishes him to cast, and that I am now home should she still wish to call on my services.' There being no more he could do after having left his message, he then took a wherry and crossed the river in search of Emma. In her house he found the woman who had earlier offered to nurse Fortunatus for her, and in answer to his query as to Emma's whereabouts she told him that she was expecting her back any time and invited him in.

'How's the child?' he asked.

The woman sighed. 'I feed him as well as I can still, but he takes so little nourishment.' A thin cry came from a basket set on a bench in a corner and she went over and lifted the baby out. 'See for yourself. He's a poor mite for nearly three months.' The red down which had covered the baby's head at birth was changing to auburn hair. He was pale of face, a face dominated by a pair of enormous weary eyes, with which he solemnly regarded Simon. 'Is there any more to be done, Doctor?' the woman asked.

Simon shook his head. 'You're doing all you can. He was born too weakly and too soon. I fear any ordinary childhood sickness is likely to prove mortal.'

There came the sound of the latch being lifted and Emma entered, mopping her forehead. 'It's like a furnace outside,' she said, then stopped when she saw Simon. 'Wherever have you been?' she asked. 'We've all given you up for lost.'

'I almost was,' he responded. 'I've been to Scotland, have twice been threatened with hanging, barely got away with my life and have lived among savage men on the wild Borders. It would take days to tell you all.' Her eyes gleamed with curiosity but he refused to be pressed further. 'And how are you? You certainly look better.'

'Thanks to you,' she replied warmly, 'for had you not come that day, I fear I'd have long been in the churchyard.'

'I did only what any physician would have done in the circumstances.'

'But how many physicians would come out without payment to a whore dying in childbed?' she returned.

'And Robin? I scarcely dare ask.'

It seemed Robert Greene was still alive – indeed, had rallied slightly after Simon had left London, but had since relapsed again and his death was now only a matter of time. He had still not relented over his refusal to recognise his child. Simon promised Emma he would visit Greene the very next day, keeping to himself the fact that at the present moment he simply didn't feel strong enough to cope with the man.

He set off home, pushing through the narrow streets and alleyways of the Bankside, relieved to hear the familiar sounds of cursing carters as they struggled to find somewhere to unload their vehicles, cheapjacks and market women calling their wares, shoppers haggling with stallholders over a bargain. No flag flew above the Rose Theatre denoting a performance for, like all the others, it was still closed. Cases of plague, Emma had told him, fearfully clutching Fortunatus, were growing by the day now rather than the week. He cut through an alleyway that brought him out beside the river, and as he looked across to the grand city houses on the other side he felt a tap on the shoulder.

'I presume you arrived home whole and that I'm not addressing a ghost?' enquired a familiar voice. It was Marlowe.

'Certainly I'm here, if not entirely whole. Apart from almost being hanged for another murder, having to escape as best I could from Edinburgh, being run through and nearly dying of blood loss, then, yes, you could say I've returned hale and hearty! Also you were right, of course, on both counts. I should have left Edinburgh with you and there *was* a God in the Machine.'

'Our esteemed Acting Secretary of State to the Privy Council?'

'The same.'

Marlowe whistled. 'This tale deserves to be heard. We are but three minutes' walk from the Anchor Tavern. If you've no more pressing business then let's repair there immediately and you can tell it over ale or wine, whichever you prefer. I'm currently in funds.'

Shortly afterwards, seated in a quiet corner with two foaming tankards before them, Simon told Marlowe what had happened after he had left Edinburgh. 'If only I'd really taken in what you told me, I might have been able to piece much of it together earlier. You even spoke of Rivers. Did you think even then that he might be behind what was happening?'

'I thought it had his mark on it, but couldn't see how that could be since when I left London I learned from Poley, the man with whom I deal, that Rivers was on business in the Low Countries. It was only when I received Tom's second letter, saying that he understood Rivers had gone north on state business, that I began to wonder if I'd been right after all. I'll admit now that I wasn't myself in a position to be absolutely frank with you, but I knew that if Rivers *was* in Edinburgh then he would soon learn of our friendship and that would put both of us doubly at risk; which is why I left when I did and begged you to come with me.'

'But I foolishly decided I could risk another couple of days by attending Dudley's Masque, and this gave him just the opportunity he needed. But one thing still puzzles me greatly. Once Cecil had decided Richard must be killed to stop him going to Scotland with me, what would have happened had I been found guilty of his murder and hanged in Carlisle? I couldn't then have fulfilled his purpose, could I?'

Marlowe drained his glass and called for more ale. 'Oh,' he said as the tapster set down two more tankards, 'from the first you were always expendable. If that had happened then he'd see the Careys were told you'd deceived them from the first, and even while you were still spinning in the wind, he'd have forced another innocent up to Edinburgh in your place. None of this was ever personal to you, Simon. Anyone would have done.'

And that, thought Simon, was the worst thing of all. 'So how did you fare when you reached London?' he asked.

'Well enough, though I doubt my masters were entirely satisfied, but when I asked Poley and had it confirmed Rivers was away in the north, then I really was alarmed for you. Anyway, I limped out my list of fortune-hunters and so far as I know that's that. For now. But for how much longer?' he added, almost inaudibly.

'You sound doubtful,' Simon commented.

Marlowe gave him an odd look. 'I didn't think when I so light-heartedly took up this trade all those years ago at university, how dirty the work would be nor, as I told you in Edinburgh, that once you've become involved, it is almost impossible to distance yourself from it. All I'm saying is that it's rare for those who undertake it to enjoy long life, for they're as like to die at the hands of their supposed friends as their enemies. I'm supposed to care for nothing and no one but, yes, sometimes in the dead of the night I fear the future. I saw Robin Greene two days ago and he said something to me that was most strange.'

'He's still with us, then? I was planning to go and see him myself tomorrow. What did he say?'

'It was a kind of warning and he'd written it down. He wrote: "I know the least of my demerits merit this miserable death, but wilful striving against known truth exceeds all the terrors of my soul. Defer not with me then 'til this last point of extremity: for little knowest thou how, in the end, thou shalt be visited".' He shook himself. 'I'm growing morbid. Let's drink to your safe return until we both find oblivion.'

'Another time willingly,' said Simon, 'but I've scarce been home yet and have much to see to.'

Marlowe accepted this in good part. 'So what of the future? Do you yet fear Cecil hasn't finished with you?'

'Not any longer. The Lord Chamberlain has assured me of his protection and has told Cecil so.' He gave a rueful laugh and looked sideways at Marlowe. 'Please God he never discovers that last year I lay with his own mistress!'

Marlowe gave out a great crack of laughter. 'Now that seems to me the best of all. What a splendid irony!'

They went out on to the river walk. A breeze had blown up and it was no longer so hot. 'Tell me one thing more,' said Marlowe as they prepared to part. 'The Masque of which you spoke. Is it true Dudley was forced to leave Scotland over it?'

Simon agreed that was true. 'It was, well . . . stimulating . . . and followed by what is described in those parts as "houghmagandie"!'

'What on earth's that?'

'Fornication, to put it bluntly.'

Marlowe was highly intrigued. 'So what form did this show take then, and who wrote it?'

'No one wrote it, it wasn't that kind of Masque. As to its form, well, according to Dudley the idea came to him from a book by one Master Grinston entitled *Divers Private Recreations*. I have been determined ever since to seek out a copy.'

'Then look no further,' said Marlowe. 'Let me lend you mine!'

Sir Robert Cecil, the official ratification of his position seemingly as far off as ever, had received Rivers' letter with great satisfaction. The successful outcome of the mission might well help persuade the Queen finally to do as he asked. Yes, everything had gone entirely to plan. He had a small nagging doubt that perhaps it would have been wiser for Rivers to have remained in Edinburgh and seen Dr Forman hanged with his own eyes, but possibly he had thought it safer to leave as he proposed.

But as time passed and no word reached him from Scotland of the death of a murderous English doctor, a creature of England's thus discredited Lord Chamberlain, the nagging doubt began to grow into serious disquiet. After nearly two weeks had gone by, still without Rivers reporting back to him he began, for the first time, to consider the possibility that his plan might have failed. Furious and alarmed, he despatched not one but two intelligencers north to discover what was wrong, but before either returned with the bad news, he found himself involved in a deeply unpleasant meeting with the Lord Chamberlain himself.

Sir Henry was of the same generation as Lord Burleigh, Cecil's father, and both had been close advisers to the Queen since she was a young woman, but neither had ever fully trusted the other and Sir Henry had always disliked the ambitious younger Cecil. The burden of his message to him therefore was straight and to the point. He knew of everything that had transpired between Dr Forman being brought to Whitehall to the present time, not least the role devised for the unfortunate doctor. He, thankfully, was alive in spite of every effort made to remove him, and was presently on his way back to London accompanied by Sir Henry's own son.

'It is no thanks to you,' he thundered, 'that he was not hanged in Edinburgh or dead of the wounds he suffered when he escaped. He is now under my personal protection, and if anything at all happens to him in the future, I shall look straight to you. You already owe me the life of my own man, Richard Wilmore. One more piece of interference in my affairs, however small, and I'll go straight to the Queen and ensure you will never have your position as Secretary of State ratified by her. *Never*!' Cecil said little but fumed secretly. 'Oh – and one more thing,' Carey added. 'Your intelligencer, Rivers. He's not coming back. He lies dead in Liddesdale.'

Cecil saw him go, concealing his fury and chagrin as best he could. Then he forced himself to calm down and look at the situation rationally. Carey was an elderly man, even older than the Queen. In the nature of things he could not hope for long life. He, on the other hand, was young and had his life in front of him. His time would come.

A few days later his intelligencers returned from Scotland confirming all that Carey had said. They also brought him other news, that Christopher Marlowe and Dr Simon Forman had been close companions while Marlowe was in Edinburgh. This was interesting if not entirely unexpected. Cecil sent for his chief intelligencer, Robert Poley, and informed him it was time they turned their attention to Master Marlowe. 'I want him watched,' he said. 'See to it!'

Simon returned home to a house at peace and where, to his surprise, two patients sat waiting for him. Word of his return had, it seemed, soon got around. It gave him a great sense of relief to prescribe medicine for the elderly woman whose persistent cough kept her awake at nights and to lance the abscess of a carpenter who was working on repairing the seating at the Rose Theatre while it was closed. It made him feel almost normal again.

But after his supper he was still restless in spite of his long day, and so went out into his neglected herb garden. He began to tidy it up, cutting back straggling plants that had outgrown themselves and clipping off the heads of those in seed, and as the day cooled with the evening, he was surrounded by pleasant aromatic smells. So absorbed was he in his work that he lost all track of time, and at first did not even notice that he had a visitor.

'Am I disturbing you?' enquired Avisa.

He rose slowly to his feet, unable to believe his eyes.

She looked at him with concern. 'You must have been through much, Simon, you look so worn and thin.'

'I've been close to death,' he told her.

She gave a cry and came to him, putting her arms round his neck. He clutched her to him as if his life depended on it. She was warm and yielding and smelled of lavender. 'You came for your horoscope?' he said unsteadily, when he finally wrenched himself apart from her.

'There's no hurry,' she said with a blush. 'My husband, as you know, is from home and will not be back for several days. I've told the household that I'd word in Kent of a sick friend and that I must visit her at once and might well stay the night.'

He could hardly take it in. He had laid siege to her for so long he had almost given up hope, and even though she had seemed to promise so much before he went away, he'd resigned himself to her thinking better of it during his long absence.

'Then we'd better creep up to my chamber,' he told her, 'without even John and Anna knowing of it.'

After they had made love he lay wakeful. Usually after such a pastime he fell into a heavy sleep, but this time it was Avisa who slumbered, curled peacefully beside him. He looked down at her. He had courted her for nearly two years and, finally, past all hope, she had come to him and given him his heart's desire. Yet now he was unable to get out of his mind the memory of another woman, beautiful, courageous and headstrong, one who had given her life for him. He was still thinking about her when he finally fell asleep.

Avisa woke him early the next morning. He was convinced he had been dreaming, something which she was soon able to convince him was not the case. Then she ran her finger lightly along the ugly scar across his shoulder and down to where it ended on the left side of his chest. 'So nearly the heart,' she whispered. He agreed and put his arm round her, kissing her again.

'I must go. I'll try and come again before William returns.'

He watched her as she dressed then felt for his bedrobe to see her out of the house. 'You talked in your sleep,' she said as she prepared to leave.

'I'm not surprised, after what I've been through,' he told her. 'What did I say?'

'Who's Kate?' she asked.

Author's Note

THE REAL DOCTOR SIMON FORMAN

Almost the only knowledge we had of him for a long time was the note in the *National Dictionary of Biography*, written by Sir Sydney Lee in the late 1870s, which is full of inaccuracies and described him as a charlatan and a quack, a view presumably he had taken after reading of the clashes Simon Forman had over a period of years with the Royal College of Physicians. Later research, for much of which we are indebted to the late Dr A. L. Rowse, shows he was very far from that and indeed that he had many new ideas gleaned from the Continent that were in advance of those prevailing in the England of his day. As an example, he did not believe in wholesale blood-letting, a common practice then and for centuries afterwards, as he considered it merely weakened the patient. Nor did the fact that he practised astrology, cast horoscopes and also used them for diagnoses make him a quack; most doctors did so then, including one of the earliest respected presidents of the Royal College of Physicians.

Simon Forman was born in Quidhampton, Wiltshire, probably in 1558, the youngest of five children. His father, who worked on the land, died when he was very young, leaving the family far from well off. After going to the village Dame school, he achieved a place at the local grammar school where he was considered a bright scholar. He was fascinated by the New Science and wanted to study medicine, and his teachers were eager that he should go to Oxford University, but, hardly surprising in her circumstances, his mother was unsympathetic towards his ambitions. The best he could manage was, when possible, to act as servant to a local parson's son who was a student at Oxford and attend some lectures, but he was not allowed to become a student himself as he had no funds and had not been offered a scholarship.

After a year he returned to Wiltshire to find work locally. He soon upset the local landowner, Giles Estcourt, as a result of which he spent nearly a year in prison. There is then a great blank after which we find him working as a medical practitioner in Salisbury (during which time he fathered an illegitimate child) before moving on to London where he set up as a qualified physician formally recognised by the University of Cambridge. He may or may not have studied in Italy, or elsewhere on the Continent.

When he first set up in practice in London he was endlessly hauled up before the College of Physicians who refused to recognise him as a doctor, even when his status was confirmed by Cambridge. They disliked his attitude, considered him an upstart who had risen from the ranks of the poor, and were the most likely source for the rumour that he was a necromancer who practised the Black Arts.

Dr Rowse dates his setting up in London as around 1593–94, and it has been suggested that on one occasion Queen Elizabeth's great Spymaster, Sir Francis Walsingham, intervened on his behalf to prevent his being sent to prison by the Royal College of Physicians. If this is indeed the case, then he must have been practising in London as early as 1590 for Walsingham died in the spring of that year.

Certainly by the early 1590s Simon Forman was living in a good house near to the Bankside (outside the jurisdiction of the City of London) with a garden in which he grew herbs and flowers for his medicines. He treated patients both at his own home and by visiting them, and he almost uniquely crossed the entire social spectrum from the publicans, actors, writers and whores of the Bankside, through the City merchants to the aristocracy and the Court. He enjoyed the theatre, leaving us the first accounts of seeing Shakespeare's plays, and Shakespeare's Bankside landlady was one of his patients as was the wife of Richard Burbage. He had a tremendous weakness for women and was candid about sex. He had a code word (*halek*) for those ladies who paid him in kind rather than in cash. He also had a brief, if stormy, affair with the strongest contender for the role of Shakespeare's Dark Lady, Emilia Lanier, née Bassano.

The long-term love of his life was, however, Avisa Allen who was married to a merchant older than she was and who also 'distilled', that is made medicines from herbs. Since he outlived her and divorce was out of the question there was no possibility of marriage. She became his mistress and their relationship continued until she died. Many years later he married Jane Baker, the daughter of a Kentish Knight. He was an expert on poisons and death, and would have been a witness in the trial of Lady Howard for the murder of Sir Thomas Overbury, but he died suddenly just before the trial, from what might well have been appendicitis.

Simon Forman, like many doctors of his age including Shakespeare's son-in-law, John Hall, kept a meticulous Casebook of his patients and their maladies, and also of the horoscopes he cast. Forman also wrote books both on medicine and astrology. While my portrayal of Simon Forman owes much to poetic licence it is clear that the original was lively, clever and energetic and never ceased to have an enquiring mind.

BACKGROUND TO THIS BOOK

The story told in this book is entirely fictional, but during the last ten years of Queen Elizabeth's reign a steady stream of hopefuls did journey to Edinburgh to make their play for future political advancement, although the Queen did not name James of Scotland as her heir until the very last. It is hardly surprising therefore that the men of power in London jockeyed with each other for position and that the Court surrounding King James in Edinburgh was deeply suspicious of them. Intelligencers from both sides, Scots and English, used the situation on the Borders to their own advantage and the Court in Edinburgh was a seething cauldron of intrigue.

I must apologise to the people of the Borders (and Edinburgh) for playing games with their history and also for infelicities in their language, but I decided that even if it were possible to translate the speech of the Borders into Lallans it would be almost impossible for the readers, at least those in the south, to understand it.

OTHER PEOPLE IN THIS STORY

The people listed below really did exist, although the part they play in this novel is purely fictional.

Sir Robert Cecil was son of the great Lord of Burleigh. He remained Acting Secretary to the Privy Council, albeit unpaid, for a further six years until the Queen finally ratified the appointment. From the first he wove a web of intrigue using informers, intelligencers and *agents provocateurs*, as the Gunpowder Plot conspirators were later to discover to their cost. Throughout the last ten years of the Queen's reign he was in contact with those around King James and on the latter's accession as King James I of England, became the most powerful man in government.

The history of the **Armstrongs** and that of the Borderers in general is a fascinating one; for those who wish to know more, the most comprehensive account of the families and their exploits is given in *Steel Bonnets* by George Macdonald Fraser. **Kinmont Willie** (famous in Border ballads) and his family did exist, as did the Armstrongs of Mangerton, though I have given them a fictional son, **Alun**. The bleak keep of **Hermitage** high up in Liddesdale still provokes shudders even in the height of summer, but all that is left of Mangerton is a piece of the ruined tower and a few stones where the house once stood. The great stone, monument to the betrayal and death of Alexander Armstrong in 1320, still stands at the corner of the track up to Millholm cemetery and the Hawick road. According to documents in the archive of the Armstrong Museum, Kinmont Willie really did have a daughter who rode out with him on border raids but I could find out no more about her than that she existed. My **Kate**, therefore, is fictional.

The Reivers with their steel bonnets and black armour (the origin of the term 'blackmail'), were feared on both sides of the Border for the best part of two centuries, claiming allegiance only to themselves. Soon after James' accession to the English throne, efforts were made to remove the Armstrongs, and the other reiving clans, from the Borders but they either hung on or returned as instanced by the Armstrong seat, in Langholm, belonging to the Duke of Buccleugh and the names on the shop façades in the Border towns: Elliot, Musgrave, Murdoch, Kerr, Douglas and so on. Long memories survive. In a recent television programme on the Borders today a man, when asked whether he supported Scotland or England, echoed a phrase in this book, replying: 'Neither. We're the Borderers!'

Sir Henry Carey, Lord Hunsdon, was Lord Chamberlain of England. He was said to be the Queen's cousin but it was rumoured he was her half-brother, his mother, Mary Boleyn, having been Henry VIII's mistress before he married her sister Anne. His family and that of the Cecils, headed by the Lord of Burleigh, never did care for each other and the Careys always distrusted Cecil. For some time he was Warden of the West March and it was then he became acquainted with Sir John Carmichael; both men respected each other. **Robert Carey** also became Warden of the West March a little after the time in which this book is set, and served there with distinction. The real Robert Carey did know the real Simon Forman.

Sir John Carmichael was considered by both sides to be a most honourable man. At the time this story is set he was indeed Keeper of Liddesdale. Later, when Robert Carey became Warden of the West March on the southern side of the Border, he was appointed to the same position in the north. In 1600 he was assassinated. A member of the Armstrong clan was hanged for his murder but there has been argument about who did it ever since.

Christopher Marlowe, the brilliant poet, playwright and wit, was the son of a Canterbury shoemaker, born in 1564, the same year as Shakespeare, and murdered in 1593. Documents prove he was recruited into the equivalent of our secret service while up at Cambridge. Scholars argue as to whether or not he continued spying afterwards, and one source suggests he might have been sent to Scotland at one time to see who was making overtures to King James. As the Rose Theatre playwright, his plays packed the theatre, though increasingly their subject-matter was considered to be dangerous. He was involved in a street-fight during which a man died and is said to be Shakespeare's model for Mercutio in *Romeo and Juliet.*

Marlowe's behaviour became wilder and ever more extreme and it is clear that someone, possibly Cecil, eventually decided enough was enough. In May 1593 he was arrested on charges of blasphemy and treason but, most surprisingly, was allowed out on bail. For centuries the story was told that he died in a pub in Deptford kept by one Eleanor Bull, during a quarrel over who paid the bill. But there *was* no tavern in Deptford at that time kept by an Eleanor Bull. Mistress Bull was a substantial householder. It was not until well into this century that it was discovered that Marlowe had spent his last day with two intelligencers, Robert Poley and Nicholas Skeres, and a petty crook with gentrified ambitions called Ingram Frizer. Sometime on the evening of 30 May, Marlowe was stabbed through the eye by Frizer, who later received a state pension from the Duchy of Lancaster while Poley received a Queen's pardon for any task undertaken for the State during that specific period. Eleanor Bull was a distant cousin of Robert Cecil. Nicholas Skeres later disappeared in suspicious circumstances.

Robert Poley was a master intelligencer and *agent provocateur* on whom the character and activities of **James Ford** are largely based. He began working for Sir Francis Walsingham and continued under Cecil. So far as is known, however, he died in his bed. There must have been rumours of his secret employment, not to mention his implication in Marlowe's death, for some time later Ben Johnson wrote a poem, 'Inviting a Friend to Dinner', in which he specifically states that if one is to talk frankly with one's friends then one must ensure there is 'no Poley by'.

Robert Greene was a popular playwright and pamphleteer of the period, also a notorious drunk, womaniser and gambler. He died in poverty in the summer of 1592 after writing to his estranged ex-wife asking her to send money for his funeral. His eerie warning to Marlowe: '. . . *for little knowest thou how, in the end, thou shall be visited . . .*' echoes down the years. His devoted mistress was **Emma Ball**, sister of a highwayman, Cutting Ball Jack, and a Bankside whore. Greene never recognised his son, little **Fortunatus**, who died of the Plague in the summer of 1593.

Master Thomas Grinston's *Divers Private Recreations* is a book mentioned by academics in *Appleby and Honeybath* by Michael Innes. I can find no trace of its existence and it was probably one of Innes's jokes.